THE BOY
WHO SET
FIRE TO THE BIBLE

by
Carl Daoust

QUANTUM IMAGINATICS
NEW YORK LONDON MONTREAL

QUANTUM IMAGINATICS is a division of
SEE THE WHO COMMUNICATIONS, Montreal, Quebec, Canada.

Visit our website: www.boysetfiretobible.com

To all talented authors struggling to get their work published.

Never give up. Do whatever you can to get your material out there.
The rest will come.

To my Adobe-addicted Dad,
whose talent, wizardry and perseverance
have made this book possible.

FOREWORD

Carl Daoust is one of nature's curiosities. Like Da Vinci himself, Carl's right and left brain each operate at full throttle, conspiring to produce the almost-unimaginable. Give him a pen and he'll blow you away.

Carl's creativity became apparent early on as he delivered one comic strip after another, then wrote an enchanting children's novel, upon which was conferred First Prize at the Montreal School Board Junior Book Awards. As a corporate branding strategist, he recently turned out a fascinating and insightful industry paper on the Cultural Code behind Gold. Though not composed in the conventional white-paper style, but rather as a story swarming with an eclectic collection of characters, it nevertheless won the Discovery Award.

This author concocts characters, places, plots and narratives that mesh together, taking you on a wild journey into the recesses of Carl's imagination. He intertwines historical facts with extreme fiction and iconoclasm, never afraid to rock time-honored dogma. If you seek fantasy, sf, alternative history, suspense, thrills and a maverick's disdain for convention, you've come to the right place.

Enjoy!

From James Halperin,
best-selling author of The Truth Machine (Random House)
and The First Immortal (Ballantine)

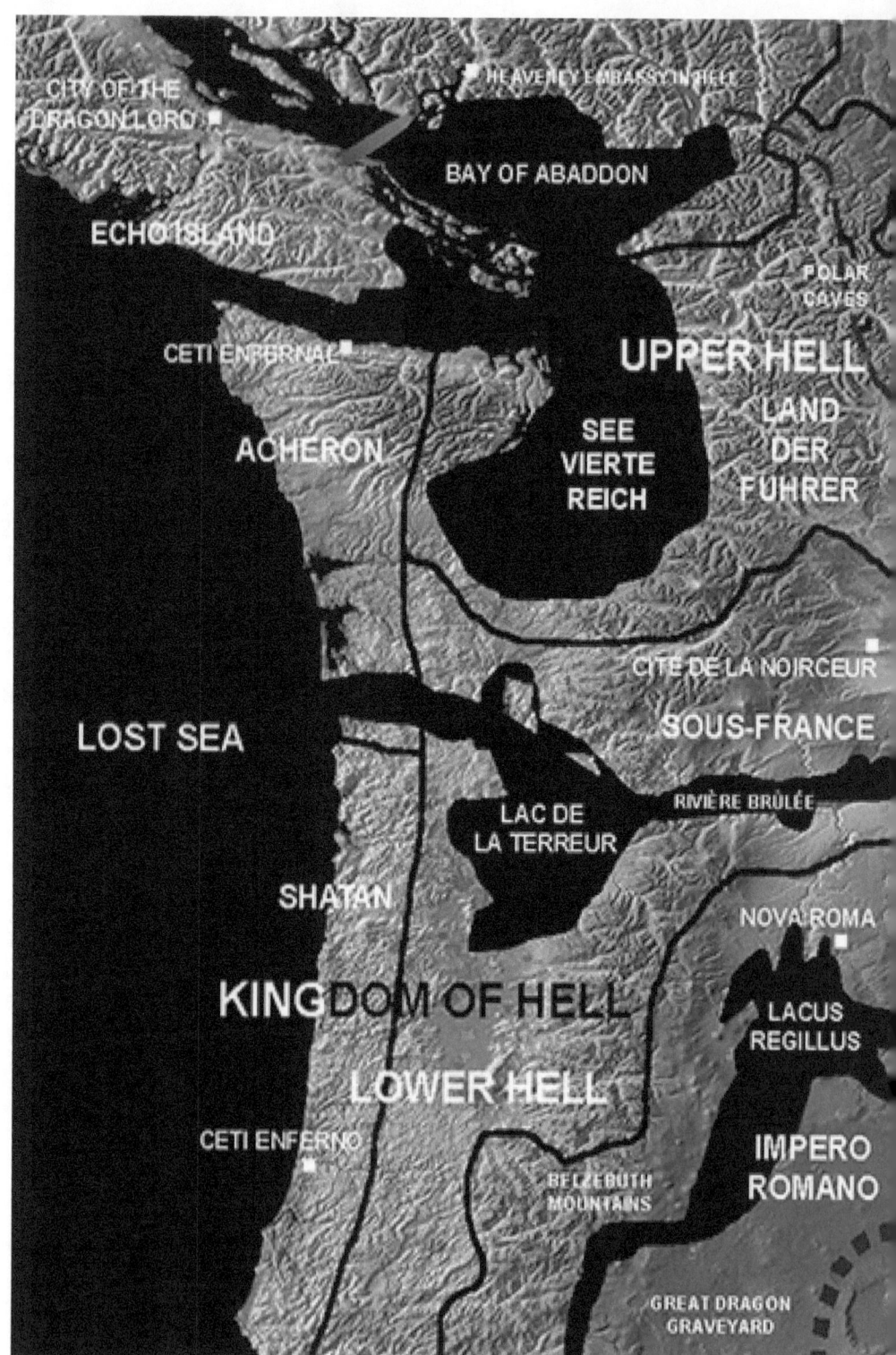

The boy who set Fire To The Bible

PROLOGUE

A long time ago; somewhere in space.

"**Back-up Control Unit N-I-4-N-I** recording status," announced the robotic being after placing his three-fingered hand flatly against a slightly raised panel whose contour exactly matched the robot's hand configuration. The artificial being was about four and a half feet tall, with an upper body made of two oval cylinders, one over the other, connected by a series of highly tensile tubes.

It had a head in the shape of a pyramid, but with rounded edges, biconvex lenses for eyes, and a triangular grid for a mouth. The lower body was composed of two parts: a concave cylinder that was narrowest at its center, and a base made of modular metal plates linked into a continuous band wrapped around two sets of wheels—much like the propulsion system of an armored tank. Its exterior body was primarily metallic and bronze in color.

N-I-4-N-I was a fine piece of machinery and electronics capable of complex analysis and decision-making—the apex of artificial intelligence. Its functions were the storage of all types of data into its heavily shielded positronic *brain*, and intervention if one or more critical systems failed. Today was its ten-thousandth recording.

"All systems of the spacecraft Audacia functioning within normal parameters," announced N-I-4-N-I as if it had an audience. This was one of its few idiosyncrasies. One would almost dare call it a human trait. "Navigation normal; propulsion normal; shields normal; course normal; life support normal," it went on. "All stasis pods, one through five-thousand-one-hundred and thirty-nine, normal."

N-I-4-N-I paused for a moment as the main computer dropped the ship out of subspace and began transmitting data on Audacia's position. "Entering a new solar system. Scanning system for candidate planet," shouted the robot in military fashion. "Compensating for variable gravitational fields. Approaching asteroid belt. 99.8% minimal density; plotting course through belt. Establishing local frame of reference; setting to unit vector 0.451 by 0.728 by 0.552. Mark. Entry in 2, 1, 0."

Dust particles bombarded the Audacia's hull as it maneuvered through the belt, causing friction and static electricity. "Electric charge building up, now at 2.7 million Coulomb," said N-I-4-N-I. "Initiating positive discharge to neutralize."

But before the discharge could be released, the spacecraft suddenly shook violently and started spinning. "Alert!" cried out the startled robot. "Charged dust particles have converged into the main plasma conduit. Plasma is no longer igniting. System corruption confirmed. Propulsion and navigation are offline."

As the Audacia spiraled off course, N-I-4-N-I took command and attempted to reinitialize the faulty systems. The main computer was no longer responding. The robot bypassed to auxiliary systems, but they too collapsed. As a last resort, it diverted power from shields to conduit flow regulators and tried to manually purge the contaminated plasma from the conduit. It worked. Systems were slowly coming back online.

A new message was now being relayed to N-I-4-N-I—a message that would have sent any human running for the airlock: "Collision imminent."

N-I-4-N-I instinctively looked up at main view screen as if to verify the message's genuineness. What was initially a speck on the view screen grew exponentially into a massive projectile of over 200 feet in diameter, headed directly for the spacecraft. The robot had just the time to issue one more command before the asteroid hit: "Initiate revival of crew."

CHAPTER 1

Present day; Center for SETI Research, California.

"ET phone Earth," softly said the voice, partially muffled by a crude rubber mask covering its owner's head. The mask, which was originally a depiction of the Incredible Hulk had been altered to look like an extra-terrestrial—two large white paper patches checkered with a black felt pen had been glued over the eyes, and two antennas made of popsicle sticks with Styrofoam balls fastened at the ends had been taped atop the head, so crudely that one antenna dangled at a 30 degree angle, ready to pop off at any moment. This, however, was of no concern to the man behind the mask whose lips moved ever closer to his victim, a rather fat man sleeping on a tattered reclining chair on the verge of toppling over under his weight.

"Wake up, fatso!" screamed the voice with excessive vigor. "The alien invasion has begun."

The portly man woke up violently, jumping out of the chair with uncanny swiftness. "I was just reflecting over the research data, Supervisor Lapierre," he reported almost mechanically. "It's quite fascinating."

"Perhaps, but not as fascinating as the gravity field generated by your fat ass," was the sharp response. "Humpty Dumpty sat on a chair; Humpty Dumpty had a great scare. All the aliens' laughter and all the aliens' chants couldn't stop Humpty Dumpty from pissing his pants."

The heavy man turned towards the author of the witty but degrading rhyme. "You scared the hell out of me, Ted."

"Better me than Lapierre," snapped back Ted as he removed his mask, revealing a wide grin. "Now put your phaser on stand-by and come and see this, Big Jim."

James never liked the nickname but tolerated it. After all, Ted was his best friend—Ted was his *only* friend. He and Ted had studied together and had been hired on the very same day five days ago as scientific investigators for the Center for SETI Research, an illustrious organization whose primary mission was the search for extra-terrestrial life in the universe. And as Ted would presently attest: "There's something there that wasn't there before."

"What's there?" asked James, following Ted to his computer terminal while he searched his pockets for the remains of a candy bar.

"I'm reading a whole basket of electromagnetic transmissions," replied Ted with an expression that betrayed his consternation laced with a good measure of trepidation. "There's a massive wave of about Pi times 1420.4 mega-hertz with amplitude of about three times the Hydrogen line."

"Life?" shouted James spitting out grossly chewed-out pieces of candy bar, landing a few on Ted's keyboard.

"There's more," added Ted pointing to the computer screen. "We've got gamma radiation at ten to the twelfth power mega-hertz and an aggregated level of energy exceeding 40 times 10 to the eighteenth power joules."

"That's equivalent to the amount of energy released from burning 500 million gallons of gasoline," pointed out James.

"I doubt we're looking at combusted fuel," replied Ted moving his finger across the data on the screen.

"Maybe an alien spaceship whose anti-matter core exploded?" chuckled James whose humor has never been amusing much less timely.

Ted glanced at James with disapproving eyes before returning to his examination of the data. "The energy seems to be contained within an inverse tachyonic field, much like water in a pipeline."

"Gushing water, you mean," remarked James. "The energy field—and the electromagnetic signals—are moving. Check out the frequencies, they appear to be increasing."

"Indeed they are," confirmed Ted. "A classic display of the Doppler effect. Judging by the variations, velocity is well beyond the *speed of light*. What the fu...warp speed?"

"There's something else," noticed James; "in the lower bands. I read two sets of eleven signatures of particular design."

"You're right," exclaimed Ted. "Harmonic waves. The fundamental tone of the first set is 8050 megahertz, with ten companion overtones — integer multiples of the fundamental tone. The other base tone is 10,070 megahertz."

"What if they're combinations," conjectured James. "Or intergalactic phone numbers?"

"If energy is being delivered to Earth from a different point of origin in the galaxy," wondered Ted, "then it may be more accurate to compare them to points of departure and destination, like addresses."

"Looks like delivery was made," noted James. "All signals have ceased."

Ted moved quickly, inputting instructions through his keyboard to connect to the array of satellites orbiting the Earth. His quality of manner was almost hysterical. "If we hurry, we should be able to detect the effects of any release of energy greater than a million mega-joules, in the atmosphere mostly, with some residuals on the surface of the Earth."

Before he could establish the connection, Ted's computer froze, sending him into a state of utter frenzy. "Not now! Please God, not now!" Desperation quickly engulfed him as he tried every bypass routine he knew. Nothing worked. Frantic, he raised his fists above his head and, much like a Kamikaze on a suicide mission, crashed them against the keyboard, sending keys hurtling in every direction.

James took no time to console his friend. Instead he rushed to his own computer. Accessing the file, the only information it relinquished was a flashing message in red that covered the entire screen: RESTRICTED FILE. "We've being shut out!"

"Damn you to Hell," cried Ted to an unknown foe who, unbeknownst to both of them, was about to appear. Pushing James aside, he entered his own access codes, but to no avail. He then began a search using key words like gamma, tachyonic, 8050 mega-hertz and 10070 megahertz, hoping to re-access the file somehow. Five files popped up on the internal browser, including the current one. The oldest file dated back twelve years. Unfortunately all were restricted.

"Who worked on the last file before ours, and when?" inquired James who, like Ted, was surprised other similar case files existed.

Calling up the information, which resided on a separate and related file, Ted was startled to find the names of two employees he knew nothing about, and who had been transferred to the Carl Sagan Center 10 days ago—the very day the last file was created.

"I don't know these guys," he told James, as if this was unusual. "John Jones and Morris Miller?"

"I don't know half the scientists who work in our department," admitted James. "So what?"

"What I mean is I don't know these *names*," corrected Ted, who immediately ordered the organizational charts for the SETI and Sagan centers on the computer screen. "I went through this on my first day, looking for old University acquaintances; and as you can see, there's no John Jones or Morris Miller."

"You remembered that?" retorted James.

"I remember the names of all the girls in my first-year elementary class," proudly replied Ted, who immediately resumed the investigation. "Let's see if there are anomalies with the other files—names, dates or otherwise."

"Gentlemen!" suddenly bellowed a rather ethnic voice behind Ted and James, who jumped like two roguish school boys caught in mischief. It was Supervisor Lapierre—or as many of the senior staff would call him: Father Lapierre. George Lapierre, holder of doctorates in theology, philosophy and theoretical physics, was once a catholic priest who held the position of Cardinal at the Vatican. He left the College of Cardinals amid bedlam after contending that the voice of God could emanate, not from a spiritual plane, but from the physical plane in which life as we know it had spawned. He also argued that the voice of the All Mighty could be measured using scientific instruments. Now, 20 years later, he was but a simple Christian capitalizing on his vast knowledge of the physical universe to prove his claim.

"We have a problem," continued Lapierre; "perhaps not of biblical proportion, but a problem none the less. SETI management suspects a security breach."

"Well there's no breach here," resentfully shouted Ted, pointing an angry finger at his computer screen. "How can there be when critical case files are restricted? Besides, who the Hell—I mean, who the heck would usurp data that'll go public eventually?"

"Need I remind you of SETI's *Declaration of Principles*, Mr. Adams?" rebutted Lapierre in an uncharacteristically condescending tone for a priest. "Any individual, public or private research institution in communication with a potential extraterrestrial intelligence should seek to verify that the most plausible explanation is the existence of extraterrestrial intelligence rather than some other natural phenomenon, before making any public announcement."

"I understand, Sir, and I do vividly remember the contents of the Declaration," assured Ted. "My point pertains more to the value of the information, especially in its unverified state, and to repercussions of premature disclosure. They're both benign."

"What about misrepresenting the information and selling it to gossip magazines," noted Lapierre. "The SETI name would surely be used as the source, and that would most certainly damage our reputation as an elite institution. There's also NASA. They've shared sensitive information with us regarding communication array design and given us controlled access to military satellites."

"With all due respect," chimed in James, "the U.S. Congress terminated all collaboration between NASA and SETI in 1993. Any data that arose out of that alliance is now obsolete. As for military satellite access, the encryption algorithms are so complex, we only receive data recursively filtered down to almost zero."

"That's enough!" roared Lapierre, his face turning violet with impatience. "This is not a debate. You *will* follow the security guard to sector nine where other researchers have been gathered," waving in the accompanying guard with a swift motion of the hand. The guard, who had been waiting outside the open door, moved forward and met the two young scientists at midpoint. "I'll join you shortly in the *interrogation* room," added Lapierre before rushing off.

"Since when do we have an interrogation room?" whispered Ted to James. "This is freakin' weird."

As they crossed the corridor towards the elevator, they noticed their colleagues working at their desks, through the windowed offices. No one seemed to be absent. Once the elevator doors opened onto sector nine, they were greeted by a second guard who joined the first one in escorting them to the interrogation room, which by all appearances, was an old supply room contrived to meet an urgent need. There were only two chairs and a small retractable round table, both made of aluminum. And there were no other researchers in sight. The guards pushed them in and locked the door, but not before taking James' cell phone. Ted, apparently, did not have his.

"No one's here, man!" nervously shrieked James, grabbing Ted tightly by the arm. "SETI's being turned into the Gestapo."

Ignoring James' emotional meltdown, Ted freed his arm from his friend's clutches and raised the right leg of his pants above his knee, revealing a cell phone tied to his ankle with a black band.

"That's where you put your phone?" said James trying to regain his composure.

"Not just my phone," replied Ted, now lifting the left leg of his pants, unveiling his wallet. "This is my countermeasure against muggings."

Stripping the phone off his leg, Ted began to dial what James assumed to be 911.

"Bill?" said Ted after a few seconds. "It's Ted."

"Bill?" repeated James, grabbing his head with both hands. "You called your brother at NASA?"

"Shut up!" snapped back Ted. "Bill, listen to me carefully, I have very little time. We discovered a corridor in space containing a vast amount of energy and emitting an odd complement of electromagnetic signals."

"A wormhole?" replied Bill.

Ted paused a moment and then resumed. "Yes, yes! Like a wormhole, but highly contained. It grazed the surface of Mars near the North-eastern edge of Meridiani Planum on its way to Earth. The data stream was downloaded on our systems, but classified before we could ascertain its termination point on Earth or its point of origin. When it passed through Mars, the corridor may have been punctured, releasing some of its energy. I'm hoping this created a unique marking on the surface and converted a portion of the energy into residual matter—of what kind I can only speculate. Can you search for this new topological element?"

"That's a tall order," pointed out Bill.

Ted pressed on with greater resolve. "Look Bill, you're the senior director on the *MER (Mars Exploration Rover)* mission. You control the path of the *Opportunity* Mars rover. Get that robotic contraption to make a minor detour. At 800 meters per day, we're talking about a 5-day delay at most."

"Can't you ask your supervisor Lapierre to declassify the data?" wondered Bill.

"You've met the man once," said Ted. "He's an asshole. Besides, he's the one who's responsible for the classification."

"I'll see what I can do, but I'm not hopeful," was Bill's grunted response. He was understandably surprised at the sudden data restriction.

"I don't know what the classification is really about," concluded Ted, "but it's clear Lapierre and likely some high-level people at SETI want to keep this discovery under wraps. Call me back with any progress."

"Are you done?" asked an exasperated James. "Who you gonna call now, your mother?"

"Science is an unrelenting task master," answered Ted in a clumsy attempt to justify his selfish behavior. He began to dial anew. "9, 1, 1. It's ringing."

Before the connection could be made, the door swung open violently, revealing a riled Lapierre followed by the two guards. The former Cardinal, in a gesture of rage and contempt, slapped the phone out of Ted's hand and pushed him onto the rear wall. "I love God, you know. I truly do. He understands why I'm doing this."

Dazed and disoriented, Ted marshaled what was left of his wavering strength and stared into Lapierre's beady eyes. "Which God are you referring to? The vengeful one?"

Lapierre smiled and turned to one of the guards. "Destroy that phone. And stay in the room with these clowns, both of you. I'll be back in a minute."

Exiting the room and closing the door behind him, Lapierre walked a few paces, breathing heavily. "Damned kids," he muttered to himself before taking his own cell phone out of his shirt pocket and dialing. "It's me. Marvelous news. I—" His interlocutor interrupted him. Lapierre pressed his forearm against his forehead and sighed. "No, I *don't* have him, but I do have something worth a million Hail Mary's. I believe I've found the address to *Heaven*."

CHAPTER 2

Present day; France.

"Sarah, ma petite, eat something," implored Gaston Sinclair, a tall and slender bearded French fellow, sitting at the end of a massive rectangular table covered with dishes, which were overflowing with a wide variety of foods. Gaston, Sarah's father, was particularly partial to ratatouille, an eggplant casserole with tomatoes, zucchini and onions.

"I've had my fill for today, Papa," replied Sarah with such deep-seeded melancholy. "You can have all of the ratatouille," she added, summoning up a discrete grin whose lack of authenticity did not escape her husband Cameron's notice.

"Chérie, starving yourself won't help anything," gently noted Cameron, in his best French.

"Cam's right," anxiously confirmed Sarah's mother Jacqueline as she deposited a bowl of chestnut soup made especially for her beautiful daughter. "It's your favorite; and it will make you stronger...*for the next time*," the last words barely escaping her quivering lips.

"Jacqueline!" barked Gaston. "Keep your place."

"It's all right," assured Sarah, raising her eyes to meet her mother's troubled stare. "We both wish for the same thing. Perhaps if we *all* wish for it as much as she does, it will finally happen."

After 5 years of trying to have a child, Sarah had at long last become pregnant. The baby due was a boy whose name had been chosen a long time ago: *Ethan*. Both Sarah and Cameron liked it very much. Of Hebrew origin, it meant "Long-Lived", which was disturbingly ironic since the child died hours after birth, two months ago. Its tiny heart just stopped beating—and doctors didn't know why. They tried to revive him, but without success. Sarah, an inveterate atheist who despised organized religion, prayed for the first time since her troubled childhood. She prayed for her boy's resurrection in exchange for her life. As she suspected, no one listened and nothing happened, anchoring evermore her atheist disposition.

"Whom do we wish to? God?" gently asked Gaston, perplexed by his daughter's request.

Sarah broke into tears, realizing that, according to her, no higher power existed. "Let's pray for each other," she quickly countered. "We are miracles of life after all; so the secret to miracles must lie within us."

Extending his arm towards Sarah, Cameron covered her hand with his. "Perhaps you're right, Honey." He gazed at her in a fashion that had become routine for him, wondering what had happened to her during her childhood that led to her disbelief of God.

"You're right indeed!" confidently spouted Gaston as he moved towards a painting on the dining room wall. The painting depicted *Childeric I*, a long-haired king of the fifth century Merovingian dynasty and alleged ancestor of his wife's family. "Yours truly's better half has this man's blood coursing through her veins, as does his daughter…and he was a true miracle worker. With an army made of far less men than any other army, he won all his battles against the Visigoths, the Saxons, and the Alemanni. Much like him and his devoted army," Gaston went on with a greater measure of zeal," you will win your next battle, little girl, and you will do it with our hearts and best spirits behind you."

Since Sarah seemed to be enlivened by Gaston's lecture, Cameron remained silent, considering pregnancy more akin to a thrilling quest than a bloody battle; but if the metaphor be effective, who was he to dispute it. As long as Gaston didn't indulge in his hyperbole about the connection between the Merovingian dynasty and Jesus Christ.

During a fishing trip with his father-in-law this past spring, the latter had brought a first edition of the controversial book, *The Holy Blood and the Holy Grail*, which he read at length and out loud to Cameron. Not only did this go against fishing protocol, but it annoyed Cameron to no end.

In the book, the authors put forward a hypothesis that the historical Jesus married Maria Magdalena, had one or more children, and that those children or their descendants emigrated to what is now southern France.

Once there, they intermarried with the noble families that would eventually become the Merovingian dynasty. Its special claim to the throne of France was championed in latter days by a secret organization called the

Priory of Sion. The organization believed the legendary Holy Grail to be simultaneously the womb of Maria Magdalena and the sacred royal bloodline she gave birth to.

Cameron was uncertain whether Gaston believed the book's claims entirely. As a Catholic, he could not truly endorse them; but he liked to entertain certain notions that reflected well upon his wife's family: being a descendant of Jesus was certainly grand, even if it was heresy. Only Gaston's immediate family was privy to his occasional, unsolicited dissertations. Unfortunately for Cameron, he was now part of the family.

"I'll be going to bed now," announced Sarah, who signaled Cameron to follow him. "I do feel a bit better," she added, producing a long-awaited genuine smile.

"We're glad, dear," said Jacqueline, picking up the bowl of soup, which had remained untouched. "I'll save this for tomorrow. Don't forget, breakfast is at 9. You'll need your energy if you're going to visit the Saint-Amboise Castle."

"There's also the Manor of Le Clos-Lucé," remarked Gaston. "That's were Leonardo Da Vinci lived and worked before he died. Did you know that Da Vinci was a Grand Master of—"

"Enough Gaston!" snapped Jacqueline. "No more stories for tonight."

"Thank God," mumbled Cameron as he gently pushed his wife up the stairs towards their bedroom. Tomorrow would be a better day.

CHAPTER 3

Present day; New York.

"Well hello there, Mister Koko," grinned the administrative nurse. "Welcome to the New York Downtown Hospital, where clowns above all others grace us with their presence."

"I beg your pardon, Madam," crisply replied the clown; "I'm *Bozo* the clown."

"Very well, Mr. *Bozo*," acknowledged the nurse, repressing her giggling. "How may I be of assistance?"

Placing his portable CD player on the counter separating him from the nurse, the clown bent over and dryly asked, "I'm looking for Mrs. Nadia Hefer. I understand she just gave birth to a delightful little boy."

"I see," realized the nurse. "You're from a signing-telegram company. How thoughtful and amusing. Mrs. Hefer will adore it, and the child will undoubtedly love those balloons you're carrying. You'll find her in room sixteen of the Labor and Delivery Unit; fifth floor to your left as you exit the elevator."

"Thank you," said the clown as he picked up his CD player and headed for the elevator. He was the tallest clown anyone had ever seen and had to bend his body slightly to enter the elevator. He was dressed in a blue costume with yellow buttons, wore 20" long shoes, and donned a skin-tight cap with bushy red hair protruding from both sides of the cap. His nose was covered with a red ball and the contour of his mouth painted in orange.

A ten-year old girl accompanied by her teenage sister studied him carefully as the elevator proceeded to the fifth floor. "Are you sad, Mr. Clown?" she asked candidly.

The clown ignored her, seemingly preoccupied with the task at hand. She tugged on his costume and resumed her innocent enquiry. "My name is Daphney," she proudly announced. "Maybe if I become your friend, you'll be happy." Daphney's sister smiled, indicating her approval of the naïve invitation.

The clown crouched at the girl's feet and scanned her face. "You're very pretty, Daphney," he replied simply, gently stroking her blond hair. "You know what makes me really happy? It's doing my job."

"I suppose it should," she wondered. "You're a clown who sings and brings balloons to make other people happy. Will you be happy soon then?"

"Yes little one," promised the clown. "I'll be quite merry in a few minutes."

As the elevator doors opened onto the fifth floor, the clown stepped out, but not before cheerfully waving goodbye to Daphney who continued on to the next floor. The moment the doors closed, he lost his new-found cheer and instantly regressed to his earlier somber spirits. Perhaps the anticipation of a job well done truly did not have any uplifting effects on him—only the deed itself did.

The clown walked in a perfectly straight line, passing room after room until he reached room sixteen. As he entered, he was immediately confronted by a short man in a blue jogging suit. "Who are you?" he asked in an uneasy tone.

"I'm here for the boy," placidly answered the clown, handing the balloons over to the man who inspected him from head to toe. "You must be the proud father."

"What is that?" went on the man, pointing at the CD player.

"I'm from Notre-Dame Singing Telegrams," replied the clown, lifting the player at the man's eye level.

"Let him approach, Abar," ordered Mrs. Hefer, who lay in bed holding her child. "Forgive my husband," she humbly appealed to the clown. "He's not used to such entertaining displays of glad tidings. It's a cultural thing."

"Indeed he's not," concurred the clown, depositing the player at the end of the bed after closing the room door. "We mustn't disturb the other patients."

Pressing the play button on the player, a familiar melody began resonating throughout the room. Abar sat on the edge of the bed next to his wife and looked at his first-born boy who appeared to respond to the music. As for the clown, he listened to it for a few seconds, his eyes shut, then cut in with the corresponding lyrics:

"You look like an angel,
Walk like an angel,
Talk like an angel,
But I got wise,
You're the devil in disguise,
Oh yes you are the Devil in disguise,
You fooled me with your kisses,
You cheated and you schemed,
Heaven knows how you lied to me,
You're not the way you seemed,
You look like an angel,
Walk like an angel,
Talk like an angel,
But I got wise,
You're the devil in disguise,
Oh yes you—"

"Stop! Please stop!" yelled the new mother. "What kind of song is that? What's the meaning of this?" She held her baby tighter, sensing something was awry.

"It's about your son, of course," casually certified the clown; "or to be more precise, it's about who he may well become." Cracking open the back of the CD player, he pulled out a Ruger SP101 revolver, equipped with a silencer, and aimed it at Abar. "It's unfortunate you are here. You're not my target, Mr. *Hafiza*."

A wave of terror overcame Abar, who released the balloons, clutched his hands together and pleaded for his life, while his wife remained frozen with fear. "I am not the man you think, and nor is this the child you seek," pointing at the baby. "I beg of you, do not—"

The shot rang out quite unpretentiously, but with impeccable aim. Abar crashed to the floor, blood trickling from the hole in his forehead. Before his wife could scream for help, a second bullet spat out of the silencer's muzzle and lodged itself right above her right eye. Her head tilted forward, with her chin coming to rest against her chest.

The only sound that now permeated the room was the melody of the Elvis Presley hit song *Devil in Disguise*. Surprisingly, the baby had preserved its quiet manners throughout the executions, unaware of what was about to transpire next.

Stepping over the father's body, the clown pressed his thighs against the side of the bed, raised his arm and placed the revolver against the boy's left temple. The child looked up at him and smiled. The clown fired his weapon.

Dropping his gun onto the bed, the clown pulled out a long blue satin scarf out of his costume pocket and wrapped it around the baby's bloodied head—much like a turban. A strange symbol made of golden silk yarn was embroidered into the fabric and was positioned in plain view.

(symbol on scarf)

"May God have mercy on your soul," he whispered.

Leaving the revolver, the CD player and the balloons behind, he walked out the door, closing it behind him. His smile had returned.

CHAPTER 4

Present day; France.

"Rex speaking," said Cameron, his cell phone pressed against his left ear. "Hey Sophie, what's up?"

Sophie was not only Cameron's sister, she was also his FBI partner. Both worked at the FBI New York office. In fact, Cameron had recommended her transfer to the New York office years ago, hoping the Assistant Director would agree to a brother-sister team-up. He did, and since that day, they've made a formidable team.

"Do you remember Abu Hafiza?" Sophie asked her brother.

"Wasn't he a high-level strategist and operational planner for Al Qaeda?" recalled Cameron. "He was also allegedly part of the Moroccan cell that provided planning for the 9/11 attacks."

"All true," confirmed Sophie. "But he won't be planning anything soon: he's dead."

"Vigilantes?" conjectured Cameron.

"I don't think he was the target," surmised Sophie. "His wife and newborn child were with him at the hospital, all three under an assumed name, and all three murdered. The child was the *real* target."

"Was the baby wearing a blue scarf around his head?" asked Cameron, apprehending the dreadful answer.

"Yes," woefully deplored Sophie. "And the golden symbol was there as well."

This was the fourth child murdered and subjected to the assassin's strange modus operandi. All four were first-born sons of high-profile tyrants and terrorists, killed either at hospital or at home. While the connection between the children was evident, no motive had been established yet, and no evidence had been found. Cameron and Sophie, the agents assigned to the cases, were understandably disheartened by their unusual lack of progress.

"I can't get involved right now," bitterly said Cameron who spotted his wife heading towards him. "As you know, I'm supposed to be on vacation. I'll talk to you in a few days." Quickly stuffing his phone in his pocket, he turned to his wife Sarah. "So, are we starting this tour of the Amboise castle?"

Sarah glared at him, suspecting a transgression, and ordered him to follow her to the castle's main entrance. They arrived in minutes. The castle guide was waiting for them.

"Bonjour," proudly cried the guide. "Bienvenue au Château d'Amboise. I am your guide, Charles." Opening the large double doors, he waived his guests in and immediately began his discourse: "Built in the eleventh century, the royal Château at Amboise is located in Amboise, within the Loire Valley in France. It was erected on a promontory overlooking the Loire River to control a strategic ford that was replaced in the Middle Ages by a bridge.

"Expanded and improved over time, in September 1434 it was seized by Charles VII of France, after its owner, Louis d'Amboise, was convicted of plotting against Louis XI and condemned to be executed in 1431. However, the king pardoned him but took his château at Amboise. Once in royal hands, the château became a favorite of French kings."

After an hour of touring, Cameron, whose mind was elsewhere for the most part, needed to be prompted into interest—perhaps an introduction to something mysterious like a hidden underground corridor.

"Can we visit the secret corridor?" avidly requested Cameron. "You know the one connecting the castle to the Le Clos-Lucé Manor. It's mentioned in your brochure."

"That is not part of the tour, Monsieur," indicated Charles.

"Perhaps a show of official authority would do the trick," thought Cameron, pulling out his FBI badge.

"What possible business would the FBI have here?" asked the bewildered guide. "Besides, Interpol has jurisdiction over French territory."

"The FBI and Interpol are working together to capture a serial child killer," confessed Cameron, pulling the guide away from Sarah. "We think he might have used the corridor as a hideout—that there might be clues about his identity."

While Cameron's former statement might have been true, the latter was complete fabrication. He often used his position of power for his personal agenda. Sophie regularly reprimanded him, but he always took his partner's warnings of formal disciplinary actions lightly. He considered himself a rebel with a cause.

"That changes everything," recognized the appalled guide. "Follow me."

Moving briskly, the guide brought them to a steel gate that protected what appeared to be an unremarkable stone wall. Unlocking the gate, Charles placed his hand over an etching on the wall of a royal scepter and applied pressure. Part of the wall—about two-feet wide by five-feet high—cracked open, creating an opening just big enough to slip through.

A few feet in, they encountered a staircase leading down into a dark abyss. Charles flipped a switch that lit the entire corridor. "That's not very medieval," humorously noted Cameron.

"Come, come," insisted Charles, ignoring Cameron's poor attempt at humor. He was now on a mission.

"I'm not comfortable, Cam." Sarah placed her hand on his shoulder, afraid to fall as they engaged the staircase. "What are we doing here?"

"This is going to be the best part of the tour," Cameron whispered to his wife. The corridor proved to be quite unmemorable, in fact: stone walls with fastened rusted candlesticks every ten feet, and a dirt floor. The ceiling was laced with wires and light bulbs.

"Well, what do you see?" asked an excited Charles, who seemed to enjoy playing detective. "Anything suspect?"

"Nothing yet," conceded Cameron, pretending to search for clues. Pulling out a pocket flashlight, he scrutinized the walls, expecting nothing, and finding nothing.

"Cam, I want to leave this dreary place," begged Sarah, who was in no mood to indulge her husband's follies.

He glanced at her and nodded his head in agreement. "Sorry Charles, It appears I was mistaken. There's nothing fish—" Cameron stopped in his tracks. "What's this?"

He noticed three indentations positioned in a circular pattern, describing a circle of about four inches in diameter. Each indentation was an inch deep and the size of a golf ball, and was equidistant from one another. The interior and the edges of the depressions were blackened with some kind of soot.

"If I didn't know any better, I'd say some type of three-nozzle launcher did this," theorized Cameron as he inserted his finger in one of the holes and swiped its surface. "The stone was charred—burnt if you will—probably by a series of small explosive missiles producing an incredibly high energy yield."

"This stone melts at over 3,000 degrees Fahrenheit," observed Charles.

Cameron looked at Charles with an air of bewilderment. "3,000 you say?"

"I'm the guide!" rebutted a defensive Charles. "I know these things."

"Honey, there are more holes here," noticed Sarah, joining in on the investigation.

Cameron examined the new set of indentations, which were approximately five feet from the first set, roughly at the same height. "There's more soot along the right half of the circumference. The shots came in at an angle, maybe 30 degrees from the wall. And the intended target was moving—running from the Manor towards the castle, I'd say."

"A *human* target?" blundered Charles.

"Call it instinct," replied Cameron who began probing the floor for foot or body prints, or empty shells. "When was this corridor last visited?"

"It's been years," answered Charles. "The last time was to evacuate excess water from a raging rainstorm."

"What about Le Clos-Lucé Manor," went on Cameron. "Who lives there?"

"No one," assured Charles. "It's now a museum. It contains forty models of machines designed by Leonardo Da Vinci."

"Can we see the museum?" insisted Cameron who was going to inspect it no matter what the response.

"Of course," plainly said Charles. "It is part of the tour."

"Lead the way, *Charley*," ordered the FBI agent.

"Can you be at least polite if not gracious?" supplicated Charles. "My name is—" His face suddenly sparkled with the boon of recollection. "Nazis!"

"I may be swaggering," said a piqued Cameron, "but far from deserving of the designation of Nazi." His wife chuckled in mock endorsement.

Charles saw an opening for a wily insult, but refrained. "I was merely weighing the possibility of the Nazi incursion of March of 1941 as a precursor to the regrettable events in the corridor. The Nazis invaded the town of Amboise, and established a restricted area that encompassed the castle, the manor and the forest behind the manor."

"What's so interesting or strategic about a small forest?" wondered Cameron.

"Urban legend has it the forest eventually served as an escape route for dozens of Nazi criminals of war, like Dr Death Aribert Heim, and the

Angel of Death Dr Josef Mengele. To avoid pursuit, many carefully selected Germans had been surgically altered to look like the runaways and live their lives as fugitives of law. It is said that even Hitler contemplated joining those he considered traitors."

Cameron was perplexed by the extraordinary tale. "A forest would only afford them a temporary haven. Where could it safely lead them except onto itself?"

"The forest was far more than a transient sanctuary," said the guide. "It was a portal to a new realm—a reality where they believed they could rule once more."

"Do you really believe that?" asked a doubtful Cameron.

Charles snapped back instantly. "There are many ways to Heaven… or to Hell."

CHAPTER 5

"Please don't touch that!" screamed Charles, his arms weaving frantically over his head.

"I didn't realize Da Vinci was into warfare weaponry," exclaimed Cameron, aiming what appeared to be an antiquated machine gun at the guide.

"Put it back on the stand!" pleaded Charles. "I'll get in trouble."

Replacing the model weapon in its original position, Cameron stared at it, much like a child would stare at a Star Wars blaster pistol in a toy store. "I suppose Da Vinci didn't design this to chase away squirrels."

"It was ordered by one of his patrons," indicated Charles. "Like all of us, he had to put food on his table." Grazing the weapon with his fingers, Charles felt a sensation of power. "It's a three-tiered machine gun. It consists of eleven barrels in each of the three tiers, into which projectiles are loaded. The aim of the tiers is that in rotation, the first tier is fired while the second tier can be loaded. This allows for the third tier to cool down before its turn in the rotation to be loaded and fired again."

"Did it actually work?" inquired Cameron.

"Indeed it did," said Charles with a certain measure of pride. "Leonardo always aimed at increasing the firepower of the weapons he worked on and maximizing their overall destructive capacity. He did this for both his patron's benefit in having superior firepower compared to his rivals and for his own personal, intellectual curiosity."

"He would have been quite an asset for our military," remarked Cameron as he began his inspection of the rest of the museum.

"There's nothing here, but the embodiment of sheer genius," he gathered after a time. "We might as well continue the tour." Cameron surmised that, if there had been foul play, it most likely occurred centuries ago, notwithstanding Charles' Nazi theory.

They left the museum and walked to the chapel of Saint-Hubert, where Da Vinci's remains were buried in a tomb covered with a marble plaque bearing his name. The chapel itself was small—under 500 square feet—and enhanced with stain glasses and late gothic carvings, a marvel of architecture worthy of a marvel of human achievement.

"When did he die?" asked Sarah who knelt and gently stroke the letters on the plaque.

"Leonardo died here, at Clos Lucé, on May 2, 1519," answered Charles. "In his last days, Leonardo sent for a priest to make his confession and receive the Holy Sacrament. He allegedly died in the arms of his close friend, King Francis I."

"Not allegedly," refuted an old man wearing a suit and tie, and a long raincoat, lurking at the chapel entrance. He walked in, followed by seven other men wearing similar accoutrements.

"Dr. Lefoux!" Charles recognized the man. "I didn't expect to see you today."

"I had some friends fly in," explained Lefoux. "You don't mind if I give them a tour of the grounds?"

"Of course not, Doctor," timidly agreed the guide.

Lefoux was an educated man who loved philosophy, history and politics. Now in his sixties, he had become intractable in his disposition and his opinions, and would never yield to dissonant persuasions.

"Please forgive Charles," he said to Sarah as he helped her up and kissed her hand. "His facts are erroneous on occasion." Ignoring Cameron, Lefoux and his guests surrounded the tomb and bowed their heads in veneration. Thirty seconds later, he concluded the quiet prayer with: "Bless you for having been the conduit towards the Light."

Cameron looked at Charles who was as mystified as he was. The guide shrugged his shoulders.

Without another word, the group of men marched out in pairs and proceeded to an area covered with short bushes, forty feet behind the chapel, at the perimeter of the château grounds.

Producing a switchblade, Lefoux cut away branch after branch until a small burial plaque—sixteen inches by ten inches—was revealed. Engraved on it was the name *Lisa Maria*. The men suddenly became alarmed and agitated. Lefoux, on the other hand, remained calm and composed, savoring the spectacle.

"This is but an appetizer," Lefoux told his guests. "The ultimate *piece de resistance* may yet grace our dinner table one day...*one day*."

CHAPTER 6

"Look at these elm trees and the fauna."
Sarah admired every detail of the forest behind Le Clos-Lucé Manor. Her sadness was finally starting to lift. Cameron's curiosity, however, had been reignited and had yet to be quenched.

"Those men are just not right," maintained Cameron, "gathering around a camouflaged grave. Moreover, what if the body of the person who was shot in the underground corridor was in that grave?"

"Charles assured us it was either a fake grave," Sarah reminded her husband, "or the grave of a villager who wanted to be as close as possible to his idol, Da Vinci. Leave it at that."

His frustration growing, Cameron sat on a tree stump and crossed his arms. He studied his wife of five years as she picked flowers spread along the side of a stream. "She's so beautiful," he thought; "and caring, generous, witty…and strong. And here I am giving her grief." His resentment melted as swiftly as it had arisen.

He sprung up and raced into the depth of the forest. "Wait for me here. I'm going to find the most exquisite flowers and bring them to you." She smiled: he was far more attractive when he spoke from the hearth rather than from the end of a gun.

Ten minutes passed, and it started to rain lightly; then twenty, the rain intensified; and Cameron had not returned. She yelled out his name repeatedly and loudly, apprehension consuming her. No answer came. Her dread became unbearable. She ran into the forest in the direction her husband had taken, shoving aside brush and branches, howling his name without respite. She came upon a stream and labored across it, and then ran faster until the ground under her feet vanished.

For a moment, she glided through the air, and then fell onto the thick rim of a stone structure, her hips and legs hanging inside the structure. She grabbed the underside of the rim and pulled herself out and onto the ground. Bruised and bloodied, Sarah stood up and contemplated the object that assaulted her: a *well*.

The well was imposing, at least fifteen feet in diameter, and featured elaborate symbols carved into the top face of the rim, and grouped into identical sets of ten symbols repeating eight times. A narrow unmarked rectangular stone rested between two consecutive groups. The well was about sixteen feet deep, four of which protruded out of the ground, with a staircase spiraling along its inner surface. At the bottom laid an unconscious Cameron.

A dirt ridge rested against one-quarter of the outer surface, effectively acting as a launch board, which was precisely how Cameron came to rest at the bottom of the well.

"Cam, I'm coming," cried Sarah as she dashed down the staircase. Summoning all her strength, she pressed his body against her back, placed his arms around her neck and secured them with her hands, and commenced her slow journey upwards. Reaching the rim, she let him drop over it onto the ground.

"What happened?" asked a dazed Cameron, suffering from a concussion. "My God, Sarah, you're bleeding."

"It's just a few lacerations," Sarah reassured him. "Can you walk?"

Cameron nodded, and they painfully made their way out of the forest. "Where's my revolver?" he asked suddenly, checking his shoulder holster twice. "It's gone!"

"It must be in the well," assumed Sarah.

"I need to retrieve it," begged Cameron. "If a child finds it…"

"You stay here. I'll go," decided Sarah who trotted back to the well. As she came upon it and was about to look in, she heard a high-pitch moan that seemed to come from everywhere. She scoured the area, but saw nothing. Then, it dawned on her. Gazing into the well, she discovered, at its bottom, a baby boy wrapped in a white wool cloth and wearing a dark linen cap on its head.

Spotting her at the top of the well, the baby freed one arm from the cloth, raised it towards her and began to cry. For the first time in her life as an Atheist, Sarah believed in miracles.

CHAPTER 7

"Rex; Cameron Rex," shouted the nurse.

"Yes?" Cameron gently helped his wife up, careful not to upset the baby.

"The doctor will see you now," indicated the nurse. "Emergency room number five. Just walk in."

"Is he awake?" asked Cameron as he pushed the door open and led his wife in.

"Yes; but he's unusually quiet," noted Sarah. "You would think a child who was dropped into a well and abandoned would be filled with anxiety."

"There's no greater safe haven than a mother's bosom." Cameron tickled the baby's nose and caressed its head, suddenly overwhelmed by a sensation of pure euphoria. He then slowly removed the cap on its head, revealing a full set of light-brown hair.

"My, my," exclaimed the doctor who emerged from the examination room's interior door. "He's got more hair than I do." The doctor had been balding for years and was left with a modest crown of grey hair.

"This child was abandoned in the woods behind Le Clos-Lucé Manor," said Sarah. "We stumbled upon it as we strolled through the woods."

"I remember you," cried out the doctor who peered into Sarah's dark blue eyes. "You were at Da Vinci's tomb this morning."

"Doctor Lefoux?" remembered Cameron whose person had failed to make impression upon the physician. He would not be discounted a second time. "My name is Cameron Rex. I'm an FBI agent."

"A police man! How quaint," sarcastically replied Lefoux before returning his attention to Sarah and the baby. A fuming Cameron held his tongue—for the child's sake.

Relieving Sarah of the bundled baby, Lefoux deposited it on the gurney, delicately removing the cloth. Freed from its restraints, the child began moving its arms and legs briskly. "You're a lively one." Lefoux slid his finger down the child's torso to its groin. The baby smiled and giggled for the first time. "There doesn't seem to be any permanent emotional damage stemming from neglect and abandonment."

"You don't appear to be appalled by this baby's predicament," commented Cameron. "It was left to die, and would have if we hadn't found it."

"Serendipitous happenings indeed," recognized the doctor as he examined every inch of the child's body, searching for bruises, cuts and broken bones. "This little creature will live while many others will die. I've had my share of misery, anguish and death...as you have, I suppose: the life of a police man must be replete with those same inevitabilities."

Cameron remained silent, deliberating on the merits of his actions today—a child had been saved. Perhaps that could earn him some measure of redemption for all the criminals who killed before he could stop them.

"This is odd," said Lefoux as he pushed back the baby's hair and exposed its left ear. "The ear is pointed, and very much so." Uncovering the other ear, he observed the very same deformation. "Devil ears," he muttered.

"What are *those*?" nervously asked Sarah, taking a step back.

"I've heard of cases like this one." The doctor was scrambling for an explanation. "They're quite incidental and benign, and are not symptomatic of any grave disease or syndrome...although, this part is quite curious: there's a bone supporting the top of the ear." Pinching the ear's extremity, Lefoux determined the bone was triangular in shape.

"All in all, I should surmise the ears are the expression of a minor genetic mutation."

Turning the baby onto its stomach, Lefoux let out a telltale gasp. "Good Lord, there's more!"

Sarah locked on Cameron's arm. "What else is wrong?"

Two vertical segments of interweaved muscle extrusions spanned the boy's back, from the lower edge of the shoulder blades to the midpoint of the lower back. Each segment was about two inches from the spine, one on each side. The extrusions were oval-shaped and a half-inch in height.

"Your baby has extra muscle fibers traversing its back," discovered the doctor as he touched and probed the extrusions. "And they're attached to two bone nassels, connected to a bony plate fused to the shoulder blades. The whole structure is perfectly symmetrical. As you can see, the fibrous bumps are clearly not positioned randomly."

"Another *minor* genetic mutation, I suppose?" guessed Cameron whose voice betrayed his growing concern over the child's health. "A flawed tangent in intelligent design no less," he added in trepid mock.

"Don't be alarmed," reassured Lefoux. "Despite the abnormalities, the baby seems to be healthy." Lefoux checked the boy's vital signs and everything fell within normal guidelines. "Perhaps the ears and the bumps are hereditary. It's unfortunate we don't know the biological parents' identity."

"Maybe the parents deserted the child *because* of his *original* features," proposed Sarah who moved closer and focused on its face. Riveted by its seductive beauty, her uneasiness and trepidation dissipated, replaced by the yearnings of a mother's instincts and the unquenched thirst of her love. She smiled at the little man and he smiled back. Cameron knew that, in that instant, Sarah had become a mother in every sense that mattered.

"He has bewitched you," said Lefoux. "Babies do possess that uncanny power—especially those as winsome and disarming as this one." He parted the child's hair in several areas, hunting for fleas and other creepy crawlers. "Nothing here…nothing here…nothing—What's this?"

Sarah and Cameron were ready for any new finding. "What have you found?" he asked.

"Markings along the upper-neck," he curiously reported. "Very faint but visible. What do you make of it, Mr. FBI Agent?"

"There are three marks, positioned horizontally," detected Cameron. "Three-quarter inches apart, one-half inch high. The one on the left looks like a slanted capital E; the middle one, an over stylish capital V; and the right one, an incomplete O or perhaps a capital Q. It could be an acronym, or some weird language."

"Greek, perhaps?" chimed in Sarah.

"We would then have Epsilon on the left, Upsilon or Psi in the middle, and Omicron or Theta on the right," replied Cameron.

"These are probably birth marks," assessed Lefoux; "of no particular meaning—and our tiny tyke doesn't appear to mind or care."

"He may not be interested, doctor, but I am," admitted Cameron. "Although I can't decipher any of it, the markings are oddly familiar to me."

Sarah was no stranger to her husband's inquisitive mind. Faced with a puzzle, he would dwell on it until every neuron in his brain had been excited to exhaustion. And many times, he saw puzzles where there were none. Doubtless, this was one of those times.

"May I keep the child for testing and analysis?" requested Lefoux. "I'll run blood work, EEG, MRI, CAT Scan, and SAGE. I estimate a week should suffice."

"What is SAGE?" wondered Sarah.

"SAGE stands for *Serial Analysis of Gene Expression*," explained the doctor. "It's a powerful tool that allows the analysis of overall gene expression patterns using digital instrumentation. I'm hopeful this type of analysis, above all others, will provide us with some answers."

"I see." Sarah's gaze moved from the baby to Cameron. Her imploring eyes begged for his assent, not so much for the test as for a far more significant and consequential issue.

"I want to keep him as much as you do," whispered Cameron to his wife, "but there is a process. It will take time—and there's no guarantee he'll be entrusted to us."

Without hesitation, Sarah engaged the doctor in a plot to secure the boy. "That could endanger my career, Madame," he answered calmly. "I can certainly speak on your behalf to the proper authorities."

"I lost a child recently," she told him, earnestly petitioning for his compassion and his assistance. "In its place, God has sent me this one. How can you oppose God's will?"

Cameron was startled by Sarah's declaration of God's intervention. Although she had succumbed to self-afflicted emotional duress and prayed once or twice in the past, she would never openly acknowledge God or his heavenly powers. Perhaps she was being manipulative.

Sarah dropped to her knees and grabbed his white coat, pulling on it firmly. "I beg of you. Grant my request. They say doctors are closest to God," she continued, now appealing to Lefoux's vanity. "Can't you bring his work to its rightful conclusion?"

Lefoux stared at her, reflecting on her plea: he was wavering. "Perhaps there is something I can do without diverging into *flagrant* illegality; but I promise nothing."

"You are a Saint," she said, bowing her head in gratitude.

"One person's Saint is another's scoundrel," muttered Lefoux as he lifted Sarah to her feet. "To accelerate things, in the event we're success-ful, I'd like to run the same tests and analyses on both of you. Healthy parents would be a definite plus in your favor."

"Absolutely!" they cried out in unison.

"I'll arrange for a room for the three of you." The doctor looked up. "You better be behind this, you heavenly prankster."

CHAPTER 8

Circa 2,000 years ago; Kingdom of Heaven.

"Queen to g-5; check," arrogantly declared the Prince of Darkness as he flapped his bat-like wings in delight. Lord God, the King of Heaven perused the Chess board, pondering over his next move. "I believe I shall move my King to c-7. A heavenly move, I must declare."

"A cowardly move, you mean to say," said Satan, attempting to destabilize his opponent. "Retreat if you will, but I will have you soon enough—and I'll have what is rightfully mine."

"You will not supplement your ranks today," King Deus assured his eternal counterpart. "It is enough that the *Act of Allocation* has favored your agenda for millennia."

"Indeed," recognized the Dragon Lord of Hell. "Of all the rulings in the Acts of Maitreya, that Statute has been my favorite. Even Erel, your faithful chief-accountant, has not expressed a grievance against it. Contrary to you, his duty has not been dulled by petty interests."

"The souls of Humanity do not fall within the realm of pettiness," retorted Deus. "They are of paramount significance."

"Knight to b-5; check," was Satan's only answer, oozing with undeserved confidence.

As Deus considered his next move, Satan rose from his plush chair and walked about the room which, apart from what appeared to be a large video screen, abounded with luxurious furniture and decorations of the human baroque era—an era whose onset on Earth would only come about centuries in the future.

"If only I had been accorded more fortuitous circumstances during the Great War," whined Satan, "all this extravagant and *sinful* opulence would have been mine." Sitting back into his chair, he lowered his head and tilted his face to capture Deus' gaze. "You live in sin, my friend. What of humility, modesty and simplicity? Have you abandoned these principles only to adopt my way of life?"

"Bishop takes over Knight," said an unflinching Deus.

"Is that conceit I see plastered over your face?" Satan was unrelenting. "What is it that poor fellow said: *the meek shall inherit the earth*? I don't detect any meekness in you. You should have never inherited Heaven."

"It was not mine to inherit," grinned Deus. "It was simply mine. Your move."

"Narcissism?" cried out Satan with amusement. "Your true nature exposed in this objectionable manner compels me to remind you: I have snatched part of Heaven from under Maitreya's sword. Even he, your appointed Holy Spirit and War General, was helpless in stopping me."

Deus said nothing, letting Satan drown in his waves of futile taunts.

"And what of human misery?" Satan redoubled his efforts. "Not only were millions of souls destroyed in your name during the War, but your greatest advocate on Earth is about to lose his mortal coil."

Leaving his chair a second time, he pressed a button on the visual screen. The image of a beaten man nailed onto a cross appeared.

"He calls himself Jesus Christ," said Satan, pointing at the center of the screen. "This man was mocked, scorned, and horribly tortured. He was forced to carry his cross over a great distance and was finally nailed to it, in between two common criminals."

"I am well aware of these events," Deus dryly informed Satan.

"His suffering is indescribable," went on Satan, "and yet he claims to love his tormentors and all the people who judge him or do nothing for him. Look upon him and tell me you are not indifferent to his plight."

As Deus, Lord God and King of Heaven, stared at the man on the cross, he heard him say something only a great Noble of Heaven would say: "Father, forgive them, for they do not know what they do."

"Love and forgiveness, is that not what you teach, Deus?" asked Satan. "He forgives them—all those nasty sinners—as he knows you would forgive any soul—or any Eternal."

"What could he know of me?" pondered Deus. "He has not yet crossed over."

"If, as you maintain, you have followed this mortal's quest, you would know of his claim," pointed out Satan.

"What claim?" demanded Deus, who now seemed a bit unnerved—a development that did not go unnoticed by Satan. His plan to impair Deus' poise and concentration was working. After all, the stakes of the Chess game were high.

"He has called you by name countless times," replied Satan. "Lord here. God there. God of Heaven…and of course, *Father*."

"I have no such Son," insisted Deus, who now rose from his chair and pressed his knuckles against the table. "Let that be clear."

"No recent fornication with a Human female?" Satan was thoroughly enjoying his mind games. It had been quite a while since he had witnessed Deus' indignation unravel in such effervescent form.

"As the Prime Noble, I would not!" declared Deus. "No Eternal would since the application of the *Act of Non-Interference*. That is the Law."

"I see," softly said Satan, moving to the screen again and raising the volume. "There's more," he added, anticipating, oddly enough, more incriminating revelations from the man called Jesus.

"My God, my God, why have you forsaken me?" cried out Christ, looking towards the sky.

"He calls you by title once again," Satan reminded Deus. "He beseeches you…and blames you. He now realizes the horror of what is happening and what he is enduring. He is about to be engulfed in the raging sea of sin."

"Evil triumphs," suddenly conceded Jesus. "This is your hour, but it is only for a moment."

"He blames you, not me," realized Deus. "You are the great begetter of Evil. I represent truth and justice."

"Where does this grand Representative operate?" queried Satan. "In Heaven or on Earth? The burden of all the sins of humanity is overwhelming the humanity of Jesus. Is that your justice?"

"His claims are hollow," asserted Deus. "No human could wield such power."

"Perhaps not, but even you can be mistaken." Satan laughed out loud before resuming his seat. "If only you admitted he was your son, such power would be explained. Oh, what other surprises await us? Only *God* knows!" He laughed again, ending his show of jocularity with a low and persistent chuckle. "Queen to c-5."

Flustered and impatient, Deus moved back his King. "King to d-8."

"Queen to c-7," countered Satan. "Checkmate."

Deus' face became red, his full lips tightened, and his skin boiled as Satan basked in his victory. But it was not so much these tokens of pent up anger that usually arrested Satan's notice as the deep-rooted sorrow he glimpsed in Deus' eyes. On this day, Lord God had failed to save many souls.

And Erel, the King's chief-accountant, would attest to this momentarily.

CHAPTER 9

Present day; France.

"I have news," announced Doctor Lefoux as he entered Sarah and Cameron's hospital room. "Good news and…" Lefoux paused.

"What's the bad news?" insisted Cameron, expecting some life-threatening condition.

"Nothing of that nature," reassured the doctor. "Let's call it weird and highly implausible news."

Sarah held her newfound child tighter. "Please doctor, no more bombshells."

"In the end, you both should be pleased," presumed Lefoux. "Well, I think you will."

"Get on with it," barked Cameron, his FBI agent persona bursting to the forefront.

"Firstly and most importantly, the child is in splendid health," reported Lefoux. "In fact, he is the quintessence of all a mother would hope for—the embodiment of perfect health. And that's despite the anomalies."

"More anomalies?" queried Sarah, holding back her joyful but cautious exuberance.

"Yes," plainly answered Lefoux. "Genetic anomalies that have never been recorded in the annals of medicine. Bear in mind, genetic analysis and mapping is a relatively new field. New discoveries are bound to happen sooner than later."

"These anomalies are not harmful, are they?" deduced Cameron.

"As I said," went on Lefoux, "the child is otherwise perfect. Let me explain. Human cells have 23 pairs of large linear nuclear chromosomes: 22 pairs of autosomes and one pair of sex chromosomes. Around the centromere, the point where the two chromatids touch, and where the microtubules attach, a short arm and a long foot extend. These are the two primary parts that make up a chromosome. Genetic anomalies affect one or both parts. Of the recorded mutations, we have phenomena known as deletion, duplication, inversion, translocation and insertion. What concerns us in this case is a strange form of insertion, where typically a part of a chromosome, usually along the long foot, detaches itself and connects to another chromosome—a transposition if you will."

"Why is this transposition *strange*?" wondered Sarah; "I mean as far as mutations go."

"Because there is no evidence of transposition," admitted Lefoux. "However, it is still technically an insertion. We've found three chromosomes: chromosome 1, 11 and 21 with extraneous chromosomal material—material that doesn't originate from the other remaining chromosomes. In effect, it is insertion without transposition. The additional chromosomal strands are completely new and have never been mapped before. Aside from the ears and the back muscle extrusions, I'm at a loss to even speculate as to their purpose or latent impact on the child's physiognomy or biology."

"So you're saying our child might grow wings, or fangs, or webbed feet?" cried Sarah in a fatalist tone, bereft of any hint of humor.

"I am saying nothing," Lefoux replied slowly, "nor do I proclaim to be the harbinger of doom. Your child is full of life and, need I say it again, perfect. And if God is looking over him as his own little miracle, your child will remain perfect."

"*Your* child!" noted Cameron. "Not *the* child. You've mentioned that twice now. Is that part of the good news? You've found a way to make this child ours?"

"I believe so," happily trumpeted Lefoux, relieved the conversation would end auspiciously. "But my influence played only a minor role in the matter: nature has a way of interceding. Analysis of Sarah's genome has revealed that approximately 23% of her genetic baggage matches that of the child. That would make you, Sarah Sinclair, his great aunt, or second cousin, or something along those lines. Believe it or not, this tiny boy is of your kin, and you are its closest and only known relative."

Thunderstruck, Sarah began to shed warm tears of joy. "What extraordinary news…but how is that possible? I'm an only child. My parents are only children; so are my grandparents. He couldn't be part of my family line."

"Yet he is," confirmed Lefoux, "and not that far removed. As I said, he is God's miracle. Barring any unforeseen event—like an unlikely distant relative claiming the child—he is yours, or rather will be once I push through the required paperwork."

"Will we be interviewed to determine our suitability as parents?" inquired Cameron.

"No need for that," confidently answered Lefoux. "DNA match aside, our week together has convinced me you'll make great parents. Congratulations."

Sarah and Cameron snuggled the boy between them and kissed him over and over again. "My little miracle," whispered Sarah, rubbing her nose against his. His deep blue eyes twinkled and he giggled. Somehow, he knew he was home.

CHAPTER 10

Circa 2,000 years ago; Kingdom of Heaven.

"Erel! How good of you to show up," gleefully shouted Satan as he reveled in his accustomed victory over Deus, Lord God. "And punctual, your most shining quality."

"May my punctuality only serve my Lord," snapped back the chief-accountant. Erel was a short stocky angel, a Sanctus Angelicum as all angels were called in the Kingdom of Heaven. He seldom smiled, nor did he ever scowl, but he was implacably suspicious of all demons, Diabolicus Terrum and Arium alike—and of Satan, the Dragon Lord most of all.

"Your punctuality, in this instance, will only expedite my delectation," assured Satan. "Your Lord has lost again; checkmate as it were. Perhaps we should switch back to poker at our next encounter," Satan suggested to Deus. "The aggressive intellectuality inherently required in the game of Chess falls to the lot of great minds, from which yours has been ostracized eons ago. The luck of the draw, on the other hand, may yet be your most dependable consort."

"Mind your words, Devil," warned Deus, "and mind your place. Do not forget whom you are addressing." Satan feigned contrition and abstained from any further aspersions. He instead turned to Erel. "I understand that many deem the vocation of *Echo Accounting* a slatternly and untidy business. Your hands must be stained with the ink of condemnation."

"Might I point out that *your* hands are blemished beyond repair." The accountant's face remained expressionless as he pulled out a ledger from under his white robe. "31,297 souls…I mean Echoes, have arrived, for a reintegration rate of 75.7%."

"Reintegration is up, this cycle," noted Deus. "That's excellent."

"Echo engineers have reduced transfer interference by 4%," said Erel. "That's a marked improvement in efficiency."

"What of the preliminary split?" eagerly asked Deus.

"As expected, *Sin Scores* are normally distributed," replied Erel, "with a mean sin score of 210 and a standard deviation of 72. It's an even split: 45% of Echoes have scored 200 or less and been directly dispatched to Heaven; 34.4% were sent to Hell-*Zone 1*; 10.6% to Hell-*Zone 2*; the remaining 10% have been temporarily assigned to Purgatory."

"Marvelous!" exclaimed Satan. "If my Math serves me well, that's 3,130 bonus souls for the taking—a solid 10% gain courtesy of my superior intellect." The King of Hell profusely exuded consummate cupidity and avarice, contaminating the air with an overwhelming stench of rancidity—a fetor of decay that was common to the kingdom of Hell and permeated its land through and through, from the South shore of Lake Spiritu Sancto to the Great Deserts beyond the Belzebuth Mountains.

"I realize I must remain dispassionate, my Lord," said Erel as he handed the ledger to Deus for an approval signature, "but I am sorry. Purgatory was once a vast realm where all Echoes without exception were *purified* for entry into the Kingdom of Heaven. Now it's nothing more than a minuscule and vulgar processing plant, a triash center where, more often than naught, Echoes are committed to Hell."

The Act of Allocation, the most controversial statute among the Acts of Maitreya, was originally professed to be a just covenant, dividing souls evenly over the long term: half destined for Heaven; the other half for Hell. This was, of course, contingent on opponents of comparable abilities and decisiveness. The passage of time had proven otherwise. Evidently, Satan had bested Deus at all games played: Chess, Strategic Squares, Kingdom Clash, Maitreya Swording, and Dragoraptor racing. At this juncture—and as disturbingly put forward by Satan—poker might be Deus' only avenue to triumph.

"Poker it is," announced Deus as he passed the ledger to Satan for his signature.

"Poker it is," confirmed a grinning Satan.

"I will provide the deck of cards," insisted Erel. "I'm certain you have no objections, Lord Satan." The accountant snatched the ledger from Satan's hand and left hurriedly, depriving Satan from the opportunity to protest.

"I'll see you at the end of the next cycle, your place," impassively said Deus to his rival. "Now get out."

Satan complied happily and went back to Hell.

CHAPTER 11

Present day; Rome, Italy.

"Archbishop Nadeau! Archbishop Nadeau!" shouted Father De Lucia, panting as he reached Nadeau, the prefect of the pontifical house, at the threshold of the Apostolic Palace, the Pope's official residence.

"I have no time for you, Father," replied Nadeau almost harshly. "I must rejoin the Pope and the American President Armstrong at once." Grabbing the primary entrance doorknob, he began turning it until De Lucia placed his hand over his, stopping its circular motion.

"I would be derelict in my duties as College administrator if I did not deliver this immediately," pointed out De Lucia as he presented a small envelope marked urgent. "The contents were given to me in confidence, although any of my efforts to decode their meaning would have been in vain."

A puzzled Nadeau foraged through his pockets. "You need only have called me on my cell phone. Where is that blasted thing?"

"The owner of this message wondered the same thing after repeatedly trying to reach you," said De Lucia as he handed Nadeau his phone. "You left it on your desk atop your out box."

Nadeau snatched the phone and then the envelope. "On top of things, as usual." De Lucia was uncertain as to the intent of the comment: the Archbishop often doled out criticism under the guise of compliments. The two Papal Swiss guards standing straight as rods on each side of the entrance dared not even blink an eye lest they also be the recipients of Nadeau's courtesies. Quickly, the latter opened the door and disappeared inside.

"Your Eminence," extolled Nadeau as he half-bowed and stretched out both arms, one hand over the other, carrying the pope's glasses. "As you requested." Evidently, Nadeau wasn't the only absent-minded priest at the Vatican.

"Thank you, Archbishop," softly replied the pope before putting on the glasses. "Perhaps I need new glasses to find my old ones." Karl Armstrong, the current President of the United States, chuckled at the pope's witty remark.

"I see that clever repartee is well within your compass, your Eminence," gleefully noted Armstrong.

"The radius of my compass is on an irreversible decline," admitted the Vatican ruler, "but what remains becomes evermore precious. Isn't that so, my friend?" now addressing Nadeau.

"Yes, your Eminence," agreed Nadeau. "I myself find new failings every day, but I rejoice in the knowledge that with every new revelation of feebleness, I am one step closer to God. May my imperfect self now retire from your Holiness and his distinguished guest?"

The pope eyed Nadeau keenly. "Let us suspend our discussions of world affairs and engage in more personal matters. Let us talk as men, as simple men." Inviting Nadeau to sit next to the President, the pope bent forward. "Tell me some things about yourselves that defined you as mortal men; a turning point in your lives."

"After you, Archbishop." Armstrong respectfully offered Nadeau the opportunity to share first. "I'm positive you can evoke a far more interesting tapestry of musings and reflections than I can."

"I assure you, my tapestry is quite plain," confided Nadeau. The pope urged him on, dismissing his humility. "I was once very much in love, only 19 at the time. Her name was Caroline. We were taking the bus from Montreal to her parents' country house in Franconia, New Hampshire. The rain was torrential and the roads dangerous. What could happen happened: the bus driver lost control and we slid into a deep ravine, tumbling all the way down until the bus crashed into a huge rock. The bus literally cracked in two."

Nadeau paused to regain his composure, his stare never leaving the ground. The pope and the President said nothing and waited. "Caroline was ejected out of the bus," he went on, "and fell onto a bed of stones. Despite my broken leg and several broken ribs, I crawled through one of the shattered windows and inched my way to her. Her bloodied body was embedded with several shards of glass—one large piece protruded from her chest. She lay there listless and quite dead. I pulled the piece out, cutting my hands further, and collapsed over her, coming in and out of consciousness. Amid the screams and cries from the other passengers, a voice suddenly rose above the chaos and spoke to me—it spoke to *me*."

Nadeau stopped, unwilling or unable to carry on. "Go on, my Son," prompted the pope. "Christ is with you."

Nadeau lifted his head and gawked at the pope with amazement and consternation. "He was. He was *with* me; and he instructed me to *wait* for him."

"Perhaps he asked you to *pray* for him," intimated the pope, who was no stranger to divine apparitions. "Christ waits for you, not you for him."

"I...I became a priest shortly after—because of this," hesitantly admitted Nadeau. "After that extraordinary experience, I could become nothing else."

"The reasons are irrelevant," said the pope. "If Christ lives in you, you need not justify how he came to do so. Perhaps we should now let our guest regale us with a story equally fertile in imagination and illumination."

"You've inspired me, Archbishop Nadeau." Armstrong gently tapped Nadeau on the shoulder. "I'm privileged to be in the presence of such devout and inspirational men."

"As are we, Mister President," diplomatically replied the pope. "Please, proceed."

"I must admit to experiencing a similar event," said Armstrong with a hesitation that rivaled that of Nadeau. "I don't profess to be more worthy than any other man, but I too heard the voice of Christ. I bring this up only because the Archbishop has already dared broach the subject."

"My, my," let out the pope. "I am indeed blessed to be sitting among men of such divine privilege."

"I claim no such privilege," corrected Armstrong. "I submit only co-incidence." The pope said nothing further and appeared eager for the tale to come. "It happened in February 1991 during the Gulf War. I was an army reservist stationed at an American military barrack in Dhahran, Saudi Arabia, when an Iraqi missile hit us hard. 28 soldiers were killed while many others were severely wounded. I was one of the latter. The force of the blast shot me clear across the barrack and against the side of a jeep, breaking my pelvis and both arms. My body was peppered with shrapnel and blood oozed from every wound. That's when a voice rung my ears: 'It's not your time,' it said gently. I opened my eyes and saw a soldier like none I had ever seen. While his outfit was clearly military, his face was heavenly—the face of Christ. He touched me on the knee and the pain vanished. Thank you, I said to him."

" 'No worries,' he replied simply. 'Wait for me.'

"Wait for what?" I asked, compelled to pose the question.

'The time when I will be in need of your mortal coil is close,' he said."

"But Christ is all powerful," remarked an annoyed Nadeau. "He is in need of nothing of the mortal sort." The pope raised his hand, signaling Nadeau to remain silent. Armstrong's account of the mysterious had apparently titillated the pope's interest.

"The mystical being began dissipating," continued Armstrong, "but not before repeating: 'Wait for me.' A moment later, he was gone. I rose and was immediately joined by a fellow reservist. 'Are you injured?' He asked frantically. I…I was, uh, no I'm fine, I blurted out, confused and relieved. Did you see him?"

"'Who?' No one, I said, thanking the soldier for his concern. Since then, I've refrained from telling the story to anyone, not even my wife. This is the first time I confess to it."

"Confession is good for the soul." The pope extended his hand, smiling. "You may kiss it or shake it. I'm not much for formalities behind closed doors. The Archbishop will see you out."

Shaking the pope's hand, Armstrong left, escorted by Nadeau. "I hope I wasn't too presumptuous," worried the President as he took place in his limousine parked in the driveway.

"As I hope as well," retorted Nadeau. "For my sake, of course. I work daily with the man."

As the presidential car drove off, Nadeau turned his attention to the envelope De Lucia had given him. He pulled it out of his pocket and clumsily opened it, revealing a short note in French on cardboard paper: **CONFIRMÉ. E = M^{2}C**. To the uninitiated eye, the message seemed to indicate the confirmation of a mathematical equation that closely resembled Einstein's energy-mass conversion formula $E = MC^2$. To Nadeau, however, it was brimming with history-altering significance. It was the message—*the ultimate sign*—he had been waiting for since his horrifying bus accident 40 years ago.

The Archbishop dropped the note, and took a few steps before his legs gave way. He stumbled to the ground and lay on his back, gazing towards the heavens. "God, forgive us for we are about to trespass."

CHAPTER 12

Present day; France.

Resting in a lavish leather chair in the study room of a luxurious 16th century house on the western extremity of *Île de la Cité*, a natural island on the river Seine, Doctor Maurice Lefoux leisurely smoked a cigar. After staring at a large envelope on his massive wooden desk for some time, he rose from his chair and walked to a painting on the wall, and opened it, much like a door, revealing a safe behind it.

Rotating the combination lock twice to the right and to the left, he opened the safe door, and pulled out a metal box, 18" by 24" by 4", and placed it on the desk next to the envelope.

Retrieving a key from his pants pocket, he unlocked and opened the top right desk drawer and secured another key from under a pile of papers, which he used to open the metal box. He sat back into the chair, and grabbed a DNA chart labeled *Subject C, degradation 48.913%*, from the box.

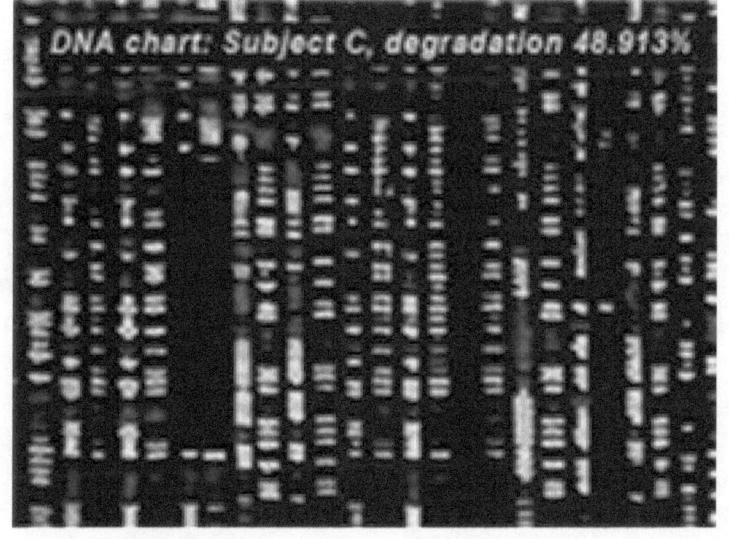

He then detached a short memo clipped onto the chart and read:

√ *Blood belongs to a group consistent with a native Jewish male.*
√ *Blood contains XY chromosomes, consistent with human and male source.*
√ *Blood is type AB.*
√ *Pattern of blood stains consistent with historical premise.*
WARNING: DNA profile is incomplete.
Mitigating factors in authentication of Subject C:
√ *Small quantity of workable DNA.*
√ *Degradation of DNA due to antiquated age.*
√ *Contamination of DNA with limestone and cellulose.*
Good luck,
LGV
Department of Microbiology and Molecular Genetics
University of Texas

Lefoux examined the chart, concentrating on the blank areas, and imagining the data that would have appeared had the DNA been in virgin condition. "I know it's you," he mumbled to himself, before depositing the chart and memo on his desk.

He then removed a second DNA chart from the box, labeled *Subject M^2, degradation 7.115%*, and scrutinized that one. "You, I have no doubt," he said. "Sing to me, darling."

Depositing the chart over the other one, he finally harvested his pride and joy from the metal box: a small five-century old wooden chest containing a triad of priceless items: a clump of dark brown hair (including follicles) tied together with a strand of silk; the phalanx bones of a female ring finger; and a gold ring.

Lefoux slowly twirled the ring between his fingers, letting the light of his Tiffany-style Victorian lamp bounce off its glistening exterior. The inner side of the ring was inscribed with *Amore Mio Lisa-Maria*. "The catch of the Millennium," thought the doctor. "You had much better luck with women than I ever did, you old Italian Casanova."

Replacing the ring in the miniature chest, he closed the cover and returned it to its favored position in the metal box, turning his attention anew to the large envelope, which had remained unattended until now. He pulled out yet another DNA chart, from the envelope, this one marked only with the mention *degradation 0.0666%.*

Grinning widely like a materialistic schmuck salivating over the picture of his newly ordered BMW-X3, Lefoux snatched a black felt pen from a container on his desk, and wrote in bold letters atop the chart: **SUBJECT M²C.** He admired the chart, comparing its subjective beauty to Da Vinci's masterpiece Mona Lisa. "Simply stunning." He found himself unable to look away.

But, as with all things, a sudden and hearty knock at the door managed to snap his concentration. "What is it, Madame Poissant?"

"Cardinal Nadeau of the Vatican is on the phone," said his longtime housekeeper as she entered the room. "Do you wish me to transfer the call to the study?"

"Please do so. Thank you," instructed Lefoux. "The good priest is either ecstatic or petrified."

"Rather petrified, I should say," humorously replied the housekeeper, before retiring. She loved giving her opinion, even if her master never solicited it.

"Probably wants to challenge my findings," assumed the doctor. "He's so weak. I should be the one heading the *organization*," he mused with pompousness. "*The Circle of the Eight* should be ruled with an iron fist and single-minded conviction."

No sooner had he picked up the phone, he heard quite clearly: "Qui est cet *ENFANT*? (who is this *child*?)"

CHAPTER 13

Present day; New York.

"Cameron, you seem preoccupied," noticed Sarah as she lightly bounced her baby off her thighs. "Young fathers always are," interjected the taxi driver who was taking back the happy family to Sarah's parents' home.

"The chain of events leading to our parenthood is so improbable," replied Cameron, disregarding the driver's comment.

"It doesn't matter, Cam," countered Sarah. "Whether by chance or by design, we have a second shot." Sarah placed her index finger in the child's palm, its fingers entrapping her own. "How's my sweetheart Ethan?"

"Sarah, I don't think it's appropriate—or healthy—to name him that," pointed out Cameron. "Ethan died, and his name died with him."

Sarah pondered over her husband's position and tendered a compromise: "Theon!"

"The name of your grandfather," remembered Cameron. "That would be a nice tribute to his memory."

"It would," agreed Sarah, buoyantly looking over her child who had now been endowed with an identity, and reinvented. "Theon Ethan Rex."

Cameron frowned. "Honey, don't trifle with my patience. Ethan is not an option."

"Not Ethan, but Theon Ethan," specified Sarah. "But don't fret. While he may be baptized as such, we'll simply call him Theon…Theon E. Rex."

Cameron knew that, once his wife set her mind on something, it was virtually impossible to alter course. She did compromise, however; and that was enough to keep his criticism at bay.

While Cameron ruminated upon the armistice over the boy's name, his cell phone rang angrily: it was Sophie, his sister and FBI partner. "Hi, Sophie, who's dead this time?"

"No one, thankfully," informed Shopie.

Cameron sighed with relief. "Some positive developments then?"

"Not really," she said uneasily. "It concerns Sarah and you. Someone seems extremely interested in your personal and professional lives."

"How do you mean?" questioned Cameron, who had been subjected to several interrogations in the past by the Senate oversight committee. "Am I under investigation again?" During his career, Cameron had been involved in the deaths of many infamous criminals. It was standard procedure to review and ascertain the implication and role of federal agents involved in high-profile—and well publicized—homicides. "And what of Sarah? Who's investigating her?"

"It's not so much a legal inquest as it is an unauthorized search," clarified Sophie. "Someone has hacked into our computer network and accessed the FBI central database. The perpetrator called up the personnel files and downloaded a copy of one of them—yours to be precise. Whoever hired this hacker now knows every detail of your life, from the name and background of your wife, the prescription drugs you take, the places you've traveled, to the quantity of cream you put in your coffee, all the way to your psychological profile."

"My wife, Sophie," growled Cameron, "my wife."

"What's going on, Cam?" nervously asked Sarah. "Who's after us?"

"Hang on, Sarah." Cameron wrapped his arm around his wife, hoping to calm her.

"We checked to see if your wife was also a person of interest," said Sophie, "and discovered that the human resource datamart of her employer, the French magazine publisher *Alerte à la Primeur*, was also infiltrated. Your wife's resumé was downloaded to the same unknown server."

"Any leads?" pressed on Cameron, determined to identify the transgressors and put an abrupt end to their illicit activities.

"Not yet," sadly replied Sophie, "but I'll continue canvassing all possible leads. You enjoy the rest of your vacation. I'll see you in a week."

"Easier said than done. Keep me posted." Cameron terminated the connection, but refrained to remand his phone to the bottom of his pants pocket. "Sarah, do you have the number of your therapist?"

"Why…why do you need my shrink's number?" Sarah's anxiety spiked.

"Just give it to me," implored Cameron. "I'll tell you in a minute."

Dialing the number provided by Sarah, a charming and engaging voice answered. "Doctor Gallagher speaking."

"Doctor, this is Cameron Rex, and I'm here with my wife Sarah Sinclair. I'd like to ask you if anybody has been inquiring about my wife lately."

"Doctor-patient confidentiality prevents me from divulging any details about our conversations," adamantly riposted Gallagher. "If someone had asked, that person would have been met with silence."

"Of course, doctor," acknowledged Cameron. "Do you keep electronic or paper files on your patients?"

"Paper files only," said Gallagher, "in locked cabinets."

"Can you retrieve my wife's file?" pleaded Cameron. "I'm not interested in its contents, only its safeguard. Please, I beg for your indulgence."

Heeding the unusual request, doctor Gallagher unlocked the drawer labeled R-S-T and browsed through the files. Moments later, she returned to the phone. "I'm confounded and quite confused, Mister Rex. The file on Sarah Sinclair has vanished."

CHAPTER 14

Circa 2,000 years ago; Kingdom of Hell.

Lord Satan paced the floor of his office, jubilant and quite full of himself. Today had been a good day. The sinister and ominous being standing in the office doorway thought otherwise. "Your glee is premature if not unwarranted." He moved forth, donning a hooded cape that concealed his macabre features.

"Master," shouted Satan to the Dark Lord. "I did not expect you."

"You never expect me," remarked the Dark Lord, "nor do you seem to desire me. I'm beginning to think I'm a source of dread and foreboding to you."

"Of all the envious and hostile tongues lashing out at me, I did not imagine yours to be the most venomous," caustically replied Satan. "Today, I repatriated thousands of souls from Purgatory: a victory for our side, and good reason for exemption from your jeering."

"Today's repatriation is tomorrow's deportation, you short-sighted fool," sneered the Dark Lord, toppling over an imposing marble statue of God and Satan in mortal combat. The effigy of the Dragon Lord towered over that of God, preparing to stab its heart with the Sword of Maitreya.

"Spare me your sermons couched in riddles," moaned Satan. "My performance against Deus has been exemplary, that you cannot deny."

"I deny nothing," stated the Dark Lord, "and I testify to everything, notably the fallacy and extravagance of your theory about the prophet *Jesus Christ*. He was brought to life for one reason and one reason alone. After serving his purpose, he should have fallen into obscurity."

"My theory was sound, Master," insisted Satan. "Once he unexpectedly embraced the role of seer of souls and human fate, my facilitation of his demonization and execution has catapulted the ignorant mobs to the apex of sin and wickedness. From it, the number of sinners and sin scores of future cycles will undoubtedly rise considerably—strengthening our ranks."

"You're sadly mistaken," cried out an incensed Lord. "Our sin monitors on Earth have registered a massive eradication of sin among the populace—immediately following Christ's death. Your plan has backfired. Lack of foresight I can forgive now and again, but failing to recognize the true state of your affairs is inexcusable."

"Undeniably a coincidence," alleged Satan, who hid his difficulty in believing his own assertion. "He was never endowed with such powers. Of all people, you should know this."

"Many things have escaped your ambit during your supposed dominion over Hell," observed the Dark Lord, who lowered his hood, revealing a horribly disfigured face, its eyes especially, having since been violently relieved of their eyelids.

"I saved you once," sharply retaliated Satan. "*Your poor* state of affairs had not escaped me then."

"Granted," conceded the Lord, "but you walk a fine line. Be warned, be proficient…and bring Christ's soul to me." Satan's master walked out, but not before glimpsing the statue he had overturned. "The sword should be in God's hand," he thought.

CHAPTER 15

Present day; New York.

Sarah sat at the outer edge of the first bench on the left side of the front hall that connected directly to the main altar of the gothic-style St. Patrick's Cathedral, New York's most revered church and seat of the Archbishop of New York. Theon, resting quietly on Sarah's knees, looked about, his attention monopolized by the beautifully crafted stained glass windows and marble sculptures.

"He seems to like Church a lot," said Cameron who sat next to his wife. "How about you?" Cameron expected a novel answer.

"It's breathtaking and amazingly peaceful," confessed Sarah. "I resisted it for so many years. And despite my defiance of God and his existence, he imparted to me this little treasure of unblemished life."

"He's also inviting him into his kingdom." Cameron pointed to the baptismal font on the altar, a critical element of a ritual that his first child Ethan would have been spared, had it been only up to Sarah. She had indeed been transformed.

"Speaking of invitation, where are Sophie and William?" worried Sarah who peered intently at the Church's main entrance. "You did tell Bill it was at 10am?" Despite his stunning memory, homed by years of training, Cameron could be absent-minded when it came to issues outside the realm of his profession. "You did, didn't you?" Her voice became increasingly critical.

"Honey, you underestimate me," he replied in a musky roundness that wavered between vexation and trepidation. "Let me check outside. They're probably searching for parking as we speak." Cameron secretly prayed that was true as he broke into an easy canter towards the entrance. "Idiot!" he called himself as he endeavored to jog his memory. How could they proceed with the baptism without Theon's godparents?

Family relatives and friends smiled and waved at Cameron as he passed them, and he, in turn, produced an unsettled grin. He began to slip his hand into his pocket, intent on pulling out his cell phone and calling Bill the moment he overtook the outside terrace, but stopped in his tracks when he beheld a man that had recently been instrumental in his bestowal of a child. Accompanied by several other men sitting on the very last bench, there sprawled an exalted Doctor Lefoux, unlit pipe in mouth.

"A most princely event," cheerfully exclaimed Lefoux to Cameron as he sprung out of his seat and extended his hand in felicitations. "Come now Mister Policeman, shake my hand. I did make the trip for the boy." Cameron complied with an equal measure of stupefaction rather than pleasure. "I'm…*honored* that you could make it, especially without an invitation, or an address."

"I'm a presumptuous and resourceful man," simply said Lefoux. "I hope you're not offended by my unsung presence?"

"I see you brought your cavalry," gibed Cameron, unintentionally manifesting his thinly veiled annoyance.

"Nothing as dignified as a cavalry," placidly retorted Lefoux; "just interested and concerned partisans."

"Of course. Enjoy yourselves." Cameron scrutinized the odd group of men for a few seconds, recording their images in his mind, frowned and then quickly stepped out of the church, almost running over his brother William.

"Where the hell have you been?" yelled Cameron. "It's 10:02 and the priest is waiting."

"Sorry Man, my fault," apologized Bill. "I had an emergency with the Mars Rover and couldn't leave Washington on time."

"Yeah, his space go-cart encountered disgruntled Martians," snapped Sophie who was right behind him. "I should have married a Martian. At least I would see more of him."

As Cameron, Bill and Sophie rushed to the altar, Sarah gave her husband a sour look before turning her attention back to the priest. "May God forgive my husband's shortcomings." The priest smiled politely, maintaining his serene demeanor.

"Let us begin," announced the priest as the foursome gathered around the holy water font. "Please hold the child directly over the font," he instructed Sarah. Despite her frail arms, she felt the power of God coursing through them as she held her boy effortlessly above the shimmering water.

The priest gathered some of it into a small flat cup made of ceramic, raised it above the baby's head and declared: "I baptize you Theon Ethan, the servant of God, in the name of the Father, and of the Son, and of the Holy Spirit." He then poured the water onto the child's forehead and wiped it gently across its temples, revealing its pointed ears. "My Lord," he gasped inaudibly.

Sarah saw his lips move. "What was that, Father?" she asked respectfully.

"Your child is most unique, my dear," observed the priest as his fingers followed the contour of Theon's left ear. "Surely, God will reserve a special place for him in Heaven."

"Right next to his brother Ethan," assured Sarah with the greatest conviction.

The remaining holy water on Theon's skin bubbled intensely and evaporated, leaving a visible reddish rash. The priest was baffled and understandably alarmed. Theon began to moan and squirm incessantly, prompting Sarah to leave the altar swiftly and head for the exit.

"She's very emotional," Cameron confided to the befuddled priest before thanking him and signaling Bill and Sophie to follow him. As they walked steadily in pursuit of Sarah, Bill noticed Lefoux and his contingent, one of which struck his interest. Sitting right next to Lefoux was his brother Ted's immediate superior at SETI, supervisor George Lapierre, the one who, weeks ago, classified the data regarding the wormhole that grazed the surface of Mars. "You did find Theon on *this* planet, right?" Bill asked Cameron, pointing to the ground.

CHAPTER 16

"These cartoons are new, aren't they?" queried Bill as he moved from one picture frame to another, hanging along the living room wall. "I see you're still bent on ridiculing religion," he added, scrutinizing one cartoon in particular depicting God sitting at a dining table while being served a bowl of soup whose vapors bore the likeness of wretched souls. Upset by the dish, God cried out to the angel-waiter: *"You call this Soul Food?!"*

YOU CALL THIS SOUL FOOD?!

"I won an award from the *National Cartoonists Society* for my series on religion," said Sarah with a conspicuous lack of pride. Recent events had irrevocably transformed her perspective on the ideologies surrounding religion. And she looked intensely at the most salient outcome of those events, resting against her bosom.

"Well, you could always go back to politics," proposed Bill, clearly detecting her newfound shame for her pagan ways. "I'm sure your publisher, *Alerte à la Primeur*, would appreciate a change in theme."

"For the next little while, we'll be concentrating on baby pictures," remarked Cameron as he, his sister and his parents appeared from the kitchen. "I'm making ratatouille," announced Cameron's mother, "your favorite. I hope it'll be as good as your mother's."

"Oh, come now Francine, your cooking is top notch," bragged Henry, Cam's overconfident father, as he sat next to Sarah holding a Pinocchio doll. "If I were lying, Pinocchio's nose would grow." And suddenly it did. "I thought you were on my side, you renegade puppet," he yelled, feigning outrage. "Just for that, I'm giving you to Theon. He'll pluck away your nose in no time."

"Thank you Henry, for the beautiful gift," acknowledged Sarah, who seized the doll and jiggled it in front of Theon. "The Blue Fairy has been very busy these days, tiny one."

"Why don't you put Theon to bed while Sophie and I prepare the ratatouille," suggested Francine who then ordered her daughter back into the kitchen. "It should be ready in about one hour."

"Good idea," concurred Henry who handed Sarah a second gift: *The Illustrated Adventures of Pinocchio*. "Read this to him. Every little boy likes adventures."

"Theon certainly has had his share of adventures," noted Sarah as she left the comfort of the sofa and made a beeline for the staircase. "I'll be back down in 20 minutes."

Cameron intently watched his wife and child as they proceeded up the stairs. He smiled radiantly and shone like a beacon.

"You're decidedly in a better mood than the one you carted around heavily in church," observed Bill. "Want to share?"

"I noticed something peculiar in church," said Cameron. "Well, I think it was peculiar. The French doctor who treated Theon attended the ceremony."

"All the way from France. That's quite a trip," remarked Bill. "He's either overly dedicated or extremely obsessed."

"I think he's been gathering information about Sarah and me," conjectured Cameron. "Perhaps to assess our suitability."

"Suitability as parents?" asked Bill.

"Not just parents, but parents *to* Theon," replied Cameron. "I suspect there's something about the child he's not telling us; something far more unique than what he's already discussed with us."

"I did recognize one of his pals," said Bill. "George Lapierre, one of the guys running SETI operations. My brother Ted was reassigned to the Carl Sagan Center for the Study of Life in the Universe, because of him."

"Have you spoken to Ted since?" queried Cameron.

"No, he's incommunicado, now working in Antarctica with the Anderson exploration team," answered Bill, quite puzzled by this new development. "The group is attempting to learn more about how life began and how its many diverse forms have survived and evolved. By investigating the ice-covered lakes of Antarctica, it hopes to learn more about the history of water, and perhaps life on Mars."

"What's the connection between Antarctica and Mars?" wondered Cameron, whose expertise was limited to the analysis and understanding of the human psyche in all its felonious glory.

"The Mars Exploration Rovers have shown compelling evidence that water once flowed freely on Mars," explained Bill. "Eons ago, as the temperature on Mars cooled, ice-covered lakes, similar to the lakes in Antarctica, might have formed. And if life did exist on early Mars, it may have continued to live even as the Martian lakes froze over. Finding such life in Antarctica could, by induction, confirm the postulate of life on Mars."

"And you find Ted working on this strange?" gathered Cameron.

"His experience is in electro-magnetic signals," replied Bill, "not micro-biology."

"Assuming you're right, how is this germane to Lapierre's presence at church?" asked Cameron.

Bill became even more perplexed. "The only thing I'm sure of is that Lapierre is determined to keep a rare wormhole discovery Ted made under wraps. Maybe he's here to find out if I know anything about it."

"Even if Ted discovered aliens," mockingly said Cameron, "that still doesn't shed any light on Lapierre's connection with doctor Lefoux," his inquiring mind now entertaining all sorts of hypotheses.

"Are you two going to talk shop all day?" interjected Henry, who was at his core a simple man with simple ideas. "Arkham's Razor states that the simplest explanation is the best: your doctor and your alien-researcher were in church to honor the child—nothing else."

"Quoting Arkham's Razor? That's amazing, Dad," said Cameron, quite impressed.

"I may be just a bus driver, but I'm no ignorant boob," huffed the old man. "Now I don't want Francine or Sarah to be burdened by your conspiracy rubbish; you got that?" As elder, Henry was always grateful for any opportunity to dispense fatherly discipline and bring order to the family—even if it was only semblance of order.

As he beamed with authority before his son and son-in-law, a bell rang crisply. "That was quick," he ascertained before peering into the kitchen.

"It's not the kitchen timer, Dad," said Cameron. "It's the doorbell."

"Of course it is," uttered an irritated Henry while he headed for the door. "Probably another conspirator who wants a piece of my grandson."

"Hello Mr. Rex," cheerfully said the so-called intruder, holding a large box. "Glad tidings and felicitations to you."

"It's your pompous neighbor," announced Henry. "Mister *Renaissance*. Should I let him in?"

"Amadeo, glad to see you. Do come in," shouted Cameron to his guest who barely had room to slip by Henry, firmly entrenched in position. "Don't mind my Dad. Old age has wreaked havoc with his mobility," he added, frowning at his father.

"The ravages of old age have not spared me either," admitted Amadeo. "Praise God my mind is still as sharp and as resilient as the Sword of Goujian."

Amadeo Da Verdi was an Italian immigrant who had moved to New York at the age of 23, after his mother, his only surviving relative, died of cancer. Carrying two large suitcases, one filled with clothes and the other with books, Amadeo lugged them around town until he found a decrepit but affordable apartment that cost him his last $20. A prolific autodidact, he learned all he could doing odd jobs during the day and reading books at the local library during the evening. And he so reveled in his mammoth knowledge, engaging anyone who would listen.

Cameron enjoyed Amadeo's company. A lover of art, literature and languages, he also considered himself a Renaissance man, albeit less learned than Amadeo.

"I saw the telltale balloons tied to your balcony," said the skinny white-haired man, moving in an unsteady uneven gait. "Thankfully my keen eyesight has yet to abandon me."

Resting in the middle of the sofa, Amadeo scanned the room. "Where is the newest member of the family?"

"Most likely asleep at this point," assumed Cameron, sitting to Amadeo's right and curiously eying the Italian's gift box.

"No matter then," said Amadeo before removing the box cover and disclosing its content—a bizarre apparatus, cylindrical with a height of 5 inches and a radius of 14 inches. "I built this, years ago. Its design is based on an obscure sketch prepared by Leonardo Da Vinci, some time after taking in a young Michel de Nostredame. He called the device *The Eye of Bedlam*."

"*Les Propheties* de Nostradamus?" exclaimed Cameron in French. "The guy with the prophecies?"

"That one indeed," confirmed Amadeo. "The 15-year old Nostredame boy had come directly from the University of Avignon after it closed its doors in the face of an outbreak of the plague. His parents—and good friends of Da Vinci—Renée de Saint-Rémy and grain dealer and notary Jacques de Nostredame hoped Michel could polish his education under the polymath's guidance. It would seem the *seer-to-be* also had some insights to dole out."

Removing the device from the box, Amadeo bent forward and deposited it on the coffee table. "The exterior body is made of wood while the top surface is comprised of two panes of polished glass, between which is contained a thermo sensitive liquid crystal. The interior of the structure houses a collection of gears, cogs and transmissions that set various pieces in motion."

"Like those two triangles and that smaller inner circle resting on the glass?" surmised Bill as he towered over the object.

"Among other things, Yes," replied Amadeo. "Let me demonstrate." Inserting a bronze key into a hole on the side of the machine, he cranked it a few times as the three unsuspecting spectators watched closely. The two right-angle triangles, with two of their respective three corners initially resting against the contraption's circumference, began to rotate, each one around its own axis, until the third corners came into contact at the very center of the glass surface. A small cylinder—a third axis—no more than a half-inch, then rose from the center of the glass while the other two original axes sunk into it. The triangles now started to rotate around this new one until they passed over the thin inner circle, and finally connected along a common edge.

Upon contact, the inner circle sank into the glass, and a burning lens appeared at the top of the central axis, capturing and concentrating light from the massive ceiling chandelier above, and delivering it to the liquid crystal. Like a tenebrous mist slinking in, the crystal's mood turned to black and the inner circle was overtaken by darkness. A tiny equilateral triangle then emerged from where the corners of the two triangles had last met, pointing towards the center of the glass. It slid down in-between the common vertices and touched the small cylinder armed with the burning lens. The totality of the glass surface was now plunged into blackness.

"Fascinating toy, don't you think?" asked Amadeo who pressed a button near the keyhole, restoring the apparatus to its initial parameters.

"What ever happened to G.I. Joes, or cowboys and Indians?" barked Henry whose patience had been sorely taxed all evening.

"I can see the educational benefits," retorted Bill. "Theon would be exposed to notions of geometric shapes, motion, colors…and *symbols*. Are those etchings on the triangle corners, symbols?"

"They were allegedly drawn by Nostradamus himself," answered Amadeo. "As you might now suspect, the device's first purpose was not the edification of understanding, but rather the premonition of theological upheaval."

"This is a religious artifact?" chimed in Cameron who glanced upstairs to check if Sarah was coming back down. "I am fascinated, but not to sound unappreciative, Sarah's had quite enough of religious illumination these last weeks."

"This thing I built only carries the significance you decide to bestow upon it," coolly replied its architect. "Religious interpretation and labeling are as fleeting as our corporeal odyssey on Earth. If you wish it to be a simple toy, then it *is* a simple toy."

"I wouldn't mind knowing more about the symbols," insisted Bill. "As a scientist, I've always been interested in the reconciliation between science and religion. Perhaps the two can be simultaneously expressed through a set of elegant mathematical equations?"

"All right then, all right; tell us about the symbols," conceded Cameron. "I'm going to hear about it someday anyway." Turning to his father, "why don't you go watch TV in the kitchen, Dad. There's bound to be something more riveting than this."

"It's about time someone rescues me from all this jibber jabber," heavily groaned Henry before dashing into the kitchen.

Amadeo rubbed his palms together, much like a weight lifter on the brink of a lift. "The large circle represents the Kingdom of Heaven while the smaller inner circle is Earth. The two triangles positioned on either side of the circle constitute the opposing Trinities: the Holy Trinity and the Unholy one. Each triangle corner and its symbol designate a member of either Trinities, namely God the Father, the Holy Spirit and Jesus Christ on one triangle, and Satan, the False Prophet and the Antichrist on the other triangle.

"When the triangles move and touch for the first time, a battle is waged between the Holy Spirit and the False Prophet. The victor then devotes his resolve to the coming to Earth of the next ruler: Christ or his opposite. When the triangles touch again, an apocalyptic war is launched; and in the wake of such a war, either light or darkness prevails."

"Darkness survives," imagined Bill, recollecting the crystal liquid turning black.

"Yes, darkness survives," confirmed Amadeo. "The False Prophet wins the battle, and with his aid, the Antichrist wins the war, spreading Evil over every horizon; and as the smaller, unassuming third triangle meets the center, Evil overtakes the Kingdom of Heaven and quells its radiance."

"And darkness abounds on Earth *and* in Heaven," concluded Cameron, who was now eminently uncertain as to the merits of Da Verdi's gift as a toy. Without admitting it, he was nevertheless quite captivated.

"It is just a story concocted by Da Vinci and Nostradamus," reassured Amadeo, "epitomized by a mechanical toy that, in and of itself, harbors no power."

"Perhaps so, but I never realized Da Vinci could be so ghastly," thought Cameron.

"While the boy Nostredame might have unknowingly exerted some influence over Da Vinci," conceded Amadeo, "another source of a more palpable and direful nature might have been the hard kernel of inspiration, channeling his engineering prowess into action; a source that also left him paralyzed on his right side."

"A stroke, no doubt," presumed Cameron, "or a heart attack?"

"An attack on his very existence would be more precise," said Amadeo as he lapsed into a grave demeanor. "There is an enigmatic tale circulating among the more pious scholars of Da Vinci's life. It tells of an assault on him and on a young woman he was sheltering, by demons carrying tridents that shot lightning bolts. While trying to escape the demons, Da Vinci was apparently paralyzed by one of the bolts while his protégé was killed. A year later, dying from a variety of ailments, he shared this fantastic anecdote with his friend, Francis I, King of France."

"That's an incredible fable," admitted Bill. Turning to Cameron, "You've got to keep that gizmo. It'll make for a great conversation piece."

"We'll see," sharply replied Cameron before snatching the toy and precipitously shoving it under the sofa. "I'll think about it." And he did, but his thoughts were only centered on his wife's predictable reaction to the bizarre toy.

A thought still lingered in Bill's mind: "tell me, what was the name of the young lady under Da Vinci's protection?" eager to relay the story to his wife, Sophie.

"Da Vinci aficionados have debated this," said Amadeo. "Some claim the name Lisa; others insist on Maria."

Cameron suddenly had a notion inspired from the grave. "Maybe it's both. Maybe her name was Lisa Maria."

CHAPTER 17

"Pinocchio, today you were brave, honest and generous," Geppetto said. *"You are my son and I love you."*

Pinocchio remembered what the Blue Fairy told him. "Father, now that I've proven myself, I'm waiting for something to happen," he whispered as he drifted off to sleep.

The next morning Pinocchio came running down the steps, jumping and waving his arms. He ran to Geppetto shouting, "Look Father, I'm a real boy!"

"Did you hear that, Theon?" Sarah said rhetorically, sitting on a stool next to her son's crib, assisted only by a dim light emanating from a small table lamp. "What a wonderful ending." She placed the children's book in the cot, inches away from Theon's incessantly twitching feet. "You liked the story, I can tell, my little muffin. Just as Geppetto wished for a boy—a boy whose wooden limbs turned to flesh—I wished for you—a boy once made of a collection of vivid dreams, harvested right from my yearning imagination. I couldn't have envisioned you otherwise."

As she stroke Theon's hair, he clutched her thumb and squeezed tightly, maneuvering it into his mouth. Nibbling its ending, he found it salty, but nevertheless pursued his raid upon the pulpous digit. All the while, his eyes scrutinized those of his mother's, dissecting their way into her soul, just beyond her intellectual paradigms, both fighting for sovereignty over her thoughts, her words, and her actions. Her unconditional love for him would conquer all, of course, but it would come at a price.

Theon seemed to be cognizant of the struggle, discerning full well the political nature of his adoptive mother's discourse. Somehow he knew he was not *exactly* as she envisioned him. Somehow he knew he was different and that he too would struggle to become a good boy—a *real* boy just like Pinocchio.

Pulling the thumb out of his mouth, Theon let out a soft whimper. He stretched his arms towards the rotating mobile set that hung above the crib. It featured four hanging pieces: a space rocket, a shuttle craft, a Mars rover, and the planet Mars.

"Uncle Bill gave you this," she told him. "Maybe one day, you can visit your uncle's workplace. It's called NASA." The mobile began to rotate under the force of a gush of wind coming through the open window. "A storm is drawing near, dear. We better close the window."

Before she could reach it, Theon let out another plaintive cry, much louder than the first, as if cautioning her against approaching the window. In that same instant, a bird crashed into the top panel of the window frame. Unnerved and disconcerted, Sarah clumsily stepped back. Before she could assess what had just transpired, a second creature came hurtling through the window, this time through the open panel: it was a bat. Its wings stretching 8 inches wide, it flew in perfect circles seven feet above the floor, emitting ultrasonic shrieks and reading the returning echoes.

Sarah rushed back to the cot to grab Theon, but the bat reached him first after quickly spiraling down at an angle. It hit him in the stomach, then flew straight up, spinning like a top—a very queer tactic for a bat equipped with echolocation, a perceptual system allowing bats to detect, localize and even classify their prey in darkness.

Crashing against the ceiling, the flying rodent broke its neck and plummeted back down into the crib, next to Theon's head. Without hesitation, Sarah snatched the animal, ran to the open window and jettisoned it, just as the wind was increasing in force. She then closed the window with such vehemence that the glass cracked in two.

"Theon!" she screamed, rushing back to his side. "Are you all right, sweetheart?" Calm and quite still, he smiled, somehow knowing the bat had been neutralized. Above him, the mobile set swung wildly under the effect of the dying wind. Immobilizing it with her left hand, Sarah cupped Theon's cheek with the right. "You're a brave boy, my dauntless darling."

Pointing anew at the set, Sarah complied with her baby's earlier wish. "You want me to turn it on? Anything for my little warrior." Before she could press the button and activate the toy, it began rotating of its own volition. Dumbfounded, she stared at it; and the longer she stared, the faster it went—faster even than the maximum setting of the master bedroom ceiling fan. "What the hell?" Walking swiftly through the door left ajar, she pressed against the hallway railing. "Cameron! I need you this instant!"

CHAPTER 18

Present day; FBI New York Office, New York.

"Mr. Dumont, there's a Doctor Maurice Lefoux to see you," said Dumont's secretary, after entering her boss' office.

"Who?" wondered Dumont.

"He says he has a message for you of the utmost importance," informed the secretary. "Do you want me to send him in?"

Dumont hesitated. It was not in his habit of granting audiences without an appointment. But since the man was a Doctor, he supposed the information he wanted to impart was of some relevance. "Send him in, please."

"Maurice Lefoux, MD, Head of Pediatrics at the American Hospital of Paris," said the doctor, vigorously shaking Dumont's hand.

"Scott Dumont, Assistant-Director of the FBI New York Office," soberly replied Dumont. "What can I do for you?"

Lefoux took a seat and pulled out a sealed envelope. "The real question is: what can you do for my *organization*…and for the enlightenment of all the Christian people of the world?"

Dumont frowned with unease. "This is the FBI, a laic concern, not a—"

Lefoux sharply cut him off. "You have a subordinate, an agent named Cameron Rex, correct?"

"Yes, why?" Dumont started regretting inviting the doctor in his office.

Lefoux gave Dumont the sealed envelope. "The head of our organization, Cardinal Pierre Nadeau, Prefect of the pontifical house and Archbishop of Marseille, would like to entrust you with a *mission* of paramount consequence to history, religion and Man's destiny. The envelope contains details of the mission, and your instructions, should the good Christian in you accept."

Dumont decided to indulge the good doctor. He opened the envelope and carefully read it contents. He then deposited the letter on his desk, and gazed gravely at Lefoux, who eagerly awaited an answer.

"Well, what do you say?" asked a fervent Lefoux. "Do you accept the mission?"

Dumont was fascinated and oddly inclined to trust the doctor. After a moment, he surrendered a faint grin. "I *accept*." He would regret it.

CHAPTER 19

Circa 37,000 years ago; Kingdom of Heaven.

The Drakus was a sea vessel characterized as a graceful, long, narrow, light, wooden boat with a shallow-draft hull designed for speed. The ship's shallow draft allowed navigation in waters only a few feet deep and permitted beach landings, while its light weight enabled it to be carried over land for short distances.

The Drakus was also double-ended with a retractable propeller at each end, and symmetrical bow and stern, allowing the ship to reverse direction quickly without having to turn around.

Lord Deus, King of Heaven, had a Drakus of his own and enjoyed evening excursions aboard it, along the canal connecting Bliss Bay and Lake Seven. He always went alone, over the objections of his personal guard, the Thronos, who feared the rebel factions of the Kingdom's past enemies, the Chimerians and the Kalidrone, might use this opportunity to strike against the vulnerable King.

But tonight, the King was not alone, and his Drakus was not negotiating the calm and restful waters of the canal. Rather it was forging ahead confidently, cutting through the turbulent waves of Lake Zion, the most treacherous body of water in the kingdom, on a heading towards the Island of Cebrus.

The contingent he chose to accompany him was composed of three Thronos; of Khrist Lesus, Prime Seraph; of the archangel—or Sanctus Angelicum—Michael, General of the King's legions; and of Satan, Primus Pilus, commander of the First Cohort, and brother to Michael.

Their mission definition was clear: recover the sword once belonging to God through his Holy Spirit: the *Holy Sword*, the *Sword of Maitreya*; but the road towards it fruition was paved with landmines.

"The sword was lost during the *Divine Journey*," said a surly Satan. "Why would we believe a captured Chimerian pig with tall tales to tell?

He knows nothing of the Sword."

Satan was a handsome archangel: blue eyes, lustrous long blond hair, strong jaw, and radiant white wings. Women would literally flock around him when he strolled in public. But his beauty was surpassed by his arrogance and narcissism. Lord Deus tolerated him not only because he was brother to Michael, his most trusted friend, but also because he was a fierce combatant whose shrewdness and aggressiveness had won the King many a battle against the opponents of the State.

"The Chimerian's tale was quite convincing and genuine, especially after you ripped his curly tail off," remarked Michael. "I would not have authorized that. Torture is not *our* way."

"You can't condemn what brings you results," snarled Satan. "If the interrogation had been left in your inept hands, you would have bored the pig to death with your empty threats."

"You have much to learn if you wish to replace me one day," said Michael, who had always been extraordinarily patient with his brother.

"I suppose you'll have to die before that happens," half-threatened Satan. "Your compassion and your clemency on the battlefield will be your undoing. When a Chimerian barbarian stands over you, sword in hand, he will not hesitate to extinguish your life, even if you spared his moments before."

Michael smiled. "I'm more concerned about you standing over me as I sleep in my tent."

"To kiss you good night, no doubt," interjected Lesus in jest. "Such poignant expression of brotherly love."

"Enough banter!" ordered Deus, who pointed astern towards the tenebrous skies. "Something is approaching."

The sound of flapping wings grew stronger in amplitude and frequency; and as the *thing* passed overhead, the gush of air rushing downwards further angered the waters around the vessel. A tempest instantly arose, violently rocking the boat sideways. The men stayed low to avoid capsizing, their eyes fixated on the beast headed for the island.

"A Great Dragon," said Michael, who measured the flying dinosaur at at least 50 feet in length, from head to tail. "It's the first one I see."

"They're coming from the far South, no doubt looking for new feeding grounds," mentioned Deus. "And their number is increasing."

"Soon, we may have a new enemy," speculated Michael.

"Or a new ally," countered Satan, "if Chimerian flesh be a more palatable solution to its dietary requirements." As the Drakus steadied, Satan rose, flapping his wings vigorously. "Perhaps I should follow it, and scout the area by stealth."

"Stay, you fool." Deus strongly signaled Satan to sit. "Great Dragons are tribal animals. Where there is one dragon, there are assuredly more. And, you may well discover that the beast's appetite fancies *angel wings* above all other delicacies."

"He's not the King we once had," muttered Satan to himself. "Where has the boldness, the audacity, the vengefulness gone?"

Lesus heard what Satan said, and knew Deus heard as well, even if he displayed no reaction to the defamatory comment. "He's always been driven by invidious jealousies and uncandid imputations, now more than ever. It may be time to remove him from service, Lord Deus."

Deus glanced at Satan. "There was once a time when I would have beheaded anyone who challenged my authority with such impudence," he told Lesus. "But while his words may have been chosen poorly, they strike at me like a blade—like the sword I wish so earnestly to return home."

"The sword of Maitreya made you the greatest and most dreaded Lord of War," acknowledged Lesus. "It gave you the might of a hundred warriors, the ferocity of a thousand, and the clout of an indomitable army. And while wielding such power struck fear in the hearts of the kingdom's enemies, it did not foster the respect and the love of the people. Forbearance, generosity, devotion, mercy, and forgiveness did that."

Deus sighed heavily. "I have been at war with so many hostile realms bent on destroying our peaceful and bounteous way of life that I had forgotten the *true* role a God must play, to not only fight for but also preserve that way of life."

"You are an instrument and a symbol of peace and freedom," reminded Lesus. "There is no other calling for the *Master of the Universe*."

"You need not speak in such grandiose terms to sway me back towards duty," gently admonished Deus. "Posturing is, after all, unbecoming of a *Lord of Peace*."

"That is exactly what the *spirit*—and not the body—of Maitreya would say," pointed out Lesus. "Does Maitreya, your Holy Spirit, still speak to you?"

Deus smiled. "Who do you think slipped me that last line?"

Lesus was pleased but surprised. "If you and Maitreya are in agreement, who then seeks the Sword the most, you or him?"

"We both seek it equally," answered Deus.

"To use its power anew?" asked an intrigued Lesus, hoping for a response that would invalidate his initial assumption.

"It has been quite some time since Maitreya has taken bodily form by way of the potency of the Sword," recognized Deus; "to experience the intoxicating appeals of the world through the senses, rather than vicariously through a *copy* of that experience, filtered and sterilized by the reductive sanity of the mind."

"Maitreya is yearning?" wondered Lesus.

"No," immediately replied Deus. "But *I* sometimes yearn for that level of corporeal communion."

"Then, respectfully, I ask again," insisted Lesus, "will you once again call upon the Sword's mystic energy, in part or in whole? As guardian of the Holy Sword, I have the *right* to know."

"We will not exact its power, in whichever capacity," reassured Deus, who decided to overlook his Prime Seraph's insubordinate albeit duty-bound belligerence. "Rather, we shall circumscribe it. Until I, or Maitreya, decide otherwise, the sword shall be retired so that no one—friend or foe—may exert its implacable force."

"We've enjoyed a long period of relative peace," said Michael, "and contrary to enemies of eons ago, the sword was not necessary to defeat the Chimerians or the Kalidrone. It is a wise decision to put it to rest."

"Such words from a General of legions border on blasphemy," exclaimed Satan. "You and I only exist for war."

"And the blood of others may yet spill again," announced Deus as the Drakus touched the shore of the island. "Stay together and march furtively."

The island of Cebrus was roughly circular with a diameter of about seven miles. At its center stood a mountain with a large cave opening along its eastern edge. According to the captured Chimerian, the sword lied within the confines of the cave, in the possession of the clan of Chimerian primates who made the lair their base.

The Chimerian race was composed of four sub-races: *bulls, reptiles, boars, and primates*. While their heads were those of animals, their bodies were humanoid in appearance; and their intelligence level was akin to that of Homo Sapiens Sapiens from the early Bronze Age.

Contrary to their sister races, the primates did not participate in the war against Deus' army. Their cultural philosophy was one of *isolationistic neutrality*. Ironically, they were the strongest and most brutish of the four sub-races, and one was never advised to disturb their order. But today, a small group of Eternals would decline that advice in favor of the salvage of a great prize.

"The ground is peppered with the bones of primates and great dragons," noted Lesus. "A fierce battle was waged here."

Satan picked up a bone fragment. "Well, it seems monkey meat *is* the dragons' food of choice."

"Or vice-versa," rebutted Lesus, who came upon the decomposing body of a dragon. "Its tongue has been cut off."

After 50 minutes of travel, they arrived at the entrance of the cave. "There is light inside," noticed one of the Thronos. "And chanting."

"Remember, all of you," soberly said Deus, "we are here for the sword. Shed blood only if necessary." He stared at Satan. "Is that understood?"

Satan gave an unconvincing nod, complemented with an insidious grin. They entered the cave, walking through a short corridor that opened onto a colossal hall, lit by hundreds of fire sticks positioned along the perimeter of the hall.

A huge camp fire raged in the center of the cave as primates danced and chanted around it. Some threw morsels of dragon flesh into the fire, only to retrieve them minutes later using the blades of spears. Their sharp long teeth easily tore through the meat, which they quickly swallowed before attending to other pieces burning in the fire.

Other primates carried the dead bodies of their brothers above their heads, reciting ritual incantations, before throwing the bodies into the fire. Strangely, some of the bodies seemed mutated: their skins reddish in color, their heads horned, and their backs outfitted with hulking bat-like wings.

A taller and more massive primate appeared from behind the fire, followed by two others tightly holding a third one—this one mutated—flapping his wings in an attempt to escape. The lead primate shouted a few words to the assembly before raising a sword, turning to the prisoner and stabbing him in the heart.

"Lord Deus! He holds the Holy Sword!" screamed Lesus in shock. The chanting immediately stopped, the attention of the Chimerians now directed at Deus' party.

Deus raised his arms in the air. "We come in peace!" he shouted in a broken Chimerian. "We wish you no harm, and seek only what is rightfully ours!"

"Keep your weapons down," Michael instructed the group. Armed with two types of weapons. Michael, Satan, and the Thronos bore stick weapons with three fire nozzles at their ends, while Deus and Lesus bore wrist weapons with three short barrels along the edge.

The larger primate—evidently the chief of the tribe—advanced defiantly towards the group, sword in hand.

"You dare intrude on our ceremony," cried out the chief, standing only a few feet away from Deus. "Do you not know who we are? We are the great dragon slayers."

"You are indeed brave warriors," humbly said Deus. "And you have done well to kill the beasts invading your territory. We, however, have not come to invade your land; we have come to seek your indulgence, to ask you to remand to our custody the sword you carry."

"Who are you to issue such a demand?" angrily asked the chief.

"I am Lord Deus," he replied with a pride and a confidence designed to incite respect if not submissiveness, "ruler of the kingdom of Heaven."

The murmurs among the assembly instantly subsided. A king greater than their own had delivered a challenge. The chief, however, did not appear swayed or intimidated by this new knowledge.

"What will you do if I refuse to part with this magnificent sword?" asked a recalcitrant chief whose capitulation would undoubtedly be interpreted as weakness by his men.

"I will take it by force," impassively answered Deus. "The choice is yours."

What could seven men do against his horde? thought the chief. He turned to his clan and shouted: "This will be a glorious day!" before facing Deus anew. "I have decided."

Without warning, the chief flung the sword forward, the blade hurtling towards Deus' heart.

Deus instinctively grabbed the blade with his right hand, arresting its forward thrust. The chief then pulled it back, slicing Deus' flesh, while the latter simultaneously activated his wrist weapon, the bolt of energy from which tearing off the chief's head.

As the Chimerians helplessly watched the decapitated body of their leader crumble to the ground, they went absolutely wild, and rushed the intruders, wielding spears and bows.

Fire bolts began raging throughout the hall, felling dozens of primates within seconds, but not before spears and arrows rained upon the group's position.

"Retreat!" ordered Deus after retrieving the coveted sword. They ran back through the corridor and, as they reached the entrance, began firing repeatedly at the rocks surrounding it, collapsing it entirely.

"This should hold them off for a few hours," surmised Michael. "Are you all right, Lord Deus?"

"It will heal quickly," replied Deus, who hid his pain. "To the Drakus, swiftly!"

The Drakus soon rejoined the unruly waters. Deus sat at the front, the sword resting on his thighs. Lesus handed him a cloth. "For your hand."

Deus used it instead to wipe his blood off the blade. "Curious. There is some dark matter, like a powder, incrusted in the blade near the handle. And the blood that has flowed to that region seems to have fused with the dark matter. Try as I might, I cannot remove any of it."

"Perhaps, if you summon Maitreya to your body, it will fade away," proposed Lesus.

"Splendid idea!" exclaimed Deus, who held the sword with both hands, raising its tip until it rested against his forehead. "Holy Spirit, Teacher of all things, defender of all life, mirror of my being, I conjure you. My body is your body; my voice is your voice."

In an instant, the sword shimmered with a trembling silver light that completely engulfed Deus' body. Then, something unexpected happened. The body of light left Deus, never losing cohesion as it stationed itself a foot away, dragging the sword with it.

The light increased in density, forming a glowing capsule that shot an incandescent lining of dark silver through the skies. The light receptacle's radiance then gradually subsided, adopting the shape of a man who looked very much like Deus. As its hands coalesced, they surrounded the handle of the blade. The entity lifted the sword above its head. "I am alive again! It has been such a long time."

Deus, whose body had failed for the first time to become host to Maitreya, gaped at this new creation with astonishment. "Who are you?"

The entity lowered the sword and softly placed its hand on Deus' shoulder. "It is I, brother. It is Maitreya."

CHAPTER 20

Circa 37,000 years ago; Kingdom of Heaven.

Lord Deus gazed outside the South window of the war room, situated at the top of the Western tower of his castle. The citizens of the *City of God* walking across the royal plaza could barely perceive him, but they knew his countenance was dressed up in woes and worries over his army, commanded by the newly appointed and highest ranked *Primus General* Maitreya, as it advanced towards the *Alps of Rawdon*, 425 miles south of the city.

"General Michael has reported in, my Lord," announced Khrist Lesus as he entered the room and activated a holographic map from a small device on Deus' desk. "The army has set up camp here," pointing at an area 5 miles from the Alps. "To date, they've sighted over a hundred Great Dragons flying overhead, none of them having attacked, or even taken an aggressive stance against them. However, they did come upon thousands of dead Chimerians along their trek, butchered by the great beasts."

"Twenty-thousand men marching in unison are a formidable and daunting pageant," remarked Deus, "even for creatures as stalwart as Great Dragons."

"Yet I cannot help but notice trepidation in your eyes and in your demeanor," said Lesus, questioning his Lord's conviction. "What thing bothers you about this pre-emptive campaign?"

"Several things do gnaw at me," admitted Deus. "The appointment of Maitreya as Primus General for one. Michael was not at all pleased or in agreement with my decision, contending Maitreya possessed no *official* battle experience."

"As King, you held that position before the appointment," pointed out Lesus. "And since Maitreya was formerly part of you, he too partook in your own war experiences—the experiences of the greatest leader who ever lived."

Deus appeared uncertain about that assumption. "You must know that I only bestowed that commission at Maitreya's behest. He seemed so eager to appropriate the position that I complied too hastily. To my surprise, I have found his strategic input in matters of State to be somewhat deficient."

"Perhaps something was lost during his excision from your being," supposed Lesus.

"Or something of controversial significance was added," thought Deus.

"True or not, this cannot be proven," noted Lesus. "All we know is that he emerged from you, and your mind does not sense his presence, or hear his words anymore. What else perturbs you?"

"Maitreya ordered this campaign against the Great Dragons," replied Deus, "against Michael's counsel. The General, an Eternal of superior insight, is convinced Maitreya's estimation of the number of Great Dragons occupying the network of caverns within the Alps is grossly understated. He claims there may in excess of five thousand creatures now dwelling there, not a mere thousand."

"You have allowed the bulk of your *skilled* army to join in this battle," indicated Lesus. "Surely, that is sufficient in number and in wit to defeat the beasts, no matter how many thousands enter into combat."

As Lesus pursued his discourse in idle optimism, none of which managing to alleviate Deus' concerns, a Thronos burst into the war room. "My Lord, Khrist; the sentinel has returned to camp. It is not as we believed."

"Tell me what has transpired," anxiously asked Deus.

"The Great Dragons do not number in the mere thousand," blurted out the agitated Thronos; "their sum eclipses that of the men…by the *thousands*."

"Contact Maitreya immediately and order the army to withdraw," commanded Deus.

The Thronos' face turned pale, and his tongue lost all ability as he stuttered mindlessly like a frightened child caught in unscrupulous enterprise. "But…but Lord…but…but…"

Deus grabbed him by the shoulders and shook him vigorously. "Speak up, man!"

"Primus General Maitreya has already ordered the troops forward," he nervously told Deus. "As we speak, they have engaged the enemy!"

Deus froze for a moment, and then released the Thronos. His fists tightening, he silently walked to his chair and sat into it heavily, staring at a plaque on the wall, which read: *Thus it is that in war the victorious strategist only seeks battle after the victory has been won, whereas he who is destined for defeat first fights and afterwards looks for victory.*

Countless good men would die today.

CHAPTER 21

It has been nine days since the clash of Armageddon between Deus' army and the horde of Great Dragons. A relatively healthy army would have made it back in six. This telltale lateness could only bode disastrous news for the Kingdom.

The King paced up and down the Royal Plaza, and with every step, his typically buoyant and self-confident air deflated, and his hopes for a safe return degraded into despair.

As he gazed at the small hill just beyond the south boundary of the plaza, he saw Khrist Lesus, who had taken post there several hours ago, wave his arms frantically. His pace instantly quickened and took on a jaunty streak, as he darted towards Lesus.

"They have returned!" Lesus yelled blissfully. "They are back!"

One legionnaire head popped over the horizon, then another, and another. Soon, thousands appeared over the hill, some standing straight, some hunching, some dragging themselves laboriously, while the rest, prostate with pain, lied on stretchers either pulled by horse-like dinosaurs or carried by other men.

The injured men were sent to the House of Healing, a large medical center counting 28 buildings that could accommodate over 15,000 patients at any one time. This questionable battle, however, had forced the center to greet close to 18,000 men.

Maitreya and Michael were among the men who had survived the bloody encounter unscaved, for the most part.

A furious but relieved King made his way to the principal building, where Maitreya and Michael were undergoing a mandatory examination.

"Was it worth it?" Deus asked Maitreya, unable to repress his indignance. "Was it worth disobeying my direct order to draw back?"

"The order came too late," simply stated Maitreya. "Besides, we dispatched over 23,000 dragons. Only a few thousand remain. I would consider that a highly successful campaign."

"And what of the dead soldiers whose wretched bodies are now scattered across the battlefield?" retorted Deus.

"Acceptable collateral," replied Maitreya, exhibiting no empathy or pity for the dead men or their grieving families. "That is the price of any war, you know that full well. When we were *One*, you *never* expressed concern or reservation about the heavy cost of warfare. To *preserve* our way of life; that is what you have always clamored. Are you now recanting the virtue of that noble objective?"

Deus grew impatient. "There is no virtue or nobility in eradicating a race that has never demonstrated any aggressive designs on our kingdom."

Maitreya was baffled. "*Who* are you? When we were merged, *I* was the one who always tempered your sword. Now that we are separate, you should be pleased that I have released you from my burdensome and intrusive doctrines of peace, and that I have, in turn, adopted your former vision of war with unstinting devotion."

Deus clamped his teeth in frustration. "You are in the wrong, persisting in decorating yourself with the title of warlock. We are at peace, and I require a Consigliere, a Royal Adviser, not a warmonger."

"Do you regret my appointment to Primus General?" insistently asked Maitreya.

"I am *concerned*," replied Deus. "But my qualms shall be contingent on redefining the nature of our roles and interactions in safeguarding the felicity of our people. And you will abide by my view of such things."

"Agreed," Maitreya smiled with an uncharacteristic lack of resistance. "Brothers should never work against each other. That being said and understood, I shall visit some of the men before retiring to my chambers."

"One more thing, Maitreya." Deus grabbed his arm. "You have ordered the Holy Sword out of retirement for the battle. Where is it now?"

"I gave it to Lesus for safekeeping," said Maitreya. "He is after all its guardian."

"Indeed he is. We finally agree on something." As Maitreya moved away, Deus proceeded to the next station where a Healer was attending to a cut on Michael's forehead.

"I did not mean to pry, my Lord," said Michael, almost asking forgiveness, "but I heard the conversation. You should know that Maitreya fought bravely…" Michael hesitated.

"But? There is something else, isn't there?" Deus turned to the Healer.

"Leave us for a moment."

"Yes, you are correct," confessed Michael. "After we assailed the enemy in the fields at the foot of the Alps, and killed most of them, I deployed the legions equally across the fifty or so cavern entrances—as my role of tactician called for in this particular battle—and was on the verge of ordering the advance, when Primus General Maitreya infringed on my authority and belayed my order."

"It is his prerogative as your superior officer," remarked Deus.

"It is not the abidance to the chain of command that troubled me," said Michael, "but the order he gave. He redeployed the men in such a way that left one specific cavern under his charge and that of Satan's. No other men were assigned to accompany them. When I asked why only two men, and why Satan, he told me that he wanted no random element present, and that Satan was the fiercest warrior…and the most deserving."

"Deserving of what?" wondered Deus.

"He would not say," replied Michael. "Perhaps Satan holds the answer. He rests in a station at the back end of the building."

"I'm glad you're unharmed, my friend. I shall see you again on the morrow." An intrigued Deus walked away, accelerating his stride as he melted within the crowd of healers bustling about.

CHAPTER 22

Present day; New York.

"Oh God! My water broke." Sarah dropped the dish into the water-filled sink and ran into the living room where Cameron was watching the morning news. "Get the suitcases," she screamed, dashing by him towards Theon, who was sitting in the corner, building a spaceship out of Lego blocks his parents had bought him for his fourth birthday.

Theon was quite precocious for his age, demonstrating uncanny abilities in the areas of engineering, mathematics, logic and drawing. His father immensely enjoyed pitting his son against algebraic and trigonometric problems designed for sixth graders. He was now eager—far too eager perhaps—to introduce him to advanced literature, like the works of Shakespeare, Molière and Hemingway, firmly convinced he could tackle these more complex subjects in a year or so.

His mother, on the other hand, encouraged him to draw. Placing one of her own cartoons next to a blank page, she would invite him to recreate it. And he would so masterfully, even adding original elements to it. Theon could observe a scene for a minute, and then, with pencil in hand, render it onto paper with even greater distinctiveness than the mental image that created it. That's why his mother liked to call him, "my little Da Vinci. We have to go. Your sister is on her way." Sarah pointed to her stomach before picking up Theon.

"Maya is coming soon, Mommy?" asked Theon. "Yes, Honey, very very soon." It had now been nine years since Sarah had begun her trek to motherhood. Blessed with Theon, she had hoped for a reversal of misfortune that would carry through into the future. Unburdened by the curse of childlessness, she had never felt so centered and serene, and she had let fate become her unconditional friend instead of her disobliging servant. Fate was magnanimous and grateful for the new rapport: Sarah was with child for the second time.

"Here, let me buckle you up," said Sarah, checking twice to make sure Theon was well secured. She slammed the rear side door of the Ford Escape she and Cameron had purchased a year ago, and waved at Theon through the window.

"What do you have in these suitcases?" wondered Cameron, throwing them laboriously into the back of the SUV.

"Everything a girl needs in a moment of crisis," replied Sarah in jest. "You drive," she ordered.

"I gathered that much," snapped back Cameron as he settled into the driver's seat while his wife took her seat and positioned the rear view mirror so that Theon's reflection appeared in plain view. "We're off, muffin."

Cameron drove steadily, both he and Sarah immersed in their own thoughts. Theon gazed at everything that came into sight. "A big bridge," he said playfully, after a half-hour of travel. "A park with grass and trees," he added a moment later."

"That's the East River Park, sweetheart," said Sarah.

"We're on Delancey Street," noted Cameron. "We should be coming upon First Avenue right about…now."

Exiting Delancey, the SUV sped along First Avenue, but was stopped by the first of twenty-some traffic lights that stood between the hospital and them. The light turning green, they sped anew to the next light that also turned red as they came upon it. "This is ridiculous," bellowed Cameron. "Can't they synchronize these lights. Instead of taking us ten minutes, it'll take thirty-five. I want green! Do you hear me, green!"

"I like green too, Daddy," interjected Theon."Green like Kermit the frog, green like Elliott the dragon, green like Wally Gator—"

"Yes, yes, you like green," interrupted an edgy Cameron. "Green like a traffic light, that's what Daddy likes. Green like a traffic light," he said again, pointing at the light above them.

"Green like a traffic light," repeated Theon, giggling and clapping his hands. "Look Daddy, the light is green."

"About time," grunted Cameron as he pressed heavily on the accelerator pedal and advanced towards the next light. "Huh! Green. Nice." Hunching forward to check on the next series of lights, Cameron made a curious discovery: all the traffic lights—as far as he could see—had simultaneously turned green.

Confounded, Cameron glanced at Theon through the mirror. "You like green traffic lights, Theon?"

"Much more than red ones," he answered. "Red ones make Daddy unhappy."

Each light Cameron passed turned promptly back to red, skipping yellow altogether, while the remaining lights stayed green, patiently waiting for Cameron's arrival.

Arriving at the New York University Langone Medical Center, Cameron parked by the main entrance. "Do you want to talk about the green lights?" he asked his wife.

"There's nothing to discuss," she replied sharply. "You should be used to *it* by now."

Fifteen minutes later, Sarah was in bed, being examined by her doctor. "Your cervix has already dilated to ten centimeters," he announced. "Are you experiencing any pain?"

"There was some mild discomfort in the car, but it's subsided," said Sarah. "Thanks to my good luck charm," she supposed, gently pinching Theon's cheek as he sat on the edge of the bed.

"We'll wait outside," decided Cameron, pulling Theon off the bed and exiting the room. "We don't want to be in the stork's way when he brings Maya to Mommy," he told Theon in the most serious of tones. "He's as real as you and I, and he's very testy when it comes to baby-delivery procedure." Theon wrinkled his brow in disagreement not only over leaving the room, but also over the veracity of his father's *fowl* deposition.

"I know where babies come from," proudly proclaimed Theon. "They don't come from storks—and they don't come from wells."

Cameron and Theon sat on chairs lined up against the wall opposite Sarah's room. He pondered over his son's knowledge of the well in which he was found. No one had told him about it. As far Theon knew—or his parents thought he knew—he came into existence in the same way and in the same place his sister would.

Theon began mumbling silently, flawlessly quoting an excerpt from *The Adventures of Pinocchio*:

"*'You can talk!' exclaimed Geppetto. 'Of course I can, silly,' said the puppet. 'You've given me a mouth to talk with.' Pinocchio rose to his feet and danced on the table top. 'Look what I can do!' he squealed.*"

Theon waggled his dangling legs hither and thither, mimicking a poorly orchestrated dance, hitting his father's thigh numerous times.

"Why don't you play on the floor," suggested Cameron. "You'll have more space."

"I don't have my blocks," sadly said Theon. "The floor is good for blocks."

"I don't have your blocks," retorted Cameron. "They're at home."

"No, Daddy, they're in Mommy's suitcase," corrected Theon. "The blue one."

"All right, son; I'll scamper in, get them, and scurry right out." Cameron walked to the door, while instructing Theon not to move an inch from his chair.

He entered the room and was immediately assaulted by the sound of an erratic heart beat emanating from the heart monitor. "That's the second time I've tried to do it from the inside," yelled the doctor. "It's too tightly wrapped. I'll have to pull her out."

Sarah was pale white and bore an expression of sheer horror. "My baby!" she wailed bitterly, sobbing uncontrollably. Cameron ran to her side and held her hand tightly.

The top of the baby's head appeared as the doctor clamped his fingers onto its shoulders and pulled gently, hoping for minimal tensile resistance from the umbilical cord. If the cord did not cooperate, he would have to perform a caesarean. "She's coming out," shouted the doctor, "nice and easy."

The baby slid out onto the bed, its neck encased in several layers of the cord. The nurse glanced at the heart monitor just as the red shimmering wave, which had resumed normalcy for a few seconds, became unmitigatedly flat. The high-pitch single tone of the monitor droned without end, assuming its most dire role: herald of death.

"Nooooooooooooo!" Sarah let out a shrill and piercing cry, and sank into unconsciousness.

"Oxygen!" ordered the doctor as he quickly unrolled the cord. "Damn it, oxygen now!" Clearing the mouth with his finger, he placed the oxygen bag over the baby's mouth, pressing the bag twice, and then proceeded to massage its tiny heart, alternating oxygen intake and massage for over a minute. The baby remained unresponsive and did not revive.

"Has Maya arrived?" inquired an oblivious Theon, who had managed to open the door and slip in.

Cameron rushed to Theon and picked him up, using his back as a visual shield. "Maya is having trouble," Cameron said ambiguously, camouflaging his acute sorrow.

"Are you sure, Daddy?" said Theon. "I can see her…and she's smiling. I think she wants me to go with her."

"You can't go where Maya is going," admonished Cameron. "It's not your time."

"Time for what, Daddy?" wondered Theon. "Maya wants to play, but I don't know if I can fly like her."

In a bold but necessary gesture, Cameron whirled around and pointed at Maya's torpid body. "Maya is not flying, Theon; she's sleeping, and she'll be living in her dreams...forever."

Theon didn't quite understand, but was moved by the sight of a despondent doctor drooping over Maya's still body, overcome by adversity and defeat, Theon insisted on being let down. His father hesitated but finally complied. He trotted to his sister and placed his hand over her left foot, hanging over the side of the bed. He stared at the foot, and then looked up at the ceiling. "I can't play with you way up there," he said quite manifestly, "but, if you want, you can play with me *down here*."

"Will she come down?" asked Cameron, stupefied and almost aghast by his spontaneous complicity in a child's whimsical fantasy. "A normal outburst of desperation and foolhardiness, no doubt," he thought.

"Yes, Daddy, she will," answered Theon; "but only if we can play with my blocks." Cameron nodded stupidly, overtaken by a sudden flood of hope and expectation. Affecting traffic lights was one thing, but this baby was not a machine ...but, then again.

"I'm showing her the way down, Daddy," reported Theon. "It's like going down a slide with lots of curves." He started describing circles with his head, accelerating the motion after each completed orbit. A light began to dawn dimly within Maya's body, evidenced by a soft glow radiating from her eyes and extremities. The doctor and two nurses floundered backwards in awe, the former toppling over the monitor.

Maya's body quivered as the glow dwindled down and finally abated. Her eyelids fluttered as swiftly as butterfly wings. 'On,' she whispered, opening her eyes widely. 'On,' she said again. Was this just a meaningless moan, or an earnest appeal for Theon's presence?

"Maya wants to see me!" Theon clamored insistently and noisily. "Pick me up, Daddy."

Shedding tears of euphoric relief and astonishment, Cameron sat his boy next to Maya, who was now waving her arms in every direction. 'On,' she said anew, staring intensely at Theon, and perhaps recognizing her timely benefactor.

"It's not possible," cried out the doctor as he regained his composure and delicately cut the umbilical cord. "She was dead, quite dead I assure you. It's a miracle."

"My wife would never beg to differ on matters of miracles," assured

Cameron, who bent over and kissed her. "Wake up, Honey, wake up. It was just a bad dream." He kissed her again, this time pressing firmly against her lips.

Drowsy and nauseated, Sarah slowly awoke. "Maya?" she murmured, distressingly upset, laden with the conviction of her child's demise.

"Look, darling, she's alive…and kicking!" Cameron signaled the bemused doctor to deposit the baby in his wife's arms. "Say Hi, Maya. Say Hi to Mommy."

Joining her husband, Sarah burst into tears. "How can this be? *How* can this be?" In a flash, she answered her own question. "My Theon," she said thankfully, arching her back forward and placing her right hand against Theon's heart. "My little miracle, my little miracle…my *big* miracle worker."

"Mommy says thanks, Theon," translated Cameron.

"It was easy, Mommy," casually replied Theon. "Can Maya and me play with my blocks now?"

CHAPTER 23

"What the hell is that racket?" wondered Cameron as he awoke from one of his many nightmares. His wife, lying in bed next to him appeared undisturbed by the noise—her gentle snoring was clear evidence of that.

"Theon's having another fit," he thought, induced no doubt by a nightmare of his own. He'd had many of those in the last year, far more than previous years. And their intensity and vividness grew in tandem with their number, so much so he never knew what to expect upon entering his son's room.

"Here goes," he said as he turned the doorknob and opened the door, only to witness the undisputable tokens of a ravaging war that had just ended: desk drawers were pulled out, their contents spread across the floor; the closet door was unhinged; six floor planks were pulled out; and the table lamp had literarily imploded, replaced by a pile of ceramic dust.

As for Theon, he stood on the bed, his eyes closed and breathing heavily. "We did it. We stopped them. We won the battle," he boasted to an invisible battalion. "Those who still dare defy us, let them announce themselves."

Cameron was familiar with this particular dream, and had become adept at taming Theon into stillness. It was critical he not upset Theon, lest the destruction resume. "Congratulations, General, on your victory. As always, you've protected the kingdom."

Theon raised his arms, his hands clamped together as if wielding a sword. "Who goes there? Identify yourself."

"Do you not recognize your emperor?" Cameron moved to the side of the bed.

Theon lowered his imaginary sword, and bowed. "My Lord; you honor us with your presence. The barbarian horde has retreated back to their hellish realm."

"Indeed." Cameron carefully placed his hand on Theon's shoulder. "With peace restored, your Lord now orders you to rest. I've taken you to the royal bed where you may lie and dream of past glories and future conquests."

"Your wish is my command. I am yours, *a capite ad calcem*." Theon lay down while his father pulled the sheets over him.

"I shall recompense you with land, General," Cameron told his little warrior. "What say you of this?"

"My Lord, I say I would petition for the fertile fields to the North of *Paradise City*," replied Theon.

"Of course, the fields are yours," confirmed Cameron, who was always fascinated by the specificities of his son's nightmares, and by the impeccable language used to describe them. But there was *one* specificity Theon had never surrendered before: the name of his alter-ego. Cameron suddenly had a novel idea to remedy this lack of information.

"I shall have the title deed prepared," he told his son, who began to doze off. "Tell me what name to inscribe on it, so that no mistake is made."

"I don't remember my name," said a sleepy Theon. "Why don't I remember my name?"

Cameron made an attempt. "Is it Theon Rex?"

Theon frowned before punching his pillow and turning onto his side. "No, I don't think so."

Cameron tried something else. "Enemies often attribute nicknames to their greatest foes. Is there such a name for you?"

"Yes," mumbled Theon. "It's *Ghost Knight*, I think. Yes, it's Ghost—" He finally fell asleep.

"Strange name," thought Cameron. "Not much to go on." After kissing his son's cheek, he cleaned up the room, reinstalled the closet door on its hinges, reinserted the planks, and replaced the lamp with that of the guest room. If past incidents were any indication, Theon would not remember his actions or their consequences.

And Cameron and Sarah would always make sure no signs of damage remained to prompt his memory. It was a never ending burden for both of them—a burden they knew would come to Theon one day since he was becoming increasingly aware that his uniqueness wasn't limited to his physique.

"Have we made a terrible error by saving this *boy's* life?" pondered Cameron as he closed the bedroom door behind him. "What kind of life will he have? What kind of life will *we* have?" He headed for his bedroom, berating himself for his selfishness and his defeatist attitude. He was *better* than this.

Someone else—or *something* else—agreed, but, through the passage of time, had come to err on the side of caution. A shadow, taking the form of a man, stood at the nexus of Theon's imagination; and its voice spoke softly to the boy's mind. "I was once *matched* to three others; you are the fourth, as powerful and benevolent as the first; as alien as the second; and as conflicted as the third. Keep the course, and one force shall prevail over its brothers. No ordinary mortal may understand this, not even the mortals who took you in; so above all, tread lightly for you may tread on their dreams of a boy made in their image."

"Stay out of trouble," it added before melting away. But the boy was already in trouble, and his path already set.

CHAPTER 24

Circa 37,000 years ago; Kingdom of Heaven.

"What say you, Primus Pilus, in the wake of such resounding victory?" asked Deus, his neutral poise indicating neither gratification nor discontent.

"I say Maitreya has lost his mind," claimed Satan. Satan pulled down the sheet covering his torso, revealing a bite mark twice the size of an adult male lion's. "This is my reward. Maitreya and I were progressing through the cavern, always back to back, separated by never more than a few feet, when the dragon bastard came at me from the rear, locking its powerful jaw onto my right flank."

"Was not Maitreya protecting your back, while you protected his?" questioned a puzzled Deus.

"I thought he did," sneered a furious Satan. "It appears the dragon wasn't the only son of a bitch in the cavern. As it shook me, I clutched the monster's upper jaw with my left hand, and his lower jaw with the right, temporarily arresting its shutting motion. Frankly, I had not believed myself endowed with such brawn."

"What of your weapon?" queried Deus. "Did you not fire upon the beast?"

Satan's anger exploded. "Of course I did! The moment it seized me. But my Rash'ta (wrist weapon) failed me. The damn thing did not function!"

"Since when do you carry a Rash'ta?" Deus' puzzlement doubled. "The Kor'ta (stick weapon) is your weapon of choice?"

"My choice, yes, but not his," told Satan. "Your brother gave me a Rash'ta, claiming it would provide more maneuverability in a closed environment. While I considered the rationale of his decision peculiar, I kept my dissent to myself. After all, he wielded the Holy Sword—a single sway of which would have stricken down the beast. If I came into trouble, he would easily prevail in my stead."

"What did Maitreya do exactly…or not do?" asked Deus, trying to make sense of it all.

Satan's eyes glared with hateful reprisal. "The scumbag watched, as if I deserved my fate. He just watched! It had been over 20 seconds since I became caught in the dragon's clutches when, no longer able to keep its jaw at bay, my flesh broke and my blood spilled, flowing down my body. Only then did Maitreya intervene, rushing to the underside of the beast, and planting the sword into its heart. Had he waited a few more seconds, I would have died."

"It almost seems like Maitreya was calculating the precise moment of his intervention," suggested Deus. "He waited for the instant between injury and death before striking."

"There is more strangeness to be accounted for," added Satan. "While the other caves each harbored hundreds of dragons, the one we penetrated sheltered only one, the largest among its kind, judging by the other slain dragons."

Deus frowned. "How did he know that?"

Satan chuckled in derision. "Oh, he knew! In fact, he *chose* that dragon, claiming some gift had been bestowed upon me by way of the assault. Something is terribly amiss here."

"Your assessment of his true intentions is pure speculation at this point," reminded Deus. "But I will pursue the matter, discretely of course. Maitreya's return has generated renewed elation among the people. I will not stifle that jubilation without irrefutable proof of Maitreya's incompetence…or underhandedness."

"I never thought we would find common ground on anything," confessed Satan. "And I never thought it would bring me comfort."

"We may yet become closer allies," agreed Deus. "Now, let us prepare for the worst, but hope for the best."

"We always hope for the best," said a healer, arriving with his team. "We'll take good care of your Primus Pilus."

As Deus left, Satan mumbled to himself, "a storm is brewing, Deus; you'd better batten down the hatches and secure the children, for Maitreya is but the silence that precedes the storm."

He would not be far from the truth.

CHAPTER 25

Satan lied bloodied next to the slain Great Dragon. "Damn your insane devilry, Maitreya! Why did you abstain from striking the beast? A second more and my body would have severed in two."

"*Devilry*!" shouted Maitreya in glee. "The word is most appropriate." He kneeled next to Satan and caressed his wing, imagining the Primus Pilus in a completely new light. "You've just received a most precious gift, the essence of which shall not only propel you to new heights of power, but also make you a critical part of a new *order*."

"What if I refuse your *gift*?" defied Satan, mocking Maitreya's nonsense.

"Your cooperation is not required," replied Maitreya. "The gift has already been accepted."

Maitreya quickly moved back when Satan tried to grab his neck and strangle him. "You insane piece of crap! My life and my future are my own!"

"Please Primus Pilus, stay calm!" cried out the Healer as he held both his arms, pushing them down onto the bed.

Satan's eyes popped open. "Where am I?"

"You're at the House of Healing," replied the Healer, "and having quite a nightmare. Everything is fine now."

"Are you certain of that?" asked a concerned Satan whose senses were being battered by the sights and sounds of overwrought Healers running frantically about, urgently screaming directives to their staff; and by the howls, the wails, and the moans of patients caught in the throes of what Healers have diagnosed as a bizarre form of physical decay.

Satan seized the Healer's collar and pulled his face a few inches from his. "Are they dying?" Am *I* dying? Speak for Heaven's sake!"

"The soldiers' bodies' main systems appear to be shutting down one by one," nervously answered the Healer. "And while this is occurring, their physical appearances are metamorphosing."

Satan shook the Healer. "In what manner?"

"Well, the skin and eyes are taking on a crimson red color," revealed the Healer; "horns are forming on top of the head; a pointed tail is growing; claws and fangs are forming; and the wing feathers are shedding, leaving only a skin membrane."

"The soldiers are becoming *dragons*!" exclaimed a disgusted Satan. "Worse…*demons*!"

"Yes, for lack of a better word," said the Healer. "But not all are transforming—you may well be spared the—"

"Systems are peeking once again!" yelled the Healer at the station next to Satan's.

"I'll return in a moment," Satan's Healer told him before joining his colleague. "What has transpired?"

"It seems the body's systems have not shut down after all," discovered the Healer. "They have, in fact, dramatically reduced in activity in order to allocate most of the body's energy to the physical transformation. This man's body is now functioning within normal parameters."

"If you call that normal," noted Satan's Healer, pointing at the completely mutated body. Pressing his hands against the bed surface, he bent forward and closer to the warrior's face. "How do you feel, soldier?"

The soldier's response was an unequivocal expression of his frame of mind—he slashed the Healer's throat with his claws.

The other Healer screamed in horror, stumbling backwards.

As for Satan, he was quick to react. He jumped out of bed, pulled away the sheet that separated the stations, and, with lightning speed, wrapped his arm around the bellicose soldier, and snapped his neck.

"Forgive me, my friend," he whispered before letting the body slump onto the bed. As he took a step back towards his bed, his legs suddenly failed him, and he crumpled to the floor.

"It's happening to me, isn't it?" he asked the Healer, the pain traversing his body becoming acute. He looked at his wound; the skin around it becoming reddish.

"I'm sorry," replied the Healer, who was filled with far more terror than sorrow.

Lord Deus would need to know about this immediately. An ominous new enemy was rising from among his ranks.

CHAPTER 26

Over 10,000 people had congregated on the Royal Plaza, 4,000 of which were human souls, branded as *Echoes* by the Eternals, a term indicative of duplication of life.

Eternals and Echoes alike waited with anticipation for Maitreya's address to the Nation. And soon enough, he appeared, accompanied by Deus, onto the balcony adjoining the war room of the castle.

Deus spoke first. "It has been Millennia since Maitreya addressed the people. While we were once One, we are now two, but always speaking with one voice. Hear him now with the same attention, the same consideration, and the same reverence you accorded him in the past. I give you the spirit of God incarnate, Maitreya."

"Greetings people of Heaven," Maitreya began. "These are dire times for all of us. It was some time ago that we were at war against the Chimerians and the Kalidrone, a war we finally won in decisive fashion. The recent war against the Great Dragons was no different: unmitigated and surprisingly swift. Regrettably, it engendered a foul side-effect, which manifested itself in the creation of a perverted species: the *Dragon kindred*.

"These demons—once brave soldiers willing to give their lives for yours—will now stop at nothing to take those lives from you. Nothing of their former selves remains; and that is the notion we must grapple with and finally concede before we fight them. Their leader, I regret to say, is none other than one of the mightiest warriors of Heaven turned to darkness: Satan, the self-proclaimed Dragon Lord.

"As we speak, Satan is building his army, which includes not only his kin, but also the Chimerians, and countless Echoes enslaved and trained for battle. At day's end, their forces will number in the hundred thousand.

"We will do the same and marshal our army of soldiers, civilians, and all Echoes willing to join their Eternal brothers in battle."

Maitreya raised the Holy Sword above his head and shouted: "Victory depends on you. Are you with me? Are you with your Lord Deus? Will you fight for Heaven and for your freedom?"

"We will fight!" the crowd screamed in unison.

"Will we prevail against the enemy?" shouted Maitreya.

"We will prevail!" screamed the crowd.

"So say we all?" added Maitreya.

"So say we all!" answered the crowd.

Maitreya lowered his sword and, without another word, retired to the war room, followed by Deus.

"That went well," said a conceited Maitreya. "My charisma has never been so irresistible."

"Save your so-called charisma for your romantic conquests," advised an irritated Deus. "There is much to discuss."

Deus and Maitreya sat at a small round table placed near the center of the room, where Michael had been waiting. "Scouting report, Michael," ordered Deus.

Michael placed a data storage device on the table and read the contents on its display screen. "The scouts have gathered the following: there are a little over 12,000 *Draco-Demons*, or *Dracs* for short, preparing for battle."

"I like the name Dracs," remarked Maitreya; "sounds vile."

Deus glared conspicuously at Maitreya, conveying his annoyance. "Go on, Michael."

Michael resumed. "About 42,000 Chimerians have joined the Dracs, and around 66,000 Echoes have been forcibly drafted, equating to an army of 120,000 able bodies."

"Hum, higher than anticipated," realized Deus. "What of the remaining Echoes?"

"Many have been killed for refusing to fight," sadly admitted Michael. "Others have left their homes and escaped to the fields and forests."

"What about the Kalidrone?" wondered Deus.

"As we suspected, no member of the subterranean race has joined the Dracs," replied Michael.

"The Dracs will never find them," believed Maitreya. "As earth tunnellers and underground dwellers, they will settle in safety deep inside the Polar caves."

"What about position?" asked Deus.

Michael punched a few keys on his device. "The Dracs and their allies are positioned in the Eastern region of the Province of Echosia, a few miles north of the Miracle Mountains. Once they start their march, they'll reach the City of God in 12 days."

"That gives us time to train the Echoes," presumed Deus. "How many have volunteered to join the fight?"

"About 107, 000," replied Michael.

Deus pondered the numbers. "While our count exceeds the Dracs', we lack in caliber and strength. Granted the Echoes are sufficiently intelligent and adaptive, but they possess neither the skills nor the ferocity of the Chimerians."

Deus pondered further. "There is one more ally we haven't considered."

"Not an option, my Lord," reported Michael, foreseeing Deus' proposition. "The *Blue Skins* are extreme pacifists; they will not participate."

"Have you actually spoken to the *Akkadians* to verify that assumption?" queried Deus.

Michael nodded. "Our scout spoke to our Akkadian contact. They say they will remain within the walls of their secret city until the war is over. They, of course, expect us to win. Otherwise, they stand to be discovered every time they set foot on dry land."

Deus was disappointed and frustrated. "One cannot relish one's freedom without paying for it. They must know this."

"A collection of cowards, that's what these blue *fish-people* are," stated Maitreya with loathing and repugnance. "If I ever get my hands on one of them, I'll have it for dinner."

"It's not our place to judge their beliefs and values," pointed out Michael. "No matter our differences, they remain a remarkable people."

"Perhaps they will have a change of heart before the Drac army amasses at our doors," fleetingly hoped Deus. "That's it for now, gentlemen. We'll regroup tomorrow morning."

As the men headed for the door, Deus called upon Maitreya. "Please stay a moment." As soon as the door closed, Deus finally confronted Maitreya on his behavior during the battle against the Great Dragons. "Why did you enter the cavern with only Satan as your backup, and how did you know a sole dragon inhabited it?"

Maitreya appeared prepared to answer. "I *sensed* there was only one dragon," he explained, "and not just any dragon—the leader of the tribe. Astonishing as it is, I can only surmise my new existence in bodily form has afforded me unique insights previously unavailable."

Deus appeared incredulous. "So, armed with that knowledge, you concluded only two men were necessary to dispatch the beast."

"Several men could have accompanied us," acknowledged Maitreya, "but I feared that a large contingent might have scared the beast into hiding within the corridors connecting the caverns. We would have lost the chance to kill the leader."

Deus went on. "All right. What about your delay in slaying the beast while its fangs and teeth held Satan prisoner, crushing him slowly?"

"I was waiting for its underbelly to be exposed," said Maitreya.

"You wielded the Holy Sword," reminded Deus. "Striking any area of the beast's body would have resulted in a death blow. You know that."

"In the heat of the moment, that fact did not occur to me," admitted Maitreya.

"That is hard to believe," said a doubtful Deus.

"That is the only explanation I have to offer," retorted an unphased Maitreya. "I am suddenly growing fatigued—the strain of the task at hand no doubt. May I excuse myself?"

Deus sighed heavily. "You may go. On your way out, tell the Healer to enter."

The Healer trotted in. "Good day, Lord God" said the Head of the medical center in quasi-singing fashion. "I live to serve, your Magnificence."

"What have you uncovered?" impatiently asked Deus, who, in dire times, grew weary of excessive displays of adoration.

The Healer nervously flipped through the pages of his report. "Well, well, it's quite astounding to say the least. Judging by the configuration of the wounds and the foreign substance found within, we've ascertained that the spontaneous mutation into a demon-like being is caused by a geno-toxin delivered either by the dragon's fangs or by the calcified ridges surrounding the end portion of its tail. Upon injection of the geno-toxin into the victim's bloodstream, a cellular restructuring immediately commences, the speed of which is almost impossible to fathom."

"Is the transformation reversible?" inquired Deus.

"Not at the moment," said the Healer. "More analysis is required."

"Can the Dracs, I mean the demons, transmit the disease to others in the same manner as the dragons?" wondered Deus.

The Healer's eyes turned to the floor. "I'm afraid so. The soldiers of my Lord must be made privy to this unfortunate development before engaging in battle."

"Leave me," commanded Deus. "I must reflect on this."

Victory against the enemy had suddenly become more elusive.

CHAPTER 27

Present day; New York.

"I can move! I can talk! I can walk!"
"Yes Pinocchio, I've given you life."
"Why?"
"Because tonight, Geppetto wished for a real boy."
"Am I a real boy?"
*"No, Pinocchio. To make Geppetto's wish come true will be
  entirely up to you."*
"Up to me?"
*"Prove yourself brave, truthful and unselfish, and someday you
  will be a real boy."*
"A real boy!"
"You must learn to choose between right and wrong."
"Right... and wrong? But how will I know?"
"Your conscience will tell you."

"What's a conscience, Theon?" Maya asked her eight-year older
brother as she sat next to him on the sofa, both watching a video of Dis-
ney's Pinocchio.

"Like the Blue Fairy says, it helps you make the difference between
right and wrong," explained Theon.

"But *what* is it?" urged on Maya, trying to imagine if she could detect
a conscience if it came up to her.

Theon yawned in boredom. This was his fourteenth viewing of the
movie; and each time he hoped to gain insight as to what it meant to be
a normal boy. Because of his unusual physique and abilities, he felt far
more empathically connected to the character of Pinocchio than any real
boy he'd ever met. If the puppet, by his actions, could become a normal
boy, why couldn't he, by similar actions.

Maya tugged on Theon's sleeve. "Well, what's a conscience?"

"It's sort of a voice inside your head," simply said Theon. "It tells you what you should do, and what you shouldn't do. Got it?"

Maya wiggled her nose as she processed the answer. "Does it look like you and me? I bet your conscience really looks special."

"Why would you say that?" Theon was miffed by his sister's gratuitous assertion. It's enough he looked *special* on the outside, he didn't want his insides—*his spirit*—to be accused of aberration as well.

"Sorry." Maya stared at her lap in remorse. "I just figured your conscience must be like a super-hero...I mean...it did tell you to bring me back to life, didn't it?"

Theon was utterly surprised by her claim of the circumstances surrounding her birth. "What are you talking about?"

Maya grinned bashfully. "Mommy and daddy talk a lot in bed. I just lie down on the floor, at the foot of the door, and I listen."

"I think you should have your ears cleaned," said Theon, relegating her account to the imagination.

"You won't squeal on me, will you?" she begged. "I do it for you, so that you would know things."

Theon knew she was just a self-indulgent snoop, but was none the less impressed by his sister's entrepreneurial albeit surreptitious streak. "I won't tell them...as long as you repeat everything they say to me; deal?"

Maya slapped Theon's open palm with hers, happy to be her big brother's informant. "We're kind of secret agents, now, just like daddy and Aunt Sophie. And they tell each other everything, right?"

"You're really sneaky, you know that," said Theon, realizing Maya had maneuvered him into indulging her request to describe his *super-hero* conscience. "But why just talk about what it looks like?" he reckoned. "Why not show you what my conscience looks like."

Theon sprung out of the sofa and grabbed his sister's hand. "Follow me, pipsqueak!"

Theon ran upstairs, his sister in tow, to the end of the corridor where the trapdoor to the attic hung over their heads. Opening the door to the closet where Sarah kept bathroom cloths and bed sheets, Theon retrieved a four-foot stick outfitted with a hook, and inserted the hook in a ring dangling at the end of a short rope tied to the trapdoor. He pulled down with all his might, and the trapdoor rotated downwards, revealing a staircase.

"I don't think this is a good idea," admonished Maya. "Mommy has forbidden us to go up there."

Theon knew this well, but decided the thrill of adventure far surpassed the possible repercussions. Besides, he never missed an opportunity to awe his sister with his clever tricks. "Mom's at the market and Dad's at Uncle Amadeo's. We won't get caught."

Working their way up the attic stairs like mice looking for that choice piece of cheese, Theon switched on the single 60-watt light bulb, which barely provided enough light to guide their steps, while Maya had already begun rummaging through all the forgotten treasures surrounding her.

"One little ducky; two little duckies; *three* little duckies! Ah, ah, ah!" cried out Maya after picking up a dusty copy of *Sesame Street's Counting with the Count*. "I am a vampire," smiling freakishly and flaunting her white teeth like the living dead on the prowl for blood. "I'm going to bite you on the neck," she warned Theon, who had proceeded to the far end of the attic.

Right under the attic window, he spotted his crib, covered with a blanket and partially hidden by Maya's crib. Only the mobile set, affixed to the head of the crib, stuck out from under the blanket. Two of the four toy replicas which originally hung from the mobile structure had been torn away. This observation disturbed Theon, who wondered why his parents would have done this. After all, he wasn't tall enough at the time to reach the toys; and had he tried to climb the bars of the crib, surely he would have toppled over.

"I'm going to bite you," reiterated Maya, who trotted to Theon and grabbed his hips.

"Get off of me!" shouted Theon, pushing her away.

"You said we were going to have fun," pouted Maya, who sat heavily on the floor and clearly expressed her sulkiness. "You're a liar."

"We'll have fun in a minute," he assured her as he rolled her crib to the side, and pulled the blanket off his own crib. "What the hell?" he hollered, quoting his father's favorite exclamation. Four of the eight aluminum bars on one side of the crib were completely ripped off, while three on the other side were severely bent. In addition, a nine-inch hole had been melted through the center of the aluminum head board.

"Wow!" screamed Maya, brandishing her arms in the air. "You *are* a super-hero with super powers. I knew it. You're Superman!"

Theon glared at Maya in reprobation. "I'm no darn super-hero."

"Hey, don't blame me," she retorted harshly. "I didn't do this. I just heard mommy tell daddy she was worried about your *unproductable power*."

Theon was skeptical about Maya's account. "She said *unproductable* power?"

"Yeah!" snapped back Maya. "I know what power means, but unproductable…beats me."

The word Maya was searching for was *unpredictable*—a word she could not have invented on her own. And Theon now knew his mother was not just guilty of acute motherly concern, but was also very concerned her son was increasingly becoming a loose cannon.

He felt very ambivalent about what to do with this new and alarming information. "Do mommy and daddy also say they love me?" he asked his sister, hoping love would conquer all.

Maya hesitated. "I, er…I,,,"

The longer Maya vacillated, the more Theon's face grew angry and ever so frightening, a face Maya had never seen before. "You're scaring me!" she cried, her lips quivering.

Theon was appalled at the ease with which he lost control, and even more aghast at the fear he provoked in Maya. "I didn't mean to scare you," he reassured his sister before sitting down next to her. "I just feel so different than everybody else. And I'm always scared people will find out I'm not like them and hate me."

Maya rested her head on Theon's arm. "I'm not afraid of you. You're the best brother in the world."

"Thanks, little sister." Theon wrapped his arm around Maya's waist. "I used to feel at home here, but now I'm not sure. I'm not even sure mom and dad love me as much as before."

"They do," said a guilt-riddled Maya, who now regretted withholding this information moments before. "They say they love you so many times in bed, a lot more times than they love me. I'm jealous. I wish I was different too."

"You are," said Theon with frank conviction. "You're the only girl with a brother like me." They both chuckled as their spirits began to lift, and their childish glee resumed its course. "Now, let's have fun."

Theon directed his attention at two stacked full-length mirrors leaning against the wall a few feet from the light bulb. Selecting the one on top—the only one with a stand—he placed it under the light bulb, directly facing the other mirror, which he straightened in a perfect upright position by shoving a box against it.

"Come stand next to me. We're going to play my version of *Bloody Mary*," Theon told Maya.

Bloody Mary was the children's game of summoning an evil and vengeful witch of the same name. This was done by standing in a room, with one lit candle or dim light, and calling the name "Bloody Mary" into a mirror three times in a row. It was only the bravest of children who would attempt to participate in this game since summoning the witch could result in: the horrific appearance of the witch; serious bodily injury; imprisonment in the mirror; insanity; or death. Using two mirrors was believed to increase the likelihood of success of the morbid experiment.

"My version is called *Ghost Knight*," remarked Theon. "That's the name I give my spirit, my conscience. If we stare in the mirror and say his name three times in a row, he'll appear in one of the mirrors. You'll be able to see what he looks like."

Maya seemed unsure. "Is it going to be scary?"

Theon coaxed her on. "You did say you wanted to see what he looked like?"

"Yeah, I guess," she conceded.

Theon held her tight. "On the count of three, we say his name together. One...two...three!"

"Ghost Knight...Ghost Knight...Ghost Knight!" They both peered deeply into the mirror, anticipating some sort of manifestation; but nothing happened. Theon stared in the mirror behind him, but there was nothing there either.

He tried calling the spirit on his own, but his second attempt was equally futile. "Why isn't this working?" he muttered in disappointment. "There has to be a way."

"Maybe he's shy," conjectured Maya, who quickly lost interest and returned to her earlier treasure-hunting.

"Or he doesn't recognize the name Ghost Knight," considered Theon. "But what else should I call him?" This was quite a conundrum.

"I have an idea," announced Maya, who had foraged through a box labeled *Cameron/Electronics*. The box contained earlier models of cell phones and i-pods, an old laptop, two bulky traditional cameras and one digital camera. "We can take a picture of the Ghost Knight with this *magical* camera," pulling the digital camera out of the box.

"It's called a *digital* camera, Maya," pointed out Theon, "not a magical camera." But then again, what did he have to lose, he thought. It was no sillier than the current rules of the game. Perhaps the game needed to be revitalized with a more contemporary component to recapture its mythical potency. "Bring the magical camera over here."

"We make a good FBI team, don't we, Theon?" she postured proudly, gladly handing him the camera. "We should take lots of pictures to make sure."

Theon checked to see if the camera had a memory stick inserted into it. It did. And the battery, to his surprise, was still partially charged—the camera probably had been put in storage only recently since Theon's father had bought a new one two weeks ago.

"Ok Maya, you stand here." Theon positioned her next to him, six inches apart. "Raise your arms above your head and hold the camera. "He placed it in her hands and flipped open the display screen. "Twist your arms a bit; ok…perfect aim," he exclaimed after checking the screen. "You're spot on the middle of the mirror. Now, the automatic adjustment is on; and the automatic timer is set to go…now!"

Theon moved in position. "Stay still, Maya. It'll take ten seconds."

"My arms hurt," moaned Maya.

"Ghost Knight…Ghost Knight…Ghost Knight. Another two, one, and—" The camera clicked sharply. "Good work, Maya," congratulated Theon after examining the picture in the screen. "Let's take one more."

"There will be *no* more pictures," suddenly roared an indignant voice coming from the stairs. A head stuck out from the attic trap. Daddy had returned.

CHAPTER 28

"You both know the attic is off limits," Cameron reminded his son and daughter. "Your mother is going to be pissed when she finds out you were up here."

"I'm sorry daddy. I won't do it again," promised Maya, who now dreaded her mother's return from the market.

"I'm not blaming you, honey," said Cameron as he glared fiercely at Theon. "Your *older* brother should have known better. Now, run along while I speak to him."

Maya scampered off hastily, but not before waving at Theon. He wasn't quite sure whether his sister was waving goodbye or good luck. Had he the choice, he would have opted for good luck, of which he needed in ample quantity to be spared his father's wrath.

"So, what now?" asked Theon, who readied himself for a draconian tongue lashing.

"Why did you come to the attic?" sternly demanded Cameron.

"I needed stuff to play a game with Maya," honestly replied Theon.

Cameron had never known his son to lie, but given the right set of circumstances, he believed he could. "No other reason?"

Theon immediately understood what his father was getting at—the crib. "I really didn't know about it, nor do I remember it, or what I did to it. I swear, dad."

Cameron stared into Theon's eyes, searching for any trace of deception. All he could report was an impenetrable layer of pleading innocence; what dwelled behind it, he could not discern. Nevertheless, what he did see was grounds enough for forgiveness.

"I believe you, Theon," said Cameron as he simmered down. "Your mother will too, I'm sure."

His father having renewed ties with his congenial disposition, Theon saw an opening and mobilized enough courage to ask a few questions of his own. "Dad, if I were to look through the boxes, would I find other stuff that I've broken as a toddler?"

"Plenty," candidly replied Cameron. "Your mother doesn't throw anything out—especially your stuff."

"But my stuff isn't broken the way other kids' stuff is broken, right?" Theon probed further.

Cameron contemplated the question, and, in that moment, decided his eight-year son was old enough to handle certain truths. He was also exceptionally bright, articulate and mature for his age—another argument in favor of admission. Whether his wife would agree with disclosure at this time, he would cross that bridge when he came to it.

Cameron took a deep breath and began. "The first thing you should know is that we found you within the walls of a damp and dirty well, and not within those of a warm and comfortable hospital. That, in combination with your unique physical attributes and abilities, has cast an ominous shadow over your unknown origin."

Theon remained unusually calm. "Are you saying the people who abandoned me did so because they were afraid of me?"

"Not necessarily," replied Cameron. "Maybe they were trying to save you from someone or something terrible."

"Someone who wanted me for my abilities," surmised Theon.

"Could be," concurred Cameron. "When you were three and four years old—and still lacking awareness of and control over your powers— you did things no one could ever conceive—most of them disturbing. It stopped for a few years, and your mother and I were hopeful, but it started again just after your sixth birthday. You may not remember, but you have done and can do far more than you think. *Far more*."

"Like raising the dead, for example," said Theon, expecting an acknowledgement from his father.

"You remember that?" said a startled Cameron.

"Not precisely," replied Theon, refraining from expanding on the subject. "Dad, sometimes I'm more worried about what's going on in my head than what I'm able to do— as scary as that might be."

"Have you discussed this with your psychiatrist?" queried Cameron, who, after four years of consultation, had not heard anything of substance from Theon's therapist. "Theon is secretive and somewhat of an enigma," the therapist often said.

"I just don't trust her," Theon said plainly; "never did."

"You could have told your mother and me this a long time ago," pointed out Cameron, who kept his cool, and for good reason—this was the first time he and his son had a semblance of an authentic, open conversation.

"My going to therapy seemed to make you and mom happy," explained Theon. "Why interfere with that…and why interfere with *your* goal of a *picture-perfect* family?"

"What's this business of a picture-perfect family?" angrily spouted Sarah as she popped up from the attic trap. "And what is Theon doing here?"

Without thinking twice, Cameron elected to preserve the confidentiality of the conversation, and protect the newfound trust established between Theon and him. "Oh, I was just showing Theon my old digital camera. I thought he could use it to take family photos."

"And we were using the mirror to experiment with lighting," cleverly added Theon, while Cameron discretely moved in Sarah's plain view of the incriminating crib.

Sarah shot a suspicious look at the dubious duo. "Riiiiight! Now put that mirror back in its place and come down. Supper will be ready in 20 minutes." She dashed down the stairs, yelling, "and Theon, go get your sister from her room."

"Tell your sister to keep quiet about the attic affair," Cameron whispered to his son. "I'll take care of the crib."

"Aye Aye, sir!" replied Theon, who was thoroughly enjoying the complicity with his father. He rushed downstairs, fully intent on reducing his sister to silence.

After putting back everything as it was, Cameron also engaged the stairs, all the while skimming through the pictures stored on the camera's memory stick. "I had forgotten about these photos," he thought to himself. All the photos involved Theon's eighth birthday, except for one—the one taken by Maya minutes ago.

When he got to it, he stopped short. The shot was remarkable and extraordinarily beautiful. By placing two mirrors opposite each other, Theon had engineered an infinite image-multiplication effect. Each reflection off one mirror traveled to the other mirror, reflecting against that one and returning to the first mirror, and repeated the process a second time…and a third time…a fourth, and so on, without end.

(example of infinite image-multiplication effect)

"I'm going to frame this picture and put it on my office wall, right above my—what's this?" While scrutinizing the picture, Cameron noticed something odd: Theon's image seemed to be distorted as of the fourth reflection. And the further down the reflections, the more distorted it became. However, after closer inspection, he concluded the phenomenon was more a case of image mutation than image distortion. He was utterly fascinated.

"I'll be in my office," Cameron notified his wife as he marched through the kitchen to his home office. "No interruptions, please."

"Supper in 15 minutes, Cam; don't forget." Sarah hoped he hadn't been called on business again. His frequent absence during supper time was becoming problematic. Despite her appreciation of the nature and the constraints of his job, her coping mechanisms had begun to fail her. He was a hero, and rightly so, but she never wanted a hero, she wanted a husband. Unfortunately, like many husbands, he was oblivious to his wife's plight; and more so today as the mystery of the bizarre photo consumed him totally.

Sitting at his desk by his computer, Cameron connected the memory stick to a USB port, and then called up the FBI intranet and entered his primary password and secondary counter codes. *Level five security clearance* read the computer screen. After navigating through several page layers, he accessed the FBI 2DARE (*2-dimensional absolute reconstruction engine*) software program, an advanced artificial intelligence program performing two-dimensional facial reconstructions based on ante-mortem photographs.

Uploading the photograph of interest into the program, he began running it. The computer was quick to respond:

"Multiple entities detected."

Cameron responded through a flexible query system:

"Number entities based on size, from largest to smallest. Stop numbering at ten." Images beyond the tenth reflection were simply too small and lacked workable resolution.

"Activity complete."

"How many entities are identical to entity #1, irrespective of relative size?"

"Entities #2 and #3 are identical to entity #1."

"Do elements of entity #1 appear in entities #4 through #10?"

"Affirmative."

"Remove those elements from entity #4 through #10, and display separately in one view, and in equal size using entity #1 as reference. Remove original background from all generated pictures."

"Activity complete."

Cameron probed each of the seven pictures, but could not distinguish anything of significance. Each picture was a motley assortment of facial features, one different from the other. He would try something specific.

"Are the elements of entity #4 congruent between themselves?"

"Negative."

"How many sub-entities are included in entity #4?"

"Insufficient data."

"Damn!" Cameron was frustrated, but would not admit defeat. "Overlay entities #4 through #10, and display. Label composite entity as #11."

"Activity complete."

"How many sub-entities are included in entity #11?"

"Four sub-entities detected. Congruence factor for each sub-entity above critical level, and calculated at 88.6%, 82.1%, 79.5%, 73.3%, respectively."

"What is causing congruence interference?"

"Each sub-entity respectively includes similar but competing residual data. Quantity not sufficient to prevent rendering."

"Specify using a random example."

"Example provided. Sub-entity includes two sets of eyes, similar in physicality but not identical."

"What is the protocol in such a case?"

"Blending of physical features is recommended."

"Apply protocol, and display sub-entities, full screen, and sequentially from highest congruence factor to lowest."

"Activity complete. Press space bar to begin display."

The first picture Cameron saw was a Caucasian man, probably in his thirties, with almond eyes, shoulder-length reddish brown hair with a short beard and goatee. By all standards, he was a handsome specimen. The man's stare followed Cameron, no matter the angle from which he gazed at him; and he felt such benevolence exuding from the man's face. If this sub-entity, as the computer called it, was part of Theon, then perhaps he could finally banish all his concerns about his son's future—surely he would become a good man, even a man of the people.

The second picture created much the same impression, but at a different level. It looked like a man covered entirely of red-hot silver, which shimmered as if the silver had just been poured over him. Although Cameron could barely make out the facial features, he was convinced the *Tin-Man* was smiling at him. "You look like a man who's just received the biggest of hearts," he mumbled, alluding to the Wizard of Oz. "But who are you? What are you?"

Cameron proceeded to the third picture. This one left no room for interpretation. It conjured the most terrifying of childhood nightmares in Cameron—nightmares that always sent him running to the safety of his parents' bed. "Good Lord, what the hell does this mean?" he uttered nervously as he examined the unadulterated manifestation of a demonic creature. Its crimson red skin oozed with sweat gorged with brimstone; its heinous catlike green eyes cursed its petrified onlookers; and its sharp teeth dripped with the blood of the sacrificial lamb.

But the disconcerting emotions these tokens of depravity and turpitude stirred in Cameron were nothing compared to the devilish ears whose pointed ends bent forwards like harpoon guns poised to release their poison arrows. The revolting ears looked so much like Theon's ears. "Let it be just a deplorable coincidence," he trusted. But he knew he was dabbling with wishful thinking. Perhaps the next picture would restore hope.

"She's beautiful," he thought as the fourth picture appeared. The woman's face was soft and lovely. Her long brown hair cascaded down her shoulders; her hazel eyes twinkled; and her slightly arched nose added character to the ensemble. But it was her discreet smile that stole the show—it was simply bewitching.

Somehow, Cameron knew this face. There was something about it that was so familiar, so much so it triggered an astute idea.

"Computer; based on the residual data, how many distinct variations of this sub-entity can be produced without blending?"

"Specify differential factor."

"20% of elements must be different from one variation to the other."

"Activity complete. Eight variations produced."

"Display sequentially."

Cameron went through the pictures, his anticipation and sense of familiarity increasing with each picture, until he reached the sixth one. All hell broke loose. "God preserve me!" He couldn't believe his eyes, nor could he fathom the meaning of what appeared on his computer screen. It was, in all its intricate and never foreseen details, a perfect picture of his wife Sarah.

CHAPTER 29

Circa 37,000 years ago; Kingdom of Heaven.

The battle had been raging for twelve days now, with heavy casualties on both sides. A command center had been set up three miles from the front, from which Deus received daily reports on the progress and the state of his army, and issued instructions accordingly.

"The war does not go well for both sides," gravely said the Tribune Augustus to Deus. "We have lost over 32,000 Echoes, 7,000 civilians, and 3,000 legionnaires. Most are dead, the rest captured. And my Lord, I must also report the disappearance of *Secundus Pilus Prior Gabriel.*"

Deus remained stoic. "What of Maitreya and Michael?"

"They are both alive and fighting at the front," informed the Tribune. "Rumor has been circulating among the troops that Maitreya alone has killed over 2,000 Chimerians and 500 Dracs. In total, our army has dispatched about 52,000 enemy fighters."

"So, the situation is not as dire as you first inferred?" noted Deus, who cracked a rare smile since the beginning of the hostilities. "We've killed 10,000 more men than they have."

"That may be true," recognized the Tribune, "but most are Echoes, their fighting skills mediocre at best. There is also the matter of Maitreya and the Holy Sword—the men's bravery and resolve seem to have become oddly contingent on his omnipotent presence and power on the field. The men measure their chances of success by the number of fighters he kills. Were he to fall in battle, the tide would assuredly turn against us.."

"If Maitreya were to succumb, I would wield the Holy Sword in his stead," announced Deus. "I have the noble blood and still carry the imprint of Maitreya, both of which investing me with the qualities necessary to conjure the Sword's might."

The Tribune vacillated. "Perhaps, but let us hope it does not come to that; a kingdom cannot survive without its king."

Deus gazed over the horizon towards the frontline. "I don't entirely trust you, brother," he thought to himself, "but if there ever was an occasion, a place, a time for restoration to favor, for vindication, it is this war, here and now. Do you hear me, brother?"

"I hear you!" shouted Maitreya to Michael as their troops advanced on the enemy. "The Chimerians and remaining Echoes are coming over the East hill, in great numbers. We have to separate. Take two legions to intercept them. I'll move the remaining legion west, to join the civilians and the Echoes who are fighting the Dracs."

In minutes, Michael's men clashed with the enemy. Fire bolts from Rash'tas and Kor'tas, immediately followed by a deluge of arrows, zipped across the battlefield, felling hundreds of men every few seconds, without discrimination for race. Swords then swung relentlessly, piercing bodies and cutting off heads, butchering those who refused to die upon the first blow.

Echoes who were mortally wounded lost cohesion and instantly disintegrated, releasing a disembodied spiritual energy Eternals had come to coin *Humanessence*. Once released, after first being embodied for the purpose of Heavenly life, the energy could never be reintegrated.

"Retreat!" screamed Michael as he stepped over dark stains on the ground, the residue left after an Echo died and decomposed. "Regroup behind the rock formations at the bottom of the hill."

While Michael prepared for a second wave of bloodshed, Maitreya and his legion joined forces with the civilian and Echo fighters. The ground was already paved with thousands of mutilated bodies when Maitreya charged the first group of Dracs in his way. With one swing of the sword, he sent eight Dracs to their graves.

Ten more Dracs rushed towards Maitreya, in triangular formation much like bowling pins. Maitreya's sword hit the ground, creating a tidal wave of rocks that grew in size as it tore the earth along its path, crushing the men so utterly nothing of them was left except for a pool of bloody organic debris.

"Impressive," said a voice stemming from his left flank.

It was familiar, *yet not*, to Maitreya who swiftly turned and intensified his defensive posture. "Satan! It was only a matter of time before we finally met on the battlefield."

The Dragon Lord responded by discharging six fire bolts, which Maitreya easily deflected using the blade of his sword. "Cease firing and call off your men! I mean you no harm!" he told Satan.

Maitreya's affirmation was so preposterous, Satan pointed his kor'ta at his opponent's head, testing his good faith. "If that is so, lower your sword gently, and we'll talk."

"You will hear me first before I place my life in your hands," staunchly stated Maitreya. "It is in your interest to do so."

Satan's expression betrayed his disbelief and his confusion. "First you toy with my life and almost have me killed by a Great Dragon; and now, you wish to impart to me some level of consideration for my safety and my survival. What manner of paradoxal jailer has sequestered your wits?"

"I am prey to no hunter of the sort," replied Maitreya. "While my logic escapes you, I ask that you heed my words. My army has made significant progress in the last few hours. Two-thirds of the Chimerian horde has been decimated, and the Echoes you recruited by force are on the brink of defection. You have 45,000 men left, while I have 67,000. If the battle persists for another day or so, my army will likely prevail; and yours will be defeated. As leader and instigator of the war, you will be tried and executed for your crime against the State. Above all else, that must *not* happen."

"You miscalculate. My men have taken control off all new Echo arrivals from Earth," boasted Satan. "We will enlist them all to our cause immediately upon arrival, one by one."

"In time, that may grow your ranks," conceded Maitreya, "but never in ample time or ample numbers."

"Don't underestimate my resolve...or my *creativity*," cautioned Satan. "There may yet be a way to swell my numbers posthaste."

"Stop your hollow posturing, and forget these trivialities," enjoined Maitreya. "Think of *yourself*."

"Why is my life so important to you?" asked Satan.

"You and I have much to do. In time, my reasons will become clear to you," evasively replied Maitreya. "For now, you will petition Deus for a truce, and then a peace treaty."

"If my army is already doomed, why would Deus agree to a ceasefire?" thought Satan.

Maitreya couldn't hold back a wicked grin. "Because the legionnaires will be so dejected and distressed by my capture, their spirit for combat will become grievously handicapped. Deus would then have no choice but to accept an arrangement."

"You seem so very certain?" noticed Satan. "No man can *perfectly* predict the actions of another."

"You forget Deus and I are brothers." Maitreya swung back his sword. "Now, before my sword sets upon its forward thrust, you must shoot me...in the leg preferably."

Satan was presented with a golden opportunity. Killing Maitreya would have the same devastating effect as capturing him, he concluded. And killing was far more satisfying. But curiosity about Maitreya's secret agenda quickly superseded blood lust, and Satan modified his aim, from head to leg.

Just as the Dragon Lord was about to discharge his weapon, the ground around them began trembling violently. The earth shook with such intensity that it cracked open in several areas, one of which was right under Maitreya's feet.

Maitreya fell in, hitting his head against the bouldery side of the chasm, and releasing his clasp on the Holy Sword, which landed partly over the abyss, in precarious balance. One more jolt and it would tip over into the crevasse.

Satan got on all fours and moved cautiously towards the sword. "The precious sword is mine, all mine," coveting it with salacious relish. But the impetuous earth would have none of it, trembling anew, causing the sword to plummet into the deep fissure.

Furious, Satan gazed into the darkness, just in time to detect a faint light twenty-five feet deep, and a cluster of shadows moving madly about, both of which faded rapidly into obscurity.

"Kalidrone!" exclaimed Satan.

CHAPTER 30

"**Welcome, gentlemen,**" Erel, Deus' chief-accountant, bid Satan's company of representatives as they entered the castle's war room. "We were expecting you sooner."

"With cautious enthusiasm, I presume," mockingly snickered Satan.

"With hopes for a quick resolution," said Erel, directing the vicious-looking group to the negotiation table where Deus and his team sat in waiting. No one at the table rose to salute the Dracs.

Once they sat, Deus spoke. His stance was neutral, revealing neither defiant aggressiveness nor lack of deep-rooted assurance. "I present to you my judicial committee formed ad hoc to address the issue of peace between our *people*."

"We use the term *people* loosely for reasons I'm sure are evident to you," added Michael with a soupcon of hatred for the monstrosities sitting across the table.

"Please, let's not compromise these talks before they begin," interjected an overly diplomatic Erel.

"Sound advice," said Deus. "I have with me people you already know, of course: Khrist Lesus, General Michael, Primus Judge Issachar, and chief-accountant Erel."

Satan immediately followed with the introductions. "These men are my newly appointed *Posterus Custodes*, the guardians of my people's posterity: Thevetat, Aurignacia, Vetis, and Sonneillon. You may address them by name. As for me, Dragon Lord Satan will do."

Michael clearly appeared irritated by Satan's self-conferred title, which did not go unnoticed by the Drac party. "Do you wish to file an objection, my *brother*?" asked Satan.

"Not at this time," grudgingly replied Michael. "However, I do protest to the term *brother* when addressing me."

"Please, gentlemen, we're wandering off topic," remarked Deus. "We must all exercise restraint and remain cool-headed. The state of our affairs, most frail in the now, will only turn to steadiness if we summon respect for and deference to the sanctity of these proceedings."

"As always, you are most wise, my Lord," said Erel, who hurriedly distributed copies of a high-level summary of a peace treaty. "This is a draft based largely on preparatory discussions between Lord Deus and… Dragon Lord Satan. The language has been simplified for the purpose of these proceedings. A formal and comprehensive document will be drawn subsequent to the ratification of the summary."

"The collection of policies and practices contained in this document has aptly been called The Acts of Maitreya," declared Deus, "in honor of my Holy Spirit, who has been sadly lost to all of us. It is no secret Maitreya and I did not always agree; I nevertheless thought the designation appropriate; and Lord Satan has no objections."

The room remained silent. Any dissent over a mere label would have been a definite intimation of the grave difficulties forthcoming in the ratification of the peace treaty.

Deus did not pause for very long and went on. "The cardinal Act: the *Act of Non-Aggression*. From this date forward, there will be no acts of aggression, or planning of acts of aggression between Eternals known as *Sanctus Terrum* and *Sanctus Angelicum*, and Eternals known henceforth as *Diabolicus Terrum* and *Diabolicus Arium*. Violation of this Act will be considered an act of war, and such war will automatically ensue."

"I prefer calling them Dracs," Michael whispered to Lesus. It was becoming evident to Deus that Michael's passive aggressive behavior stemmed from the loss of his brother's former identity. As far as he was concerned, nothing of him—with all his qualities and faults—survived in Satan, the transformed Drac.

Deus glared at Michael. "If this process is too difficult for you, I'll excuse you without prejudice. No one will judge you."

"My apologies, Lord Deus," said Michael, realizing he had gone too far, and expressing genuine contrition. "My conduct is unbecoming."

Satan smiled at his brother. "It appears the monsters you think we are have better control over their emotions."

Michael looked down, feigning reading, and kept his tongue in check.

Deus was glad Michael was staying. "Second Act: the *Act of Division*. The Kingdom of Heaven shall be divided into two parts, according to the geographical specifications detailed in the document. Bodies of water, such as lakes, rivers and seas, affected by the new boundary shall retain their original names. The names of lands now belonging to the Diabolicus shall be determined by said Diabolicus. And the entire collection shall be called the *Kingdom of Hell*, as per Lord Satan's request."

"What of the Sanctus living in that kingdom?" wondered Thevetat.

"They will be relocated," answered Issachar.

"And the Echoes?" added Thevetat.

"We will come to that," said Deus. "The third Act: the *Act of Non-Trespass*. No Sanctus or Diabolicus shall trespass on the other's land, unless prior authorization has been granted by appointed officials. Violation of this Act will be considered an act of war, and such war will automatically ensue.

"The fourth Act: the *Act of Free Exploitation*. Echoes residing in or assigned to the Kingdom of Heaven shall continue to enjoy the freedom to pursue their aspirations, the right to land and shelter, and the privilege of our unwavering protection. Echoes residing in or assigned to the Kingdom of Hell shall be treated according to Hell Law; and such law shall be determined and described at Lord Satan's discretion."

"There are over 200,000 Echoes currently in Hell," estimated Michael, based on the geographical division. "What does Satan's *discretion* entail exactly? Slavery, torture, extermination?"

"No dispositions have been put into place as of yet," disclosed Satan. "None of which is your concern anyway…or anymore. However, as a courtesy, I will inform you when I make a determination," he added mockingly.

"Why you overbear— " Michael stopped in mid-sentence, calling upon every ounce of will power to regain his composure. After a moment that seemed like a lifetime, he managed another question. "Can someone explain to me this *assignment* business?"

"It concerns new arrivals of Echoes from Earth," specified Deus. "They shall be either assigned to Heaven or to Hell, depending on the calculation of a certain *score*. The precise nature of the score proved to be a matter of great debate and contention between Satan and me. You see, I postulated that the way of the Eternal Sanctus was to always appeal to the best of us and to the best of Humanity."

"I, on the other hand, given the youngness of our race, could not yet lay claim on any philosophy," recognized Satan. "I knew, however, that our instinctive disposition, albeit ill-defined for the moment, drew us towards the exploration of our dark sides. I believe the thriving of our race resides in the exploitation of our passions, our lust, our greed, and our voracity for subjugation and dominance. What you call sinfulness, malevolence and devilry, we, the Diabolicus, shall call self-expression and self-actualization."

"We are at opposite extremes of the spectrum," summed up Deus. "And the newly uncovered polarity of our life philosophies spawned the essence and qualitative nature of the elected score: the *Sin Score*."

"I was given the task of creating a hierarchy of sins," explained Erel, "and attributing a numerical score to each sin identified, based on its variable gravity rate and duration. The hierarchy comprises seven major categories of sins, 42 minor categories, and 356 sins in total. The structure of the score was built using the sin history of the current Echo population as a base sample. On average, the population scored 210, with 49.8% scoring above 210. In the interest of equity, that score was used as a centralized reference point in establishing three assignment classes: *Destination Heaven* for scores of 200 or less; *Destination Hell* for scores of 220 and greater; and *Interim Purgatory* for scores greater than 200 and less than 220."

"This collection of assignment classes for new Echo arrivals," added Deus, "including the assignment provision for current Echo residents, shall be ascribed under the fifth Act: the *Act of Allocation*."

"This is grotesque," spouted Michael. "You can't reduce a living, sentient being to a mere arbitrary number that could very well send him to a rotting abyss."

"It is equitable," said Deus, "and the only way. It is done, Michael. Say nothing more of it." His tone was not especially convincing. Deep down, he shared Michael's disgust, but, as supreme leader, he had to consider the greater good.

"What is the significance of the Interim Purgatory class?" queried an equally uneasy Lesus. "Is it a temporary assignment?"

"Indeed it is," confirmed Deus. "After each time interval, the length of which shall be determined shortly, Satan and I shall compete in a mutually agreed upon contest, the winner of which taking ownership of all the purgatory-assigned Echo arrivals, occurring during said interval. Until a winner is declared, Echoes remain in Purgatory."

"Respectfully, this procedure seems somewhat extravagant and puerile," noted Lesus. "*Playing* with people's lives is a frivolous undertaking unbecoming of the King of Heaven."

Deus brimmed with a confidence more akin to sheer fabrication than faith in his own instrumentality. "Not frivolous, but rather astute and advantageous, when victory proves to be your King's lot more often than naught."

Deus' brief incursion into arrogant territory only fuelled Satan's cockiness. "That remains to be seen, my brash friend. Games are after all the trademark of the fiendishly cunning."

"How this peace treaty unfolds when it is in force remains to be seen," cleverly retorted Deus. "Now, there is a critical *Article of Exception* we passed over –also a corollary of the cardinal Act. It states that no Echo under Sanctus or Diabolicus jurisdiction shall be taught or trained in the art of war. Violation of this Article will be considered an act of war, and such war will automatically ensue."

No one reacted, so Deus went on. "The sixth Act: the *Act of Extradition*. Any and all Echoes, without exception, in particular those having committed a crime against the State—either State—seeking refuge to the other jurisdiction shall be promptly returned to their own jurisdiction.

"The seventh Act: the *Act of Non-Interference*. No Sanctus or Diabolicus shall ever travel to Earth again using the transport device, the *Trans'Kartum*, for whatever reason, including but not limited to: societal study and surveying, guidance, teachings, pleasure, benign interaction and copulation. To that effect, the *trans-world* portal shall be forever buried.

"And finally, one prerequisite annexed to the treaty, whose fulfillment is obligatory for and shall precede the ratification of the treaty: all Eternal prisoners of war shall be immediately returned to their jurisdiction."

"And that includes Gabriel," categorically stated Michael.

"We know nothing of Gabriel's whereabouts," insisted Satan; "nor do we know if he's alive or dead."

"I don't believe you," barked Michael.

Satan replied by signing his copy of the summary, and he and his men rose. "Your dog has difficulty heeding your orders, Deus. You best hold him back," the Dragon Lord advised. "It would be a shame if his ill humor and lack of trust tainted the goodwill you and I have demonstrated and carefully nurtured throughout the peace process."

Satan then nodded in salutation, and the Diabolicus promptly left the room.

"I'll prepare the official peace treaty," said Issachar, who picked up Satan's copy and left, followed by Erel, then Lesus, who halted at the door, stared at Deus for a moment, his air saturated with somberness and worry for his King, and left.

"You put on a brave act," said a gravely concerned Michael, who saw

Deus' weariness and torment forcefully confined within his core rise to the surface. "You question this treaty and its consequences, as I do, don't you?"

"It's a question of *relativity*," Deus had concluded a while ago. "The absence of such a treaty would have led to complications far more dire for our race—its obliteration perhaps. Must I press this argument on you yet again?"

"Your insight and intuition have served us well in the past," recognized Michael; "and you have seldom been wrong. Let us hope you are not wrong *this time*." Michael bowed and left, quite dissatisfied and troubled.

As for Deus, he was left to wrestle with his conscience.

CHAPTER 31

Circa 2,000 years ago; Galilee.

"Joseph, what are you doing here?" asked a flustered Mary. "You know full well you cannot see me without my parents' oversight."

"What is there to oversee?" Joseph, one of the most skilled carpenters in Nazareth, pulled out a clay angel from the sack he carried and presented it to Mary. "It took me a day to carve this for you with my special knife. Consider it a symbol of our imminent union before God."

Mary's guard fell as she seized the small sculpture and scrutinized it meticulously, admiring every minute detail. "You are quite the wizard of carpentry, my love. It's exquisite."

"Where shall we set it?" deliberated Joseph, inspecting every potential location in the modest house. "Perhaps the locus of our humble abode will do it justice." Joseph deposited the work of art in the middle of the table of the main room. "From there it shall stand, and from there it shall bless the food that you share every evening."

"Let it also reveal to all the love that binds us together," added Mary. "Let it be our messenger, that all shall come to know of our perfect rapture."

"Beware of messengers carrying false prophecies," warned a stranger who abruptly erupted into Mary's parents' domicile. The mysterious outlander wore a thick oversized robe and hunched forward, bearing a hump than spanned the entirety of his back. In contrast to his badly misshapen form, his facial features were nothing less than angelic.

"You have no business here," screamed Joseph who moved between the intruder and his wife-to-be. "Take your place in the dirt and the dust that fill the cracks of the decaying streets, among your brethren, the beggars."

"I am here to beg, but not for subsidization," pleaded the man. "I beg only for thy consideration and thy deference."

"You have the wrong house," barked an unflinching Joseph. "No one will listen to you here."

"I will listen," said Mary as she appealed her bethroved to restraint and tolerance. She proceeded past Joseph, coming face to face with the stranger. "Speak," she ordered him, her eyes never leaving his. He felt the warmth and kindness concealed behind her brazenness. "Do not make fools out of me and my beloved," she cautioned him. He remained unaffected by her admonition.

"I am Gabriel the Archangel, and I once stood at the Throne of Glory, at the left hand of God," staunchly proclaimed the outsider, removing his robe and unveiling his majestic white wings.

Both Mary and Joseph dropped to their knees. "You are God's servant," cried out Mary, holding her hands in prayer.

"I was at one time," sadly said Gabriel. "Now I am but a slave—a slave enjoying a brief reprieve from his cage."

"Has God turned against you?" queried Joseph whose incredulity quickly faded away.

"My temerity and my recklessness were ultimately my undoing," avowed Gabriel without expanding on the subject. "As for thee, take heed. Thou that art highly favored, the Dark Lord seeks thee: cursed art thou among women."

Mary was shocked by his saying, and cast in her mind what manner of salutation this should be. Gabriel went on and said unto her, "Fear much, Mary: for the darkness thou sustains within hast long found disfavor with the God of Light. And, beware, thou must not conceive in thy womb and bring forth a son, for he shall be troubled and be drawn into the darkness a hundred fold, and shall be called the emissary of Destruction, the bedrock of begotten bedlam. The Dark Lord shall launch unto his spawn his sword and release the Darkness upon God's kingdom: on Earth and in Heaven. The suffering shall know no end."

Confused, Mary asked to the angel, "How shall this be, must I deny my bethroved?"

And the angel answered and said unto her, "Do not mind Joseph. Instead, guard against Evil under the guise of The Holy Spirit; he shall come upon thee, and the power of the Darkest shall overshadow thee; deny him, repel him, cast him out."

"What if Evil has already crossed the threshold of our dwelling?" bravely postulated Mary who was becoming weary of the angel's allegations. "Having taken the semblance of an angel bearing a false omen."

"What are you saying?" interjected Joseph. "Believe your eyes, woman, lest he strikes us down."

"My eyes can be deceived, but not my heart," replied Mary as she stood up while Joseph kept to the ground. "Who sent you? Was it our Lord God?"

Gabriel hesitated before answering. "I come of my own volition, but if my Lord were privy to my task, he would sanction my actions. Believe what thou will; perhaps thy kinswoman shall judge otherwise, and the ponderous chain of havoc shall be broken."

"Of what kinswoman do you speak?" asked an intrigued Mary.

Ignoring Mary's query, Gabriel moved to the entrance and peeked outside. "They know of my escape and they are coming for me. I can waste no more time here." And as suddenly as he had appeared, he disappeared, claiming his robe on the way out.

Joseph sat at the table and picked up his angel sculpture and slowly rotated it, scouring every curve for likenesses to Gabriel. "An omen mayhaps," he thought. He then gazed at Mary and sighed, "What must we do now?"

"Wait for this Spirit," she simply said. "If I am to be the handmaid of a Lord…good or evil, I fancy knowing which." Mary contained her dread as best she could.

CHAPTER 32

Circa 2,000 years ago; Galilee.

"Hear this, cousin, and believe as I do in the supernatural, in the authority of godly beings," Elizabeth entreated her cousin Mary.

"I do believe in godly entities," said Mary as she rubbed her pregnant belly. "But to whom do they swear allegiance? What must *you* say to put the question to rest?"

"I can only nourish the question," replied Elizabeth, "and any answer will only beget more questions. In truth, I am as bewildered as you are, but while youth comes with the promise of posterity, old age tenders only solitude and abject resignation."

"Yet you are with child," stated Mary, "despite your coming of age. What manner of creature has intervened in your favor…or disfavor?"

Elizabeth stared empathically at Mary, who had left Galilee three days ago and traveled south to her house in Judea, seeking refuge and protection from her fiancé's family. She feared her in-laws might kill her because of her apparent adulterous transgression. Fortunately for Elizabeth, her husband Zechariah was an influential member of the priestly order of Abijah. After some initial consternation and objection over his own wife's miraculous condition, he had decided to side by her.

"Like you, I was visited by the Holy Spirit—or his likeness," claimed Elizabeth. "Although I could not glimpse him, I felt his overpowering presence enter me, depositing his seed and summoning it to life—a life I shall name John."

"But what of Zechariah?" earnestly asked Mary. "Does *he* believe in this?"

"He cannot do otherwise," said Elizabeth, "for he was witness to a clash between angel and demon. Days before my pregnancy, Zechariah had been chosen to enter the sanctuary of the Temple of Herod and offer incense as part of the daily worship. It was a pivotal moment for him, since the large number of priests, about 8,000 at that time, meant that any one priest could only expect to offer sacrifice once or twice in his lifetime. As he prepared the offer, an angel appeared at the right side of the altar in front of him.

"'Be weary and watchful,' warned the angel. 'Thy wife shall conceive a child; and this child shall—' The angel suddenly collapsed onto the ground, hit by a triad of lightning bolts. Zechariah kneeled by his side and turned his head towards him only to see his pleading and dimming eyes. He was still alive. A second round of bolts detonated, its charge engulfing my husband as well as the angel. Zechariah fell to his side, finding he had become deaf and mute. A demonic creature emerged from the shadows, holding a strange weapon. He spoke to Zechariah for a moment, and then picked up the angel's body and vanished."

"But your husband was deprived of hearing," pointed out Mary. "What could he have heard?"

"Not heard but seen," clarified Elizabeth. "Battling his fear, he gazed intensely at the demon, making out a few of his words: God, spirit and catalyst; such were the words."

"Have you or your husband speculated as to the nature of the angel's warning?" Mary was eager and equally anxious to hear the answer. It might shed some light on her own situation.

"We concluded the angel was either warning us about the imminent arrival of Satan's spawn, or about the advent of God's instrument, whose rise could be interrupted and quashed most entirely by the dark forces. I *choose* to believe I carry the messenger of God, and he *shall* overcome, only to preserve my sanity if not my faith. What do you believe, Mary?"

"I am uncertain," admitted Mary. "And my uncertainty has weighed heavily upon me. I did *see* the Holy Spirit, however. He catered to all my senses as he engaged me in sexual congress."

"Did it feel wrong or depraved?" queried Elizabeth, implicitly directing the question at herself as well.

Mary closed her eyes, embarrassed and hesitant. "I could not say."

Elizabeth pressed on. "You could not say, or you *would* not say?"

"My twin sister would never say," shouted a voice in derision. "She's far too genteel for that."

Mary and Elizabeth gaped at the intruder who had crossed the doorway. "Bethel?" screamed Mary.

"In the flesh, if I do say so myself." Bethel paraded around the room, bareheaded, barefooted and scantily clad. "Dear Mary, how about a kiss, or a peck, for your roguish and unprincipled twin sister?"

"Is Gamal with you?" asked Elizabeth as she stepped outside and scoured the immediate vicinity, searching for Bethel's husband. "You've come without him?"

"He certainly wouldn't have come willingly," casually said Bethel. "His family ostracized me; and he banished me." From childhood, Bethel had been a difficult and defiant child, unable and unwilling to abide by the exacting demands and social conventions imposed upon women. When she reached the age of betrothal, only one man from a good family, beguiled by her beauty and her charm, would choose her. Now, he had forsaken her.

"What have you done?" Mary was infuriated, although not all together surprised.

"I did what you did, what you both did: I made love with another man," replied Bethel, who had spied on their conversation a moment before revealing her presence. "And it was *heavenly*. But it was not so much this act of betrayal that incensed my pitiful husband as the pregnancy that ensued."

"You foolish child," cried out an aggravated Elizabeth. "We were not speaking of copulation with mortal men."

"Nor was I," vigorously rebutted Bethel. "I too have been intimate with the most sensual and lecherous being delivered onto me from the heavens: the Holy Spirit."

By all accounts, this was the strangest, most implausible, most preposterous case of polygamy in the annals of biblical times—of all times.

CHAPTER 33

Present day; Germany.

"Calling the police was a very risky move,"

remarked Sophie as she and her brother Cameron reached the outskirts of the Reinhardswald forest, an impressive range of hills in the Weser Uplands in the German district of Kassel, and home to countless myths and legends, like the Grimm's Fairy Tales.

"I doubt very much misses Lorenz knew her husband's true identity," assumed Cameron. Adalia Lorenz was wife to Adam Gardner, a gentle and quiet man who, unbeknownst to the townspeople of Beverungen, had been formerly known as Adam Yahiye Gadahn, a prominent terrorist involved in a number of al-Qaida missions. He had been placed on the FBI's most wanted list shortly after 9/11.

He was also on his wife's wanted list since he had failed to return from a business trip to London, five days ago. This was the first time he had been this late. Her distress was compounded by the recent presence of an unknown man who strolled by her house numerous times a day, and the subsequent disappearance of Roy, her 8-year old son. She was convinced the two events were connected—as were Cameron and Sophie after identifying Gadahn from family photos. It was likely to them that the serial child killer had struck again, now for the ninth time.

"I don't know how much longer I can tolerate this," said Sophie bitterly. "While all the murdered children might have been the sons of terrorists, they're innocent, more so even than the children of upstanding parents."

"How so?" asked Cameron.

"Well, these poor children have been protected from a truth *far more* monstrous and revolting than the trivial truths most parents suppress," said Sophie, "presumably for the children's sake and not their own."

"Innocence is fleeting, Sophie," noted Cameron, "especially when it's prematurely extinguished. Let's hope Roy hasn't met with the lethal pay-load of a speeding bullet—at least not yet."

Aided by eight other search teams, spreading out in other directions, the FBI duo marched towards *Tilly's Lair*, a stone tower built in 1885 in memory of Johann Tserclaes, Count of Tilly, who commanded the Imperial forces in the seventeenth century Thirty Years War. Originally designed as a military outpost, the tower has since become a tourist attraction.

"Hello!" shouted Cameron. "Anybody in the tower?"

"In the back!" a voice answered loudly. "The restaurant is in the back!"

Circling the building, they came upon an old man wearing a dirty apron, and tending a modest cafeteria-style bistro, attached to the foot of the tower. "I recommend the bretzels, the specialty of the house," said the cook, shoving the local delicacy under Cameron's nose. "Smells good, doesn't it?"

"Another time," replied Cameron with the utmost tact. "Have you seen the boy in this photograph?"

"Hum, I think I most certainly have," believed the cook, after snatching the photo from Cameron's hand. "This is the Gardner boy. He comes here every week; bought himself a cheese burger just yesterday; said he was going to the crash site; made me swear not to tell his mother."

"What crash site?" interjected Sophie.

"A Messerschmitt Me 323 Gigant—a German military transport air-craft of World War II—crashed in the hills of Reinhardswald in the Fall of 1941," explained the cook. "Of the crew of five, only Colonel General Ernst Udet survived. Rumor has it Udet caused the crash landing and killed the surviving flight engineer and radio operator."

"Why would a high-commander kill his own people?" queried Sophie.

"For the oldest reason in the world," said the cook: "Greed. The plane was apparently carrying merchandise worth millions, stolen from the Polish aristocracy, and earmarked for Hitler's personal fortune. Udet wanted it for himself and hid it somewhere in the Weser Uplands, an area spanning over ten thousand square miles."

"Hitler must have been outraged by Udet's betrayal," surmised Cameron.

"Udet told Hitler the plane had been pillaged by villagers," said the cook, "and as a lone and injured man, he could not prevent it. Udet died a week later, lauded as a hero who had perished in flight while testing a new weapon. He had, in fact, committed suicide, probably petrified by the savage torture that awaited him."

"The Grimm brothers would have made quite a fairy tale out of your story," thought Cameron. "Just add a dragon and a tribe of trolls, and you're off to the races."

"Speaking of races," said Sophie, "We're racing against the clock. Aside from the crashed plane, where else would you suggest we search?"

"The plane is two miles up the hill over there." The cook pointed upwards in a North-western direction. "If you don't find him there, look to the surrounding caves; many of them are deserted *brown coal* mining shafts, sealed for the most part. He might be in one of them."

"Thank you!" Cameron shook his hand. "You've been quite forthcoming." And off they went, onwards and upwards, all the while praying for the boy's welfare.

CHAPTER 34

"**Roy!**" cried out Cameron as he entered the broken body of the plane and searched every nook and cranny. "Roy, are you here?" he persisted with greater intensity, moving frontwards to the cockpit. The boy was nowhere to be found.

"Let's proceed to the top of the hill," proposed Sophie. "We'll zigzag downwards in horizontal strips half a mile long, and inspect every cave along our path."

"Makes sense," acknowledged Cameron. "Lead the way." They walked for hours, scouring cave after cave without success, until they came upon the entrance of a century-old mine. The wooden beams lodged along the entrance perimeter were somewhat rotten, and threatened to collapse under any further pressure applied against them. The wooden door, however, had been strengthened with steel rails, its padlock lying on the ground broken.

"If these beams are any indication of the mine's overall condition," uneasily said Cameron, "we might find ourselves buried under a thousand pounds of earth and rock."

"Someone wasn't at all concerned about that." Sophie crouched and examined the dirt by the entrance. "Fresh footprints. Two sets going in, one about twelve inches long, the other about five inches long. And one set coming out, also about twelve inches long—presumably the same person—and very tall to boot."

"That certainly matches misses Lorenz's and the NY Downtown Hospital nurse's description of the suspect," recognized Cameron. "The small print undoubtedly belongs to a child."

"Yes, it does," agreed Sophie, probing the print closely. "The child was running. See how deep the indentations are, and how wide apart they are. The tall man, however, seems to have entered and exited at a leisurely pace. Not uncommon for a predator brimming with confidence over securing his prey."

"Are you ready?" Cameron said rhetorically as he and his partner pulled out their revolvers and flashlights, opened the door, and penetrated the cave stealthily. The circular projections of lights danced gracefully along the walls—an overture to a performance that would hopefully climax with the safe recovery of a child. Thirty feet in, they faced their first dilemma: a fork in the passage way.

"I recommend we stay together." Cameron took a few steps into the passage on the left. "I have a feeling this is the way. We can always backtrack if it's no—" Without warning, the steel blade of a shovel rocketed downwards, bashing the unsuspecting FBI agent on the forehead. He keeled over, hitting the ground heavily.

Sophie fired four rounds into the darkness before being violently pushed to the ground face first and pinned down by the assailant's knee. "I have no quarrel with you. We have the same purpose: to cleanse the world of evil before the grapes of the apocalypse ripen. I am sorry you are *here*."

Dazed, Sophie looked up and saw the man bounce to his feet and run to the entrance. She crawled to her pistol, grabbed it, and aimed at the entrance. The man was already gone. Turning on her back, she lay there and called out: "Cameron! Cameron! Are you conscious?" She rubbed the back of her aching neck, and discovered blood on her fingers. "I got him, Cameron. He's bleeding."

"As am I," groaned Cameron, who withdrew his walkie-talkie and tried to alert the other search teams. "No signal. Must be the rocks." Cameron pushed himself up and sat, while Sophie made better progress, finally standing.

After running out of the cave and notifying the search teams, she returned and entered the left passage, pointing her flashlight directly ahead. "I see a wall of loose rocks blocking the passage, about fifteen feet away."

"Coming," said Cameron as he rose and lumbered erratically behind Sophie. Aiming his flashlight at the bottom right of the rock wall, he spotted an old mining cart, lying on its side and firmly pressed against the rocks. To the left of the wall, Cameron discovered a vertical shaft about ten feet in diameter, and plunging twenty-five feet deep. Hanging over the mouth of the shaft was a wooden platform held in place by a series of ropes and pulleys that could be operated to lower and raise the platform.

Testing its sturdiness, Cameron then gazed at the bottom. "There's another level."

"You're not going down there, not in your condition," ordered Sophie, who often exhorted him not to delve into reckless behavior. "Help me with the cart instead."

"What about it?" asked Cameron. "You want to ride in it?"

"No, you dork," retorted Sophie. "Look at the dirt marks behind the cart. It was pushed against the wall." The FBI duo mustered the strength they had left and pulled the cart away, revealing a small cavity that extended to the other side of the wall, just big enough for a young child to crawl through.

"Roy!" Sophie yelled into the hole. "Are you in there?"

A faint voice riddled with fear answered: "You won't let me go home if I come out now. You want to hurt me. Go away!"

"Don't be afraid, Roy," Sophie pleaded. "My name is Sophie, and I'm here with my brother Cameron. We're from the police."

"I don't believe you," Roy shouted. "That's what the man said when he found me playing in the plane. He tried to grab me. I asked to see his badge—you know, like in the movies—but he didn't have one. So I ran through the forest and the hills, to my hiding place."

"He found you, didn't he?" Sophie aimed the flashlight at her badge. "Peek into the hole, Roy, so you can see my shinny badge."

"I want to see your brother's face first," demanded Roy, desperate for proof the mean stranger had not returned. "The man had a bushy mustache. Do you have one?"

Indulging the boy's request, Sophie moved aside while Cameron prostrated himself before the cavity, squirming in pursuit of a comfortable position. His left foot kicked a few times, striking a small pile of rocks resting at the base of the wall.

"Be careful, Cam," implored Sophie as she shed light on the crumbled pile, only to reveal an object wrapped in all too familiar blue satin cloth with a golden symbol on it.

Releasing the object from the cloth, Sophie was appalled by she found: eight military issue M112 blocks of C-4 explosives, connected to a detonator, and a timer counting down—there were three seconds left before detonation.

CHAPTER 35

Three seconds; two seconds. Sophie, reacting strictly on instinct, threw the bomb into the vertical mining shaft. "Stay put!" she screamed at Cameron, throwing herself onto the ground. One second; zero. The bomb exploded two-thirds way down the shaft.

The force of the explosion shook the entire mine, triggering a massive cave-in. Earth and rocks fell everywhere, tumbling over each other, and a thick suffocating cloud of dust rose, instantly saturating every passage way. It took 20 seconds until the last chunk of rock plummeted to the ground, rolling over Cameron's left leg.

"Cameron! Speak to me!" shouted Sophie, covered in dust and powdered rock, and looking like a very creepy ghost. She had been fortunate: only pebble-size rocks had showered her body. Apart from several bruises, she was otherwise unscaved.

Cameron, on the other hand, had been battered by larger rocks, severed from the stone wall. While his upper body and head had been largely spared, his legs had been severely pelted. "I think my left leg is broken...and I can't feel my right one. What about the kid?"

"Roy! ROY! Are you ok?" Sophie cried out loudly. "ROY! Answer me!"

"I'm ok," replied Roy, in a trembling voice that was far clearer and more distinct than before; "but it's kinda hard to breath; I can't see through the dust."

"Don't do anything, Roy. We'll find a way to get to you," promised Sophie before moving on to her other patient. "Hang on, Cam, I'll free you." She scrawled to her brother on all fours, and began removing the rocks pinning him down. The stones she could not lift, she rolled, hoping not to exacerbate his wounds. "There, it's done," she announced, now flapping her arms to chase away the remaining mist. "How are your legs?"

"Feeling in my right leg is coming back," said a relieved Cameron. "The left one hurts right below the knee."

Placing her hand over the designated area, Sophie applied pressure. "Does that hurt more?"

"Only slightly," replied Cameron.

"You have a partial fracture," concluded Sophie. Flashlight in hand, she looked around for the blue cloth, finding it among the rubble, and tied it around Cameron's leg as tightly as she could. "Can you get up?"

"No problem," bravely said Cameron as he grabbed on to his sister, using her as a crutch. "There! Straight as an arrow." Spotting the handle of the shovel protruding from the debris, he had Sophie retrieve it—it would make a fine crutch, far more robust than his sister's delicate frame.

As the haze finally dissipated, Cameron and Sophie noticed that the light emanating from the mine entrance had grown faint. Half of the main passage way was congested; only the top half was clear, providing enough space for escape. The immediate area around the stone wall had resisted mostly, having being reinforced by additional wooden beams that extended over the vertical shaft, no doubt to prevent rock falls into the shaft. The stone wall, however, had swayed and foundered, creating a large opening in the left side of the wall.

"Bingo!" hollered Cameron, thanking Saint Christopher, the patron saint of good luck. "We're coming through, Roy. You're safe now."

"Safe," thought Sophie, fully recognizing that if the bomb had detonated where it had been originally placed, the whole mine would have completely caved-in—and no one would have been discharged from an early demise.

They entered a chamber twelve feet wide by twenty-two feet deep. The first thing they spotted was the freckled face of a nine year-old boy. "Hi!" he said bashfully and nervously, holding a Batman comic book. "I'm not that afraid of explosions, you know. My father lets me light up the fireworks every fourth of July."

"You're a courageous boy, Roy," said Sophie, noting a dozen or so lit candles spread over a five feet radius in the center of the chamber. "So, this is where you hide...and read?"

"Yes, it's *my* place, and nobody knows about it...except you and the mean man." Roy ran to the lit area. "Do you want to see my collection? I have Superman, Spiderman, Iron Man, and my favorite: the X-Men."

"Really, my son loves the X-Men too," said Sophie. "In fact, he says he's a real X-Man, with powers and all."

"I wish I had powers," admitted Roy. "I could have fought the mean man. I bet he was as mean as Mister Hyde."

"Mister Hyde?" wondered Cameron. "As in Doctor Jekyll and Mister Hyde?" He was surprised a boy so young would know of the 19th century tale.

"I'll show you," gleefully said Roy, running to the back of the tenebrous chamber, and returning with a hand-written manuscript. The cover page read: Strange Case of Dr. Jekyll and Mr. Hyde; First Draft; August 1885; Robert Louis Stevenson.

"Good Lord!" exclaimed a stupefied Cameron as he riffled through the document. "This is the first version of the story, the one the author presumably burned."

"There are more stories," revealed Roy, "but they're either too complicated or in a language I don't understand."

The injured Cameron lurched towards the back, haphazardly sweeping the zone with his flashlight, its light first coming into contact with a perfectly stacked load of rectangular items enclosed in individual burlap bags marked *Ernst Udet*. "It's damn solid," he said, tapping one of the bags. Sitting on the pile, he removed one of the items from its bag. "Gold! 400 troy-ounce gold bars! There must be over a hundred bars, worth about $50 million."

"Udet's hidden stash." Sophie passed her fingers over the bar. "Talk about dumb luck."

Scanning the area further, Cameron came upon what appeared to be paintings wrapped in wax paper. He tore the paper off the closest one. "I must be dreaming; *The Medusa* by Da Vinci." Agitated and aroused, he ripped the paper off another one. "*The Poet's Garden* by Van Gogh." And another one. "*Portrait of a Young Man* by Raphael."

"All right, Mister Art critic, I get the *picture*," yammered Sophie, thinking how clever and witty she was. "Can we please get the boy out of here." She was also eager to find out if the other teams had spotted or captured the killer.

"Roy, show me the stories, now!" Cameron, giddy as a drunk coming upon his next drink, was deaf to his sister's plea. And Roy was more than happy to oblige; he had found someone—an adult no less—who was not only agreeable to his juvenile secretiveness, but also impressed by *his* treasure trove, *his* cavern of Ali Baba. This more than offset the adversities of moments past.

"Open Sesame," exclaimed Roy in delight, handing Cameron an 18-inch stack of papers. No password was necessary to enjoy his fortune.

"*Ur-Hamlet* by Thomas Kyd," announced Cameron; "it's an earlier version of the play *Hamlet* predating William Shakespeare's version. *Le Fagotier* by Molière. And the cantata *Per la ricuperata salute di Ophelia* by Mozart and Salieri."

"Cameron!" wailed an irate Sophie. "Let's go! We'll contact FBI headquarters to impound all this stuff."

Just as Cameron was finally about to comply, he met with a manuscript whose existence was unknown even to the most invested and most fervent historians, antiquarians and archeologists: the missing *quatrains* of Nostradamus.

Born in December of 1503, in France, Michel de Nostredame grew up to become a notorious prophet and visionary known to this day as Nostradamus.

He wrote a book of one thousand mainly French quatrains (four-line poems), grouped into ten sets of 100 called *Centuries*, constituting the largely undated prophecies responsible for his fame. Feeling vulnerable to opposition on religious grounds, he devised a method of obscuring his meaning by using *virgilianized* syntax, word games and a mixture of other languages such as Greek, Italian, Latin, and Provençal. For technical reasons connected with their publication in three installments, the last fifty-eight quatrains of the seventh Century had not survived into any extant edition.

"Ten," counted Cameron, turning the page. "Twenty," counting and turning again. "Thirty…Forty…Fifty…Sixty…Seventy…Eighty…Ninety…and One Hundred. They're all here. The missing fifty-eight quatrains are included. I have a *complete* set of the seventh Century." Cameron vaguely recalled the quatrains, having reviewed some of them, interpreted them and written about them, as the yield of a high school assignment. His teacher hadn't been at all pleased by the poor quality of the work, or by his choice, given the macabre nature of Nostradamus' masterpiece, and had given him a 'C'. In truth, his amateur fortune teller of a mother had chosen the subject matter for him, and he resented that.

Flipping back the pages, he arrested his heed on quatrain forty-three, the first of the missing quatrains, and read:

(translated from the original French version)

43

He shall be born of humanity and inhumanity;
Cast into a well only to be risen from a well;
He shall prosper among the innocent and the oblivious;
And the people of the New Land shall call the Evil friend.

Deeply disturbed, Cameron read the next few quatrains:

44

Begotten by the Son of Mohammed and Daughter of the
Dragon;
He shall become the dark destroyer of all, The One King;
Mabus will die by the sword and resurrect onto himself;
A thousand times more powerful, he shall raise hatred and
virulence.

45

The well from which he sprung shall be filled with human
darkness;
As those who seek the mark of Mabus shall be seared by it;
The souls driven by deception shall plunge into the pits of
perdition;
And the bloody war of seven and twenty years on Earth
shall carry through into the Heavens.

"Let's get a move on!" yelled Sophie, interrupting Cameron's reading.

"Right, right," said a troubled Cameron as he rolled up the document and shoved it in his vest pocket. Noting his sister's expression of disapproval, he assured her, "I'll return it in a few days, swear to God."

"*Cast into a well only to be risen from a well.*" Cameron kept repeating the line in his mind, terribly disconcerted by it. He was equally unsettled by the phrase: "*The One King,*" although he didn't quite know why. In French, it read: "*Le Roi Unique,*" which he suddenly realized wasn't the true source of his concern—it was *his* English translation of it that bothered him.

"The One King," he whispered to himself as Sophie picked up Roy and headed for the opening in the stone wall. "The One King; The One King," he kept on obsessively. Then, it hit him; he pronounced it differently. "TheOn e King. Theon e King. Theon E. King. Theon Ethan King," expanding on the middle initial. "King," he muttered anxiously. "King, King...*Rex!*" It occurred to him that *Rex* was the Latin translation for King. "Theon Ethan Rex! That's it. THEON ETHAN REX!" His son.

Cameron was shocked by the parallel. "Theon Ethan Rex: The One King." Was this the product of pure coincidence or of purposeful design?

CHAPTER 36

"We'll have to crawl over the rocks all the way to the entrance," Sophie told Roy. "Are you up to it, son?"

"I can crawl faster than Spiderman," boasted the boy, who immediately took the lead.

"Hang on, Sophie!" yelled Cameron. "I see something."

"That's enough *seeing* for today. Let's concentrate on doing." Sophie intentionally accelerated her pace.

"It's not the work of an artist, I'm seeing," remarked Cameron, "but more likely the work of a slayer." Dangling from one remaining rope above the vertical shaft, the wooden platform was punctured with a distal phalange, the end bone of a human toe. The middle and proximal phalanges were still connected to the distal phalange, adding to the grisly semblance of the spectacle.

Cameron stood by the edge of the shaft and peered downwards. The force of the explosion had created a huge concave depression along the circumference of the shaft, three-feet deep at the mid-point of the indenture. A collection of small bones lay spattered onto the bottom, torn away from larger bone structures imbedded in a 60-degree section of the damaged wall. "There are several skeletons down there," counted Cameron before hacking the rope with his shovel and throwing the latter into the shaft. "Sophie, give me a hand." He pointed at the rope.

"Do you really expect me to lower you into the pit?" objected Sophie.

"No. Tie one end of the rope to that large boulder." Cameron tied the other end around his torso. "You will have to pull me up, however," he said, producing a feigned smile; "at least a little, when I'm done, of course." Despite his personalized interpretation of some of Nostradamus' fatalistic quatrains, Cameron kept his misgivings to himself. For the moment, his mind would be engrossed with this new discovery.

As soon as he touched the bottom, Cameron began examining every bone fragment. "They're human, all human," he gathered correctly, now shifting his inspection to the enclosed bones. "One…two…three." I detect at least three partial skeletons, two adults and one child," he reported to Sophie. "There are probably many more deep inside the rock."

"Any signs of foul play?" asked Sophie.

"I can't say," replied Cameron. "The axial skeleton," formed by the vertebral column, the rib cage, and the skull, "of one of the bodies—the child—is only partially encased. I can probably *pop it out* with the shovel."

Before Sophie could instruct him to wait for forensic investigators, Cameron was already hard at work, chipping at the back of the rib cage, eventually reaching the vertebral column. Using the shovel as a lever, he pushed on its end vigorously and repeatedly, until the bone framework relinquished its resting place and ejected onto the ground, leaving only the skull and the upper limbs still firmly stationed within the wall.

Cameron picked it up by the clavicles and shook it like a dusty jacket, releasing the detritus lodged inside the rib cage. He recognized an all too familiar bone configuration along the back: two nassels, connected to a plate fused to the shoulder blades. "Christ O' Mighty!" he spouted in disbelief; "the same anomaly as Theon's."

"What's going on down there?" shouted Sophie, who noticed her brother's curiosity turn to dismay. "What have you found?"

"Answers," he thought. He picked up the shovel and violently stabbed the rock next to the small skull, pushing only once to dislodge it. "I'll be damned," he gasped, noting the triangular bone extremities that once formed and supported the flesh of pointed ears—exactly like Theon's.

Cameron sat, gazing at the skull in utter stupor. Had he inadvertently discovered the burial ground of Theon's breed?

CHAPTER 37

Present day; New York.

"Well Doc, what's the verdict?" asked Cameron Rex as he entered the autopsy room at the FBI New York office.

"These bodies you've brought me are fascinating," said the jubilant forensic pathologist. "The perfect climax to an often dreary career. The pinnacle to—"

"I get it, Doc," interrupted Cameron. "What have you got?"

"A mystery, no less," excitedly replied the doctor, who placed the point of his scalpel on one of the two bony nassels on the back of one of the nine bodies retrieved from a cave in the hills of Reinhardswald, Germany. "This bone structure appears to be an unformed arm—an upper arm and a forearm partially connected to each other by incidental bone matter. Looks like the joint linking them is severely underdeveloped."

Cameron took a closer look. "Are you saying the body of this man has *four* arms?"

"Not precisely," replied the doctor. "However, had this species been allowed to in-breed, its descendants might have developed fully formed dorsal arms, and hands perhaps."

"What would Darwin and natural evolution say about this?" said Cameron. "What advantage could extra arms along the backside possibly provide?"

"Perhaps the extra limbs were eventually supposed to support *flight*," conjectured the doctor. "The evolution of the species might have also led to a tensile skin formation attached to the arms and body—much like a flying squirrel."

"Or a *bat*," suggested Cameron. "Have you detected the same anomalies on the other eight bodies?"

The doctor appeared perplexed. "While I believe they are all from the same root species, four are normal while five exhibit varying degrees of the peculiarity. Two of the bodies, one female adult, one male child, have smaller nassels with no apparent separation into an upper arm and fore-arm. The remaining two, a male and a female adult, only have tiny bone extrusions—most likely the first stage of this particular mutation."

"We suspect there are dozens more bodies buried in the rock where we found these nine," remarked Cameron. "We could excavate them immediately and supply you with more organic material."

"Not necessary for now; I'll have my hands full with these for the next few months. They have so much *more* to tell me," gleefully declared the doctor as he picked up the fossilized brain from his dead patient. "Do you know that this brain is about 9% greater in volume than the modern man's brain?"

"An unknown race of geniuses," speculated Cameron; "but not smart enough to avoid extinction." And while he said this, he did not believe it entirely--Theon may well have come from this race, and may well be its only survivor.

"Indeed; there does appear to be a paradox," consented the doctor, "but it's not attributed to an *unknown* species. This brain, this body, all these bodies belong to *Homo neanderthalensis*, a species that coexisted with *Homo sapiens sapiens*, commonly known as the modern man."

"How do you reckon?" Cameron's personal interest in the matter was piqued evermore so.

"Homo neandertalensis were very different according to DNA studies," said the doctor. "They lived in Europe and the Mideast between 150,000 and 35,000 years ago, alongside modern men, likely never merging into the Homo sapiens sapiens gene pool. Their brain size averaged larger than modern man but the head was shaped differently, being longer and lower than modern man. The nose was large and was different from modern man in structure, and their skin was golden yellow, resembling somewhat to contemporary Mongols. They were massive men with an extremely heavy skeleton and huge muscles, far stronger than modern men."

Another question, a very precise one, was burning Cameron's lips. "Tell me Doc, have you noticed extraneous chromosomal material on chromosomes 1, 11 and 21?"

The doctor was puzzled by the specificity of the inquiry. "Do you have a particular human subject in mind?"

Cameron was, of course, referring to his son, Theon. "Just answer the question."

"No," said the doctor with conviction. "The anomalies stem from the standard genome. What you're describing is most likely an exceptional case of extra noncoding DNA, describing components of an organism's DNA sequences that do not encode for protein sequences.

"While many geneticists might call it *junk DNA*, there are noncoding sequences whose functionalities have yet to be determined." The doctor stared intently at Cameron, hoping for a clue that might explain his line of questioning.

Cameron would not afford the doctor this privilege. Instead, he focused anew on the balance of power between Neanderthals and Homo sapiens sapiens. "Anomalies aside, how could men who were superior in intellect and physical strength be decimated by an inferior race?"

The briefly disappointed pathologist had a few theories about that. "Well, contrary to the gentle and peaceful Neanderthals, modern man was aggressive and cunning, and would devise method after method to ease his lot. He would remove his enemies without compassion. He would learn to enslave other animals and even other men. He would greedily take from the world around him and from those who were weaker. He would make his life easier, and evolution would degrade him to match."

"Degrade him into us—into the world we know of today," sadly concluded Cameron.

And while the doctor's expression also conveyed a bit of sadness, scientific inquisitiveness quickly quashed it. "Radioactive carbon dating indicates the remains are approximately 37,000 years old—the tail-end of this species' existence, which supports the theory that a particular branch of *Homo sapiens sapiens* was responsible for the genocide: the *Aurignacian culture*. It's an archaeological culture of the Stone Age, located mostly in Europe, especially noted for its well-developed art tradition, including engraved and sculpted animal forms and female figurines thought to be fertility objects. The earliest fully developed cave art, such as the painted animals in the Lascaux cave in southwest France, dates from this period."

"What does the term *Aurignacian* mean exactly?" queried Cameron.

"It's supposed to relate to the time period and artistic capabilities," replied the doctor. "But there are other ideologies espoused by minority groups—radical ones, I should say. Some Christian religious fanatics believe one of the four horsemen of the Apocalypse, the one symbolizing *War*, rode to Earth on his red horse to survey the state of mankind, sometime between 35,000 BC and 34,000 BC. The zealots called him

Aurignacia."

"I'm only familiar with the traditional story," said Cameron; "the one in which the four riders, commonly seen as representing *Conquest*, *War*, *Famine* and *Death*, set the stage for a divine apocalypse upon the world as harbingers of the *Last Judgment*."

"Yeah, well, one horseman was apparently itching to visit Earth early, it seems," chuckled the doctor. "And he did more than visit—he, and presumably an army of devilish soldiers, exploited the evil of modern men, recruited troupes of them, attacked the friendly Neanderthals, killed the men and raped the women. The latter, in turn, gave life to these monstrosities," waving his arm across the room and across the bodies that lay within its walls.

"That's quite a claim," thought Cameron, who was disturbed by the pathologist's qualification of the bodies—his own son, after all, also fit the criterion. "These religious fanatics have a wild imagination."

The doctor stabbed one of the bony nassels on the skeleton's back. "Perhaps not as wild as we would presume."

Cameron was boggled by the doctor's contention. "As a man of science, you wouldn't surrender to such a notion unless you had scientific evidence to defend it."

"Follow me to the next body," invited the doctor, "and hold on to your hat."

The skeleton was that of a young boy. Apart from the nassels, he had triangular bone extremities around the ear areas, and his vertebra was torn apart just above the pelvis.

"What could possibly inflict such damage?" asked the doctor, pointing at the vertebra.

"The vertebra was not just snapped," observed Cameron; "it was *blasted* apart by a high-yield energy weapon," pointing at the charred endings. "Like a concentrated laser, or a miniature missile."

The doctor noted a look of recognition on Cameron's face. "You've seen this before, haven't you?"

Cameron nodded. "I've seen this kind of scorching in France. Same type of weapon used here."

"Perhaps, but no such technology existed then," stated the doctor. "It must undoubtedly be *alien* technology—demon weaponry wielded by the hordes of the demon *Aurignacia*."

"Don't go religious on me, Doc," said Cameron with a smidgen of levity.

The doctor picked up an item from an adjacent table. "What about this? I found it lodged within the rib cage of one of the bodies. There's nothing religious about *this*."

"It's the metal head of a spear," deduced Cameron. "Given the size, it's likely the spear of an arrow. A common weapon. So what?"

"Not common around 35,000 BC," rebutted the doctor. "It's made of bronze. The earliest trace of *ore smelting* dates back to 6,000 BC, not 35,000 BC. The men who collaborated with the demon army used this type of weapon to kill Neanderthals. They were seemingly taught to smelt ore Millennia before their time; and taught to construct and operate a bow."

"A fanciful hypothesis," remarked Cameron. "But blast marks or premature bronze weapons are hardly irrefutable proof of alien intervention."

"What about an unknown metal," proposed the doctor; "something made from an entirely exotic molecular construction?" He walked to a nearby cabinet and pulled out a soldier's helmet boasting a familiar symbol—the one found on the silk scarf the serial child killer always left behind after the morbid deed.

"Whom does it belong to?" asked a baffled Cameron with a frazzled insistence that was unbecoming of his normally stolid FBI façade.

The doctor examined it a moment, rotating it slowly. "If you concede the premise, as we've laid it out to date, the helmet belonged to the horseman and demon *Aurignacia*."

CHAPTER 38

Circa 2,000 years ago; Galilee.

"Mary! Mary!" hollered a woman as she hurriedly strutted towards Bethel. "Come to the market, have you?"

"I beg your pardon," replied a slightly miffed Bethel, as the woman's hand locked on to her shoulder. "Are we on familiar terms?"

"Oh, stop your joshing, silly girl," quipped the woman. "It's me, Rebecca." Probing about the area, she gave Bethel an inquiring look. "Where's little Jesus? At home, perhaps, making a chair or a desk with Joseph? He's very talented, you know."

Realizing for whom she had been mistaken, Bethel set her straight right away. "My name is Bethel. I'm Mary's twin sister."

Rebecca gave Bethel a suspicious stare. "Mary never said she had a twin sister." She stared closer, rolling her eyes left and right, up and down, trying to ascertain if she was being made a fool of. "Are you certain?"

"If you asked my parents, they would deny it," admitted Bethel. "If you ask my sister, she would confirm it, reluctantly perhaps, but she would. We have been on better terms since the birth of my daughter. "Lisa! Come here, darling," she bid her daughter, who stood by a merchant's apple stall near the center of the open air market of the town of Nazareth.

"This is Lisa, my child and niece to Mary." Bethel wrapped her arm around her daughter's shoulders."

"And where do you come from, you gorgeous thing?" Rebecca bent forward and pricked her nose.

"I was born in Magdala," Lisa said. "It's a town on the shore of the Lake of Tiberias, near the base of Mount Arbel, many leagues to the North-East from here," she specified in a patently rehearsed manner.

"You obviously know your geography," congratulated Rebecca. "If I ever need a guide, I'll be sure to call upon you." The girl grinned shyly, happy to be of service.

"Now go and walk about, Lisa," urged her mother. "Hurry back with a list of what you'd like to purchase." No further incentive required, Lisa ran back to the apple stall, made a mental note, ran to the next one, and the next, and so on, adding figs, pomegranates, olives, dates, almonds, black mulberries, and an assortment of herbs and spices, such as bay leaves, coriander, cinnamon, mustard and salt. Her list was quite exhaustive.

"Are you planning to visit your sister? I could go to her now and announce your imminent arrival," offered Rebecca, blatantly emphasizing her intrusive nature.

"I'm bringing her food from the market," said Bethel; "and I'd like it to be a surprise," praising her speed and dexterity in deflecting Rebecca's disguised act of altruism. No doubt, she would impose herself and scrounge a supper invitation off her sister.

"I understand," Rebecca retorted, spotting Lisa halfway through her round of the stalls. "Maybe Lisa and I could get better acquainted. Lisa!" she cried out in high spirits, and then, a moment later, quite besides herself, cried out in panic, "LISA!"

The almond merchant had tackled the child to the ground, screaming obscenities at her. He kicked her twice in the stomach before emptying her robe pocket, which was filled with stolen almonds. "She is a thief!" he loudly warned the other merchants and the surrounding customers. "She is a bandit, a trespasser!" he pursued without reprieve. "She is a sinner to God!" waving a fistful of almonds above his head. The merchant—evidently cheated on more than once—sought retribution. And the child was now his hapless victim.

"Don't touch my baby!" angrily shouted Bethel, sprinting like a ravenous cougar exposing her fierce temperament. Many a lover who had paid her for sex in her younger years, and turned to molestation, had tasted her pugilistic rage—some never having recovered from it.

She hit the crazed merchant so hard, fists clenched and forearms locked in lateral position, he literally flew three feet in the air, landing heavily on his back a full eight feet away. "Mamma, it hurts," sobbed Lisa.

"I know, my love, but you're safe now." Bethel's tears intermingled with Lisa's as she leaned over her daughter and pressed her cheek against hers. Before she could embrace her child and lift her up, countless hands grabbed the mother by the robe and dragged her to the center of the market. "The sins of the child are the sins of the mother!" exclaimed one man, who picked up a stone and threw it at her. Many merchants and customers, driven by a bogus sense of righteousness, soon followed suit, mercilessly battering her with hundreds of stones until she moved no more. It was utter frenzy.

Rebecca, finally gathering her nerve, carefully approached Lisa, but was pulled back by a bystander. "One step further and the mob will kill you. This is *not* you affair."

Fortunately for Lisa, someone thought otherwise. A statuesque man, robed in black and wearing an odd amulet, intervened, appearing from nowhere. He rushed to Lisa's side, almost seeming to float inches from the ground. Saying nothing, he picked her up and stood tall, his mettle and total absence of fear spurring on the mob, and stones flew about once again. One stone struck the amulet dead on, as the good Samaritan suddenly rose above the ground. His robe vanished, replaced by a peculiar but splendid white military outfit, the amulet firmly integrated into the chest plate. His skin took on a crimson red color, giant bat like wings sprouted from his back, and horns grew inches above pointed ears. He looked demonic—he *was* a demon.

"I am *Thevetat*, and I stand at the Throne of Infamy, at the right hand of Satan, the Dragon Lord," he clamored. "As you have paid for your crimes and your transgressions in the past, you will pay for them again, more dearly and more abjectly than your imaginations could ever devise, on Earth and in the *Nether Land*. I shall wait for you all." Bounty in hand, the demon flapped his wings and soared briskly and gracefully into the skies, melting away among the clouds.

The crowd had never felt such unbridled terror—not until today.

CHAPTER 39

Present day; New York.

"Do come in," said Amadeo to Cameron and Theon, "and welcome to my humble abode." Amadeo's home was rather eclectic, each room's furnishing and decoration having been inspired by a different culture. The oriental style of the living room was the highlight of the house, overflowing with statues, candles, paper lamps, bonsai trees, and a wide array of strange Chinese and Japanese artifacts.

"Theon, your Dad and I have things to discuss," Amadeo kindly informed Theon. "I have some clay, paper and charcoal crayons in the play room, or you can watch TV. Now off you go," gently pushing Theon towards the room. The boy was quite unaware he was going to be the subject of discussion, and knew nothing of his father's dual disposition: an unrelenting need for the truth; and an agonizing fear of it.

'I can make it on my own," growled Theon, who darted across the living room and into the play room.

"He's building quite a temper," remarked Amadeo as he reminisced about his own testiness and petulance at Theon's age. "But I'm certain it will pass."

"It's not so much his temper that concerns me," said Cameron, "but what it might leave in its wake."

"Unyielding discipline, guidance and vigilance are the price we have to pay," reminded Amadeo, "if Theon is to navigate and function within society. But this does not imply that he must forfeit his individuality; he must simply summon those parts of it that will help him manage and master the situation at hand."

"He's only eight," pointed out Cameron. "Despite his intelligence, I doubt very much he can manage any powerful emotions, much less master the more daunting ones."

"Ah, but he is unique, far more than you and I can fathom. He might surprise us." Amadeo picked up a document from the coffee table, and shook it a foot from Cameron's face.

"You uncovered something from Nostradamus' missing quatrains?" avidly replied Cameron, who had passed on the manuscript to his learned neighbor a few days ago.

"Nothing precise or definite," reported Amadeo; "just a good deal of conjecture and subjective interpretation. I did, however, cross-reference the data with quatrains belonging to other Centuries, and with popular sacred texts."

"And?" A tense Cameron limped quickly to the sofa and sat heavily onto it, resting his elbows on his thighs, interlocking his fingers, and rocking his upper body back and forth.

Sitting next to him, Amadeo spread out pages across the coffee table. "Don't you want your wife to hear what I have to say?"

"She's out shopping with our daughter and my mother," snapped Cameron. "Besides, your findings are based *only* on speculation, and not worth alarming anyone…not for now anyway." Cameron, in a misguided effort to protect his wife from chilling notions, had refrained from acquainting her with his clandestine inquest into Theon's true identity. This was not his first foray into covertness.

"You're right, of course," said Amadeo quite unconvincingly. "She would eventually find out anyway," he thought. "Now, here's what I've done; I based my preliminary search on specific key words like: *well, Dragon, Mohammed, Mabus,* and *New Land.*

"The word *well* did not appear anywhere other than in two of the missing quatrains:

> Cast into a <u>well</u> only to be risen from a well;
> The <u>well</u> from which he sprung shall be filled with human darkness;

"Now the word *well* can be interpreted literally or it might signify something like a *pit* or a *prison*, or even *resurrection*—having died, and been buried or entombed only to have risen from the grave."

Cameron listened attentively, quite impotent and unable to supplement Amadeo's hypothesises. The particularly religious quality of the exercise was just beyond the scope of his investigative skills. Nevertheless, Amadeo would press him to share his insights.

"Thinking like an FBI agent," said Amadeo, "how would you explain Theon's sudden appearance in the well? According to your wife, he wasn't there one instant, and then was the next one."

"Perhaps he was partially buried, or covered in dirt," conjectured Cameron. "That would explain why Sarah, in a frenzied state, didn't see Theon when she first rescued me from the well. Alerted to our presence, Theon must have shaken the dirt off his body, becoming visible."

"More or less plausible as a theory, but in the absence of alternate explanations, we'll go with it for now." Amadeo went on. "The word *Mohammed* turned up in one other quatrain: the missing quatrain, first:

> *Begotten by the Son of <u>Mohammed</u> and Daughter of the Dragon;*
> *He shall become the dark destroyer of all, The One King...*

"And then the other:

> *Out of the country of Greater Arabia shall be born a strong master*
> *of <u>Mohammed</u>,*
> *He will enter Europe wearing a blue turban.*
> *He will be the terror of mankind Never more horror."*

Born in 570 in the Arabian city of Mecca, Mohammed grew up to become the founder of the religion of Islam, and was considered by Muslims to be a messenger and prophet of God, the last law-bearer in a series of Islamic prophets, and, by most Muslims, the last prophet of God as taught by the Qur'an.

"This means something to you, doesn't it?" Amadeo clearly saw Cameron's expression of recognition and prompted him into answering. "It doesn't have to do it with Mohammed, does it?"

Compelled once again by the term *The One King*, Cameron intuitively merged it with another quatrain line. "As you know, the FBI has been hunting a prolific serial child killer whose sickening record is now up to *eight* victims." Cameron exhaled deeply and longly in weariness and in pining for the capture of this monster. "What you don't know is that the killer always leaves his calling card: a blue satin scarf wrapped around the dead child's head—in effect, a blue *turban*. *The One King will enter Europe wearing a blue turban."*

CHAPTER 40

"Fascinating!" uttered Amadeo, quite aware of Cameron's suspicion that *The One King* was code for *Theon Ethan Rex*, his adopted son. "And this One King has entered Europe from Greater Arabia, finding his way into a well," added the old man.

"He was born in France, and did not *enter* it," insisted a torn Cameron, who found the idea absurd, "so he certainly wasn't born in any of the Arabian countries, or born of Arabian parents. The line: *Out of the country of Greater Arabia shall be born a strong master of Mohammed,*" simply does not apply." Deeply conflicted, he was now attempting to debunk his own position on the term The One King. If one quatrain line did not apply, then perhaps none of the others did either.

"You don't know that at all," rebutted Amadeo. "He may have been born in Arabia and brought to France prior to his abandonment. Or he might have been conceived in Arabia, and been born in France—Nostradamus might have used the word *born* to metaphorically mean *conceived*." Amadeo placed his hand on Cameron's thigh. "This is difficult, I know, but I'd like you to keep an open mind and remain impartial. After all, you're the one who requested my help."

Cameron nodded silently.

"Good." Amadeo resumed. "While no blue scarf—or turban—was actually found near or on Theon, would you nevertheless consider the boy to be among the killer's prospects?"

Cameron regained his calm, allowing his dispassionate FBI persona to intervene. "Theon may have lost the blue scarf during transport to the well, or he may wear one later in life. In any event, he is a supernatural child and a likely threat to any psychopathic religious extremist."

"All possibilities," agreed Amadeo. "Anything else?"

"There's also the issue of Mohammed's grandson," indicated Cameron, quoting the phrase: "*...Begotten by the Son of Mohammed.* "How can this son of the son be an offspring (a pupil) *and* a master to Mohammed?

"I would submit premeditated truncation." Amadeo produced a pencil and added a word to the phrase: *Out of the country of Greater Arabia shall be born a strong master of Mohammed,* extending it to: *Out of the country of Greater Arabia shall be born a strong master of Mohammed's teachings.*

"For what purpose?" wondered Cameron.

"Perhaps because Nostradamus relished being *overly* cryptic," theorized Amadeo. "His method promoted a pseudo-reasonable although contrived veracity of his prophecies to the people, without commitment or condemnation when arbitrary connections were made between events and predictions." Amadeo began to move his papers around the table. "The next key word is *Dragon*.

Begotten by the Son of Mohammed and Daughter of the Dragon;

"The word *dragon* appears in many sacred texts, including the Book of Revelation:

The Dragon persecutes the people of God.

"It generally refers to the demon Satan."

The word Satan stirred vehemence in Cameron, immediately recalling his troubling experiment with Theon's multi-faceted photograph. "So the child in question's lineage included a human prophet and an inhuman creature of evil?" surmised Cameron. He couldn't erase Theon's face from his mind.

"He shall be born of humanity and inhumanity," said Amadeo, quoting line one of quatrain 43, 7th Century.

"Mohammed was born in the latter part of the sixth century," pointed out Cameron; "so any immediate descendant of his would be long dead."

"Or such a descendant might have resurrected," replied Amadeo, "as per one of our earlier diagnosis of the word *well.* Let's move on to the word Mabus. We have:

> *Mabus will die by the sword and resurrect onto himself;*
> *As those who seek the mark of Mabus shall be seared by it;*

"And quatrain 62 of Century 2;

> *Mabus then will soon die, there will come*
> *Of people and beasts a horrible rout:*

Then suddenly one will see vengeance,Hundred, hand, thirst,
hunger when the comet will run.

"Again we speak of resurrection. Many are convinced Mabus is the name of the third and most hideous Antichrist, the other two being Napoleon and Hitler. They also believe Mabus will be killed by the sword, releasing an energy greater than all the nuclear power in the world; an energy that will be harnessed and used to destroy most of humanity. The war will last 27 years. Mabus will then resurrect and take its place by the King's side, leaving its generals to rule over the territories that could still bear fruit, and over the people who could still labor the land."

"Mabus sounds more like a weapon of mass destruction," remarked Cameron. "The One King's doomsday machine."

"Or Mabus is the King's dark side unleashed," said Amadeo; "pure evil, unchecked, uncontrollable, unstoppable. Can *you* put a face to such darkness?" he goaded Cameron.

"If the eyes of murdered children could tell the tale, I could." Cameron's safe answer was generally apropos, but not germane to the specifics of the current discussion. He was being purposely evasive.

"What about this *comet* business?" Cameron became intrigued by the last line of the quatrain.

"Nostradamus could be referring to a Great Comet, which only enters the inner solar system once a decade. Its tail made of ice and dust is exceptionally bright, and visible to the naked eye." Amadeo pondered further. "Or he could be unknowingly describing the tail of visible matter produced when a small wormhole collapses."

Cameron immediately recollected his NASA brother-in-law Bill's saga of a wormhole grazing Mars and connecting with the Earth's surface. "I can certainly entertain the possibility of a wormhole breaching the Earth's atmosphere."

"You can?" said a skeptical Amadeo. "The odds against the formation of a wormhole in our solar system are astronomical."

"Nevertheless, I won't discount it. It might be the only warning sign of this impending 27-year war." Cameron gazed at all the papers. "What's next?"

"Well, there's the concept of *New Land*." Amadeo pointed at the line: *And the people of the New Land shall call the Evil friend.*

His finger then traveled to the quatrain: *When two great leaders of the Northern Pole are united, In the East will be great fear and dread...*

Their great powers will be seen to grow. The <u>New Land</u> will be at the height of its power. "While this text might seem to indicate some kind of alliance against the power of Mabus," said Amadeo, "it may in fact suggest the reverse. Consider this: two of Mabus' most Machiavellian generals, both of Northern origin, unite by the king's command to rule the land spared from the devastation of war—the New Land. And in the East, the survivors drown in fear of deportation to the North and enslavement."

"Could the *New Land* also signify some kind of *Post-War Heaven*," speculated Cameron, "while the East alludes to Heaven prior to war?" He was instantly taken aback by his output of nontrivial religious insight.

"Interesting take," deemed Amadeo, who expected little from Cameron. "What exactly instigated that thought?"

"Quatrain 45, Century 7," said Cameron: "*And the bloody war of seven and twenty years on Earth shall carry through into the Heavens.*"

"Poised to bring Hell to Heaven, the diabolical King and his two wicked sons, as it were," Amadeo reckoned metaphorically. "*The ungodly triumvirate.*"

CHAPTER 41

"So, what do you really think of Nostradamus' prophecies?" asked an ambivalent Cameron whose prior circumvention of the evidence was becoming a formidable burden, not only personally but also professionally—as a career lawman, he was used to asking straight questions, and getting straight answers. "Are they proof of my son's eventual descent into hell?"

Swayed by the many inferences drawn from the quatrains—a definite and evident source of emotional turmoil for Cameron—Amadeo decided to err on the side of caution. "Proof might be too much of a *momentous* word. Throughout the centuries, Nostradamus enthusiasts have credited him with predicting numerous events in world history, but only ever in hindsight. Skeptics have suggested that his reputation as a prophet was largely manufactured by modern-day supporters who fit his words to events that have either already occurred or are so imminent as to be inevitable, a process sometimes known as *retroactive clairvoyance*."

"Granted, but what are *you*, an enthusiast or a skeptic?" persisted Cameron.

"I do believe some of Nostradamus' quatrains foreshadow certain events that will come to pass," wholeheartedly confessed Amadeo, "but," he lifted his index finger in the air, "I'm still on the fence about any connection to Theon."

"So, there *might be* a connection?" pressed on Cameron, who, despite his lingering unrest, wanted to make sense of it all. Not unlike a confused child, he so wanted Amadeo to assure him everything would be all right. Otherwise, he would have to do something about it.

"If you insist, then yes, there might be, however unlikely." Amadeo gathered all his papers and arranged them in a neat stack. "Even if there was a chance—and you acted accordingly, what possible course of action could you adopt that would not culminate into harm or violence against your son? Don't let ignorance stamp out innocence."

Cameron reflected on Amadeo's stance while the erudite old man lay back and waited for his friend's impending conclusion that any impulsive action presumably favoring Theon's welfare would be reckless. Two minutes passed when Cameron was suddenly endowed with a clever albeit likely sterile idea. "What if we attack the problem at the source?" He looked into the play room at his son, who was absorbed in artistic endeavor.

"Has Theon not been seeing a psychiatrist?" wondered Amadeo. "What can we as laymen accomplish that a professional has not already?"

"Theon trusts me above all others and he has long since taken a shining to you." Cameron gazed at Amadeo with persuasive eyes. "I'm very skilled at interrogations. "This is something *I* can control…something more reliable than 500-year old prophecies. Theon will be fine; I'll make sure of that." He hoped for nothing extraordinary, just normal kid stuff. But he suspected he would be mistaken.

"I suppose we'll tell Theon the *game* we'll be playing will be our little secret," said Amadeo in anticipation of Cameron's foreseeable request.

Cameron grinned in response—his friend knew him only too well—before popping his head into the play room. "Theon! Bring your stuff in the living room. Uncle Amadeo and I want to play a round of *Imagination Station* with you."

"Cool!" shouted Theon as he carried his unwieldy work into the living room and dumped it on the coffee table. "Where's the computer?" He swiftly moved about the room and raked it with intense stares.

"You don't need a computer to play this version of Imagination Station," Cameron told Theon as he escorted him to the sofa. "Sit in the middle—that'll be your *station*."

"Curiouser and curiouser," blurted out Amadeo as he examined Theon's drawings, which seemed to come straight from *Alice in Wonderland.* "Well, my dear Alice," he continued in jest, "what wonderful things has your imagination conjured up. Can you describe what this is?" handing the boy one of the skillfully rendered drawings. Impressed, Amadeo's curiosity had easily supplanted his own call for caution.

Cameron glared at his impudent accomplice, but decided to follow his lead…this one time. "Go ahead, son."

"That's me," Theon said, "pointing at the drawing of a boy posing proudly in front of what appeared to be a knight in a shimmering armor wielding a sword above his equally shimmering head, his facial features were largely imperceptible.

"Who's that?" asked Cameron, planting his finger on the flickering head. He recognized the character instantly from Theon's photograph.

"It's the *Ghost Knight*," sharply replied Theon without hesitation, counting on his father's trust. "He's a good spirit who lives inside me. And his sword is where his power goes when he's fighting his enemies."

Cameron also recognized the name as Theon's alter-ego from nightmares of years ago. Perhaps the dreams of the Ghost Knight had subsided because the character had somehow migrated from his son's unconscious mind to his conscious one.

"Does he come out sometimes; to join you in *your* daily battles?" chimed in Amadeo, hinting at schizophrenia. Cameron glared at him once more.

"Not really," assured Theon, who wondered whether Amadeo was joking or not. "He does help me make decisions; but it's not like he talks to me—it's just something I feel. And he protects me, most of the time anyway."

"Protects you from whom?" queried Cameron, keeping his growing concerns in check.

"From some of the others in my head," casually answered Theon.

"Multiple Personality Disorder," Amadeo whispered to Cameron, who pushed him away, struggling with the possible diagnosis. "Have you talked about this with your psychiatrist?" Amadeo went on.

"I told my dad before, I don't trust her. And besides, I have a feeling the Ghost Knight doesn't want me to," believed Theon. "He said Jesus talked about the spirit living in him. You see, Jesus said the spirit was his friend, and that he was his King. And the people tortured him and killed him for it. He also said I was still too young to master it all, that there would be ample time for that in the future. I don't want to be tortured, dad." Theon grasped his father's hand, appearing nervous for the first time.

"No one will ever hurt you," promised Cameron and Amadeo in unison, as they sat on either side of Theon. "As for Jesus, he never really died; he was just pretending," added Amadeo.

"I don't see Jesus walking the streets," retorted Theon half-smiling; he knew what Amadeo meant.

"Grab the other drawings," Cameron ordered his unruly assistant. The word King rang in his ears.

Putting the drawing aside, Amadeo flipped through the other four drawings, all fairly intriguing, except for one, which was extraordinary. "If your dad doesn't mind, maybe we can talk about this one," passing it on to Cameron, who immediately recognized the illustration.

Cameron hesitated but finally agreed. "You've put a great deal of work in this one. It's beautiful. Do you feel up to talking about it?"

"Only if you both stay next to me," begged Theon. Cameron and Amadeo both edged closer to the boy.

"You can't get closer than this," smiled Cameron as he deposited the drawing on his son's lap. "You know you can trust me."

Thirteen characters—eight adults, four children, and one strange beast—sat at a long table, much like Da Vinci's famous painting, *The Last Supper*, depicting Jesus and the twelve apostles dining on the night of Christ's arrest. "This is me," said Theon, pointing at the child sitting in the middle.

"You've got the best seat in the house," proudly said Cameron. "That's where the King sits. How does it feel to be the king?"

"The king of what?" asked a puzzled Theon.

"The King of imagination, of course," quickly recovered Cameron. "As such a king, you can have and do what you want."

"If that's true," figured Theon, who went along with the ambiguous metaphor, "then I want my own computer in my room. Might as well milk this for all it's worth," thinking like a typically crafty kid of eight once again.

"What if I say No?" submitted his father. "As king, you could punish me…persecute me."

Theon immediately became confused and upset. "I don't want to hurt you, dad. I don't want to hurt *anyone*. Do you really think I would do that?" he cried out. Evidently, child interrogations were far more complex and precarious than adult ones, Cameron realized.

Cameron crouched and gripped his son by the arms, regretting his line of questioning. "I'm sorry Theon. What I said was stupid. You're the greatest boy in the world, honest to God." Kissing his son on the forehead, Cameron invited him to continue his description of the drawing.

"Ethan is sitting to my left while Maya is at my right," revealed a jittery Theon.

"Ethan, your dead brother?" asked Cameron.

"Who else, Dad?" replied Theon as if it was obvious. "Next to Ethan is Sarah."

"Why did you draw your mother as a child?" wondered Cameron.

"Mom is over there," noted Theon, pointing at the adult character next to Maya. "This is Sarah, my sister."

"You don't have a sister named Sarah," remarked a puzzled Cameron, expecting his son to concede his mistake.

"I think I once had," said Theon. "It's very confusing to me."

Cameron moved on. "Is this me?" pointing at a figure boasting a police badge on its chest.

"Yes, sir," proudly confirmed Theon. "And mom is right next to you."

"I noticed you drew two characters *exactly* the same," interjected Amadeo. "Why is that?"

"Because they're twin sisters, of course," explained Theon.

"Of course they are," said Amadeo in a patronizing tone. "I suppose this rather large person—or persons—bearing a normal head in front and the head of the Ghost Knight in the back is you?"

"No!" snarled Theon. "I told you, I'm in the middle. That's Jesus... well, I think it is."

"Who is the woman next to the two-headed Jesus?" asked Cameron.

"A good friend." Theon looked closer. "She's known Jesus for a long time. I like her a lot, and I think she likes me. And like the Ghost Knight, she wants to protect me."

"And what about this ugly man holding a big *dog* on a leash?" Cameron could not find any better word to describe the animal.

"I don't know," confessed Theon, "but he scares me." The interrogation was starting to take its toll on the boy. "As for his pet, it's some sort of dragon—like the one I made out of clay." The detailed figurine lay on its side at the edge of the coffee table.

"Tell me, Theon, what are all these people meant to represent?" Cameron studied the drawing meticulously, searching for some overarching connection.

Theon marshaled his thoughts during a moment, then provided the best answer his mind could afford: "These people—*all* these people—are my family."

CHAPTER 42

"I'm at a loss in pursuing this matter," admitted Cameron as he pressed his lower back against the kitchen counter and interlocked his arms. "We're no closer to the truth than we were when we initiated our cloak-and-dagger investigation. Theon's candid deposition is laced with strange ambiguity and fantastic folly, and devoid of any actionable element."

"At least there's nothing truly daunting or menacing about Theon's chimerical account," reminded Amadeo. "Besides, why would you want to act against and invalidate a child's imaginary world? That would be unconscionable."

"All right, smart man," scoffed Cameron, "what else do you suggest we do?"

Amadeo thought about it, then his eyes lit up. "Do you have any experience with hypnosis?"

"Some of my FBI colleagues do, but no me," replied Cameron, who had always considered the technique dubious at best. He preferred a well-structured tactical interrogation catering to the conscious mind—although in this case, he rated his intervention as futile.

"I have a basic understanding of its practice," said Amadeo. "While serving as a corporal at a MASH unit during the Vietnam War, I assisted the local psychiatrist in its application to soldiers who suffered from shell shock. The shrink was particularly fond of the *Eye-Fixation Hypnotic Induction* method."

"The oscillating pocket watch business," guessed Cameron. "I have reservations about the effectiveness of *any* form of hypnosis."

"Children have incredibly vivid imaginations and are highly susceptible to suggestions," retorted Amadeo, confident in his abilities. "You may yet be surprised by its impact on a child as creative and as inspired as Theon, even when administered by a neophyte like me." Staring at the floor, Cameron slowly raised his eyes, meeting his friend's hungry ones, begging for a sign of consent.

"There is no danger to Theon?" Cameron's stare intensified, combing Amadeo's countenance for any iota of doubt.

"I foresee *no* danger at all. Any memory, real or imagined, we elicit should be more innocuous than anything else." The amateur hypnotist was ready and eager to return to the living room and begin.

"Proceed." On the heels of Cameron's assent came quick preparation and instructions to solicit Theon's imagination and make him responsive to suggestions.

Using a metronome, a clicking pendulum indicating the exact tempo of a piece of music, to support his hypnotic monologue, Amadeo gradually induced a state of *nervous sleep*. "Theon, I want you to close your eyes now and listen to the clicking sound. After every click, you'll feel more comfortable and relaxed." Click, click went the metronome, emitting a sound every 1.5 seconds.

"How are you feeling, Theon?" softly asked Amadeo.

"I'm good, a bit sleepy though." Theon yawned and scrunched deeper into the sofa.

"That's fine, Theon," said Amadeo. "Now, I want you to go back to the well where Mommy and Daddy found you. Do you see it?"

"Yes. There's a bright light. It's all over and around me." Theon placed his hands over his closed eyes. "Oh, now it's gone. It's dark. I can see mom at the top of the well."

"Do you know who placed you in the well? Go back to before the well. Do you see anybody?" Amadeo repeated the question. "Is anyone with you?"

"Someone's holding me; it's a woman. Her hair is tied in the back of her head, and I can see her pointed ears...they're like mine!" Theon extended his arms outwards. "Mom, is that you?"

"Where are you both?" went on Amadeo. "Look around, Theon, and tell me what you see."

"We're in a garden," said Theon, grinning. "The flowers, the grass and the leaves are all red. The tree trunks are orange; and the sky is blue with reddish clouds. The birds are all sorts of colors. Come here, little birdy." Theon's head rotated about, following the birds' flight pattern. Then, his grin vanished. "We're not alone; four knights on horses are coming towards us...but the horses look more like dinosaurs. Each knight has a different-color armor: white, red, black, and green."

"Is there something else particular about the armor or about the knights themselves?" Amadeo urged on Theon, quite engrossed by the boy's account.

"They have red skin, horns on their heads and big bat wings," observed Theon. "And they're all wearing helmets with a weird sign on them, like two bumps over a straight line. They're stopping now...and saluting the woman. I think they're supposed to protect *me*. But the woman fears them; she doesn't trust them. The red-horse knight is approaching. 'Begone Aurignacia !' she tells him. He's turning away."

"I've heard that name before. Wait! Something just occurred to me," Cameron told Amadeo before pulling out a photograph from his wallet and unfolding it. "Can you tell Theon to open his eyes for a second?"

"Theon, I'd like you to open your eyes just for an instant," ordered Amadeo. "Your father wants to show you a picture."

Theon easily complied. "Does the weird sign on the helmet look like the one in the picture?" asked Cameron, holding up the photograph by his son's eyes.

"That's the sign, dad," exclaimed Theon. "That's the one on the helmets." Cameron had shown his son the symbol that appeared on the blue satin scarf the serial child killer always left behind. The *exact same* symbol—and the one that appeared on the alien helmet found among the mutated Neantherdal bodies in the burial ground of the hills of Reinhardswald, Germany.

CHAPTER 43

"Close your eyes again, Theon, and relax."
Amadeo made a downward movement with his hand. "In this red garden that surrounds you, is there a well?"

"The well is elsewhere," said Theon; "in or near a castle." Theon paused and frowned. Amadeo noticed rapid-eye-movement behind the boy's eyelids.

"Is something happening, Theon?" queried Amadeo.

"There's a man—it's the ugly man, the one with the pet dragon," claimed Theon. "He's screaming at the four knights. I…I can see his name. It's swirling around him."

"What name is that?" Amadeo gently insisted. "Tell me his name; a name can't harm you."

"It's spinning too fast." Theon heightened his concentration.

"I have an idea," Amadeo muttered to Cameron. The old Italian turned the dial on the metronome, reducing its rhythm to 3 seconds between clicks. "Listen to the clicks, Theon. They've slowed down just as the *flying* name is slowing down. Can you read it now?"

"Yes. Now it's just vibrating." Theon raised his arm and began writing in thin air. "It's kinda reversed."

Amadeo snatched one of the drawings and placed it upside down on Theon's lap. "Here's a pen," slipping it in the boy's closed hand. "Write the name down."

Theon scribbled seven capital characters: an inversed D; an inverse E; an M with an extra line segment ending with a hook; an A; an H; an O; and an inverse N ending with a hook.

Amadeo and Cameron dissected it in minute detail. "My first thought is DEMAHON," proposed Amadeo. "Does that mean anything to you, Theon?"

"Sounds like DEMON to me," said Theon. "The Ghost Knight doesn't trust demons, and neither do I. I wish the ugly man and his dragon weren't part of my family. Maybe that's why I'm different. Maybe that's why I'm bad sometimes."

"You're *not* bad, and they're not part of your family," assured his father. "They only exist in your imagination. They're not real."

"Don't contradict him," whispered Amadeo to Cameron. "It might interrupt the trance."

A disinclined Cameron nodded, resuming his analysis. He was bothered by the odd M and N. "If you extend the hook on the M, it might read as two consecutive M's. And if you do the same to the N, it becomes an M. It would now read as the inverted-letter word: DEMMAHOM."

Reclaiming the paper, Amadeo wrote the new word in the same fashion the original word appeared. "Do you see what I see?" passing back the paper to his partner in crime.

"I do." Cameron walked to a mirror, positioning the paper at shoulder level. Amadeo followed. "What do you see, old friend?"

"MOHAMMED," a fascinated Amadeo read aloud before returning to Theon's side. "Does *Mohammed* sound familiar to you?"

"I heard it in school," said Theon. "My friend Aasim talks about him sometimes. He's a Muslim." His answer wasn't very helpful.

Amadeo then recalled lines from two of Nostradamus' quatrains: "*Begotten by the Son of Mohammed. Born a strong master of Mohammed's teachings,*" substituting Demahon for Mohammed: "*Begotten by the Son of Demahon. Born a strong master of Demahon's teachings.*"

"Do you think Nostradamus used Mohammed as a code name for this Demahon?" speculated Cameron.

"Since he was an aficionado of word games, it's certainly possible," surmised Amadeo who decided to test Theon with a bit of logic. "Theon, you said all the people in your picture were part of your family, including the ugly man called Demahon. We think Demahon had, or has, a son. It then follows that his son must be in the picture. Is that true?"

Theon pondered the question, his facial expression sinking into a state of quandary. "I'm really not sure, I can't say. And if I give you a wrong answer, you'll be mad at me."

"Can you give us your best guess?" Amadeo handed Theon the drawing. "Just guess, and don't worry about it. No matter what answer you give, I won't be mad; promise."

Theon opened his eyes, slowly scanned the picture from left to right three times, and finally placed his finger over one of the twelve heads. The head he chose belonged to the one he called *Jesus*.

CHAPTER 44

"Theon, I want you to go back to the woman
who held you in the red garden," suggested Amadeo. "Look at her closely. Do you recognize her?"

"She looks a lot like mom," replied Theon.

Amadeo dug deeper. "Does she look like mom, or *is she* mom?"

Cameron abruptly pulled Amadeo back. "What are you doing, old
man?"

Amadeo gave him a searing glare. "We've been avoiding the question. He did call *her* mom. Let me do this."

Cameron glared back, but finally acquiesced quite reluctantly. In his
heart, he did not want Amadeo to cast doubt on the identity of Theon's
real mother—the mother who raised him and loved him as her own.

"Theon, is the woman *your* mother?" Amadeo asked again with
greater urgency.

Theon moved to the edge of the sofa, stuck out his neck, and tilted his
head to the left and then to the right. "I can see her better now, much better." His heart started racing and his body jittered. After 20 interminable
seconds, he slumped back into the sofa, exhausted and bewildered. "It *is*
mom!" he declared loudly.

"*Your* mom?" said Amadeo, pressing for confirmation.

"*Our* mom!" vigorously replied Theon.

"You mean you and your sister's mother, right?" clarified Amadeo.

"No, that's not it," said Theon. "The woman is my mother *and* is my
mother's mother."

Amadeo and Cameron were baffled by Theon's assertion. But the old
Italian would get to the bottom of this. "Theon, are you saying the woman
is not only your mother, but *also* the mother of Sarah, the woman who
raised you?"

"Yes." Theon scratched his nose nervously and crossed his arms. "You don't believe me?" The boy did not like being challenged, and Cameron knew this all too well.

"I believe you, son, as does your father," softly replied Amadeo, who was afraid Theon's vexation might interfere with his state of nervous sleep. "Now I want you to put your arms to the sides and relax; and I want you to realize that I'm not as smart as you, so I have to ask questions, sometimes lots, to understand."

His ego flattered, Theon immediately calmed down. "I'm ok now. Go ahead."

"All right." Amadeo rubbed his palms together as a prelude to his next question. Its manner of delivery would be crucial in keeping Theon's temper at bay. "Have you ever been to Saint-Amboise? That's a place in France, not too far from Pappy and Mammy's house."

"For sure," said Theon with absolute certainty. "That's where the well is. I've visited fifteen times now."

"Good for you; you're quite the traveler, far more experienced than I am," acknowledged Amadeo. "I bet your Grandma makes the best food in the world."

"Her ratatouille is the greatest," confessed Theon, liking his lips as he reminisced. "I can see her serving a big bowl of it at Thanksgiving."

"Tell me, Theon; what's your grandmother's name?" asked Amadeo.

"It's Jacqueline," said Theon, now recollecting her famous coconut pie.

"And Grandma Jacqueline is, of course, your mother Sarah's mother, right?" Amadeo eagerly awaited the response.

"Of course," replied Theon without any hesitation.

The opening Amadeo hoped for arose. "Then tell me Theon—because I'm not smart enough to understand—how can Grandma Jacqueline *and* the woman in the red garden *both* be Sarah's mother?"

Theon mulled over the question, searching for a reconciliatory explanation. His imagination went wild as he invoked scenario after scenario, image after image, until one was finally promoted to the rank of distinct possibility. "The woman is also Grandma Jacqueline's mother." Theon paused, and then added, "And the lady is also the mother of Grandma Jacqueline's mother."

Amadeo was clueless. "Go on Theon, I need to hear a bit more."

"Something's happening. Everything is white except for the red garden, which is far far away and tiny to the eye," said Theon. "There's a white brick road that leaves the garden and stretches towards me. I'm in the lead, standing at the end of the road. Sarah is behind me, and Jacqueline is behind her. And a hundred or so men and women stand in line behind Jacqueline. Although I can't see her, I know the woman is the last one in line, standing in the red garden. The men and women are all fathers and mothers of other fathers and mothers, all standing in line. It's like a mom and dad parade."

Theon became still; even his eyes stopped in their erratic course. "I'm back in the garden with the woman. 'Your sister Sarah is well hidden and safe, as safe as you'll soon be,' she tells me before letting a drop of her sweat fall onto the road. A red line starts to form along the middle bricks of the road, all along the road. It's very weird. I think it's blood. *I hate the sight of it.*" Theon placed his forearm over his eyes.

"A line of blood connecting fathers and mothers to others like them," opined Amadeo. "A bloodline!" he then shouted, suddenly enabled with a solution to the conundrum.

"How do you mean?" Cameron asked Amadeo, struggling to comprehend.

Amadeo seized Cameron by the shoulder. "The woman in the garden is not just a mother, but a *foremother*—the ancestor of all the men and women in line, including your wife Sarah, and Theon."

"Theon is adopted, I remind you," said Cameron.

"Yes, yes, yes, I know," barked Amadeo. "Theon is not only last in line; he's also first right after...no, right *next* to the woman. Theon is *her* son, and this Sarah—Theon's supposed sister—is her daughter. Had she appeared in Theon's vision, she would have been positioned right after the lady."

"So this missing Sarah, is not only Theon's sister, but also my Sarah's ancestor?" concluded Cameron. "It makes sense."

"I'm glad you now think so," Amadeo said derisively. "What's got into you?"

Cameron grimaced at his friend's cheekiness. "I'm referring to a diagnosis a doctor once made about Theon's and Sarah's DNA. The doctor's analysis of Sarah's genome had revealed that approximately 23% of her genetic baggage matched that of Theon. That could only happen if Theon and my wife were biologically related—just as Theon's fantasy contends."

"Astonishing!" Amadeo, the home-grown scholar, clapped his hands together in exhilaration. "Theon, the son, is also Theon, the brother to the ancestral Sarah, and the great great great...great uncle to the contemporary Sarah—and given the length of the ancestry, an uncle closing in on his two-thousandth birthday."

Before Cameron could abate Amadeo's tactless excitement, the doorbell rang. He jogged to the window and peeked outside. "Damn it, it's Sarah."

"Which one?" Amadeo shouted jokingly before directing his notice at Theon, who appeared completely worn out. "At the count of three, Theon, you'll wake up and remember nothing. One…two…three."

"Hi, uncle Amadeo," innocently said Theon, now seeming quite refreshed.

Cameron opened the door. "Hey honey. Bought me anything nice?"

"I knew you were here with Theon." Sarah was half-smiling. "You guys never miss a chance to visit crazy uncle Amadeo, the man of a million wild stories."

"Not as wild as the one we've just heard," muttered Cameron, who moved aside.

"Theon, my treasure!" she screamed in joy.

"Mom!" Theon ran to his mother and jumped in her arms. "Did you get me anything, mom?" kissing her repeatedly.

Cameron sighed in relief. "Everything is well again," he thought. *Time would tell.*

CHAPTER 45

Circa 2,000 years ago; Galilee.

Joseph was proud of his son, Jesus, while Mary remained leery of her boy's extraordinary stamina and wisdom. Joseph and the people of Nazareth were convinced the favor of God was upon him.

Mary had no doubt he had been favored, but by which supernatural force: God or his greatest nemesis, the ruler of the valley of the shadow of death, Satan. The Archangel Gabriel had indeed dispensed fair warning that the latter might pre-empt the former in planting a seed within her womb. Besides, if God had really wanted to beget an heir, why choose an imperfect, sinful, mortal woman as a carrier. It made more sense to her that Satan would do so in order to create a human-like being whose soul was black as coal, and who would infiltrate the land and dupe its denizens into embracing the Dark side.

"That *would* be the way of the Dark Lord," she thought. And she was evermore convinced of this during the yearly festival of Passover in Jerusalem, when her boy would go to the temple despite her forbidding, which, throughout the years, turned into reluctance, and finally into abdication.

Joseph was of no help. He enjoyed watching his son sit among the teachers, and trounce them in argument at every occasion. Mary, on the other hand, maintained no child should master such alleged knowledge of the word of God, except to deceive those who would listen. Satan was, after all, notoriously underhanded.

By the age of thirty, Jesus had marshaled quite a following. But he found that the greater his following became, the more conflicted he became. He was becoming self-aware and deeply introspective.

"Mother, there has always been *one* voice guiding my path," Jesus told her; "but now there are two. I could not hear the second as I suspect it was being silenced by the first."

"I have known about the first voice for a very long time, my son," confessed Mary. "And I have questioned its purpose to the same degree that, I fear, you have not. There are disturbing elements that surround your coming into this world, of which I have never spoken to you."

"I know, mother," admitted Jesus. "I could always sense your concern and mistrust."

"It is not solicitude for your reputation I feel, but for the spirit in you that has contributed to its nurturing," remarked Mary.

"You err in judgment," rebutted Jesus. "The second voice is the *enemy*, not the first."

Mary frowned. "You cannot claim otherwise since the first is controlling you."

"Control is irrelevant since the first voice and I are the same," said Jesus. "If there is to be imposed superintendence, it will irrevocably stem from the second. And that I dread above anything else. Perhaps, it is only a test of my resolve. I must confront this dilemma and make a choice."

"What will you do?" wondered a worried Mary, who always knew her son to solve problems in grandiose ways.

Jesus thought about it. To Mary, it looked like her son was having a soundless conversation with himself. "It is settled. I shall cross the desert, where each grain of sand that grazes my feet shall carry a message."

"That is foolishness," exclaimed Mary. "You will not survive. Someone must accompany you. And you must bring food and water. I will prepare something for your journey."

"A flask of water will do to sustain my body," said Jesus. "Do not be troubled, I will not be alone—the Holy Ghost will travel at my side."

"Your traveling companion may not be as holy as you think," asserted Mary. "He may well be the one you spurn at the conclusion of your quest."

"We shall see, won't we, mother," supposed Jesus, surrendering a comforting smile at Mary.

The next day, Jesus began his trek. He walked slowly, but with steadfastness. The sun rays hit his body hard, and it seemed to shimmer under their influence.

"Courage, my son," said the familiar voice inside him. "I will not abandon you."

Every time the voice spoke to Jesus in the past, guiding him, it always referred to him as *my son*. Jesus assumed it was the voice of God, or its spirit—God's highest representative. Now he wasn't so sure. The answer lied ahead, he hoped.

On the seventh day, the second voice made its presence. If this was truly a test, perhaps it was the Holy Ghost taunting him in a different voice he would describe as baleful, but entrancing—a paradox in his mind.

The voice said to him, "If you are the Son of God, command this stone to become a loaf of bread."

Jesus answered him, "It is written, 'One does not live by bread alone.'" He then looked up at the Sun. "Reveal yourself. Are you Satan, the king of all demons?"

"The game is afoot, *my son*," replied the voice. "No amusement would be procured by disclosing my true identity. Torment is the only rule of this game."

On the eleventh day, as Jesus closed his eyes and drank from the flask, he felt the wind carry him into the sky. He opened his eyes and found that the being hiding behind the sinister voice had posted him above all the kingdoms of the world.

And it said to him, "To you I will give their glory and all this authority; for it has been given over to me, and I give it to anyone I please. If you, then, will worship me, it will all be yours."

Jesus answered him, "It is written, 'Worship the Lord your God, and serve only him.'"

"I may well be the one supplying you with the answers you dole out so with such arrogance," said the being.

"Stay the course," said the voice of the one Jesus called Holy Ghost. It was immediately followed by the being's voice, "How can you know it was not I who said that?"

"I shall learn to make the difference," replied Jesus. He suddenly fell to earth, but discovered he was not injured.

On the twenty-ninth day, the being took him to Jerusalem, and placed him on the pinnacle of the temple, saying to him, "If you are the Son of God, throw yourself down from here, for it is written, 'He will command his angels concerning you, to protect you,' and, 'On their hands they will bear you up, so that you will not dash your foot against a stone.'"

"I am *still* in the desert," Jesus cried out. "Know this, 'Do not put the Lord your God to the test.'"

The being laughed. "The Lord is not being tested, you poor fool; you are."

Jesus was desperate for a sign, for a revelation that would erase all doubt from his mind. He only had water left for another eight days. Even with rationing, he would not make it to the end of the desert.

"Stay the course," the voice of the Holy Ghost said again. "Salvation awaits you."

"What does that mean?" wondered Jesus. "Will the hand of God come down and scoop me up, carrying me to my destination?"

No heavenly hand was to be found. He was losing faith. "This was not a test," he was forced to conclude. "This was a trick, cleverly formented by Satan." Still, he refused to declare forfeit, and went on.

It was now the fortieth day of Jesus' journey. He was gravely weakened due to lack of nourishment, and had run out of water three days ago. He could no longer stand, dragging himself forward on all fours. But he found reason to rejoice as he glimpsed the end of the desert a mile away. He had not been enlightened in the manner that he hoped, but at least he had successfully crossed the desert. "A meager consolation prize," he muttered to himself, "but I shall take it, for whatever worth it brings with it."

As he neared the edge of the desert, a voice spoke to him: "Congratulations. You may now claim your reward."

Jesus could no longer make out the author of the voice. It sounded both like the voice of the Holy Ghost and that of Satan, and strangely like neither of them. Jesus attributed his inability to recognize the source to his advanced state of physical decay.

He finally reached the perimeter of the desert. Half-blinded by a 40-day onslaught of the Sun's rays, he scoured the area, hoping for something, but expecting nothing. "What have I gained?" he shouted towards the heavens.

"You need no longer look beyond the confines of this earthly realm," said a soft, melodious voice. "I am the recompense for your arduous labor, my intrepid Jesus. I have been called to duty to serve *only* you. I am the *one* who can soften your sorrows. I am your ally, your consort, and your soul."

Lying prostrate with his arms outstretched, Jesus painfully turned on his side and bent his neck backwards to lay eyes on what he discovered to be the most beautiful woman he had ever seen—a goddess by any and all accounts.

"Who are you?" he sorely asked.

"I am yours," she pleasingly answered. "I am *Maria Magdalena*."

CHAPTER 46

Present day; France.

The *Musée du Louvre* is one of the world's largest museums, the most visited art museum in the world and a historic monument. A central landmark of Paris, it is housed in the Louvre Palace, and is located on the Right Bank of the Seine in the 1st arrondissement (district). Nearly 35,000 objects from prehistory to the 19th century are exhibited over an area of 652,300 square feet.

"The museum was built in the late 12th century," Gaston Sinclair informed his adopted grandson, Theon. "It was a fortress then."

"It's a pretty big place, Pappy," realized Theon after visiting most of the exhibition rooms and galleries.

"Yes, it is," agreed Gaston, whose daughter, Sarah, was on the phone and lagging behind. 'Hurry up, Sarah. You're going to miss the best part."

Gaston and Theon entered the *Salle des États* where Da Vinci's masterpiece, *Mona Lisa*, hung alone on the back wall, behind non-reflective, unbreakable glass to protect it from climatic changes, camera flashes and willful damage.

"Mother wants you to buy bread for supper tonight," said Sarah after hurrying her pace and joining her party. "She'll be making Coq-au-Vin."

"Excellent choice," shouted a very old man wearing an impeccable suit and tie, standing a few feet away. "But make sure you use *Burgundy* wine, and just a bit of crushed garlic," he warned candidly as he extended his hand and shook Gaston's. "I am Doctor Didier Dresdner, General-Administrator of Le Musée du Louvre."

"Gaston Sinclair," replied a surprised Gaston. "This is Sarah, my daughter, and Theon, my grandson. To what do we owe the honor of your interpellation?"

"Oh, for no grandiose reason," said the jolly old man, "if only to bask in the enthusiasm of young people who've embarked on an exploration of the wonderful world of Art."

Rubbing Theon's hair briskly, Dresdner leaned downwards. "What do you think of that painting?" he asked, pointing at the Mona Lisa.

"She smiles just like mom," thought Theon, who moved closer to the painting, wanting to slip under the rope preventing visitors from touching the glass.

"Theon!" roared his mother. "Keep your place." Theon shot a look at her that pleaded leniency.

"Quite understandable for a boy on such a noble quest," noted Dresdner, who joined Theon's side. "The lady's name is Mona Lisa," he told Theon; "and I think she has a pretty smile and pretty eyes."

Mona Lisa (also known as *La Gioconda* or *La Joconde)* was a portrait by the Italian artist Leonardo da Vinci. It was a painting in oil on a poplar panel, completed circa 1503–1519.

The painting was a half-length portrait depicting a seated woman, whose facial expression had been frequently described as enigmatic. The ambiguity of the subject's expression, the monumentality of the composition, and the subtle modeling of forms and atmospheric illusionism were novel qualities that had contributed to the continuing fascination and study of the work.

Most scholars believed M*ona Lisa* was named for Lisa del Giocondo, a member of the Gherardini family of Florence and Tuscany, and the wife of wealthy Florentine silk merchant Francesco del Giocondo. The painting had been commissioned for their new home and to celebrate the birth of their second son, Andrea.

Over the years, there have been several alternative views. Some scholars have argued that Lisa del Giocondo was the subject of a different portrait, identifying at least four other paintings as the *Mona Lisa* referred to by Vasari. Sigmund Freud believed that the famous half-smile was a recovered memory of Leonardo's mother. Other suggestions have been Isabella of Naples, Cecilia Gallerani, Costanza d'Avalos, Duchess of Francavilla, Isabella d'Este, Pacifica Brandano, Isabela Gualanda, Caterina Sforza, and Leonardo himself.

"You know, Theon, nobody knows for sure who Mona Lisa really was," Dresdner whispered to Theon. "But I think she was a *mother*, at the very least—a young mother in her mid-twenties."

Theon stared at the painting for evidence of motherhood, but nothing about it testified to it, except for the smile. With his finger in the air, he traced her smile, going back and forth. "She *was* a mother," he finally concluded. "And she was thirty-three in this painting."

Dresdner grinned with indulgence. "Jesus Christ died at the age of thirty-three, I'll concede that, but this is not a painting of Jesus Christ. My dear boy, this is a painting of a woman." Granted, Mona Lisa's beauty was strangely bewitching and unconventional by most standards, but she could hardly be mistaken for a man.

"I know that," said a vexed Theon, now tracing the shape of eyebrows, which were missing from the painting.

Mona Lisa had no clearly visible eyebrows or eyelashes. Some researchers claimed that it was common at that time for genteel women to pluck these hairs, as they were considered unsightly.

"You must be confused by the absent eyebrows and eyelashes," surmised Dresdner. "Ladies used to remove them a long time ago, to look… *younger*." Dresdner suddenly and unexpectedly found himself reconsidering the age of the Mona Lisa. "You're a very perceptive boy. Your *growing* reputation precedes you."

"What do mean by that?" interjected Sarah, who had approached to fetch her child.

"Nothing at all," reassured Dresdner. "Just the ramblings of an old codger who appreciates our youngsters' great potential. I'll see you around, Theon," tapping the boy on the shoulder.

"Come on, honey; Mammy is eager to feed us—she's even made your favorite dessert: cream puffs with dark chocolate." Sarah pulled him by the arm, but could not budge him. She pulled harder, but even then Theon remained inexorably anchored in place.

"Theon, I order you to come with me…or else," menaced Sarah, but no physical might would remove him, and no threat, move him. He was completely intractable.

Gaston saw this and became upset. "Now, you listen to your mother," he loudly barked, firmly clamping his hands onto Theon's shoulders, inadvertently hurting him. Theon's animal instinct immediately galvanized into action, and before Gaston could dispense any degree of patriarchal dominion, a powerful invisible force struck him and threw him ten feet back onto the marble floor.

At the same instant, the protective glass cracked into thousands of pieces, and plunged to the floor. For the first time ever, the alarm system went off, and armed guards soon followed, aiming their guns at Sarah and Theon. "Watch your boy," screamed Dresdner, who rushed towards the guards.

"Lower your weapons," he commanded. "Do it now!"

"But sir…the paint…the painting," stammered the closest guard.

"It's an accident," Dresdner clamored. "Now lower your guns." He ran to Gaston, who was dazed, and bled from the back of the head, but was conscious. "And call an ambulance."

Gently taking her son's hand, Sarah softly pleaded with him. "Theon, darling, it's mom." His eyes were cold and blank. "I don't know where you are, but come back to me. Come back to mommy."

Since Theon's last visit at their neighbor Amadeo's house, Theon had been exhibiting early symptoms of Autism. She knew in her heart it was not autism, but rather something related to the origins of his *unique* abilities, recently unleashed, intentionally or not, after years of relative tranquility.

"I beg of you, Theon, come back to mommy." Sarah began stroking his arm. "Feel my hand, muffins; it's mommy, it's mommy…it's *mommy*."

Theon's vacant expression suddenly became vibrant and agitated. "They're hurting us, mom," he said with a voice trembling with profound apprehension. "You're hurt, mom, oh no, you're hurt!" He grabbed his mother's face with both hands and frantically probed it, passing his fingers over her frontal hair, her eyebrows, and her eyelashes. "They burnt your face, mom; they burnt it."

"Mommy's fine; mommy's okay," she assured him, wiping her tears and putting on a brave smile. "Look! Mommy has all her hair, her eyebrows, and her eyelashes."

Theon appeared totally confused. "They were gone. The fireballs burnt them off."

"He's referring to the Mona Lisa painting," explained Dresdner, who had returned to their side. "*Receded* hair line; *no* facial hair."

"Of course; where is my head?" Sarah pointed at the painting. "You were thinking about her, honey. Not me, not your mommy." Theon was now quite alert and aware of his surroundings, albeit still befogged with ominous images, which were dissipating only too slowly.

"Your father is fine, by the way," informed Dresdner. "Nothing a few suture points won't fix."

"Dad!" cried out Sarah, who, saddled with a crisis of her own, had forgotten about him. "Please watch my son for a moment, while I tend to my father."

"You're a remarkable boy, Theon," he complimented the boy as he surveyed the pile of *unbreakable* glass at the foot of the painting. "Truly remarkable—in every sense of the word."

"So *was* my mother," Theon replied in odd impromptu fashion, looking at the Mona Lisa, and then at Dresdner.

"You mean: so *is* your mother?" corrected Dresdner.

"That's what I said," insisted Theon, who easily escaped the old man's care and ran to Sarah and Gaston.

Dresdner watched the child embrace his grandfather. He was obviously oblivious of his role in Gaston's injuries. But of all things transpiring today, here in this timeless room, "how many of them had truly remained oblivious to this remarkable boy?" wondered Dresdner. Perhaps some answers were on the way—he was certain of that.

CHAPTER 47

Present day; France.

Eight men sat around a wooden table in a room spanning the entire length of a rustic log cabin, located in an isolated area of the commune of Le Lavandou, near the shore of the Côte d'Azur. Each man had been served with a jug of spring water and a plate of local fruits, which, for the moment, remained untouched. The lead man sitting at the end of the table adjacent to the kitchen area appeared in waiting of an imminent event, twirling his thumbs and eying two bottles of 2003 Haut-Médoc French wine, placed in the middle of the table. No one dared touch the bottles until the lead man had broached them.

"Mes excuses," said a ninth man, after entering the room through the back door of the cabin, plainly facing the lead man. "My plane from New York to Marseille was slightly delayed," he quickly explained in French.

"If you were an agent of Interpol, you would be summarily flogged," remarked the lead man with a hint of humor. The men at the table chuckled candidly, tearing through the sedate and solemn atmosphere that permeated the room. "Messieurs, I present to you Scott Dumont, Assistant-Director of the FBI New York office. As most of you know, this is his first face-to-face meeting with *Le Cercle des Huit (The Circle of the Eight)*, the board of administration of the Priory of Sion."

"Is this wise?" asked one of the men, concerned about his anonymity.

"As our principal informant on the matter of *Subject M²C*, I felt it was appropriate that he finally meet us in person," explained the lead man, untroubled by his decision.

Subject M²C was a code name for a person of interest the Circle had been observing for several years now.

"I'm honored to be among such esteemed gentlemen," Dumont declared with all the diplomacy he could muster, glancing all the while at a small flag flatly pinned to the cross-beam above the lead man's head. The flag featured a stylized fleur-de-lys (lily flower), beaded at its bottom, and interlaced with a figure eight.

"Your French is impeccable," noted one of the men at the table.

"As is my name…French that is," replied Dumont. "I was born in New-Orleans to a French father and to an American mother. Despite my blatant *shortcoming*, I still made it to the FBI," he quipped without malice.

"I understand," replied the man. "Being American is *problematic* indeed." All the men burst into laughter.

"Allow me the introductions," offered the lead man. "For those whose memories have been clogged by a lifetime excess of *La Piquette* (cheap French homemade wine), I am Cardinal Pierre Nadeau, Prefect of the pontifical house and Archbishop of Marseille. As for my associates, we have clockwise:

"Cardinal Umberto Romeo, Archbishop of Bologna, Italy, Ph.D. of theology;

Cardinal Matak Pubudu, Archbishop of Khartoum, Sudan, Ph.D. of theology;

Doctor George Lapierre, Head Supervisor at the Center for SETI Research, Ph.D. of theology, philosophy and theoretical physics;

Doctor Sean Ramsay, Provost and Chief Academic Officer of the Massachusetts Institute of Technology, Ph.D. of Mathematics, Science and Engineering;

Doctor Maurice Lefoux, MD, Head of Pediatrics at the American Hospital of Paris;

The Honorable Claude Blanchard, *Keeper of the Seals* and French Minister of Justice and Freedom; ex-special agent of Interpol; and the elder of the group, Doctor Didier Dresdner, General-Administrator of Le

Musée du Louvre, Masters of Social Science, Ph.D. of Renaissance Art and Literature."

"I see," blurted out Dumont. Impressed by the international intelligencia that surrounded him, the FBI agent, tempted by his ego to glamorize his own status, succumbed to it miserably.

"I too hold a degree: a Masters of Arts in Criminology," he announced with a false sense of modesty. "It has served me well in my career…you know, catching bad guys."

"Good for you," said Nadeau dismissively, before wavering in a man who had been standing in the kitchen shadows. "This is Jean-Luc Normand, Doctor Dresdner's great-grandson-in-law, and the Secretary to the Grand Master. He has been in my service for…for…"

"For five months as of tomorrow, Master," indicated Normand, rescuing his boss from a faltering memory. "I shall be the one taking the minutes of the meeting…and serving the wine of course." Without further ado, he skillfully opened the bottles and began serving the elite group. Upon completing his round, he pulled a glass out of his vest pocket, placed it on the table, nearest Dumont, and filled it. "Yours to enjoy, Monsieur du FBI." Dumont ignored it.

"What became of the previous secretary?" Dumont couldn't help noticing how young Normand was.

"Our last secretary died quite tragically," Nadeau told Dumont. "An unfortunate overdose of heroin," he added reluctantly, pressed by Dumont's inquiring gaze.

"Was it self-administered?" queried Dumont, who had seen his share of dead drug addicts.

"The police thought so." Nadeau's debonair charm melted away, replaced by a brief bout of melancholy. "His name was Arthur Nadeau, and he was my nephew."

"I'm sorry for your loss, Cardinal." Dumont was itching to ask another question, as any self-respecting FBI agent would. And the more personal the question, the better he could expose his opposition. Nadeau detected this and became bothered by Dumont's implicit impertinence. "Let me save you the trouble, Monsieur Dumont. The answer is *no*. I don't believe Arthur killed himself."

Dumont remained expressionless. "Did he have any enemies? Someone who held a terrible grudge against him?"

"Not against him…against *us*," supposed Nadeau. "Our *organization* is deeply rooted in non-traditional beliefs that are exceedingly unpalatable and repugnant to Christian purists. Some would gladly have us exterminated by *any* means. That is also why we never mention the name of *Subject M²C*, or exchange on any details that might readily betray his identity or his whereabouts. In fact, the only people who know the name of *Subject M²C* are The Circle of the Eight."

"Don't forget *Subject M²C's* family," pointed out Dumont. "They *certainly* know his name," stating the obvious in mocking fashion. "Wouldn't you agree?"

"Of course." The overly sensitive Nadeau now appeared thoroughly annoyed by what he perceived to be an insult to his intellect. "They know his name, but not *what* he might represent." He brooded for an instant and then resumed. "Perhaps it was a mistake to invite you here."

Dumont appeared unaffected by Nadeau's change of heart. "Why *did you* invite me here? Isn't that against protocol?"

Nadeau became a trifle more sullen and surly. "I relieved myself from that particular rule because I believed your allegiance was wavering, and needed to either confirm or refute that hypothesis—in person."

"Let me guess," said Dumont. "You didn't appreciate my last report on *Subject M²C*?"

"In so far as the facts of the report were accurate, I had no issue with that aspect of it," conceded Nadeau. "It is your editorial commentary, which by the way was never required nor desired, that kindled and fuelled my suspicions." Nadeau pulled a report out of his suitcase. "I have a copy, if you need to refresh your memory."

"No need." Dumont pulled the one empty chair pressed against the wall, dragged it very slowly to the end of the table opposite Nadeau, and sat on it, in clear view of everyone. He felt like a convict during a parole hearing—his words would need to be compelling if he was to be spared the Cardinal's prison of distrust.

"I assume you all read it?" Dumont scanned the men's faces, which all remained impassive. "Yeah, ok! Let's get this over. After *monitoring Subject M²C* for far too many years, I've finally come to the conclusion that he is just an *ordinary* person subjected to the extraordinary imaginations of the people who are privy to his life and times—and that includes you gentlemen."

The men appeared perplexed, now expecting the FBI agent to expand on the elements that led to his conclusion.

"That's it, boys," said Dumont, dismissing their need to grasp his meaning. "I've nothing to add."

"Is it in your habit to not finish what you've started?" asked Nadeau.

"I'm not sure you would *really* listen," replied Dumont.

Nadeau pondered on that. "You're right. Curiosity aside, your opinion should be of no importance to us. You're just a lowly henchman whose job—whose only job—was to gather information, not interpret it?"

Dumont, piqued by Nadeau's derogatory commentary, now elected to speak, ignoring Nadeau's rhetorical directive. "I believe you've all been blinded by your mission. You must know that, for all intents and purposes, you've put a *kid, a boy,* on a holy pedestal with all the religious trappings that go with it?"

"Do *not* make any reference to the *age* of *Subject M²C*," ordered Nadeau.

Looking beyond Nadeau to Normand who was furiously scribbling in a note book, Dumont called on him. "Well, Normand, now you know we're not talking about an old geezer waving his cane at the ungrateful family that left him in a senior center. That knowledge may spell your death."

"Monsieur Dumont!" Nadeau rose violently, toppling over his chair, and hit the tabletop with his fists. Normand, like a good servant, replaced the chair in its upright position, and dusted off its seat area.

Dumont did not flinch. "Sorry. It must be the fatigue from the long trip," he said mechanically. "What I'm trying to say is that every miraculous event you've attributed to *Subject M²C*'s supernatural powers can be explained rationally. A newborn baby's heart stopping and restarting shortly after resuscitation efforts is not uncommon. Things like a mobile set or a toy truck moving on their own can be explained by a gush of wind or an uneven floor. School bullies getting nose bleeds at exactly the same moment can be explained by very dry air. Unbreakable glass shattering mysteriously can be explained by a manufacturing defect."

"I saw a sturdy old man being thrown violently to the ground by an unknown force," noted Dresdner, recalling the incident at the Louvre; "a force emanating from a child."

"The boy's adrenaline was at its peak," said Dumont, "and his strength augmented dramatically."

"Enough! None of this is new information," said an impatient and furious Nadeau. "You do not agree with our conclusions, fine. But what more has clearly happened to you to prompt this wanton incredulity?"

Dumont, in turn, became impatient and furious—far more than Nadeau. "You want to know what happened? A child—yes, *a child*—being exposed to psychologically aggressive and potentially dangerous procedures like interrogation and hypnotism; that's what happened. And by whose approval; the father's no less, a man I've always known to be kind and loving. If he could be driven to this in the name of *Truth*, then so could I; and so could all of you."

"Those procedures were quite revealing," noted Nadeau: "evidence of biological parents from biblical times—whose DNA no less we've retrieved and adequately matched to *Subject M*; evidence of a hallowed family; and evidence of a heavenly garden—perhaps the Garden of Eden itself. Need I say more?"

"Evidence is based on verifiable facts," replied Dumont. "Even this DNA matching business is questionable when you consider the unproven origin of the genome source material, and its degraded condition."

"Are you a medical geneticist?" chimed in Lefoux, intent on injecting a dose of humility into Dumont. "I thought not. It is best you limit your sermon to areas you fully grasp."

"Listen, *I* get it," said Dumont who was not the least deterred. "I really do, but you, Monsieur," pointing at Nadeau, "are carrying this too far. I strongly suspect past trauma has been clouding your objectivity for some time now."

The men around the table knew nothing about Dumont's assertion. Nadeau was incensed and Dumont gave him no opportunity to rebut. "Cardinal Nadeau has claimed that Jesus appeared before him during a tragic bus accident 40 some odd years ago."

"He did not appear before me," cried Nadeau. "He *spoke* to me. He instructed me to wait for him."

"And this child is the second coming of Christ?" defiantly retorted Dumont, testing Nadeau's state of mind. "Back from Heaven to conveniently validate your claim."

"He is *not* Christ!" Nadeau turned red with anger. "You know that as well as I do."

"There's very little I know with any degree of certitude." Dumont pushed on. "Hell, the child could be the Antichrist, the dark destroyer of all; the One King, cast into a well only to be risen from a well. Since Nostradamus, the great seer, wrote this, why not include it in your collective delusion? His trash is as believable as a child under duress' pipe dream."

"We do believe his *trash*," interjected Doctor Didier Dresdner, General-Administrator of Le Musée du Louvre.

The whole room became silent.

CHAPTER 48

"You do?" exclaimed Dumont, after shrugging off his stupor. "You believe in Nostradamus' quatrains?"

Dresdner looked over at Nadeau for approval to take the floor. A relieved Nadeau nodded. "To be precise, we believe *some* quatrains do have merit in providing insight on the child and on the circumstances surrounding his arrival (Dresdner had decided to dispense with the cryptic term *Subject M²C*).

"Go on!" Dumont bore down on Dresdner.

But Dresdner was not a man to be rushed—he had been rushed too many times in his life, with dire consequences, and his tolerance for it had run out. In fine fashion, he took a sip of wine; his hand shook as he carried the glass to his lips—an unwelcome token of old age. He was otherwise quite healthy for a man of ninety-three. "Hum, good wine; not German, but quite acceptable."

Didier Dresdner was born in Berlin, Germany. His father was a Lieutenant Colonel in the German Army, who had married a French showgirl he met during R&R in Paris. At the age of 10, Dresdner had been forced to join the *Deutsches Jungvolk (German Young People)* until the age of 13 when he transferred to the *Hitler Jugend (Hitler Youth)*. His Youth-Commander, *Baldur Von Shirach*, was particularly hard on him, calling him *half-breed*, and accusing him of being soft and weak.

Every morning, Shirach would tell him that, "the weak must be chiseled away. I want young men who can suffer pain. A young German must be as swift as a greyhound, as tough as leather, and as hard as Krupp's steel." Dresdner couldn't care less. He preferred drawing and writing to senseless combat.

At the age of 18, he joined the Air Force as Private First Class, under the command of Colonel General Ernst Udet. On his second mission in the Fall of 1941, he was dispatched to Warsaw, Poland, to help secure the spoils of a raid on the Aristocratic community. He was overjoyed to discover that part of the stolen treasure was a collection of Renaissance and Contemporary works of art and literature; and he took his sweet time appraising the items before loading them on Colonel Udet's plane bound for Berlin.

At the last minute, Udet told him he would not be joining the crew because of weight capacity. His frustration over the decision quickly turned to relief when he heard of the plane's fate, and of Udet's betrayal and murder of the crew. Since then, he has been living life to its fullest.

"Is your life full?" Dresdner asked Dumont.

"What?" Dumont wondered what the old man meant.

"Is your life full?" he asked again.

"I *guess* so," answered Dumont.

"Are you comfortable with your answer?" Dresdner took another sip of wine.

"Yes, of course." Dumont had nothing inspirational to complement his brief response.

"Well, that's what we do all day," said Dresdner. "We *guess*! We guess the meaning of things, and hope we are right. And once we agree on a guess, we immediately become comfortable with it."

"Your *guesses* should at least be educated," pointed out Dumont.

Dresdner smiled. "Son, at my age, any kind of guess is good enough for me. That being said, would you allow me to make some guesses on the matter that assembled us here in this quaint cabin?"

"Certainly." Dumont calmed down. He had fallen prey to the soothing effect of Dresdner's serenity and wisdom.

Dresdner began quoting a few significant lines from Nostradamus' quatrains:

"Cast into a well only to be risen from a well; Quatrain 45, Century 7.
The anointed one shall return on the Feast of Trumpets; and, *Raugon the third of October shall be set loose*; Quatrain 62, Century 9.

"Now, here are my guesses about those lines: a child—a very special child—traveled from Heaven to Earth on a mystical ship sailing on an ocean separating the two realms. He disembarked on the Earth's dock represented here by a well. And the Earth trembled as it trumpeted the arrival of the dragon-child, on the day of October 3rd."

"I'm afraid your fable is a little too poetic for my taste," confessed

Dumont.

"Let me translate some of it in more scientific terms," offered Lapierre, the ex-priest turned scientist. "I believe the well acted as the *exit point* of a wormhole, a corridor that spanned great distances across space. What made this wormhole unique was its *stationary* exit point—the great majority of wormholes have random exit points."

"What about the wormhole's entry point; is it stationary as well?" wondered Dumont.

"I would gather it is," said Lapierre. Entry and exit points usually exhibit the same characteristics. Now, if we assume the traveler had heavenly powers, we could further assume the reality he came from was Heaven-like, if not Heaven itself. Furthermore, if my wormhole theory is correct, then the world at the entry point must exist in the *same* physical reality as Earth."

"That is absurd," growled Cardinal Umberto Romeo. "Heaven lies beyond all physical realities."

Lapierre grinned faintly. "As you can see, we don't always agree on our *guesses*. Now if my distinguished colleague would indulge me a bit longer, I'll continue. When a wormhole connects, it releases energy in the form of light, sound and vibrations. While light and sound might be difficult to track or measure, when it is not anticipated, vibrations are not."

"Vibrations like those produced by Earth's trumpets," chuckled Dumont in mild amusement.

"Did you know the Bible associates the *Feast of Trumpets* with the trembling of the earth?" asked Lapierre.

Dumont couldn't recall. "No, but I *guess* I'm not surprised."

"I left my surprise at the door, and opted for confirmation," said Lapierre. "My employer, the Center for SETI Research, enjoys an informal relationship with USGS, an organization that owns and operates a global seismographic network. It's a permanent digital network of state-of-the-art seismological and geophysical sensors connected by a telecommunications network. On the day of October 3rd, 2007, its seismic station in Schiltach, Germany, detected a mild and shallow earthquake at the center of the forest in the town of Amboise, France. It measured at 3.2 on the Richter scale—barely perceptible, and had a focal point of about 70 feet deep."

"Exactly where the well was," acknowledged Dumont.

"And where it still stands," added Lapierre.

Dumont mulled over it all. "I agree this is very fascinating...and the date is quite significant—the child was found in the well *on* October 3rd, 2007.

"Indeed," exclaimed Lapierre. "Do you now see why we are so enthralled by this child, whomever he might turn out to be."

"I still don't understand this dragon-child business Doctor Dresdner mentioned." Dumont looked towards him for an explanation. "I thought the dragon was an *archetype* for Satan."

"Not necessarily," replied Dresdner after sipping some wine. "You see, I am convinced the word *Raugon* appearing in the quatrain is an anagram for *dragon, the life force*. In many Asian cultures, dragons were, and in some cultures still are, revered as representatives of the primal forces of nature, religion and the universe. They are associated with wisdom—often said to be wiser than humans—and with longevity. They are also commonly said to possess some form of magic or other supernatural power, and are often associated with *wells*, *rain*, and small bodies of water like *rivers and streams*."

"Mention of the *well* again," noted Dumont. "This is freakin' weird."

"Don't overlook the mention of *rain* and *streams*," said Dresdner.

"What do you mean?" Dumont didn't see the connection.

Dresdner took yet another sip of wine, emptying his glass. It now became evident he always prefaced his answers with an intake of alcohol. "There was a stream of water only ten feet away from the well, *and* it was raining when the child was found in the well." Dresdner began eying Dumont's untouched glass of wine. "Are you going to drink that?"

CHAPTER 49

"There is another reason I invited you here,"
announced Nadeau—"at Doctor Dresdner's behest, if you must know."

"Do you also want to drill me on my loyalty to your cause?" Dumont gibed at Dresdner.

Dresdner passed his finger along the rim of his empty glass, attempting to produce a detectable sound. "A good scientist proposes hypotheses as explanations of phenomena, and designs experimental studies with observable and measurable results to prove or disprove these hypotheses."

Dresdner pushed away his glass as Normand deposited Dumont's glass in front of him. "Doctor Lapierre, Doctor Ramsay, and I understand and appreciate the language of science, more so than anyone else in this group. You, Monsieur Dumont, must also; your job is predicated on that understanding. So, I propose we leave Nostradamus and Asian beliefs in peace, and surrender ourselves to science once again, just for a brief period."

"Normand!" loudly yelled Dresdner.

"But, Monsieur, your glass is full," said Normand.

"Not the wine, you silly simpleton." Dresdner patted the secretary on the arm like he would a confused child. "I require the document."

"My apologies." Normand strutted into the kitchen and returned with a short stack of papers, which he quickly distributed to the group and Dumont. Each person received two pages, 15 inches by 21 inches.

"I want to thank you and your FBI department for returning this document and many other priceless works to my care after seventy years," the old German said to Dumont. "Had it not been for your agents' diligence and fortitude, Colonel General Ernst Udet's hidden cache of stolen treasures in the hills of Reinhardswald would never have been discovered."

"Of course, Le Musée du Louvre." Dumont had ordered the array of works of art and literature delivered to the Louvre, to the attention of the

General-Administrator, seven weeks ago. The topic of Udet's stockpile having been introduced, jogging his memory, he just now realized Dresdner was the one who had been awarded custody of the works.

"I've relished many a day of delight and delectation appraising each and every item," timidly admitted Dresdner, as if the euphoria that had overtaken him bordered on sin. "And I've privileged a few that may shed light on our path towards illumination." He exhaled in satisfaction and looked at all the men. "Gentlemen, you each hold a *photocopy* of one of those favored items. Now, tell me what you see."

"The Vitruvian Man!" gasped Cardinal Matak Pubudu, as he reviewed the first page.

The *Vitruvian Man* was a world-renowned drawing created by Leonardo da Vinci circa 1487. It was accompanied by notes based on the work of the famed architect, Vitruvius. The drawing, which was in pen and ink on paper, depicted a male figure in two superimposed positions with his arms and legs apart and simultaneously inscribed in a circle and square. The drawing and text were sometimes called the *Canon of Proportions* or, less often, *Proportions of Man*. It was currently stored in the *Gallerie dell'Accademia* in Venice, Italy.

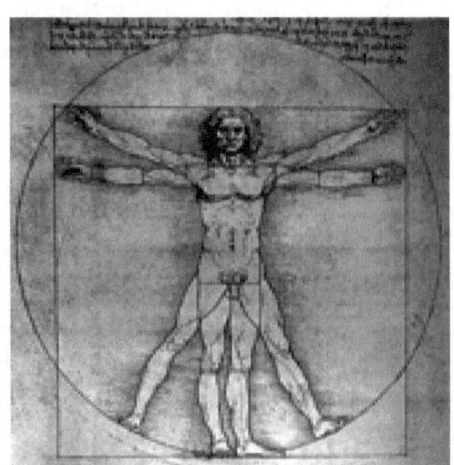

"It is, in fact, a *second* version of the Vitruvian Man," reported Dresdner. "The position of the arms and legs are slightly different, and the drawing is entirely in pen. Apart from that, it's identical. I suspect Da Vinci sold the first version to one of his patrons before deciding to produce another version."

"For what purpose?" inquired Minister Claude Blanchard.

"While Da Vinci was known to make copies of some of his works," said Dresdner, "he had a very specific reason to create this near-identical copy of the Vitruvian Man." The men waited for Dresdner's disclosure of the reason with bated breath. "Look to the second page." The men slid the first page to the left, exposing the one under it.

The top two-thirds of the second page depicted a ring cut into 80 equal sections along its circumference, plus one additional, narrower section, half the width of the others—a point of origin of sorts.

The sections were grouped into eight sets of ten sections, each section within a set featuring a unique symbol, forming a series of ten symbols repeated on each set.

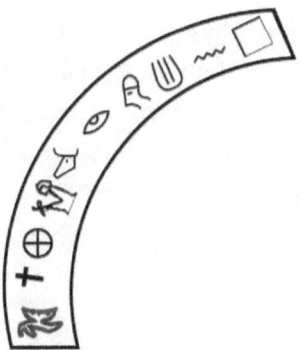

Immediately below the ring appeared a sequence of eight pairs of symbols, four of which having faded away beyond recognition.

✝ � *-faded-* 𐤍𐤍 *-* 𐤍𐤲 *-faded - faded -faded -* 𐤧✝

Doctor Lapierre was the first to share his observations. "The symbols appear to belong to some variant or extension of *Proto-Sinaitic* script." Proto-Sinaitic was a Middle Bronze Age script argued to be an alphabet and the ancestor of the Phoenician alphabet, from which nearly all modern alphabets descended. Due to the extreme scarcity of Proto-Siniatic signs, very little was known with certainty about the nature of the script.

"I would agree," said Dresdner. "Ten intriguing symbols:

"A square, or a house; □. Water, or a river; ∿. A hand; �. A head; 𝒜. An eye; ◉. An ox; 𝒟. The Sun; ⊕. A priest; 𝖬. A cross; ✝. And a *dragon*; 𝖭."

"The ring with its inscribed symbols is a *representation* of the top surface of the well in Amboise Forest, isn't it?" recognized Lapierre. "I haven't seen this in over eight years."

"Tatsächlich!" cried out Dresdner in German, confirming his friend's astute determination. "This schematic of the top view of the well was found on the back side of the Vitruvian Man drawing. It's therefore reasonable to postulate that there is a connection between Da Vinci's sketch and the symbols. Would anyone dare venture a *guess*?"

The men furiously examined the symbols, then the perfectly proportioned man, their stare moving rapidly and repeatedly from one page to the other. Dresdner sat back in silence and in peace, as though he had already solved the puzzle. Despite his previous efforts, he had not. He did, however, have a sneaking suspicion a mathematical perspective to the problem would propel the group to the brink of a solution. "Doctor Ramsay, you are a mathematical genius in your own right, isn't that correct?"

Ramsay radiated with equal measures of pride and embarrassment. "*Genius* is somewhat of an overestimation of my aptitudes. I would rather say—"

"What if we interpreted the symbols as *numbers*?" Dresdner cut him off short, sparing everyone the hardship of a self-gratifying dissertation on Ramsay's qualifications.

"I was just about to propose that," remarked Ramsay, "given the sequence of symbols (implicit numbers), and the algebraic data appearing under the string of symbols."

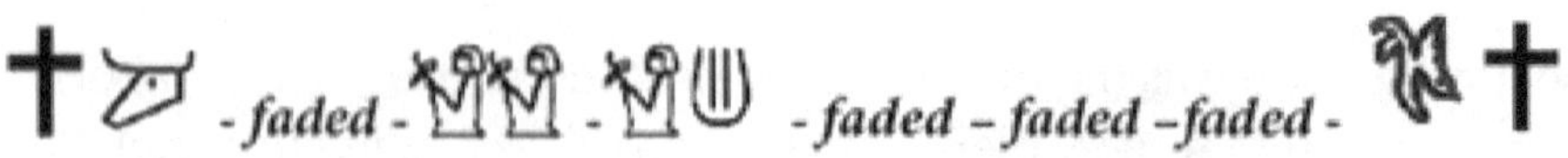

✝𝒟 *-faded-* 𝖬𝖬 *-* 𝖬III *-faded-faded-faded-* 𝖭✝

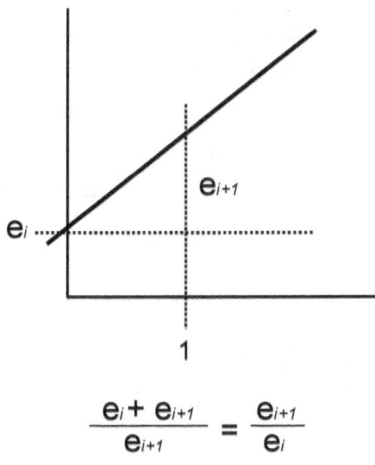

$$\frac{e_i + e_{i+1}}{e_{i+1}} = \frac{e_{i+1}}{e_i}$$

"It looks like *gobbledygook* to me," admitted Cardinal Nadeau. "I can make far more sense of sacred scriptures."

"Well, it's music to my ears," countered Ramsay. "Can you not hear the symphony of numbers?"

"Doctor…symbols as numbers, please," interjected Dresdner. "We don't have all day."

"Yes, yes, of course." The CAO of MIT resumed his dissection of the document, pushing his glasses up along the ridge of his nose. "The series of ten symbols, repeated on every set, can be viewed as natural numbers—ordinal numbers to be precise, indicating order:

"The symbol $\square$ represents **0**; $\sim\!\sim$ represents **1**; $\text{\small⫼}$, **2**; $\mathcal{R}$, **3**; $\oplus$, **4**; $\square$, **5**; $\oplus$, **6**; M , **7**; $\dagger$, **8**; , **9**."

"The decimal system, our everyday system of numbering, measuring and counting," said Lapierre.

Ramsay nodded. "Yes, and it has been used to devise a combination lock. I believe the sequence of eight paired symbols below the ring is, in fact, a combination that unlocks the well and activates a wormhole between it (entry point) and some other well (exit point), presumably situated at the place from which the child originated."

"I examined the well myself," said Lapierre; "quite thoroughly, and found no movable parts—nothing to indicate a combination mechanism."

"Perhaps there's a *camouflaged* unblocking system," submitted Ramsay, "not unlike child-proofing a bottle of prescription drugs."

"It must be damn well cloaked then," presumed Lapierre. "Hidden from sight, I would gather." Ramsay scrutinized the half-faded sequence of symbols further. "Converting symbols to numbers, we have: (8 and 5); (7 and 7); (7 and 2); and (9 and 8). But why pairs of numbers?" he mumbled. "Why, why…why not!" He pulled out a pen from his shirt pocket and began marking the ring, placing four X's on it.

"I've got it," he bellowed. "The first number in every pair is the rank of the set. The second number in every pair is the rank of the section within that set. For example, pair (8, 5) means set number 8, and section number 5 within set number 8." Ramsay raised his drawing of the ring, in view of all, pointing at the four X's he added to it. "Do you see?"

"I only see half the positions of a potential combination lock," chimed in Dumont, whose mind jumped into high gear, calculating the number of groupings of four positions the missing pairs of numbers could occupy. "Given the four unaccounted pairs, I estimate close to *1.3 million* possible combinations for activation of the wormhole. If testing one combination took a minute, testing all of them would take about two-and-a-half years."

Dumont grinned. "Anybody up to spending a long vacation in Amboise?" No one laughed.

Ramsay now directed his attention to the algebraic data, hoping to deduce the link between the data and the sequence of paired numbers—after all, they were both written using the elegant language of Mathematics. "I think it's worse than we think," he announced after a minute or so. "The combination we're searching for is *encrypted.*"

CHAPTER 50

Dumont snickered. "Not only are we missing four paired numbers, but those we have are also encrypted. We're basically screwed. Nice work Doc."

Ramsay barked back. "I said the situation was worse, not impossible. Everyone, look at the algebraic graph and only the graph. It's our first clue to solving the combination."

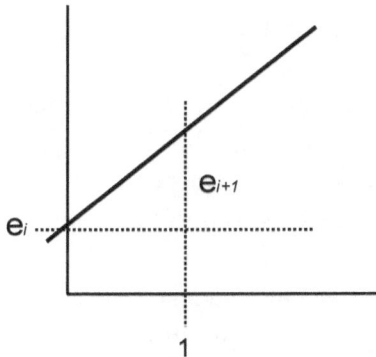

"It's a simple linear equation," surmised Lapierre.

A linear equation typically takes the form: $y = ax + b$, where a and b are constants, x is the *input variable*, and y is the *output variable*. For example, if we let $a = 2$, and $b = 3$, we then have the equation: $y = 2x + 3$. If you assign the value 1 to the input variable x, then the value of the output variable y would equal to: $y = 2$ *multiplied by 1, plus 3, equaling to 5*. When $x = 6$, $y = 2$ *multiplied by 6, plus 3, equaling 15*; and so on.

"It *is* a linear equation," agreed Ramsay. "In fact, it is not just a linear equation, but an *encryption formula* as well. In view of the notation on the graph, the equation should take the form: $C = (e_{i+1})P + (e_i)$, where (e_{i+1}) and (e_i) are constants, P is the input variable—in our case, an input *Plain-number (non-encrypted number)*, and C is the output variable—an output *Cypher-number (encrypted number)*."

Lapierre recalled the *known* pairs of numbers. "So, what you're saying is that the numbers (8 and 5); (7 and 7); (7 and 2); and (9 and 8) are the output Cypher-numbers."

Dresdner pointed is thumb upwards in agreement. "Behind those numbers hide other numbers that *are* part of the combination—numbers called Plain-numbers."

Dumont, for his part, instantly recognized the encryption method called *Affine Cipher*, where plain numbers are encrypted using a linear function, producing cypher numbers. "Julius Caesar often employed this encryption method to communicate with his generals," he recollected. "What I don't get is the kind of notation Da Vinci used, this i and $i+1$ scribbling." [*recall the notation of the constants* (e_{i+1}) *and* (e_i)]

Ramsay was quite familiar with this type of notation. "The notation is associated with infinite sequences of natural numbers (0; 1; 2; 3; 4; 5…). It specifies the positions of numbers in a sequence.

"The notations i and $i+1$ clearly indicate the two constants we're looking for are immediate neighbors in an infinite sequence of natural numbers."

"Would you care to provide us with an example of an infinite sequence?" requested Cardinal Nadeau. "Just so we're all at the same place."

"Of course." Ramsay wrote a sequence of numbers on the back of page 2 of his document, and exposed it to the group. It read: 1; 3; 5; 7; 9; 11; 13; 15; 17; 19; 21;…

"Those are odd numbers," said Nadeau.

"One of the simplest sequences of numbers known to Man," pointed out Ramsay. "And using Da Vinci's notation scheme on that sequence, we would have:

$$(e_1) = 1; \quad (e_2) = 3; \quad (e_3) = 5; \quad (e_4) = 7;$$
$$(e_5) = 9; \quad (e_6) = 11; \text{ and so on.}"$$

"Got it!" said Dumont, beaming with satisfaction. "In such a sequence, the numbers 5 and 7, for example, would be immediate neighbors, right?"

"Right on." Ramsay was pleased with the progress. "And, using your example, the linear equation/encryption formula $C = (e_{i+1})P + (e_i)$—or more precisely $C = (e_4)P + (e_3)$—would become $C = 7P + 5$.

"However, the odd number sequence is but one sequence among countless others," warned Ramsay. "In fact, the choices of logic to apply to sequences are infinitely diversified."

"So, how do we figure out the values of (e_{i+1}) and (e_i) if we don't know what sequence they belong to?" wondered Nadeau. "And even if we knew the sequence, which two neighboring numbers would we choose from that sequence?"

"We look towards our second clue," simply said Ramsay, pointing at the equation Da Vinci wrote below the algebraic graph:

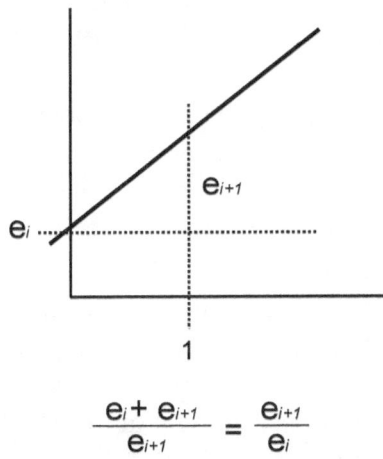

$$\frac{e_i + e_{i+1}}{e_{i+1}} = \frac{e_{i+1}}{e_i}$$

"Doctor Lapierre, you should get this," assumed Ramsay. "As an accomplished astro-physicist, it should be well within your *orbit*," baiting him further. "Orbits, Doctor, orbits."

Lapierre scratched his temple. "Orbits, hum…oh yes, orbits. I get it now. The ratio of the Earth's orbital period over that of Venus. *The Golden Ratio!*"

In mathematics and the arts, two quantities are in the *golden ratio* if the ratio of the sum of the two quantities to the larger quantity is equal to the ratio of the larger quantity to the smaller one. The golden ratio approximately equals 1.6180339887.

$$\frac{Smaller\,Quantity + Larger\,Quantity}{Larger\,Quantity} = \frac{Larger\,Quantity}{Smaller\,Quantity}$$

(The above equation describing the golden ratio is identical to Da Vinci's equation)

At least since the Renaissance, many artists and architects have proportioned their works to approximate the golden ratio—especially in the form of the golden rectangle, in which the ratio of the longer side to the shorter was the golden ratio—believing this proportion to be aesthetically pleasing. Mathematicians have studied the golden ratio because of its unique and interesting properties. The golden ratio was also used in the analysis of financial markets and related investment strategies.

"The Golden Ratio is the ticket to isolating the right sequence, gentlemen," said Ramsay with assurance. "Why? Because it is intimately related to the *Fibonacci* sequence of natural numbers, namely:

"0; 1; 1; 2; 3; 5; 8; 13; 21; 34; 55; 89; 144; 233; 377; 610; 987; 1597;...

"By definition, the first two Fibonacci numbers are 0 and 1, and each subsequent number is the sum of the previous two."

"Where's the intimate relationship with the golden ratio?" inquired Nadeau. "I know I'm lousy at Math, but even a pudding-head like me should be able to see a glimpse of it."

"Think about ratios," hinted Ramsay. Lapierre winked at him—he knew the answer, but abstained to extend the suspense. "Try dividing one Fibonacci number by the one preceding it. Oh, and by the way, skip the zero; dividing by zero will only get you in trouble." Ramsay took out a calculator and handed it to the Cardinal. "Do as many divisions as you want."

Nadeau began punching numbers.

"1 divided by 1 equals 1;

2 divided by 1 equals 2;

3 divided by 2 equals 1.5;

5 divided by 3 equals 1.67;

8 divided by 5 equals 1.6;

....

610 divided by 377 equals 1.618037135;

987 divided by 610 equals 1.618032787;

1597 divided by 987 equals 1.618034448..."

"That's enough." Ramsay swiftly retrieved his calculator. He was impressed by Nadeau's zeal. "In this instance, you seem to be more a man of *Calculus* than a man of the *cloth*." Nadeau dismissed his compliment with a wave of the hand.

"I see where this is going," interjected Cardinal Pubudu. "The divisions, the ratios, are converging towards the number 1.6180339887—the golden ratio."

"Precisely!" roared Ramsay, slamming his palm onto the table top. "Da Vinci utilized the golden ratio equation to lead us to the

Fibonacci sequence, two consecutive numbers of which are the constants for the encryption formula: $C = (e_{i+1})P + (e_i)$."

"But which two?" asked Nadeau, who found himself increasingly riveted by the nature and the progress of the analysis. "Are the Fibonacci numbers we're searching 1 and 1; or 2 and 1; or 3 and 2; or even 1597 and 987?"

"Should we proceed by trial and error?" mused Ramsay. "If the two numbers are far down the sequence, it would take days, if not weeks, to identify them."

"Well, Doctor Ramsay, what's the next step?" Nadeau's newfound eagerness shone brightly.

Ramsay tilted his head upwards, perhaps praying for an answer to fall from the skies, and arrested his attention on the small flag Nadeau had pinned to the crossbeam. He gazed at its emblem intently, hoping it would engender an extra provision of inspiration. Suddenly it did, to his amazement. "Am I that lucky of a bastard?" he thought.

CHAPTER 51

"Da Vinci was quite the trickster, gentlemen," said Ramsay. "As former Grand Master of our organization, he used its emblem as the third clue in establishing the combination. Can you extract two consecutive Fibonacci numbers from the emblem?" he quizzed Nadeau.

Nadeau surveyed the emblem from top to bottom. "Well, I clearly denote the number 8—the reference to the Circle of the Eight. And, hum…let's see…I can see..hum…"

"The second number is as obvious as the 8," hinted Ramsay. "Look below the 8."

Nadeau rose from his chair and planted himself inches away from the flag. "The *thirteenth apostle*," he cried out moments later, turning towards Ramsay. "There are 13 beads, each representing an apostle; and the thirteenth bead, the larger one, pertains to the preferred apostle, *The One Jesus Loved*. 13 is the number we're looking for."

"Bravo, Cardinal, well done. 8 and 13 are indeed two consecutive Fibonacci numbers." Ramsay wrote down the encryption formula, replacing (e_{i+1}) by 13, and (e_i) by 8, giving the formula:

$C = 13P + 8$, that is, Cypher-number equals to 13 multiplied by Plain-number, 8.

"Our task isn't done yet," cautioned Ramsay. "Please remember the paired numbers of the combination: (8, 5), (7, 7), (7, 2) and (9, 8), are encrypted. They're cypher-numbers—the output of the equation. What we need to do now is transform the encryption formula into a *decryption formula*, where the cypher-numbers become the input into the formula." Using what is called *Modular Arithmetic*, he began working out the transformation:

$C = 13P + 8$;

Subtracting 8 from both sides of the equation: $C - 8 = 13P + 8 - 8$, giving $C - 8 = 13P$;

Multiplying by 7 both sides of the equation: $7(C - 8) = 7 \cdot 13P$, giving $7C - 56 = 91P$.

In modular arithmetic base 10, (using base 10 since the decimal system was at the core of the symbol scheme), $56 = 6$, and $91 = 1$, substituting the numbers,

giving $7C - 6 = P$,

or $P = 7C - 6$.

"The decryption formula is $P = 7C - 6$," declared Ramsay. Using the formula, he converted the four pairs of cypher-numbers into plain-numbers—the real numbers to the combination.

(8, 5) became (0, 9);

(7, 7) became (3, 3);

(7, 2) became (3, 8);

(9, 8) became (7, 0).

Ramsay borrowed Nadeau's unmarked drawing of the ring, and wrote four X's onto it. "Set 0, position 9; set 3, position 3; set 3, position 8; and set 7, position 0. There, how does that look?" he asked the men, displaying the marked drawing.

"Looks good," said Dumont, "but still looks like half the combination."

"Not for long." Ramsay dropped his drawing on the table and snatched the Vitruvian Man sketch. "All we need to do is to *cut* through the clutter. And nothing cuts better than a sharp pair of *scissors*. Normand! Scissors!"

Ramsay cut the Da Vinci drawing along the circumference of the circle that encompassed the Vitruvian Man. "Da Vinci was truly a puzzle-virtuoso. He created very clever puzzles whose answers always dwelt at the nexus of simplicity. Often, all that was required to solve the puzzle was a keen sense of observation."

The circle Ramsay cut had a diameter of 12.4 inches, which he overlaid on the drawing of the ring. The inner diameter of the ring measured at 12.8 inches, allowing for a near-perfect fit of the Vitruvian Man circle inside the inner circle of the ring. "This is the fourth and most telltale clue to uncovering the entire combination," he tendered to the group for consummation of the solution.

Ramsay rotated the Vitruvian Man until four of the Man's eight members (4 arms and 4 legs) each pointed respectively to one of the known pairs of numbers. The left arm in the higher location coincided with the pair (0, 9), the set ranking as 0, and the position within set 0 ranking at 9. The left leg in the higher location matched the pair (3, 3); the left leg in the lower location matched the pair (3, 8); and the right arm in the higher location matched the pair (7, 0).

"Amazing!" exclaimed Dresdner. "The implication here is that the four remaining members point to the four missing pairs of numbers of the combination. Let's see what we have: the left arm in the lower location is pointing to pair (1, 3); the right leg in the lower location is pointing to (4, 1); the right leg in the higher location is pointing to pair (4, 6); and the right arm in the lower location is pointing to pair (6, 6)."

"Correct," said Ramsay, bathing in a perfect rapture that accompanied a great sense of accomplishment. "Reverting to symbols, the complete combination is therefore:

$$\square \,\text{𓀠}\text{𓏲}\,\text{-}\,\text{〜}\,\text{𓃀}\,\text{-}\,\text{𓃀}\,\text{𓃀}\,\text{-}\,\text{𓃀}\,\dagger\,\text{-}\,\text{𓂀}\,\text{〜}\,\text{-}\,\text{𓂀}\,\oplus\,\text{-}\,\oplus\,\oplus\,\text{-}\,\text{𓀠}\,\square$$

Lapierre jumped in jubilation as he marveled at the significance of the discovery. "Eight years ago, I thought I could calculate it, but miserably fell short. Today, its stands before me."

He walked to one of the windows, through which he could see the Sun setting over the horizon, and then looked up towards the stars. "Gentlemen, we now possess the address, so pack up your bags, we're traveling to Heaven, first-class."

CHAPTER 52

"Heaven can wait," said Dresdner. "There is still much work to do on Earth. Normand!"

"Yes Doctor." Normand raced from the kitchen, where he had been washing the dirty fruit-plates. "We're out of wine, sir."

Dresdner glared at him. "Are you stupid on purpose?"

"Only slow…or so my mother says. The remaining items, of course." He raced back to the kitchen and returned with a book and three items wrapped in wax paper, placing them one next to the other, on a long bench pressed against the wall, a few feet away from the table. "Ready, Doctor," depositing the book on the table.

"Hand me the item labeled *DEMON KISS*." Dresdner unwrapped the item, revealing an oil painting 18" by 32", depicting a demon embracing a woman.

"Just like the coded Vitruvian Man sketch, this painting, and the other two items on the bench, were also part of Colonel General Ernst Udet's hidden cache of stolen treasures."

"Is it Da Vinci's work?" asked Dumont. It seemed like a logical assumption to him since the Vitruvian Man was part of the lot.

"My appraisal of it confirms it is." Dresdner opened the book before him to page 383, and read: *'And they came, demons all, seeking the traitor. I cherished her more deeply than any other; she had beguiled me. The first demon embraced her naked soul, bestowing upon her the kiss of death; she would not be forgiven for her trespass against the Dark Lord. And our flight was barren of prosperity. She died in the burning light. I shall pursue her anew in the Kingdom of Heaven.'* This is a text from a copy of *The Notebooks of Leonardo Da Vinci*, published by Dover Publications. It references a painting, created in 1518—a year before his death, that was never found—until today."

Dumont found the text familiar. "It does coincide with an anecdote I heard during my monitoring duties. It spoke of an assault on Da Vinci and a young woman he was sheltering, by demons carrying tridents that shot lightning bolts." Dumont got closer to the painting. "What's that symbol on the demon's head...or helmet?"

The resourceful Dresdner screamed out, "Normand! Magnifying Glass!"

Dumont probed it closely. "That's what I thought. It's the same symbol as the one on the blue satin scarf the serial child killer always leaves behind; and it's the symbol the child saw on the demons' helmets, while under hypnosis."

Dresdner thought about it. "It could be that the biblical mother the child saw during hypnosis is *also* the woman Da Vinci sheltered; which means the demons who once guarded her and her child ended up hunting her down and killing her."

"A 2,000 year-old woman reappearing 1,500 years later as Da Vinci's girlfriend," said a clueless Dumont. "I'd love to have her genes."

"The plot thickens, my friends." Dresdner ordered Normand to hand him the item labeled *TLS-version one*, before tearing the paper off of it. "You all recognize the painting? It's a 32" by 17" version of the famous mural painting *The Last Supper*."

The Last Supper (*L'Ultima Cena*) was a 15th century mural painting created by Leonardo Da Vinci for his patron Duke Ludovico Sforza and his duchess Beatrice d'Este. It represented the scene of The Last Supper from the final days of Jesus as it was told in the Gospel of John 13:21, when Jesus announced that one of his Apostles would betray him.

The Last Supper measured 29 feet by 15 feet and covered an end wall of the dining hall at the monastery of Santa Maria delle Grazie in Milan, Italy. Leonardo began work on *The Last Supper* in 1495 and completed it in 1498.

"There's something *off* about the painting," noticed Nadeau. "John the Apostle, allegedly at Jesus' immediate right is different—manlier somehow."

Dresdner flipped through the pages of his book and placed it flatly in front of Nadeau, displaying a two-page spread of a photography of the mural painting. "Now, you should be able to compare."

"They're not the same!" shouted Nadeau in dismay. "Are you sure *this* oil painting was produced by Da Vinci?"

"There is absolutely *no* doubt," replied Dresdner. "In fact, I would submit the painting was created and *used* as a *template* for the mural painting, and that the mural was subsequently modified by Da Vinci, following the death of his mysterious consort, in 1518. Gentlemen, the person on Jesus' right could be *that* woman—the woman who stole his heart."

"Da Vinci chose to include *that* woman in that *specific* mural painting—and specifically *next to* Jesus—for a reason," conjectured Nadeau.

"And that would be?" queried Dumont.

Nadeau gawked at the men, one after the other, expecting them to take cognizance of his long-suppressed epiphany. The men remained cautious. "Do we finally dare entertain certainty rather than possibility?" he challenged them, his own heart beating faster than an army drum roll.

Dresdner smiled like a child in a candy store. He knew what Nadeau was thinking. "Go ahead, Cardinal, say it."

Doctor Lefoux whispered to Blanchard, "I was right. You all challenged *my* proof, but *I* was right."

Nadeau grabbed his head with both hands. "The woman next to Jesus *is* Maria Magdalena."

CHAPTER 53

Dresdner placed his hand over Nadeau's trembling one. "Let's not get ahead of ourselves. *Certainty* is quite a big word. Let us simply replace possibility with probability. The woman next to Jesus is *probably* Maria Magdalena."

Some writers and historians have indeed identified the person to Jesus' right not with the Apostle John, but with Maria Magdalena. Furthermore, they pointed out that the absence of a chalice in Leonardo's painting meant Leonardo somehow knew that Maria Magdalena was the actual *Holy Grail* and the bearer of Jesus' blood. They went on to explain that this idea was supported by the shape of the letter *"V"* that was formed by the bodily positions of Jesus and Maria, "V" being the symbol for the *sacred feminine*, a concept that assumed women, through the ability to bear children, were more sacred in God's eyes than men. The absence of the Apostle John in the painting was explained by knowing that John was also referred to as the *Disciple Jesus loved*, a code for Maria Magdalena.

"So, it seems we have many possible scenarios," surmised Dumont. "The woman in the painting may or may not be Maria Magdalena; may or may not be Da Vinci's girlfriend; may or may not be the woman the child saw during hypnosis. She may well be all these things, or she may be *none* of these things."

"In identifying this woman, I count eight possible scenarios," interjected Ramsay.

"When interpreting the portrait of history, nothing is black or white; just countless brushstrokes of shades of gray." Dresdner screamed once again. "Normand!" Let's move on. Get the last one, and take the paper off, I'm tired."

"Yes, Doctor." Normand handed him the last item on the bench, after quickly ripping the paper off and revealing yet another version of The Last Supper—this one measuring 19" by 10", and enclosed in a protective wood and glass casing.

"I believe this painting was created as Da Vinci drew nearer and nearer to death," contended Dresdner, who gently set it down on the table.

"It's identical to the mural painting," noted Nadeau after meticulously examining it through the glass panel, which pressed against the canvas.

"Visually it is," said Dresdner, "but technically it is not. Normand!" he screamed for the last time. He was going to miss hounding his half-witted great-grandson-in-law. "Bring me the board."

Normand scampered into the kitchen yet again and came back with a giant cardboard, about 6 feet by 3 feet, placing it upright on the bench.

"This is a blow-up of the painting I used to analyze its details and intricacies," informed Dresdner. "To verify authenticity—or forgery—and to detect anomalies, we divided the painting into 2.5" by 2.5" sections. Each brushstroke within each section was compared to a computer model devised from scans of twenty-two unquestionably authentic Da Vinci works—a training database, if you will, for Da Vinci's unique style. The strokes were examined based on their length and steadiness."

"Looks all the same style to me," admitted Dumont, disappointed his keen FBI eye couldn't detect any incongruities.

"Look at the sections enclosing the woman's upper body," suggested Dresdner to Dumont.

"I see what you mean," replied Dumont. "There are a lot more cracks and creases in that area than anywhere else on the painting. Some of it almost seems to be peeling off."

"That's because the area in question was painted with oil, then covered over with an acrylic resin," pointed out Dresdner; "two very different types of paint. The vehicle and binder of oil paints is linseed oil, whereas water serves as the vehicle for a suspension of acrylic polymer that is the binder in acrylic paint. That's why oil paint is said to be "oil-based", while acrylic paint is "water-based"".

"So what?" Dumont didn't understand the issue; neither did the other men.

Dresdner was patient. "Oil paint takes a long time to dry, while acrylic paint dries very rapidly. In fact, an oil painting takes over 9 months to dry, and even then, there is still moisture trapped within the paint. So, applying acrylic paint over dried oil paint—even after years of dryness—would eventually cause the acrylic paint to crack and peel. And, while applying several layers of varnish might retard the degradation, as was the case here, it would not stop it."

"That sounds like a rookie mistake, especially for someone as accomplished as Da Vinci," remarked Dumont.

"He couldn't have applied the acrylic paint," announced Dresdner, "since I suspect he was dead at the time. And, had he been alive, he would never have allowed anyone to defile one of his works so grotesquely."

Dumont took a second look at the blow-up of the area painted with acrylic paint. "So, who could have done it?"

"His favorite pupil, *Francesco Melzi*, did," argued Dresdner. "No doubt about it."

Francesco Melzi was an Italian painter, and favorite assistant and pupil of Da Vinci. The son of a Milanese noble family, Melzi joined the household of Leonardo da Vinci in 1506. Melzi accompanied Leonardo to France in 1517. As a painter, Melzi worked closely with and for Leonardo, and he was quite gifted. In fact, some works which, during the nineteenth century, were attributed to Leonardo were now ascribed to Melzi.

Upon Leonardo's death, Melzi inherited the artistic and scientific works, manuscripts, and collections of Leonardo, and had henceforth faithfully administered the estate. Melzi wrote to Leonardo's brothers to notify them of his death, and in the letter, he described Leonardo's love for his pupils as *sviscerato e ardentissimo amore, a selfless and incandescent love.*

Dresdner placed his finger on one of the acrylic-painted squares. "Upon close inspection, you'll notice that the brushstrokes are longer and steadier than Da Vinci's. They *perfectly* match Melzi's style."

"Why would Melzi, favored by Da Vinci above all others, do this?" queried Dumont.

"To protect Da Vinci's shining reputation and legacy from secular controversy and heresy," retorted Dresdner. "There is something behind the acrylic paint that is so contentious Melzi felt compelled to conceal it."

"Why not have used oil paint instead?" wondered Dumont. "That way the concealment would be permanent."

Dresdner ruminated upon it. "I believe Melzi thought that there would come a day, centuries later, when people would tolerate, if not embrace, the notion hidden behind the patch of acrylic paint. He therefore wanted the patch to be temporary and removable."

"*C'est de la merde, votre bande,*" suddenly said an uncharacteristically vulgar Normand as he walked to the main window next to the front door, and lit up a cigarette.

"Our gang is bullshit?" shouted Nadeau. "One more insult like that and your probationary period with the organization will end badly." Nadeau felt abashed at his secretary's unexpected boorish behavior.

"You think this is wrongful conduct?" said Normand in a spiteful tone. "This is a trifle compared to murder."

Nadeau's choler turned to consternation. "What in heavens has gotten into you? And what are you talking about?"

"*I* killed your previous secretary—your dear nephew," stoically confessed Normand. "Since I was next in line for the secretary job, it seemed like the most expeditious way of infiltrating your band of dissident renegades."

Nadeau was thunderstruck. "Who the hell do you work for? Tell me!"

"*Non nobis Domine, non nobis, sed nomini tuo da gloriam (Not to us Lord, not to us, but to Your Name give the glory),*" clamored Normand as he pulled out a *Mateba Autorevolver*.

"The pledge of the *Knights Templar*!" Nadeau's face turned white when he heard the motto, and whiter when he saw the gun.

The *Knights Templar*, or the *Order of the Temple* (*Ordre du Temple* or *Templiers*) were among the most famous of the Western Christian military orders.

Officially endorsed by the Catholic Church around 1129, the Order became a favored charity throughout Christendom, and grew rapidly in membership and power. Templar Knights, in their distinctive white mantles with a red cross, were among the most skilled fighting units of the Crusades—a series of religiously sanctioned military campaigns, called by the Pope and the Church of Rome, whose main goal was the restoration of Christian control over the Holy Land.

The Order was later suppressed by the same Church of Rome it protected, under the hands of a greedy French King, Philip IV, controlling a weak French Pope, Clement V.

"Take your gun out of its holster and throw it over here," Normand commanded Dumont, who failed to comply deliberately. "Do it now, FBI man, or I kill Nadeau."

Dumont finally obeyed. He crouched and slid his weapon towards Normand, who shoved in the back of his pants.

"Thank you, Dumont," wept Nadeau, scared out of his wits. "We're all pacifists," he told Normand. "No one here is a danger to—"

A bullet suddenly sped through the air, ending its course in Nadeau's parietal lobe. The Cardinal fell off his chair and slumped onto the floor, quite dead. The Circle of the Eight—now down to seven—was frozen with fear, with the exception of Blanchard, who appeared ready to pounce on the shooter.

"You fucker!" cried out Dumont, who took a few steps towards Normand.

"Make my day," replied Normand, directing his gun at Dumont. "I never had myself an FBI man before; it's tempting."

"*Eight* men against one," observed Dumont. "Clearly, we have the advantage. You might get one more of us, or maybe two, but we *will* kill you."

"I suppose I need to even the odds a little bit," contemplated Normand, who threw the remainder of his cigarette on the floor, raised his left hand at eye level, and clenched his fist. Almost instantly two men emerged from the darkness outside, and barged in the cabin, one through the front door, the other through the back door. "The cavalry always arrives in the nick of time."

The two men were wearing Italian army camouflage suit fatigues, covered in green and brown patches, and emblazoned on the right shoulder with a white circular patch adorned with a red cross, the crest of the Templar Knights. They both wielded deadly FN-P90 submachine guns—and they looked *serious*.

CHAPTER 54

Dumont remained still, studying the type of weapon the soldiers carried. "Impressive, and an expensive arsenal for an underground Holy militia. I suppose the Pope let you dip into the Vatican coffers."

Normand shrugged his shoulders playfully, avoiding an answer.

Cardinal Romeo, however, mustered the courage to provide one. "Many Popes of yesteryears supported the cause of the Knights Templar; and the soldiers supported their reigns with honor. A Templar Knight is truly a fearless knight, and secure on every side, his soul protected by the armor of faith, and his body by the armor of steel. He is thus doubly armed, and need fear neither demons nor men. If a *true* Templar ever lived today, it would not be you." Romeo spat on the floor in disgust.

"Oh, but we are Templars," rebutted Normand; "and killing heretics is our most sacred duty—a duty sanctioned by a very resolute *Pope*. You should be honored; you're at the top of his hit list."

"Pope Benvenuto may often be an inflexible man, but he is no murderer," insisted Romeo.

"All Nazis are murderers, in one way or another," said Normand. "Don't be fooled by the white skullcap and the nice dress; the killer instinct is very much there."

Pope Benvenuto was German and his real name was *Carsten Maximilian Reiniger*. As a boy subjected to the demands of the Nazi regime, he attended the elementary school in *Aschau am Inn* for several years. Following his 14th birthday in 1941, Reiniger was conscripted into the Hitler Youth. And in 1943, he was drafted into the German anti-aircraft corps as *Luftwaffenhelfer (child soldier)*, and then trained in the German infantry.

Not many people knew of these events, but Normand did—and it was only the tip of the iceberg. He knew how *deep* the iceberg really went.

Normand, quite full of himself, rotated his aim 45 degrees away from

Dumont, now pointing his revolver at Dresdner. "Tell Romeo, and the others, what you know about Reiniger. I'll kill you if you don't."

"You'll kill me no matter what," replied Dresdner.

Normand grinned. "I'll kill somebody else if you don't loosen those lips."

Dresdner acquiesced and confessed to a ghastly story. "Reiniger and I spent three months in an American POW camp in 1945. I was twenty-two and he was only eighteen, and looked towards me for guidance and protection. We were the youngest of the camp. One night, while we sat on the balcony of our barrack, an American soldier we had befriended gave us a bottle of moonshine. He told us to drink it quickly since curfew was almost upon us.

"In no time, we became heavily inebriated. Reiniger then began telling me of his tour of duty in the Hitler Youth. As part of his initiation, he had to prove his devotion by ending an unworthy life. While he refused to kill of his own hands, he did divulge the place where one of his cousins, a fourteen-year-old boy with Down syndrome, was being hid. The boy was found and was taken away by the Nazis and killed as part of the *Aktion T4* campaign of *Nazi eugenics*."

Nazi eugenics were Nazi Germany's racially-based social policies placing the improvement of the Aryan race through eugenics at the center of its concerns. Those humans the Nazis identified as *life unworthy of life (Lebensunwertes Leben)* included criminals, degenerates, dissidents, the feeble-minded, homosexuals, the insane and the weak, all marked for elimination from the chain of heredity. More than 400,000 people were sterilized against their will, while 70,000 more were killed under Action T4, a *euthanasia* program.

"How can you say such things about the Pope?" shouted Romeo to Dresdner. "We may not agree with him on several matters, but that is no reason to sully his good name."

Normand waved his gun up and down as a gesture to continue the damaging account.

Dresdner went on reluctantly. "Reiniger also told me that, as part of his infantry training, he had to practice shooting moving targets. He had just turned eighteen, and his *commandant* informed him that it was time to become a real soldier.

"A Jewish man was ordered to run across the field. The commandant put a gun to Reiniger's head and said he had to choose who would die. Reiniger aimed his firearm and shot the man through the heart. A Jewish woman and her ten-year old son were then ordered to run across the field as well. He shot her through the neck, and the boy through the head.

"His gruesome tale ended, a smiling Reiniger came to me. He said shooting *sub-humans* was a cathartic experience, an emotional purging of sorts; something he never expected to feel. I was appalled and so angry at the boy-turned-sadist that I never spoke to him again."

"And there it is," exclaimed Normand. "Reiniger was never an unenthusiastic member of the Nazi army, and nor did he ever desert back to his family's home in *Traunstein*, as many would attest. He was as indoctrinated and as conditioned as any other young German soldier. And now, this Nazi rules Christendom. He is a man to be feared and obeyed."

Dumont appeared unswayed--he had faced far more terrifying men in the line of duty. "What's your real interest in all of this?" What have these men done to you or the Pope?"

"They offend me and they offend the Pope. As devout Christians, we cannot let them fester and multiply," retorted Normand. "They threaten the very tenets of our faith."

"All I see here is a ploy to maintain power," said Dumont. "Being the instrument of the Church of Rome—the valiant Knights Templar—must be very *lucrative*. What ever happened to the *Templar Oath of Poverty*?"

"Protecting the faith doesn't come cheap," laughed Normand, who replaced his revolver in its holster. "Now, enough about my *employer*. Let's get back to business." The two armed soldiers moved closer, while the traitor picked up all the copies of the Vitruvian Man document, and walked to the stone fireplace right next to the kitchen area, depositing the stack over a pile of wood, and igniting it with his lighter. "You don't have to worry about the original document; I've taken care of that."

At the sight of destruction of such paradigm-shifting information, Dresdner lost it and rushed at Normand. "You ignorant fool!" He was immediately pelted by a dozen machine gun bullets, and crashed to the ground.

Normand stared at Dresdner's prostrate body. "What a shame." He then pulled out a knife and cut out the canvasses of the *Demon Kiss* and *Last Supper-version one* paintings, throwing them into the burning fireplace.

As Normand crouched before the fireplace, enjoying the heat of the fire, and reveling in his superiority, Dumont noticed the handle of his own gun sticking out of the back of Normand's pants. He glanced at Blanchard, who gave him a quick nod, hoping the ex-special agent of Interpol was not only signaling his approval to act, but was also indicating he had a weapon of his own. In a flash, Dumont barreled towards Normand, while the two soldiers instinctively aimed their machine guns at him.

Simultaneously, Blanchard pulled out his weapon and shot six rounds, three at each soldier, emptying his gun. One soldier collapsed and died instantly, a bullet to the head. The other, wounded, fired randomly at the group. Blanchard had just enough time to deck below the table. Romeo and Pubudu were shot dead, while Lefoux and Lapierre were shot to the arm, and Ramsay to the thigh.

Dumont had now tackled Normand to the ground. He grabbed his revolver, twisted his upper body a full 180 degrees, and shot the injured soldier in the head. In that same moment, Normand kicked Dumont off balance, who dropped his gun, and pulled out his own weapon. The men struggled, somehow both getting up. Dumont latched on Normand's gun, and violently pushed his assailant over the table and onto the glass-framed painting, shattering the glass. Both men then rolled over and fell to the floor.

As for Blanchard, he wasted no time. He picked up Dumont's weapon from the ground, and rushed to Dumont's aid. Without hesitation, he pressed the barrel of the gun against Normand's temple and fired. The blood spat over Dumont's face.

"Thanks for the shower," said a groggy Dumont, who clumsily got back up. "What's the damage?"

"Lefoux, Lapierre and Ramsay are the only ones who made it, present law enforcement excepted," replied Blanchard.

Shaken and disoriented, Lefoux, Lapierre and Ramsay wept in relief. The only graphic violence they had ever witnessed before today came from cable television.

"We need to call an ambulance," insisted Dumont.

"No!" sternly replied Blanchard. "I'll take care of everything. As for you, get as far away from this place as you can." He grabbed Dumont by the arm. "This is not finished, not by a long shot."

Dumont headed for the front door and just as he reached the threshold he stopped in his tracks and turned around. "I have to know."

"Go ahead, but be quick about it," said Blanchard as he examined the wounded. "Dresdner was going to do it anyway."

Dumont walked back to the table and pulled the bastardized painting towards him. He removed the larger shards of broken glass, and swept the rest to the side. "*What* are you hiding, mystery girl?" he whispered to himself as he stared at the woman to Jesus' right.

Blanchard handed him Normand's knife. "This should help."

Dumont peeled off two large chunks of acrylic paint, and then began carefully shaving off the rest until he could clearly make out what had been shrouded by myriad brushstrokes of imposturous paint. "Holy Moses!" he suddenly cried out in astonishment.

What he saw, he never would have expected to see in such explicit and manifest fashion: a *baby boy* nestled in the woman's arms, sucking milk from her breasts.

CHAPTER 55

Present day; New York.

"Does anyone know what a molecule is?"
asked the 6th grade chemistry teacher during class at Rocky Point Middle School, in Rocky Point, New York.

Theon E. Rex, now a stout boy of twelve, sitting in the first row, raised his hand. Like all students in the room, this was Theon's first year at Rocky Point Middle School. In fact, it was only his eighth week at the school, and already, he had built a solid reputation as the brilliant class nerd—something that had not gone unnoticed by the academically-challenged class bullies.

"The *freak* has the answer again," said one of the hooligans in a spiteful manner. "You're making us look real bad, ass-kisser."

"You're doing just fine on your own," rebutted Theon, who closed his raised hand, with the exception of his middle finger. The gesture was quite clear in meaning.

"Gentlemen, there will be no insults or obscenities in my class," firmly proclaimed the teacher. "If you dare pursue the matter, detention awaits you both."

"I'll see you *later*, Rex," slipped in the bully before resuming his sulky silence.

The teacher frowned at the ill-tempered boy, but refrained from any further threatening declarations. "Go ahead, Theon, tell us—*all* of us—what a molecule is."

Theon, unconcerned and unafraid, shot a cocky and ostentatious smile at the bully before answering. "A molecule is a combination of atomic nuclei and electrons sufficiently stable to possess observable properties."

"And what would be one of the most prevalent, stable molecules?" asked the teacher. "One that is vital to all life on Earth."

"That would be H_2O, water," replied Theon.

"Go on," urged the teacher.

Theon was only happy to oblige. He enjoyed any opportunity to shine in public. "Well, in water, each of two hydrogen nuclei is bound to one central oxygen atom by a pair of electrons that are shared between them; chemists call this shared electron pair a *covalent chemical bond.*

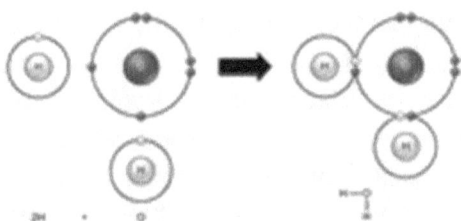

"H_2O is in effect a super-molecule—a sort of *holy triad*—far greater in power than the sum of its parts."

"I appreciate your *stylish* analogy," said a somewhat perplexed teacher; "the father, the son, and the Holy Spirit; but there is no room for theology in chemistry."

"That's how I see it," remarked Theon, quite comfortable with his illustration of chemical sanctity. "That's how I *sense* it."

The teacher had been advised beforehand of Theon's singular quirks and twists, but this mindset was beyond anything she'd confronted before. "Perhaps a bit of tutoring after class might broaden your scope of—"

The school bell suddenly rang loudly. Theon did not wait for her to finish, not the bit interested in tutoring.

He grabbed his school bag and books, and ran out the room, quite satisfied with himself. In fact, he often considered himself an observer looking in and onto the world, experiencing things far differently and more clearly than anybody else. This was *his* gift—or his *curse.*

He trotted to his locker, one of 120 located along both walls of the main corridor, and slammed it open after swiftly unlocking it. A photograph of his 8-year old sister Maya, siting on Amadeo Da Verdi's knee, was crudely taped to the inside of the locker door—they were his best friends. He would have added a picture of his mother had it not been for his fear of being called a *Momma's boy*. The nickname *Teacher's pet* was already quite enough to handle.

As he swung his bag to the bottom of the locker, and placed his books on the shelf, he looked forward to his weekend stay at Uncle Bill's place in Forest Hills, Washington D.C.

Uncle Bill, or as Theon called him: *The Master of Mars*—because of his work at NASA—promised his nephew a day of cycling and bird-watching at Rock Creek Park, bordering the East side of Forest Hills. He imagined the aggregation of intoxicating smells from the multi-colored fallen oak leaves, and from the crisp Fall sweeping the entire park.

Even the horse manure along the equestrian trails he and his uncle usually traveled had an especially balsamic scent that lost more and more of its offensive quality as they cycled deeper into the forest. But this was not the case with the rancid odor that flowed from the mouth of the most terrifying bully of Rocky Point Middle School. The more he breathed on the back of Theon's neck, the more Theon's nostrils were assaulted by a putrid fetor akin to a basketful of rotten eggs.

"Hey *Spock*!" snarled Joey the bully. "Didn't I see you in Star Trek; Captain Kirk's *bitch*, I think?"

"Didn't I see you in Animal Kingdom?" sharply replied Theon as he turned around to face his would-be oppressor. "You were the dim-witted gorilla drinking his own *piss*, I believe?"

"Them are fightin' words, freak," said one of the other two tough guys, standing behind Joey.

"*Those* are fighting words," mockingly corrected Theon. "Kindergarten is offering extra classes. You should consider it."

"Not just an ass-kisser, but also a smart-ass," remarked Joey. "I've had my eyes on you for a while, Rex; thinking about cutting off those pointed ears of yours. They would make a nice addition to my sideshow collection."

As usual, Theon's bravery far outweighed his trepidation, believing he could back out at any time. He knew this was a mistake, but still opted to aggravate the confrontation. "How could I possibly compete with the jewel of your collection: your revolting elephant-man face." Theon moved a step closer, his gaze never leaving Joey's. That, also, was a mistake.

Without warning, Joey's fist flew like lightning and crushed Theon's stomach. "You're right, Rex; I am an animal—and animals give no quarter to their prey."

Theon took the hit and did not waiver at all. He smiled instead. "Do you know what Bruce Banner always told his enemies?" referencing the comic book character who transformed into the monstrous *Hulk* when under extreme duress. "He told them that: *"you wouldn't like me when I'm angry."*

The bullies all laughed, like foolish pedestrians unaware of the out-of-control truck hurtling towards them. "You should be more concerned with *my* anger," barked Joey before throwing Theon to the ground.

"Keep control...keep control," kept repeating Theon, recalling a promise to his mother. "Made a promise to Mom, no fighting." He rose to his knees. His departure now seemed opportune.

"Mommy doesn't want you to fight," said an overconfident Joey as he towered over Theon's body. "Well, it's a bit late for that." He grabbed Theon by the hair, intensifying his rant. "I always wondered why you never took a shower with the boys after gym class. You got some other freak show hiding under those cloths?"

"Waste him, man! Do it!" encouraged one of Joey's buddies. "Or everybody's gonna know you backed down in front of freakazoid here."

Joey thought about it, but his pause only lasted three seconds. "Let's have us a good show first," he announced brashly, releasing his victim's hair before gripping his shirt and pulling it off. "What the fuck is that?" noticing the extraneous muscle fibers traversing Theon's back from top to bottom.

Taken aback, Joey did the only that came to mind, the only thing he was programmed to do most of his turbulent life: he hit! Both fists came down like guided missiles, hitting the frightening anomaly.

The searing pain cut across Theon's whole body, as if the two abnormal muscle nassels, violently stimulated in concert, became the hub of his entire nervous system. He screamed so stridently, the shrilling sound carried through every corridor in the school. Every student stopped what he was doing, startled and looking at each other for answers.

Theon's head tilted down, revealing three symbols on the back of his neck, which burnt like gun powder. The flames from each symbol touched each other, pulling the symbols closer together, from three-quarters of an inch apart to half an inch apart, and they turned dark as coal.

Joey stumbled backwards onto his accomplishes, and all three tumbled to the ground. The students in the immediate vicinity ran away, followed by Joey's friends. But the show, as Joey had put it, had just begun. The unnatural muscle strands each split into two, forming some sort of gruesome upper and lower arm. The bone wrapped in the muscle fibers became exposed, but was quickly covered with new muscle, tendon and nerve growths.

While the upper-arm portion remained rooted to the back, the lower-arm was mobile, moving up and down within the plane defined by the stationary upper-arm. At the free extremity of the lower-arm, five tiny digits sprouted.

Theon, now crouching like a tiger on a hunt, raised his head and turned it towards a frozen Joey, his eyes gorged with blood and with the lust of the killer. "I told you not to make me angry," he screamed in regret mingled in with anticipation, before leaping onto a terrified Joey.

His strength multiplied many folds, Theon raised his fist above Joey's head. "No one will miss such a menial, stupid creature. Now, let's have us a *real* show!"

"Don't move, kid!" suddenly shouted a Washington police officer assigned to perform several rounds of the school every day. He stood fifteen feet away from Theon, facing him, his hand over his weapon still nestled in his unbuttoned holster. From his vantage point, he could not see what protruded from Theon's back.

"Why must I always be the one to back off?" shouted Theon. "No one looks after *my* back." Theon glared deeply into the officer's eyes, infuriated and conflicted. "Where were you five minutes ago? Where the hell were *you*?"

The police officer immediately recognized Joey the trouble maker, having dealt with him several times in the past. "I promise you he won't bother you again. I'll talk to the Principal myself and see to it he's punished severely."

Theon's fist trembled, wanting so much to smash the bully's face, but he kept it at bay. He thought about his mother, and how distressed and saddened she would be if he broke his promise to her. But, on the other hand, he yearned for retribution against the people who persecuted him, and against the universe, which, evidently during a bout of puerile frivolity, made him the way he was.

Theon finally made his choice. He began to calm down, his eyes cleared up, and his fist came down peacefully. He stood up and signaled the officer to approach. "He's all yours."

The officer helped Joey up, his weeping quickly turned to forebodings of dire straits. "He's not human! He's a monster, a demon; and he'll come after me!"

Theon put his shirt back on—the strange extrusions on his back had receded, resuming their original form. Joey was at a loss to understand. "I tell you, he's a freak, look at him!" Joey screamed more vigorously.

"Shut your trap," ordered the officer, who pushed Joey forward, towards the Principal's office, while Theon walked freely next to the bully.

As the two boys turned onto the next corridor, briefly out of sight of the officer, Theon whispered into Joey's ear: "You had better confess your sins sooner than later because you've awaken the *beast*. It will come for you."

Theon's prophetic warning struck greater fear in Joey; and the ease with which it was delivered stunned even Theon—he realized he had crossed a new line.

CHAPTER 56

Present day; New York.

"I have new data regarding Theon," announced the doctor at the New York University Langone Medical Center. "Let's look at the brain scan first," he told Cameron and Sarah.

"The prefrontal cortex, which helps with focus, decision-making, organization, and the control of emotional impulses, appears to be overactive. The same can be said about the temporal lobes, which drive memory, cognition, and language understanding, the combined effect of which translates into a boy both brilliant and temperamental. In short, your son is a *smart bomb*."

Sarah was perplexed. "The doctor who first examined Theon as a baby never told us this."

"It's not surprising," said the doctor. "The original brain scan revealed nothing out of the ordinary. The genome analyses, on the other hand, original and new one, have both revealed extraordinary anomalies—anomalies that have progressed in a direction that I can qualify as neither better nor worse." The doctor put both gene charts on the table, one next to the other. "Do you see what I mean?"

"I'm a lawman," said an irked Cameron, "and my wife is a cartoonist."

"Sorry, folks, I read this stuff like I read the newspaper." The doctor pointed to a few areas on the first chart, then on the second. "The extraneous chromosomal material from chromosomes 1, 11 and 21 has relocated. The material from 1 has attached itself to chromosome 12; the material from 11 has attached itself to 13; and most amazingly, the material from 21 has moved to a location between chromosomes 12 and 13 without attachment—it is essentially free-floating. Furthermore, it is in the process of duplication."

"So, what does this all mean?" queried a frustrated Sarah.

The doctor grabbed his chin and puckered his lips, musing over an answer. "This is wild speculation, but if I was compelled to explain, I would say the extraneous chromosomal material is moving towards each other in order to merge. I predict the extra material currently on chromosomes 12 and 13 will eventually detach and become free-floating. And when the currently free-floating material between 12 and 13 duplicates, one copy will form a pair with the material from 12, the other copy will pair with the material from 13. In effect, your son will graduate from a human being coded by 23 pairs of chromosomes to a *super-being* coded by *25* pairs of chromosomes."

"You only speak of cause and not effect," irascibly cried Cameron. "There are the ears, and the arms on his back, growing and receding at will. What else is there? What is our son becoming?"

"I fear you misunderstand," said the doctor. "The physical manifestations stem from your son's *original* genome—mutated genes most likely, and possibly activated by the extra DNA. The additional chromosomes themselves, which are in irreversible formation, are something else totally, the net effect of which I dare not even guess. There is *no* precedence in medical history."

"What of the three marks on the back of his neck?" vigorously rebutted Cameron, while his wife held her head in anguish. "They're moving closer together, just like the extra genetic material. Surely they offer some clue."

"Perhaps they do," entertained the doctor, deciding to dwell beyond the ambit of medical science and into mysticism. "Your son may be the next step in Man's evolution—perhaps a godlike being capable of ushering in a new level of consciousness. God may be letting us know this by the marks on his neck, the *junction* between body and soul."

"We used to believe God played a part in this," said Cameron. "This is not God's work, even on his worst day. It's someone else's entirely."

"Would you love your son any less if you knew who the true *artisan* of his existence was?" queried the doctor with all the seriousness in the world.

"No, we would not," instantly answered Sarah, wiping her tears. "He is *our* son, no matter what happens."

"Then go with God." The doctor led them to the door. "And remember: *One who loves the vase loves also what is inside.*"

Had the doctor known the truth about Theon, he would have been wiser to dispense the proverb: *Love is like Heaven, but it can hurt like Hell.* And nothing hurts more than Hell.

CHAPTER 57

Present day; Rome, Italy.

To the world you may have been just someone.
To me you were the world and the only one.
You watch me evermore from the great above.
And as I stumble and as I fall.
You raise me and restore me with all your love.
And tell me to always stand tall."

The epitaph on Flora Da Verdi's tombstone had been written by a man full of regrets, who desperately sought his mother's forgiveness for his sins.

"Mother, I thought I was doing the Lord's work. I thought I was protecting his Son's legacy, through secrecy and through manipulation." Amadeo Da Verdi, the only child of Flora Da Verdi, placed a rose on his mother's grave in *Cimitero del Verano*, a cemetery in Rome, and wept. "When I was asked to commit the unthinkable, I saw the errors of my ways, and wanted to tell you of the son you thought you had; and of the son he had become as you released your last breath in his glaring absence."

"Very touching and heartfelt, Signor Da Verdi," said a man in a dark elegant suit and glasses, approaching Flora Da Verdi's grave. "The pope shares in your grief and would like to offer his condolences…*in person*."

"The pope and I have nothing to say to each other," replied Amadeo whose irritation at the intrusion rivaled his misery.

The man placed himself right next to the tombstone. "The pope would remind you that it is not advisable to deny a man to whom you are so indebted—especially if that man is the most powerful religious leader in the world."

"That's a matter of interpretation," rebutted Amadeo. "And looking at you, you should know that the suit—or the *robe*—doesn't make the man."

"Nevertheless, he wishes a consultation with his former *agent*, his *Seeker*," insisted the man, "to renew ties as it were."

Amadeo glared at him. "Get out of here and let me mourn in peace."

"My orders prevent it," remarked the intractable man. "I'm to bring you to him...in whichever state necessary."

Amadeo knew what this man was capable of. After all, he used to be like him. "I suppose you'll have to frisk me first?"

"Not necessary, *old man*." He invited Amadeo to follow him to the limousine parked a few hundred yards away. The car had been washed recently and was in pristine condition.

"Only the best for the best," mocked Amadeo as he stepped into the back of the car.

"I wouldn't know," replied the man before slamming the car door shut. "You're just *ancient* history to me."

CHAPTER 58

"Please take a seat, Amadeo," invited Pope Benvenuto (born Carsten Maximilian Reiniger). "I was so pleased to learn of your visit to Rome. It saved me much time and effort."

"God forbid you would make an extra effort, Reiniger," harshly replied Amadeo as he scanned the pope's office. "Where's your statue of the Virgin Mary? Couldn't stand her accusatory gaze anymore?"

"*Your* incriminatory look is quite enough," jokingly said the pope, "and quite sanctimonious." The pope picked up a remote control device from his desk and activated a recording on the giant LCD screen affixed to the wall. Amadeo immediately recognized the man on the recording: the 35th President of the United States, *John F. Kennedy*. And he was in the midst of his 1961 inaugural address to the nation.

"...the belief that the rights of man come not from the generosity of the state, but from the hand of God," Kennedy stated emphatically.

Reiniger advanced the recording to the next salient segment, cringing as he did so. "Ask not what your country can do for you—ask what you can do for your country," Kennedy said, finally ending with: "…let us go forth to lead the land we love, asking His blessing and His help, but knowing that here on earth God's work must truly be our own."

"I'm quite familiar with Kennedy's speech," remarked an impatient Amadeo. "I was there when he made it."

"You were *more* than there." Reiniger slammed the remote onto the desk. "You were there to ascertain the threat. *And*, you were under orders from pope Paul VI, the man who provided your ill mother with the best care money could buy; and you betrayed him."

"The price was simply too high," Amadeo said in his defense, now regretting his agreement to meet. He was finally going to hear the whole sordid story—a story best forgotten.

"Yet you accepted his help," retorted Reiniger. "You made a deal, reaped the benefits, and then reneged on it. As you stood by that window on November 22nd, 1963, your rifle aimed at Kennedy's head, you failed to pull the trigger. You failed to eliminate the greatest threat to Christianity since Jesus Christ's resurrection."

"He was only a threat to the people in power," said Amadeo. "He was in fact a true godsend to the suffering people of the world—a blessing whose nature and origin you could only quash by his death. Kennedy knew this about himself, yet he did not fear. As for me, my fear of him fortuitously turned to fear *for* him in the nick of time."

"Blasphemy!" cried out Reiniger. "Only the appointed servants of God could read between the lines, could hear his unsung claim to divinity—a claim that, had it been brought to the forefront, would have wreaked havoc, disorder and confusion onto the entire world."

Amadeo smiled. "Not the *entire* world, just the close-minded and increasingly fragile *ecclesiastic* world."

"He was the Antichrist, you fool!" screamed Reiniger; "*his* enemy," pointing at the cross of Jesus Christ on the wall behind him.

"This *Son* was not the enemy of his Father," exclaimed Amadeo. "Only yours."

Reiniger's accusation was gratuitous and had been designed by Paul VI to justify Kennedy's assassination. In truth, like hundreds of popes before them, Reiniger and Paul VI feared the emergence of a great leader out of the descendants of the Merovingian dynasty, pretender to the throne of France, and sacred bloodline of Jesus and Maria Magdalena.

And Kennedy was such a leader—and rightful claimant not merely to the throne of France, but to the throne of Humanity. This incredible revelation first came to *John Vernou Bouvier III* descended from Michel Bouvier, a French cabinetmaker—*and secret member of The Circle of the Eight*—who left France in 1813 after Napoleon ended his 10-year decimation campaign of the Priory of Sion.

In 1795, Napoleon had petitioned the secret organization for official recognition as descendant of Jesus and leader of the world. The Grand Master at the time, Archduke Maximilian Francis of Austria, agreed to the entitlement on three conditions: strict adherence to Sion protocol; marriage to Josephine Beauharnais (a true Merovingian descendant); and capture of the French throne. Napoleon kept his promise on all counts, finally becoming Emperor of France in 1804.

The new Grand Master, however, did not keep the promise of his predecessor. Maximilian Francis, having died in 1801, had been replaced by Charles Nodier, a prominent author, who denied Napoleon his due. Nodier believed an Irishman named James Kennedy was in fact the best contender to rule the new Merovingian dynasty. A betrayed Napoleon retaliated by hunting down and killing Nodier and every Sion member he could find. Only a handful was spared Napoleon's fury by escaping to North Africa and America. Michel Bouvier was one of them, settling in Vermont. The Priory of Sion would eventually rebuild 40 years later and reclaim France under Victor Hugo.

In January 1951, John Vernou Bouvier III (descendant of Michel Bouvier), a lover of French antiques, discovered a hidden compartment in a recently bought 19th century cabinet built by his ancestor. It contained various documents prepared by the Priory of Sion, including a list titled *Prétendants à la couronne de France (pretenders to the throne of France)*. Four names and places comprised the list, all crossed off except for the last one : James Kennedy of Dunganstown, who, after extensive research by Bouvier, proved to be the influential and politically outspoken father of Patrick Kennedy, Irish immigrant to the United States, and more surprisingly, the great-great grandfather to John F. Kennedy.

Bouvier was familiar with the Priory of Sion and their agenda, and was puzzled by James Kennedy's candidacy to the French throne. He pursued his research with greater fervor, hiring a team of genealogy experts who worked around the clock. After a year of research, the team discovered a clear ancestral link between James Kennedy and *Dagobert II*.

Dagobert II was the son of Sigibert III, an Austrasian king of the Merovingian line. When Sigebert died in 656, Grimoald, mayor of the Austrasian palace seized the throne for his own son and had Dagobert tonsured, (hair shaved completely), thus marking him unfit for kingship, and exiled.

Dagobert was given to the care of Desiderius, Bishop of Poitiers, where there was a cathedral school. The boy was sent on to a monastery in Ireland to be further trained as a page at an Anglo-Saxon court in England. Years later, he met and married Mechthilde, an Anglo-Saxon princess of Irish descent.

At Mechthilde's request, they moved back to Ireland and soon had a child, a boy bestowed the proud and virile Gaelic name of *Cinnéide* (pronounced Kennedy). Since the name was often used as a family name, it became such after a few generations. Thus, the Kennedy bloodline was born.

Armed with this providential information about John F. Kennedy's royal past, John Vernou Bouvier, an acquaintance of the Kennedy clan, saw an opportunity to raise his standing and influence with that clan, and organized a diner party during which he introduced his daughter, *Jacqueline Lee Bouvier*, to John. They fell madly in love to Bouvier's delight, and married a year later.

In 1954, during the celebration of his daughter's 25th birthday at his home, Bouvier, quite intoxicated and no longer able to keep his secret, invited John Kennedy and his trusted old friend and dispassionate sounding board, *George de Mohrenschildt*, a petroleum geologist and professor, to his study. He told them everything he knew.

Somehow Kennedy strongly suspected he was meant for great things, his thirst for a better world never having been quenched; but he never expected its manifestation in the form of latent royalty. He would later exploit this knowledge carefully and strategically, behaving and operating as a King, but never explicitly revealing the glowing ember that lit the fire of change within him.

As for George de Mohrenschildt, he uncharacteristically refrained from initiating a debate and simply acknowledged the possibility. Unbeknownst to Bouvier and Kennedy, Mohrenschildt was a Knights Templar on Pope Pius XII's payroll. Upon hearing of Kennedy's secret origin from his agent, the pope advised caution, restraint, and surveillance of Kennedy's movements and intentions. No aggressive actions were commissioned.

It was not until June 1963, when Pope Paul VI, a far more *militant* man, came into power, that the orders changed from simple surveillance to assassination. The pope hired his best Templar—a Seeker: a man responsible for the location and destruction of considerable amounts of material evidence supporting the surviving Merovingian bloodline. He hired *Amadeo Da Verdi*.

CHAPTER 59

Amadeo Da Verdi sat in his chair watching the blood of angst torment every pore of Reiniger's face. "What does it matter that I abstained from shooting Kennedy, you had another man, *Lee Harvey Oswald*, posted in an apartment a few floors up from mine."

"You can thank, or curse, George de Mohrenschildt for that," said the flustered pope. "He did what you could not." Mohrenschildt had in fact befriended Lee Harvey Oswald in the summer of 1962. A former US Marine who had briefly defected to the Soviet Union, Oswald found an unlikely friend in 51-year-old Russian émigré George de Mohrenschildt—and found in him a means to supplement his meager revenues.

Indeed, Mohrenschildt, a well-connected *intelligence* man, had convinced Paul VI to hire a second man as a backup to Da Verdi because he did not trust the latter to complete his mission. After all, seeking and destroying evidence was a far cry from murder. Despite his initial reluctance, Paul VI had a change of heart and agreed to use Oswald—and rightly so, given the subsequent turn of events.

"Oswald completed his mission," said Amadeo. "Why did you have *Jack Ruby*, a lowly club manager and Italian Mafia operative, kill him a few days later?"

"You obviously don't know this, but Oswald was also a Mafia operative," revealed Reiniger, "and an astute FBI informant who, after his cover was blown, had been sent to the Soviet Union in 1959 for his protection. In 1962, upon meeting Mohrenschildt at a symposium in Moscow, Oswald was offered lucrative work for the CIA and a safe return to the US."

"So, in effect, the CIA killed Oswald?" wondered Amadeo.

Reiniger grinned at Amadeo's deficient acumen. "The CIA work was legitimate, but was only a ploy to keep Oswald in the country—and keep him *in clear sight* of those who had business to settle with him. You see, my dear Amadeo, Mohrenschildt was not only doing the Vatican's bidding, but was also in league with the Mafia. In exchange for a generous donation from the Mafia to the Vatican, Mohrenschildt promised the Mafia two things: easy access to Oswald, and Kennedy's death."

Kennedy, above all men, was most hated by the Mafia. Not only did this President sanction an unprecedented legal assault on organized crime, but he also led a failed invasion to overthrow the Cuban government of Fidel Castro. Since several Mafia families had long-standing ties with the anti-Castro Cubans through the Havana casinos operated by the Mafia before the Cuban Revolution, these families counted on the success of the invasion.

"So I guess the Mafia got what they wanted—on both fronts," scoffingly said Amadeo.

"It was a close call," admitted Reiniger.

Following Kennedy's death, it took, in fact, two attempts to kill Oswald. A corrupt police officer first failed to kill Oswald as he fled through the streets of Dallas, being gunned down instead by Oswald himself; while a second shooter, Jack Ruby, succeeded during Oswald's transfer from police headquarters to the county jail.

"Speaking of close calls, I have a plane to catch," remarked Amadeo. "So, if you plan to kill me, do it here. We're close to my mother's grave; you can bury me next to her."

Reiniger smiled faintly as he called up an audio file from his computer and activated it:

"...you've all been blinded by your mission. You must know that, for all intents and purposes, you've put a kid, a boy, on a holy pedestal with all the religious trappings that go with it...

"...A child—yes, a child—being exposed to psychologically aggressive and potentially dangerous procedures like interrogation and hypnotism; that's what happened...

"...Exactly where the well was...

"...The woman next to Jesus is Maria Magdalena...

"...You might get one more of us, or maybe two, but we will kill you..."

"How much longer is this recording?" asked Amadeo, "and what does a deadly encounter between the Circle of the Eight and the Templars have to do with me?"

"It has everything to do with *you*," snapped Reiniger. "You're going to pick up where you left off fifty years ago. You're going to bring me this *boy*—the next pretender to the throne of Humanity, and the most dangerous Merovingian descendant ever to be born."

"You've seen one dangerous Merovingian descendant, you've seen them all," countered Amadeo. "What's so special about this kid?"

The pope's intolerance grew rapidly. "The evidence The Circle of the Eight have mounted in favor of this boy's true identity is overwhelming. It towers above everything the Vatican and Templars have ever gathered. In fact, this boy is *far closer* to Jesus and Maria Magdalena than anyone could have conceived. I feel it; I know it."

Amadeo sighed in frustration at the pope's frivolous ranting. "Well, I *feel* like leaving; and I *know* I won't take this absurd mission. The worst you could do is kill me."

"Ah, but there is worse," said Reiniger in a Machiavellian tone. "You may not have family anymore, but you have close friends, the *Rex family*, I believe."

"You would kill an innocent family?" cried an angered Amadeo; "for a conjectural cause? Choose another chump to wash your dirty laundry."

"You're the best *Templar Seeker* the Vatican has ever known," pointed out Reiniger. "Only you can find the surviving members of The Circle of the Eight, no matter where they're hiding now. Find the FBI Assistant-Director Dumont; he certainly isn't hiding under a rock. Find them all. Find the boy!"

"What would you have me do with any of them?" queried Amadeo, who appeared to be faltering.

The pope was pleased. "Contact me when you've located one or more of them. Do nothing else. Further instructions will follow."

Amadeo rose from his chair and left. "Don't bother, I'll call a taxi," slamming the door behind him.

Amadeo knew something the pope obviously didn't: the boy of which Reiniger spoke so fearfully was none other than *Theon E. Rex*, boy extraordinaire—his neighbor and best friend. Amadeo figured two things: anonymity can sometimes be better achieved by standing in the light instead of cowering in the shadows; and luck smiles upon well-meaning fools. Indeed, the Circle of the Eight's obsession with secrecy had kept both Theon's identity and the clandestine aspect of Amadeo's relationship with the boy hidden. But for how long? He had to choose a course of action quickly...and a side.

CHAPTER 60

Circa 2,000 years ago; Galilee.

"Oh, Maria, what have done to yourself?"

rhetorically asked Mary, as she brought pieces of cloth and warm water.

Maria Magdalena moaned as the pain seared and traveled up her spine. "I have done no worse than you, producing a child born of an ambiguous father. How Joseph could ever come to terms with that is indeed a miracle."

Mary gave her an incredulous stare. "Do you think me so obtuse, child? I am fifteen years your elder. Tell me, if I were to query Jesus as to his knowledge of the child's father, what would he say?"

"He would naturally say the child belongs to God." Maria coughed, making her belly jerk as it rose and receded rapidly.

"My son and you have known each other for three years," remarked Mary. "I have seen the love in his eyes. It does not *lie*, nor could it forever resist the guile of such a seductive woman. Why have you never wed? People talk, you know."

"Jesus is a *career-man* first and foremost," said Maria.

"Yes, he is," agreed Mary; "and his job is to *love* is kin—you and me above all others, of course."

Both women burst into laughter. "Oh, my, it hurts," gasped Maria.

"God is punishing you for denying me the truth, and the joy that it brings," said a joking Mary. "How can you deny your own mother-in—"

"Please, Mary," cried out Maria as she placed the palm of her hand against Mary's mouth. "I would rather certain things not be put into words, whether they be true or not. Tell me instead of things you have seen of me. Withhold nothing."

Mary wavered over the difficult request. "All right. To be quite blunt, I have not liked you for a long time. Since the very first time Jesus brought you over, I could not see or feel love inside of you; lust perhaps, but not love. I was certain you were driven by some sort of agenda I could not fathom. All I knew was that it was not in my son's best *interest*."

"Have you ever spoken to Jesus about your fears?" nervously inquired Maria.

"I sense anxiety in you, child," noticed Mary. "Is it for your sake, or my son's?"

Maria looked lost and remorseful. "I only think of *him*, now. My thoughts have taken me off guard for some time now."

"Indeed they have," said a nurturing Mary; "since the very first second life shone from the child you carry. I have witnessed the *change*. With that child came an outburst of immaculate love that you could never contain. From nothingness sprung the allness of God, wrapped in the stillness and consciousness of new life."

"I am so filled with love, that I could not describe it," admitted Maria. "It has been such a long time since it had been sponged away from my heart." Utterly surprised and disturbed by what she had just said, she suddenly felt very weak, her body going limp, and became overwhelmed by hundreds of images flooding her mind.

"What is the matter, child? Is it the baby?" Mary placed her hand on Maria's stomach, trying to detect signs of distress. "Talk to me."

Maria closed her eyes and raised her arms inchmeal towards the ceiling, as if in a trance-like state. "Oh, Mamma, they could take my body, but they could not take my soul." She repeated this three times, sobbing as the words slipped from her mouth. "They took my name, but they could not take my heart."

"Maria! Wake up!" implored Mary. "You've drifted into nonsense."

Maria remained unchanged. "Evil killed you on Earth, and Evil kept you from me in the Nether Land. I tried, mamma. I tried so hard."

Mary became distraught at Maria's enigmatic discourse, and held her by the shoulders. "Maria, you are becoming feverish. I don't understand what you're saying."

Maria's eyes were now wide open, gawking stupidly at Mary, but seeing only her mother. "With every stone that struck you, you should have been one step closer to Heaven, but they denied you its pleasures, when God was not looking. Oh, Lord Deus, why did you not look?"

"Maria! Maria!" screamed Mary. "You're losing your head! Take hold of your senses."

"I went looking for you!" yelled Maria. "I wanted to find you and bring you to Heaven; but they stopped me! I was just a child, frail and helpless. They took the Evil inside my body, and with it, infected my mind."

Powerless to arrest Maria's hysteria, Mary opted for the only solution her mind could conjure: she slapped Maria so hard, she lost consciousness. "Oh, God, what have I done?"

Quickly soaking a piece of cloth with water, Mary gently passed it over Maria's face. She did this again, and again. She then held her face between her hands, and whispered: "Maria, come back, now. It's time to come back," crowning her murmurs by the humming of a children's song."

"Mamma's here, darling," she finally said every so lovingly, adding in desperation, "Mamma wants her baby back."

Maria's eyes popped open so abruptly, Mary let out a piercing shrill, and fell back onto her bottom. "Maria? Maria? Do you know where you are?"

"I'm on a bed, and I'm as fat as a squealing sow," she replied weakly. "What's happened?"

Mary was hesitant to tell her. "Well, you began speaking of your mother, and then became somewhat crazed."

A look of confused recollection glazed Maria's face. "I remember," followed by one of guilt. "Yes, I remember now. And through it all, I saw your face and felt your strength—you look just like my mother."

"What do mean?" asked a rattled Mary. "I have nothing to do with your dream."

"I'm sorry if I did anything to frighten you," said Maria. "The imminent birth of my child seems to have triggered very vivid memories that had never surfaced before."

"Or *could not* surface before," suggested Mary.

Maria threw a suspicious look. "It seems I've said too much."

"Or you've always said too *little*," countered Mary. "But for now, let's leave things of the past for later. A baby awaits us."

"Ow! The baby is pushing," growled Maria. "Evidently, it heard you; it has its father's ears—hearing all, from the faintest whisper to the loudest cry."

"What did you say?" a grinning Mary asked her patient, who instantly realized she had revealed something incriminating about the father's identity.

Maria grinned as well. "As you just pointed out, let's leave things of the past for the future. Oh, Lord!" she hollered. "The baby is coming!"

"Spread your legs and push," said Mary in a commanding tone. "Push, child. Push! Push!"

Maria huffed and puffed like the proverbial wolf, spitting strands and pellets of saliva on her surrogate nurse's face. She arched her back, and pushed and pushed, wailing all the while, ending her concerto of pushes with a mighty one that precipitated the baby's head through the vagina.

"The head is out!" Mary shouted in joy. "I can see the shoulders now." Before she could maneuver the baby's tiny torso, it slipped out like a wet soap from an overzealous hand. Mary hastily cut the umbilical cord, wrapped the baby in cloth, and handed it to Maria.

"Isn't *he* beautiful?" declared Mary, "and with a full set of hair," stroking the boy's hair from front to back.

"He's gorgeous; the most handsome boy in all the land," agreed the proud mother before noticing Mary's expression change from exhilaration to consternation. "What's the matter, Mary?"

Mary's trembling finger pointed at the child's left ear.

Oddly, Maria did not react as her sister-in-crime expected. "He's got another one just like it on the other side," she jested with a disarming calm. "And, what do you know, they don't look like daddy's ears one bit."

"Are you not concerned at all?" a stunned Mary asked. "They look like…like…"

"Like his mother's ears," Maria said quite matter-of-factly, pulling her hair back to reveal the same kind of pointed ears. "Are you afraid of me now because of them?"

"No, no, of course not. I was…I mean…it just took me…" Mary's words stumbled one over the other. "How?"

Maria grabbed her hand. "How does one woman have long fingers, while another has short ones? How does one man have dark eyes, while another has light ones?"

"Did your mother have the same ears?" wondered Mary.

Maria turned her head away from Mary's stare. "No, she did *not*," she admitted evasively, releasing Mary's hand.

"Perhaps we should examine the rest of the baby's body," proposed Mary, who began to unfold the cloth around the child.

"No!" angrily screamed Maria, pushing Mary's hand away. "There's nothing about my boy that should concern you."

"I meant no harm, dear." Mary moved back a few steps in a gesture of reconciliation. "May I ask another question?" she treaded carefully.

"Go ahead," answered Maria. "I'll try not to be so cross, I promise."

Mary paused as she formulated her question. "In the years I've known you, you never spoke of your mother, except to say she married and lived in *Magdala*; nor have you ever mentioned her name." She paused again for a moment. "Maria...what is your mother's name?"

Maria gazed at Mary intently. "If one person ever deserved to know, it would be *you*. My mother was named—Oh my, oh my...the pain is back! Something is happening."

Before Mary could ascertain what was transpiring, a head emerged from Maria's vagina. "Maria! There is another child!" she yelled. "Let me have the boy. Don't worry, I'll let him be." She snatched the baby and placed it on the table. By the time she returned, the child was already out.

"It's a girl!" shouted Mary, who dutifully processed the child and handed it to Maria. "You have twins, dear, one as beautiful as the other."

"Its ears look like yours...as *normal* as yours," Maria quipped. "That should please you."

Mary sat next to the fortunate mother. "This has been hard on you; I mean, *all* of it?"

Maria smiled, letting out a gasp of air in relief. She pulled on Mary's robe, drawing her face next to hers, and she whispered softly in Mary's ear.

Mary drew back, swiftly and decisively, her complexion turning completely white. Maria couldn't determine whether she was delighted or outraged. Before she could ask, Mary ran out the house, and leaned heavily against its wall.

She crossed her fingers in prayer and looked to the skies. "What Evil has taken away, God has brought back. My poor, poor sister Bethel, you did *not* die in vain."

CHAPTER 61

Circa 2,000 years ago; Galilee.

"Who may I say is calling upon the Master?"
humbly asked the servant.

"Tell him Sonneillon is here to see him," answered the man in a choppy Aramaic dialect. He was scrawny and underweight and wore a grayish-brown robe, which hid his ectomorphic physiology. However, nothing could conceal his large and close bloodshot eyes, peering intently at the servant as he crossed the hall of the sumptuous house to a backroom, knocking gently on its wooden door.

The balding head of a heavy-set man emerged, its eyes—equally bloodshot—appraising the Visitor From afar and his possible reason for being here. "You're early!" he bellowed.

"I am *late*, oh Caiaphas, High Priest of Judea," remarked Sonneillon in a tone more akin to sarcasm than reverence. "Please grant me an audience."

"Fetch him," Caiaphas grunted to his servant before retreating back into his study.

Upon entering the study, Sonneillon sat on a marble chair facing another that remained vacant until Caiaphas could evacuate the bulk of his frustration over his visitor's carelessness and cavalier attitude. After marching to and fro several times across the room, the High Priest finally sat, slumping into the chair.

"What could possibly have possessed you?" he irately asked. "Calling yourself by your real name. Among these humans, you are *Judas Iscariot*."

"What does a lowly servant know of Judas Iscariot?" laconically replied the impostor. "My dear Vetis, *you* should be more concerned about preserving *your* identity. What would the chief priests say if they discovered their Commander is an inhuman—and a dark one at that?"

Pressing against the center of a medallion resting on his chest, Sonneillon instantly shuffled off his human façade and transformed into a devilish creature—as ghastly-looking as one's worst nightmare could conjure. "We are what we are, Vetis," he roared pompously, batting his gruesome wings and levitating from off the chair.

"Stop this immediately!" ordered Vetis, the false holy man masquerading as the High Priest, grabbing his accomplice by the shoulders and pushing him back onto the chair. "I'll replace you if I have too."

"I suppose you would," acknowledged Sonneillon, who resumed his disguise. "But that would expend too much time—time we do not have."

"Something is transpiring?" concluded Vetis.

"Yes! An opportunity." Sonneillon touched Vetis on the knee in a gesture of reconciliation. "But what of your progress?" He would make Vetis linger just a short while before sharing his own headway.

"It has been difficult," admitted Vetis, "but after many a gathering with the Sanhedrin, the Jewish Council, I have finally convinced the Council of Jesus' seditious ways and his subversive plans to overthrow the Sanhedrin."

"Are there still resistors?" Sonneillon hoped for unanimity. Once the Council's position against Christ was made public, he fully expected the gullible people of Judea to side with the Council and manifest their hate in the most unequivocal of manners.

"There are still a few," believed Vetis, "but they are among the least influential. Word of the Council's position has also spread to the Sadducees and the Pharisees. Most are with us."

"Ah, greed, egotism and political gain, what a potent concoction," observed Sonneillon. "Most flavorful among the rich and powerful."

"Do not presume so quickly," warned Vetis, shaking his finger at his partner in crime. "Without my intervention and my prowess as an orator, we would not have achieved what we have—whether it ultimately proves sufficient or not. Remember, it is the people—Jewish and Roman alike; citizen and soldier alike—who must believe in the end. Do not underestimate their dominion over mind and self-determination, even under the most dire of fortunes."

"Poverty and destitution are powerful motivators," pointed out Sonneillon. "Promise them food and lower taxes, and they will gladly choose these materialities over the obscurity of a seat next to God. The people of Judea—and other lands—will yield to the words of the Council if they are intertwined with carnal assurances. Soon enough, corruption of the soul will be at its apogee. The Dragon Lord will be pleased indeed."

"That remains to be seen." Vetis knew this better than any other diabolicus. This was not his first mission commissioned by Satan. "Now, what of this opportunity?" he urged on.

"Jesus and the apostles are gathering for a supper tonight at the Cenacle on Mount Zion, just outside the walls of Jerusalem," announced Sonneillon. "The supper will be followed by private prayer in the Garden of Gethsemane. No one knows of this outside of our group."

"Good!" Vetis rose and took a few steps towards the only window in the room. It was large on the inside and narrower on the outside. Surprisingly, sunlight came through in abundance. He passed his hand through it. "Little light will survive on this world when we are done." Turning to Sonneillon, "at supper's end, you will join the Sanhedrin police waiting by the walls of Jerusalem and lead them to Jesus. They will take him into custody and bring him here. I'll alert members of the Council to prepare for trial."

"What if the apostles intercede in Jesus' defense," asked Sonneillon, foreseeing some degree of retaliation.

"They are as docile as sheep," simply answered Vetis. "Nevertheless, one can never be certain," he pondered further. "I shall double the police force to thirty men." He walked to his desk and grabbed an *amphora*, a hand-made ceramic container, whose neck and body formed a continuous curve. Reaching in several times, he pulled out thirty silver coins and placed them in a cloth bag.

"Promise them a coin each upon Jesus' capture." Vetis threw the bag at his comrade. "Oh, and kiss Jesus on the cheek when you come upon him. If he is as intuitive and insightful as many claim him to be, he will know who has really done this to him."

"It shall be done," grinned Sonneillon, who made a beeline for the door.

"Wait!" yelled Vetis, stopping his associate in his tracks. "Once our assignment is complete, I shall produce Caiaphas' body. He will appear to have succumbed to a heart attack during sleep. What of the true Judas Iscariot?"

Sonneillon paused before providing a response, inviting Vetis' spiteful glare. "He's neutralized for the moment," he replied almost apologetically. "I was planning on a bit of torture after we were done—as an added benefit."

"An exemption from Satan's wrath is benefit enough," spouted Vetis.

"It is always *enough!*"

"I will kill him tomorrow then," promptly assured Sonneillon.

"You will kill him tonight," demanded Vetis. "Immediately after Jesus' arrest."

Sonneillon complied and rushed off, thinking hanging might be a good way to die. It would be dramatic if not spectacular—and quite fitting for a traitor.

Now to find a strong rope and a high tree.

CHAPTER 62

Present day; Washington D.C.

Theon's school week ended on a rocky note.

His parents knew the fight at school had not been instigated by their son, but that was of little comfort to them—they realized how close Theon came to exposing his unique abilities to the school administration. And they would have suspended Theon, and demanded an investigation into the danger Theon might represent to the other students.

Luckily for the boy, only his nemesis, Joey, had clearly seen the chilling physical manifestation of his rage; and as far as school authorities were concerned, Joey would say anything to get off the hook. Theon's parents, however, believed every word. Upon hearing of the bully's fantastic account, they feared any new catalytic event might trigger even more gruesome expressions of his growing powers. For the first time since Theon's arrival, Sarah Sinclair was *afraid* for her safety.

Theon knew nothing of his mother's leap into trepidation beyond the fact that she worried about him constantly. As for Theon's clueless uncle Bill, who had promised his nephew a weekend of fun, he refused to cancel Theon's sleepover at his place despite Sarah's sudden indisposition. Cameron had to intervene to calm his wife down. "We can't lock him up in the house forever," he told her. "He has to live his life on his own two feet, whatever that entails. And we'll be there for him at every turn."

Bill had been warned to watch over Theon closely, and not be surprised or frightened by any unusual development concerning Theon's *condition*. He didn't quite understand what that meant, chalking it up to parental exhaustion.. "Theon must be a handful," he simply concluded.

"Are you ready to head back home?" Bill yelled to Theon, trailing behind on his bicycle. They had just completed a full tour of Rock Creek Park, and were back at the park entrance.

"Betcha I can reach the sidewalk before you," yelled back Theon, stopping twelve feet behind Bill. The sidewalk was forty feet away, down a 15-degree inclined hill. "Too dangerous, Theon," said Bill. "Besides, my old legs are no competition to—"

Theon was off before Bill could finish his sentence, passing him at full speed. "There's nothing wrong with this kid," thought Bill. "Just as bold and reckless as any boy of his age."

"Theon!" he screamed loudly. "Slow down! Break ten feet from the sidewalk, you hear me? You're not above the laws of Physics." Little did Bill know, he might just be—in some respects anyway. Gravity, however, was not one of those.

Five feet from the sidewalk, Theon applied the brakes just as he shifted his body forward and crouched over the handle bars, imitating professional cyclers at the Tour de France. The bike immediately flipped over, throwing Theon clear of the sidewalk onto the two-way street.

He fell heavily a few feet from the center line, instinctively raising his head to check oncoming traffic. A small SUV driven by a young woman, with her baby fastened in a baby seat in the back, raced down the street towards him. She was on her cell phone telling her teenage daughter to start preparing supper, and wasn't looking straight ahead.

When she finally did, she saw, in horror, a boy lying on the pavement, his arm raised and his hand in a *stop* formation. The SUV swerved wildly to the left onto oncoming traffic from the inverse direction.

A grim thought instantly popped in Theon's mind: "Did I do *that*?" He had just the time to turn his head to behold an 18-wheeler truck smashing into the passenger side of the SUV, sending it spinning on itself multiple times, off the street and onto a large grass area, where it turned over twice before impacting a tree, ending its deathly course upside down and in a burst of flames that quickly surrounded the outer body of the SUV.

Bill rode down the hill swiftly and crossed the street, screaming at Theon to stay away from the burning car. He reached the vehicle at the same time the truck driver did, and without a second thought, pulled on the door handle on the driver's side, singeing the skin on his right hand. He yelled in agony. "Damn, it's stuck!"

"Let me try, I have gloves!" offered the stocky truck driver before placing his foot against the door as leverage, grabbing the handle, and pulling with all his might. The door did not budge.

"I have a hammer in the truck," he shouted, running back to his truck.

"This is my fault, this is *my fault*," Theon kept repeating as he got up and, against his uncle's strict orders, ran to the SUV. Something came over him, much like a trance. He became an observer of his own actions, unable to control thought or behavior of the veritable steamroller he had become. The dissociative sensation was far beyond that which had over-taken him during the school fight.

Theon pushed his uncle, who literally flew back five feet onto the grass. "Don't, Theon! It can blow up any second now!"

Theon latched on the handle and pulled, tearing it off. Undeterred, he smashed the window with his fist, grabbed the lower edge of the window frame and yanked the door off its hinges like it was made of soft plastic. His uncle watched in awe and consternation, marvelling at his nephew's superhuman prowess. There and then, he recanted his earlier statement that Theon was just like any boy his age. This boy was a genetic wonder.

"I'm here lady! You're safe," he told the semi-conscious woman bleeding from lacerations to the head. Ripping out the safety belt, he dragged her out of the car to a safe distance.

"My daughter, my daughter," she mumbled. "She's in the back. Save her." At that moment, Theon heard sobbing, which quickly turned to high-pitch wailing.

Theon rushed back to the car, jumped through the flames, and made his way to the back seat. The child was hanging upside down in the baby seat. Theon easily cracked open the buckles, removed the child and pressed him against his body.

He had just enough time to look up and see the gas tank explode. All the windows shattered, and the car instantly became a blazing inferno.

"Theon!" cried out Bill, who ran to the SUV, and circled it as the flames danced and stroke his body. He backed off, helpless, and called to the onlookers, "Call the fire department!" They were already on their way, arriving a minute later.

"There's a boy and a baby in there!" he frantically informed the fire chief, who took charge of the head of the water hose, and dowsed the car thoroughly. As the flames began to subside, the fire chief saw something strange, something he had never seen in his career: some sort of giant egg, more akin to a *cocoon*, greyish in color, almost luminescent. It lied there in the back area of the car, seemingly impervious to the fire.

"I see something," he said loudly, momentarily turning his attention to Bill, "but it ain't no kids!"

"What do you mean?" retorted Bill. "My nephew is in there. Can't you—Theon!!"

Theon suddenly popped out from the broken back window area, holding a completely unscathed baby in his arms. As for him, he appeared no worse for wear. Apart from his cloths that were scorched, and his shirt that was torn in the back from top to bottom, he was miraculously unscarred.

"This ain't possible," exclaimed the fire chief. "They weren't in the car. I swear it."

"The miracle child," thought Bill. "The mysterious child who rose from the bottom of a well. Boy, do I have questions for Cameron."

"What's everyone looking at?" innocently asked Theon. "What did I do now?"

"You don't know?" said a bewildered Bill.

"Well, sort of," replied Theon. " It's not at all clear."

"I can't quite explain it," admitted the fire chief, who took the child from Theon, "but you're a hero, son."

Theon did not feel like a hero. What he knew for certain is that he had been the cause of the accident.

One particular onlooker did not agree. He had filmed the latter part of the incredible event on his cell phone. It was without a doubt worthy of broadcasting on tonight's news. Theon was about to become the flavor of the month—something Cameron and Sarah Rex had tried so desperately to avoid, until now.

CHAPTER 63

Circa 2,000 years ago; Galilee.

Maria Magdalena arrived at the foot of Mount Zion. From her vantage point, she could clearly see the houses peppering its side. The largest house stood the highest amongst them—it was there that Jesus and his apostles had congregated for Passover supper.

If she hurried, she could make it before supper began. "Not to worry, little one," she told the baby boy she was carrying; "there shall be enough food for both of us."

In truth, she hoped Jesus would grace the child, and accept him for what she believed him to be. Once Jesus laid his eyes upon him, all doubts would dwindle as quickly as they had set in. He would *know* as she did.

Halfway to the house, Maria came upon a large boulder, which she easily circumvented to the left, only to hear a low whimpering sound behind her. She turned and was horrified by what she saw: John, the apostle, lying against the base of the rock, bloodied at the side.

"John! Oh, John! What has happened to you?" she asked in earnest as she deposited the child and inspected the disciple's wound.

"I was attacked and left for dead," John labored to say, grabbing Maria's robe with his bloody hand.

"For money?" Maria assumed as she wrapped John's waist with an extra piece of cloth from a small basket she bore.

John coughed painfully. "No, not for money; for knowledge. I come from the city, where I saw *Judas* leaving the house of Caiaphas, High Priest of Judea. He must have spotted me. They're plotting against Jesus!" he bellowed; "Judas is a traitor!"

"Why would they do this?" wondered Maria, who glanced at her baby boy. "They have *what* they want."

John was perplexed. "What do you mean, Maria?"

Maria brought the boy to him. "This is my child, blessed among all children—and forever cursed, I'm afraid."

John was overcome with zestful enthusiasm. "Is it mine?"

"I do not know," shamefully confessed Maria. "I have betrayed my oath of fidelity many a time."

"With others?" firmly asked John. "Are you a *whore*, Maria?"

"You are the *only* other, my sweet," insisted Maria; "but that does not make me any less of a whore."

"Jesus would understand," claimed John whose conviction vacillated like the tide. "You have said it yourself, he was seldom there for you, in a way that would have soothed your passions."

"Then you blame him for being so driven by his mission?" asked Maria.

"No, I do not," retorted John. "I admire him. I simply admit the fact. A saint does not have carnal urges."

"*He* does," Maria whispered as she embraced her child. "And when they arise, their appetite is insatiable."

"What are your plans?" tensely queried John. "What will you do, once you reach the house?"

"I will ask him if this is *his* child," she answered in an unflappable manner. "His eyes will not lie."

"And, what of Judas?" added John. "Will you tell Jesus of his treason?"

Maria stood, staring longingly at her boy, and then at the house. "No. I will speak to Judas instead."

"That is insanity!" cried out John. "He is deceitful and dangerous."

"Nevermore than I," Maria replied. "I will tell him that neither he nor his patrons shall strip away the ones I love."

"If Judas, and those for whom he procures, discover the child is truly his, they will kill them both," warned John.

"The child may well be too important to them," exclaimed Maria— "the source of *ultimate power*. As for Jesus, the traitor Judas will tell me what purpose his death shall serve."

"Maria, the meaning of what you say escapes me," said John. "The source of ultimate power is God."

"*Not anymore.*" Maria kissed John on the cheek, secured her baby, and picked up her basket. "Rest. I shall see you perhaps on the morrow; *alive and well.*"

"Are you speaking of my wellbeing or yours?" groaned John as he pressed against his wound.

"Farewell, dear friend." A resolute Maria resumed her trek up the mountain, neither saying another word, nor ever looking back.

CHAPTER 64

Bartholomew, James, son of Alphaeus, Andrew, Judas Iscariot, and Peter sat to Jesus' right, while Thomas, James the Greater, Philip, Matthew, Jude Thaddeus and Simon the Zealot sat to his left. There was only one unoccupied seat, the one immediately next to Jesus' right—the one reserved for John—whose absence was plain and disquieting to all, except for Judas, who ridiculed John for his lack of punctuality.

"Late once more," satirically cried out Judas. "You call that a devoted disciple? I call it an offence to our master. Perhaps I should take his seat."

"Or perhaps I should," struck back Maria Magdalena, who walked in the room in militant fashion, and sat next to Jesus.

Some instantly became disgruntled with her petulance. What had she done to merit such privilege?

"She sits where she will, because I have said so," proclaimed Jesus before taking a loaf of bread, and when he had given thanks, broke it and gave it to each apostle, saying, "This is my *body*, which is given for you. Do this in remembrance of me."

Maria touched his hand as he passed on the last fragment of bread. "I may have something that is also of *your* body, my love," she whispered to him, unveiling from the cloth a fetching baby boy.

"She has brought a new-born child to our proceeding," yelled Judas in outrage. "The gall of this insolent woman."

"Better innocence than duplicity that shall add to the trappings of this holy conclave," said Jesus. "Keep your place, Judas…if you can."

"Look at him," softly asked Maria of Jesus. "See how he hungers for nutrients, and for the provisions of life." She exposed her bare breast and brought it to the child's yearning mouth. "Gaze upon him as he suckles heartily, and tell me what you see."

Jesus gleaned at him, quite cognizant of the answer Maria sought. "He is not of my flesh," he whispered to her impassively. "A child deserves a father, not an ideal or a paragon built, in truth, on impaired virtues. A child deserves a father who shall remain among the living, and not one soon be bereft of breath. Tell John, he is the father."

Maria was dumfounded by Jesus's denial, shedding tears of disappointment. "I have never known you to lie. I shall hate you for it for as long as I live."

His indifference suddenly melted away, revealing a profound sadness. "There is much of me that is wholly estranged from the spirit of God—a darkness I cannot erase. I suspect you know this, and have counted on it in the past."

Maria bowed her head in self-disgust. "I have been deceitful, that is true, but this child was not born out of subterfuge. He was born out of love, I swear it."

As quickly as he lost it, Jesus regained his composure, and he picked a cup he had filled with wine. "This cup that is poured out for you is the new covenant in my blood. But see, the one who betrays me is with me, and his hand is on the table; for the Son of Man is going as it has been determined, but woe to that one by whom he is betrayed!"

"Please believe me; I have not betrayed you, Jesus," begged Maria. "Why unmask me so unjustly?"

"I speak of Judas, not you," he whispered to Maria.

"You know this?" said a baffled Maria.

The men began to ask one another, which one of them it could be who would do this. A dispute arose among them, each one accusing the other. "It is Maria!" shouted Judas. "And she has come to Jesus for forgiveness. She must leave now!"

"In that, Judas is right," Jesus told Maria. "You must go now. The father the child deserves awaits you. Make John well again; make him whole."

Maria complied reluctantly. She wrapped her child, and stood; and as she was about to leave, Jesus grabbed her arm and said: "Among all my disciples, you are the one I loved the *most*."

Maria smiled faintly and left in silence. She was about twenty-five yards from the house when someone pushed her violently to the ground. As she fell, she rotated her body to protect the child from the impact.

"What did you tell him, you mortal whore?" screamed Judas, who had also left the house, in her pursuit.

Maria clumsily got up, groaning in pain. "Why don't you show your ugly face, Sonneillon? A human appearance does not befit you well."

"Ah, I see you're partial to the horns and long tail," boasted the demon in disguise. "It has been said that I'm finer-looking than Satan himself."

Sonneillon stepped forward, facing her squarely. "Are you trying to fuck up our little business with this world?"

Maria's expression turned fierce with defiance. "You have the child... my child. Your affair with Jesus is completed."

"You're so dense, Maria Magdalena," squawked the demon. "When Jesus dies, by the hands of humanity, its sins will come full circle, and the Kingdom of Hell will fill with the souls of millions of sinners. Lord Deus of Heaven will not know what hit him."

"It will not happen as you say," claimed Maria. "The Spirit of our Lord God will see to it."

"The Spirit of Lord Deus has been lost for Millennia," harshly rebutted Sonneillon. "Now, stop your rubbish and go wait for me at the appointed place. The Dark Lord and Satan will be pleased to see you again—and ecstatic to take delivery of the child."

Sonneillon began dancing, twirling like a star ballerina performing before a sold-out crowd of self-absorbed bourgeois. "Praise *The One King* whose quintessence shall rip through space and time, and suck all that was, is, and will be into a tiny speck resting in the Lord's hand, only to be reseeded and bloom into the eternal Dark Empire."

"Go to Hell, you monster!" shouted Maria as she held her baby tighter.

"I'll see you *there* shortly, my pretty, for its consummation and its new beginning," laughed the demon before turning foot and regaining the house.

Maria spat in the demon's direction. "Hell will *remember* me; that I vow on my mother's grave."

CHAPTER 65

Present day; Boston.

"Ladies and gentlemen, what we're seeing is a cell video clip of an out-of-this-world rescue of a woman and her child," reported the anchorman from the W-X-P-T television news station of Washington D.C.

"The boy, who has yet to be identified, has just torn off the side door of the SUV, and is pulling out the injured driver," went on the anchorman. "It's an astounding feat of strength. I've never seen anything like it. Good Lord! He's just dashed back into the burning car. Oh my God! The car just exploded." The anchorman appeared genuinely surprised and horrified.

"Where are the firemen?" he shouted to the TV audience. "Where are the—they've arrived, ladies and gentlemen, and they're trying to extinguish the flames. It's a ghastly scene. No one could survive such a blast... wait! Something is coming out through the back of the car. It's the boy! And the baby! They're alive!"

"Alive...and well," said a tall, well-shaven man, sipping a glass of 20-year Scotch, as he watched the news report on his 50" inch plasma TV, in his plush apartment.

A book lied next to him, quite old judging by the worn out cover and the split spine. It lied there, opened near the middle; and a paragraph on the left side page had been highlighted in yellow:

> *Out of the country of Greater Arabia*
> *Shall be born a strong master of Mohammed,*
> *He will enter Europe wearing a blue turban.*
> *He will be the terror of mankind.*
> *Never more horror.*

Additionally, the words *blue turban* had been circled in red ink. The man glanced at the words before returning to the newscast.

"Our news reporter tells us the boy has just been released from hospital," announced the anchorman, "and he is in good health, as are the woman and the baby he saved. It's nothing short of a miracle. Although police and hospital have not revealed the identity of the boy, relatives—possibly his parents—have taken him home, on Orchard Avenue. We'll have more information soon; please stay with us."

The man's cell phone suddenly rang. "Yes…yes, I'm watching it right now. He's our strongest lead to date, I agree. In fact, I'm positive he's the one. Yes, I've said that many times before, but given this boy's nature, as it has now been revealed to us, he cannot be otherwise. I'll do what's necessary."

The man picked up his antique book and walked to the kitchen table, depositing it next to a wooden box placed at the center of the table. The book cover featured an indented symbol right below its title: *LES PROPHETIES DE M. MICHEL NOSTRADAMUS.* He pulled out of the box one of several blue satin scarfs, embroidered with the golden symbol that had become the signature mark of the serial child killer. It was also the same symbol as the one on the book cover. "We shall finally meet."

CHAPTER 66

Present day; Washington D.C.

"How is he?" asked a worried Cameron as he drove towards Washington D.C., accompanied by Amadeo Da Verdi.

"Theon is surprisingly calm and detached," replied Bill on the phone. "I'd almost say he's in denial, but then again, he's not my son."

"Keep him away from reporters, ok?" pleaded Cameron before shutting his cell phone, and then glaring at Amadeo. "We trusted you. You're our dearest friend." Cameron pressed his palm against his forehead in dismay. "What should I do about your crazy story? And, what should I do with you now?"

"You can trust me *now,* as you always have in the past," implored Amadeo. "I've come clean with you, told you of my Knights Templar past. More importantly, I've vowed to myself—and *to you*—to protect Theon against the slimy tentacles of the Vatican. What else must I do to regain your confidence?"

Cameron stared at him for a few seconds, peering into his tired old eyes, in search of extant remnants of valor, virtue and integrity. He probed deeper and deeper, but could not find what he hoped for—Amadeo was either too broken or too deceptive to summon those fragments of his former self.

"Don't make a fool out of me, old man," he gently warned Amadeo. "When it comes to betrayal, my forgiveness is fleeting at best."

"Then, in the interest of full disclosure *and* my redemption, there's more I can tell," added Amadeo. "Have you ever heard of the Priory of Son?"

CHAPTER 67

"I can't reach Sarah," Sophie told her husband. "Her phone must be off." She paced the living room floor nervously, attempting to reach Sarah over and over again.

"Cameron can't reach her either," said Bill. "It's not like her, not at all."

"Where are mom and dad?" wondered Theon as he finished reading a comic book from Bill's large collection. "Are they coming to get me?"

"Yes dear," reassured Sophie, who sat next to him on the sofa. "Dad is coming; and mom will be waiting for you at home."

Theon knew, of course, that, for the moment, his mother was nowhere to be found. Perhaps she was angry at him for creating all this commotion. Perhaps she was sick and tired of dealing with his strangeness. Perhaps her reservoir of love and affection had finally bottomed out, and was now rapidly filling with the sour liquor of apathy, revulsion and fear.

"Do you hate me, Aunt Sophie?" asked Theon. "Do you fear me?" Recent events were beginning to sink in. His eyes began to swell, and he attempted to conceal them by bowing his head.

"Why would I feel anything but wonder and pride at such an incredible boy," replied Sophie. "I love you; your family loves you, and not in spite of your uniqueness, but because of it. If it wasn't for your gifts and the beautiful heart that orchestrates their deployment, two people would be dead today."

Unconvinced, Theon met her gaze. "But I'm the one who—"

"Tut, tut," interrupted Sophie. "Stuff happens every day to all of us, as it did to you today, but you did something about it, something noble and brave. Remember that."

"Speaking of stuff, something has happened at NASA," announced Bill as he completed a call with one of his NASA supervisors. "Something totally unexpected and unexplainable. Theon, want to see something neat?"

Theon welcomed the change of pace, jumping off the sofa and accompanying his uncle to his home office, adjacent to the living room. Bill activated his computer and accessed a secure site dedicated to the *Mars Exploration Rover* mission.

"These are photos of the surface of Mars," Bill told an awestruck Theon. "They were taken by two rovers called *Spirit* and *Opportunity* over the last eight years."

"Wow! It looks like the Sahara desert, but much redder," noted Theon. "I bet NASA spotted Martian camels walking across the desert. That would be so cool."

"Yes, it would," acknowledged Bill. "That would certainly be unexpected and unexplainable. Let's see what Opportunity—the only rover still roaming around—has really discovered."

Calling up the most recent photo file, dated this morning, and opening it, Bill observed a Mars surface marking near the North-eastern edge of Meridiani Planum that looked nothing like a crater. It resembled more a giant skid mark, or a landing strip, about 15 feet wide, 130 feet long, and 2 feet deep.

"Maybe a meteor hit the surface?" theorized Theon, who had read a lot on Astronomy.

"Possible, son," retorted Bill. "Although, a meteor would impact the surface at a significant angle and form either a circular or an oval crater; and there would be debris. Whatever did this, meteor or other, only grazed the surface."

"What about a wormhole passing by the surface," proposed Theon; "like a space-train riding on energy tracks."

"What in blazes made you think of that?" wondered Bill, who immediately recollected his SETI investigative brother Ted's similar theory.

"I read a lot of science-fiction," grinned Theon. "Am I right?"

Bill was glad to see Theon smile again. He was resilient and would make it through the day. "You could be right. A good scientist doesn't endorse or discard any hypothesis until it's been thoroughly researched and tested."

"How are we going to do that?" queried Theon, who began clicking through the photo set.

"Hang on, Theon," said Bill as he swiped the computer mouse from his nephew and went back a few photos. "I noticed something. Do you see that rock near the start of the strip, just a few feet away from its farther side? There's a dark stain on it."

"It's probably just a shadow," surmised Theon.

Bill was skeptical. "Could be. It is consistent with the Sun's position. But its shape is off; too narrow compared to the rock. Let's isolate the image and enlarge."

"Anyone for milk and cookies?" offered Sophie as she entered the office carrying a tray. "Exploring Mars has undoubtedly built your appet—" Sophie abruptly dropped the tray onto the floor, shattering the two glasses of milk.

"What the hell is *that* doing there?" she cried out, pointing at the enlargement of the rock shadow. Theon also recognized it, but could not precisely recall its source or its meaning. It did, however, make him uncomfortable.

Ignoring the mess, Bill scrutinized the shadow, which, in fact, appeared to be a piece of cloth with a symbol in its center—the ominous symbol associated with the serial child killer. "This artifact is *man-made*...and quite intricate. What does it mean?" turning to his wife, clearly familiar with it.

Sophie passed her fingers over the image on the computer screen, her blank facial expression frozen in time. "The killer is from *Mars*."

Bill never knew when his wife was joking. But this time, he dared not ask; he was afraid the answer might reflect poorly on her lucidity.

CHAPTER 68

Present day; New York.

The Archbishop of the Roman Catholic Archdiocese of New York was distraught by Sarah Sinclair's request. He barely knew the Rex family, having only performed the baptism of both its children, Theon and Maya, a long time ago. Beyond that, he had seen them at church on two occasions at most, Christmas Mass he recalled.

"I rarely consult with my parishioners," he told Sarah. "The parish priest is usually the one who hears confessions."

"This is not a *confession*, Father," she remarked sharply, taking a seat without permission, and looking around nervously. The Archbishop's office at the Cathedral of St. Patrick was stunning and generously supplied with religious tokens.

"Are you intimidated, dear?" he asked. "There's nothing in this sanctuary of which you should be afraid."

"I'm afraid of the darkness beyond these confines," Sarah admitted.

"You mean, you're afraid your *son* might penetrate these walls," pointed out the Archbishop. "His evil spirit, as it were."

"Yes, Father," she answered. "Am I a terrible mother for fearing my son; for questioning what I once believed to be a gift from God; for seeking your intervention?"

"You're confused, Sarah," said the Archbishop. "The *exorcism* you seek is liberation from evil, not a punishment. It is a public and authoritative demand in the name of Jesus Christ that a person be protected against the power of the Evil One and be withdrawn from his dominion."

The Archbishop thought it odd that Sarah's husband was not at her side during this dire time. "What is your husband's position on your son's alleged nature?"

Sarah hesitated. "My husband protects him, but knows a lot more about Theon that he lets on. He's convinced he's protecting me as well by withholding harmful information."

"Harmful to your peace of mind, or harmful to Theon's safety?" queried the Archbishop.

"Both," she forcefully replied. "My husband is a *good* man."

"A good man owes his wife honesty and respect," softly said the Archbishop, "just as a good woman does," hinting at the impropriety of Sarah's approach. "Perhaps, you should return with your husband; better yet, discuss this with him; you may well resolve this without my assistance."

"Please, Father, don't patronize me," she snapped. "I'm an intelligent rational woman. I'm not imagining any of this. I've seen *things*."

The Archbishop quickly realized she would not yield to common sense, so he decided to indulge her suspicions and misgivings about her son. "All right then, I'll ask you questions, and you answer as clearly and as plainly as you can."

Sarah nodded hurriedly and straightened her back in preparation for the battery of questions, like a school girl who had been called to the principal's office.

"Does Theon eat well?" the Archbishop began.

"As well as any boy his age," Sarah replied.

"Does he cut, scratch, or bite his skin?"

"No."

"Is his bedroom sometimes abnormally cold?"

"No."

"Does he appear to be afraid of religious objects?"

"He did react negatively to holy water when you baptized him."

"I remember. A skin rash is hardly evidence. Nothing since then?"

"No."

"Do you see a pattern, Sarah; or rather lack of?" The Archbishop was beginning to realize the futility of the exercise.

"Go on!" adamantly ordered Sarah.

"Very well. Has he ever spoken in a different voice, or in a different language?"

"No, but he sometimes talks in his sleep. He pretends to be some war General, answering only to a Lord, and saying things like *a capite ad calcem*. He calls himself Ghost Knight."

"That's Latin for *from head to heel*. One foreign phrase is hardly cause for concern. As for the term Ghost Knight, it sounds like the name of a comic book superhero. You know, dear, children have wild imaginations, especially during sleep." Sarah frowned impatiently at him. He got the message and went on.

"Does Theon sometimes exhibit unnatural body postures?"

"No, but he has unnatural body features."

"You mean the ears?"

"Not just the ears. He has limbs on his back that pop out and move about when he's angry."

The Archbishop did his best to conceal a smile as he picked a book on his desk and opened it, revealing the picture of a demon on the left page, and an archangel on the right page. "Both these heavenly entities have limbs supporting their wings. Do you believe your son to be one of these creatures? And, if so, why would he be one more than the other. Your son could very well be an angel."

"You're making fun of me, aren't you?"

"You're making it very easy for me."

"What *kind* of priest are you?"

"The kind who believes levity is the shortest path to the truth. Now, tell me, have you actually seen these *limbs*?"

"Another child at Theon's school did during a fight."

"Children will say anything to get out of trouble, or get someone else in trouble—especially if that someone else is different. And I will agree that Theon is different, but not in the way that you would have him described."

Sarah was becoming increasingly irritated at the Archbishop's dismissal of her claims. She stood up and shook her fist. "What about his supernatural powers? What about those?"

"Please sit down, Sarah, or I'll have to ask you to leave. Now, explain what you mean."

Sarah promptly sat. "I'm sorry, Father. I meant no disrespect. You see, my son can make things move with his mind. He can alter their functioning; he can break things without touching them."

"If he doesn't touch them, how can you be certain he's responsible?"

"There are so many instances, and he was present every time. How can this be pure coincidence?"

"I can't answer that. I'm not in charge of the course of things. What else does Theon *do*?"

"He can break his crib like it was made of twigs; he can throw a heavy man ten feet away with one thrust of his arm. And…and he can bring a stillborn baby girl back to life."

"You witnessed all these things? Other people witnessed them as well?"

"Yes on both counts." For the first time since her arrival, Sarah saw a glimmer of sincere empathy and concession in the Archbishop's eyes.

"Assuming your son is truly the author of these deeds, his powers seem to have been equally used for good. What more benevolent act is there than the blessing of life from death? It rescinds all blame for paltry mischief."

"There is more," noted Sarah as she presented a series of photos she pulled out of an envelope. "From what I can gather, these are computer enhancements of mirror reflections of my son. This one is the base photo used to create the others."

"You did this yourself?" wondered the Archbishop. "Mighty impressive."

"Credit goes to my husband," said Sarah. "I found the photos hidden in a drawer of his work desk while searching for a pen.

The Archbishop appeared slightly miffed. "While I have no doubt your husband and you love each other, you definitely have trust issues when it comes to your son. Perhaps the severity of your problems would abate if you simply talked to one another."

"Yes, yes, Father," she replied in a dismissive manner. "Now look at the photos."

"Of course." The Archbishop kept his cool as he examined the photos. "This one looks like you; very pretty. This one is a demon. This other one is a handsome man." He probed it more closely and then facetiously exclaimed: "Well, what do you know, it's Jesus Christ himself. Your son is indeed among *distinguished* company."

"Don't be condescending, Father," retorted Sarah. "These photos mean something, they must."

"These photos are arbitrary fabrications," concluded the Archbishop. "The product of your husband's own imagination. They're jokes; a clever prank at your expense."

"I don't believe that; it's not true," insisted an irked Sarah.

The Archbishop substantiated his argument. "They're all representations of familiar figures: You, his wife; Satan; and Christ. Not at all difficult to conceive and forge."

"What about the last photo?" Sarah separated the fifth photo from the fourth, joined together by static electricity. "Is that a familiar figure?"

"God O'Mighty!" shouted the Archbishop. "Now, we're in business." He was gazing at the picture of the shimmering red-hot silver covered man. "I can't quite make out the facial features, but that's to be expected."

Sarah was perplexed. "What are you saying? You recognize this blurry figure?"

He raised his index finger, signaling patience and emotional restraint, before walking to his library and selecting one of the many bibles. Nestled within its pages was another book, soft-covered and barely a half-inch thick. This one he brought back with him, laying it on the desk.

"This is a copy of a rare book preserved at the Vatican library," disclosed the Archbishop. "It's the journal of a Roman soldier named *Plaxus Aurelius*, who was a witness at both Christ's birth and Christ's death. The events chronicled by the soldier are unverifiable, of course, but then again, the same thing can be said of the Bible. It's in Latin, so I'll translate as I go."

The Archbishop flipped through the pages. "Hum…ah, here we are." He cleared his voice as a matter of habit before any lecture.

"Rightness is the one value that guides my life within the sphere of soldier hood. I obey and insist upon obedience with inflexible regularity. But what is right about a King who orders the massacre of infant boys born in Bethlehem; and why must I obey? In the absence of rightness, there is only blind duty. Perhaps that is why I have been blinded in battle. I can no longer delight in the Sun's red robe, gaze in awe at the golden idols, or celebrate the beauty and diversity of fields of roses. My sense of sight has been numbed to spare me from the haunting crimson red of blood spills by the hundreds, innocent all."

The Archbishop suddenly stopped his reading of the journal. "In case it got passed you, the soldier became color-blind following a battle injury." He resumed immediately, moving ahead a few paragraphs.

"The three Magi follow the star, which takes refuge behind the hill top. I order my unit to return to base while I furtively shadow the three wise men to a manger where a boy is being born. Strangely, the parents and the sheppards who surround the boy do not fear me as I make my presence known. No one but I sees the star, which has been reduced to a shimmering red-hot silver speck of light. Perhaps my condition has finally afforded me some advantage whose practicality escapes me in the imme-

diate. But the enigmatic moment is short lived.

Among the dancing shades of gray, the silver point of light swells, shimmering evermore as it takes the likeness of a man in its sum, but not in its minute parts. I can ascertain no specific feature, if only a faint smile directed at the child. Untroubled and quite content, I raise my arm to touch it, but it loses form as swiftly as it took it, and disappears into the child. I am condemned to be the only witness to this wondrous event."

"That is an incredible tale," said an ambivalent Sarah, unsure whether to be grateful or fearful of her own son's apparent possession by some sort of holy entity.

"There's more," announced the Archbishop, moving near to the end of the journal.

"I look upon the man on the cross. Truly, this is a Son of God. His suffering, his heroism, his courage and the discipline manifested in submission are Godlike. He acts in the realm of order, submissive to authority, and therefore authoritative, keeping time with eternal principles in the quiet majesty of His submission, a righteous Man by all measure.

Men and woman prostrate themselves at the foot of the cross. One woman holds an infant boy as she gazes sadly at the man on the cross, who draws his last breath, his jaw dropping into stillness. To my amazement, a filament of red-hot silver light leaves his body through the mouth, shimmering and expanding into the phantom creature I had laid eyes upon in the manger 33 years ago. It becomes clear to me that it had never left him, not until now. Indeed, this holy semblance of a man smiles as it did long ago, and enters the body of the infant boy. No one notices; no one sees. I am once again the only witness to this spiritual event. Perhaps one day, I shall be the one to sustain this holy presence. Even a poor Roman soldier, albeit one whose sight can behold the godly realm of cosmic consciousness, may be blessed."

"That's it," said the Archbishop. "Comments, opinions?"

Sarah's first instinct was to try to debunk the story. "Even if the soldier's account is precisely as he experienced it, how do we know he wasn't just imagining it? According to him, no one saw what he saw."

"Perhaps his disability is the reason for his special insight," assumed the Archbishop. "There are situations where color blind individuals can have an advantage over those with normal color vision. Some studies have concluded that color blind individuals are better at penetrating certain color camouflages, which allow otherwise visible things to remain unnoticed, by blending with the environment."

"Maybe what the soldier experienced was nothing more than some natural phenomenon," contended Sarah, "explainable by scientific means."

"You insist on discrediting any premise that invites divine intervention," pointed out the Archbishop, "the nature of which may have transcended time and space, and culminated with the auspicious possession of *your* son."

"You're not making sense," harshly replied Sarah.

The Archbishop knew he had brought her to the brink of argumentative failure. "And why not? You claim without any proof that Theon is caught in the throes of demonic possession. Why would that be any more likely than possession by an intemporal altruistic spirit who champions the cause of good—a Ghost Knight, as Theon would put it."

"Because God is not forgiving," vehemently said Sarah. "When Theon first came to us, I thought God was forgiving—even bountiful, but I was wrong. My son, the prodigy of times past, has turned into my reprimand, my penance."

"What have you done to God to come to believe this?" wondered the Archbishop.

Deep, piercing emotion imbued Sarah's eyes with warm tears. "I cursed his name; I renounced him and spat on the cross. I did this because no benevolent, protective God would have let me be *defiled* the way I was. No compassionate, righteous God would have let a young girl of seven be ravaged by another she trusted so completely."

It became quite evident to the Archbishop that Sarah had been raped as a child, perhaps several times, by a close relative. "May I ask who did this to you?"

She sobbed uncontrollably, wrapping her arms around her legs. "I damned him only to be damned in turn."

Sarah would not, could not answer. The words in her bosom's core would not reach her mouth, intercepted by a mind laced with shame and contempt.

"Tell me then, does anyone know?" carefully inquired the Archbishop. "Your husband, perhaps."

"No one knows," admitted Sarah. "And no one will. It's my burden, and I carry it alone."

The Archbishop left his seat and walked to Sarah, placing his hand on her shoulder. "God has not cursed you. He loves you no matter how many times you've spoken ill of him. This traumatic event of your youth, and the manner in which you've retaliated, have clouded your thoughts. If Theon came to you, and no other, it's because Theon could be in no *better* hands than yours."

Sarah gazed at the Archbishop, wanting to believe him, but riddled with so much painful confusion. "God has not punished me with Theon?"

"God does not punish," said the Archbishop. "People inflict enough torment onto themselves as it is. God rewards instead in ways that are often unclear. You said it yourself minutes ago: Theon is a gift of God. Help your son, as he has and shall help you."

"How has my son helped me, Father?" asked a perplexed Sarah.

The Archbishop smiled. "Oh, in many ways, I'm sure. He's brought you to *me*, hasn't he?"

Sarah smiled back. "I guess you're right." She got up. "What must I do now?"

"Go home and love your family," he said simply. "Love Theon. Hell, love him to death," he added, laughing as he escorted Sarah to the door. "Goodbye Sarah, and good life."

As soon as the door closed, the Archbishop's grin vanished. He sat once again and opened the soldier's journal a few pages farther from where he had left off, and read:

"The woman and the infant boy, who had been gifted with the holy entity, pass by a band of beggars and brigands who know her seemingly since they call out her name in derisive fashion. Maria, the prostitute, I would have a word with you, one of them cries to her. Let me see the bastard you hold against your breast. Perhaps, it is mine. They all laugh as the belligerent hoodlum rushes to her and grabs the child by the face. I move to intervene, but am struck by a stone thrown no doubt by one of them, and fall flatly on my bottom, quite dazed, but not enough to be exempt from the hostile spectacle.

What is this, the hoodlum screams as he pushes back the child's hair. Behold the offspring of the devil. His ears are those of Satan, their sharp points reaching for the heavens. The rogue violently pushes the woman named Maria, who falls to the ground without relinquishing her devil-like child. The men pick up stones and begin battering them.

Suddenly, something miraculous happens. A large bull brakes out of its pen yards away, and barrels through the men, stopping inches from the child's face. The child caresses its snout and the bull bows its head as if acknowledging some command, and then goes on a rampage, viciously trampling and horning them repeatedly, killing four and injuring five. Surprisingly, all innocent bystanders are spared. The bull resumes its former quiet demeanor and returns to the pen.

Something inside this infant boy ordered the bull to kill. But it was not the holy entity. If anything, the shimmering silver spirit tempered the bull's fury, countering to a degree this other force dwelling within the boy. I am but a layman in matters of the supernatural, but I prophesize a great war will be waged between Good and Evil, and this child's soul shall be the battlefield."

The Archbishop closed the journal and sighed heavily. He stared at the cross on the wall and whispered: "This boy's soul belongs to *you*, Lord. Beware of the Devil and his devious devices. As he lusted for the prostitute's son, he lusts for this soul, *more so* than any other he has feasted upon."

CHAPTER 69

Present day; Boston.

"Ain't that somethin'," said the aging bartender of a busy bar in Boston. "I never seen such a rescue. The boy or the baby ain't got no burns. You seen somethin' like this before, Mac?" pointing at the newscast playing on the television set anchored above the bar counter.

The man facing the bartender said nothing. He sat quietly, slowly drinking his Dry Martini and fiddling with his swizzle stick. The man was well dressed, handsome, and oozed with confidence. "More olives," he asked, having decided to talk only when necessary.

"I ain't seen someone eat so many olives," remarked the bartender. "They don't have olives where you come from, I bet?"

Gulping down three olives in one shot, the man rose from his seat. "Lavatory?"

"In the back, to your left," replied the bartender. "Strange fellow; he don't smile any," he added when the man was well out of range.

Before crossing the threshold of the men's bathroom, the man turned, gazed at the bartender, and smiled. The barkeeper waved, realizing the man had heard him despite the distance.

"Guy's not normal," the bartender mumbled. "As long as he tips good."

The man surveyed the whole bathroom, checking under every stall to insure he was alone. They were all pay-stalls, so he couldn't open the doors, but he was satisfied with the conclusions of his search.

A strange odor, however, permeated the bathroom. It was not the smell of cigarette smoke, that much he knew. After verifying the vent for any foreign substance, he was now certain it was perfectly safe to conduct his business.

Unbuttoning his shirt, he exposed an exotic amulet affixed directly to his chest. He removed its cover and deposited it on the bathroom counter.

Pulling out what appeared to be a small circular power source, he raised it at eye level and pressed a few buttons along its rim. The apparatus began humming.

As he was about to affix it to the amulet, he heard a loud thump behind him, breaking his concentration and dropping the power source onto the ceramic floor. It rolled into a stall in which a man was now lying flatly on his side, wrapped around the toilet bowl.

"Sorry, man, I slipped," he said as he clumsily got up and opened the stall door, holding a joint in one hand and the power source in the other. "I was afraid you were the owner. You're not going to stool on me, are you?"

"The owner would have been preferable in your case," answered the man as his body began to glimmer and glisten, and transform into the epitome of demonic incarnation: red skin, horns, tail, claws, and bat like wings.

"It appears my *batteries* are dead," said the man-turned-demon before slashing the other man's throat with his index claw.

Picking up the power source, he fastened it to the amulet, reenergizing its batteries. A minute later, his human disguise had been restored.

Walking out of the bathroom, he stopped by the bar and dropped $200 on the counter, far more than the amount of his tab. "Orchard Avenue, Washington D.C. That's South from here?" he asked the barkeeper.

"I don't know no Orchard Avenue," replied the bartender, who quickly pocketed the money; "but Washington D.C. is South-West from Boston. Got some friends there?"

"Only one friend," he said, straightening his tie. "A friend to die for."

CHAPTER 70

Present day; Washington D.C.

"You guys have been here long enough," Bill told the reporters and cameramen who had assembled on his front lawn, eager to get a statement about the amazing rescue.

One reporter, more ambitious than the others, rushed towards Bill. "Mr. Adams, your neighbors tell us the boy is actually your nephew, Theon Rex. Tell me, how long have you known your nephew to possess superhuman powers?"

"My nephew is just like any other boy," maintained Bill. "You're making a mountain out of a molehill. Get out of here before I call the police."

"No need, sir, the police is here," said a policeman, who joined the exchange after parking his police car by the sidewalk. "I want everybody off the lawn; this is private property."

"Maybe you should call backup," proposed Bill. "One cop may not be enough to handle this rowdy crowd."

"You would be surprised how influential and how *motivated* I can be," said the policeman before pulling out his gun and shooting in the air.

The startled news people immediately liberated the lawn, surprised by the cop's bold action.

"Is that tactic in the policeman's handbook?" asked Bill, semi-humorously.

"Anything to protect the innocent citizens of Washington D.C.," impassively replied the cop. "Now, may I enter the premises and check on the boy?"

"Uh…sure," hesitantly said Bill. "He's with my wife, in my office, first floor, next to the living room. I'll accompany you."

"No need. You stay here," ordered the cop.

"Why should I?" wondered Bill.

"Procedure, sir," replied the cop, who failed to replace his gun in its holster, waving it sideways in what appeared to Bill to be a gesture of intimidation.

"All right, I'll stay," complied Bill.

Without any further words, the cop headed for the front door and entered, leaving the door open behind him.

"Cocky prick," muttered Bill as he stood there like an idiot. "Sophie's going to set him straight, FBI style."

Pacing the lawn impatiently, Bill noticed a second car park in front of his house, followed immediately by a third one. Three men emerged from the second car, and two from the third. The first three he did not recognize, while the other two he did: it was Cameron Rex and his neighbor, Amadeo Da Verdi.

As soon as these men spotted each other, the trio's lead man pulled out his revolver and aimed at Amadeo. "Don't make a move, Da Verdi. I know why you're here."

The man aiming the gun was Scott Dumont, FBI Assistant-Director, who had learned from Claude Blanchard of Da Verdi's recent Vatican-mandated mission to locate Theon Rex.

"Lower your weapon, Scott," implored Cameron. "He's on our side."

Dumont slowly lowered his weapon. "Your side, not mine, Rex. Where's the boy?"

"He's in my office, in the house," interjected Bill; "with an *odd* cop. A bit of a loose cannon, if you ask me."

Cameron and Dumont stared at each other, instantly grasping the gravity of the situation. They simultaneously darted for the house, crossing the front door as a loud gunshot resonated throughout the house.

Cameron entered the office first, and saw, in horror, his sister Sophie collapsing over Theon onto the ground, wedging Theon between her bloody body and the floor.

"You son of a bitch!" screamed Cameron, who shot the cop repeatedly in the back, emptying his barrel. Surprisingly, the policeman was not dead. Lying flatly on his front, bloodied and moaning, he mustered his fading strength, and turned his body onto its back.

He stared at Cameron while Dumont tended to his sister. "It's serious…an inch from the heart; but I think she'll make it if she gets medical help immediately."

Dumont pulled Theon up, checking for wounds as he did. "You're ok, kid. You'll live."

Dazed, Theon looked at his father, and saw such wanton and rampant hate in his eyes, the kind and quantity of which only he could understand and empathize with.

Cameron felt the connection with his son as he retrieved bullets from his pockets and proceeded to reload his weapon. As he lodged the final bullet, Amadeo and Bill ran into the office. "Good Lord!" exclaimed Amadeo as he took in the gruesome sight. He also noticed Cameron cocking his gun.

"What do you intend to you, Cameron?" Amadeo asked gently. "It's not worth it."

The cop began chuckling, exacerbating the blood flow escaping his mouth. "As an agent of Good, you know what you must do, as I have always done. As long as the boy lives, the world will be in danger. As long as I live, he will be as well. He is the *one*, truly the one. If you do not kill me, I will survive and I will return."

Theon walked by the cop's body to his father, held his left hand and looked up. "I can do *this* for you, Dad."

Cameron said nothing. Amadeo and Dumont understood the implications of the offer, while Bill remained clueless.

"Let me do this one thing for you, Dad," insisted Theon. "You've done so much for me. Let me return the favor."

Theon was quite sincere in his request to dispatch the cop. It was offered out of principle, devotion, and appreciation, and not out of malice, revenge, or even hate. Even Amadeo, the most principled among the men, was not appalled by Theon's overture.

Cameron looked down at his son. "Thanks, Theon, but it's the thought that counts." He then aimed his gun and shot the cop through the head.

CHAPTER 71

"**The ambulance is gone,**" reported Amadeo. "Bill went with Sophie to the hospital. As for Theon, he's in his bedroom."

"We have to call the police—the *real* police—and report this *incident*," urged Dumont. "There's no point in waiting any further."

"Maybe there is," insisted Cameron, who was already busy manufacturing a statement for the police. He began searching the body, finding lodged in a pocket what he expected to find all along: a blue satin scarf boasting a strange golden symbol embroidered in its middle.

"Congratulations, Rex," said a happy and relieved Dumont. "You've finally caught the serial child killer. Given his identity, I'm sure I can get the authorities to overlook the *nebulous* circumstances surrounding his death."

"Much obliged, Scott." Cameron pursued his search, padding the body from top to bottom, but found nothing else. "He's clean."

Amadeo crouched next to Cameron. "What's this here, on the side of the neck?"

"A tattoo," easily surmised Cameron. "What about it?"

"It continues below the neckline," noted Amadeo, pulling down the shirt collar. "Help me take off his vest and shirt."

After completing their task, the men were quite surprised to find an impressive tableau of tattoos covering the entire upper body. The bodily landscape included an assortment of demons, a depiction of Adolf Hitler and Napoleon Bonaparte, and an image of a boy trapped in a sphere of light being pierced by a sword. Right below the boy appeared the infamous golden symbol.

"The sketches are intermingled with writings," observed Cameron. "It's French poetry, I think."

Amadeo quickly read a portion of the writings. "It's not just some poetry; it's a compilation of Nostradamus quatrains. I count about fifty or so. This man must belong to a radical faction of Nostradamus worshipers. The cornerstone of their faith revolves around the eventual and inevitable arrival of the third Antichrist."

"Hitler and Bonaparte were the first two Antichrist," quickly figured Dumont, based on the presence of their likenesses on the body's chest."

"There's a pattern with the colors," detected Cameron. "All the writings are in black ink, while the drawings are in red and blue, except for the symbol, which is in dark *yellow*."

"There's another exception," noted Amadeo. "Look at the paragraph right below the symbol:

> **Mabus** *then will soon die, there will come*
> *Of people and beasts a horrible rout*
> *Then suddenly one will see vengeance*
> *Hundred, hand, thirst, hunger when the comet will run*

The word *Mabus* is also in dark yellow."

"You're right," said an intrigued Cameron, recalling Amadeo's words about Mabus: *He will be killed by the sword, releasing an energy greater than all the nuclear power in the world; an energy that will be harnessed and used to destroy most of humanity.*

"There's a connection between the symbol and Mabus," conjectured Amadeo. "Just as the cross is a symbol of Christ, this hieroglyph could be a symbol of Mabus." Armed with this new information, Amadeo analyzed the symbol's every detail. "That's exactly what it is," he exclaimed moments later. "Do you see?"

Cameron and Dumont stared at it, but saw nothing particular. "You'll have to enlighten us," confessed Cameron.

"It's sort of a self-contained rebus," guessed Amadeo. "Imbedded in the symbol is a series of letters: the two bumps represent the letter M; the first bump combined with the curve within it represents the letter A; the two bumps combined with the horizontal line represent the letter B; either bump rotated 180 degrees represents the letter U; and the curve within the first bump represents the letter S. That spells *MABUS*."

"The equivalence between word and symbol seems too convenient and too decipherable to have been conceived by the master of dark prophecies himself," thought Cameron. "Perhaps the worshipers of Nostradamus had a bout of creativity, prompted by a need to revel in what was really an undeserved and counterfeit understanding of Nostradamus' writings."

"This symbol is much older and much more meaningful than that," rebutted Amadeo. "The subconscious of a special boy suggested it was the symbol of a supreme guard of demons, perhaps watching over a being named Mabus."

"Da Vinci also knew of the symbol," said Dumont, "having painted a demon with the symbol on its forehead."

"The symbol was found among the bones in a burial ground…and the symbol has also presented itself 100 million miles away on planet Mars," added Amadeo, pointing at the Mars image on the computer screen. "No, gentlemen, there's something mystic about this symbol, and something so dreadful Nostradamus was compelled to impart prominence to it in a fashion that eludes us for the moment."

"The serial killer knew of it," pointed out Cameron. "He may have been privy to some part of Nostradamus' work that was never publicized, just like the missing quatrains we found in the cave in the hills of Reinhardswald."

"No matter how he came upon it, the killer thought Theon Rex was this Mabus," assuredly said Dumont; "and he believed the symbol was his mark—the mark of the destroyer of all life on Earth."

"The killer was insane, obviously," asserted Cameron. "Theon is not the next destroyer, or princely leader of humanity."

"I've always had my doubts," claimed Dumont, "doubts I expressed to the Circle of the Eight. Perhaps I could see the child, just to confirm what I've always known, that your boy is unique, but no world dictator."

To put the matter at rest, Cameron agreed. What would be the harm? He walked to the foot of the staircase and called out: "Theon, can you come down for a second?"

Theon didn't hear a thing with his earphones on, listening to his favorite music on his computer. He did, however, suddenly sense the arrival of a sinister presence. A peculiar shadow etched itself on the wall before him. It resembled a giant bat.

Theon swirled his chair around and peered at the open window. Nothing was there. He sprinted to the window, stuck his head out and looked around. "No giant bats in sight," he whispered to himself.

He made it back halfway to his computer when he felt something cold and metallic pierce his skin on the right side of his neck. He attempted to free himself from his unknown assailant, but immediately discovered he could no longer command his body. He was paralyzed.

"Greetings," said the creature as it turned Theon around so he could see he who had turned him to stone. Theon laid eyes on the lead character of his many nightmares: the devil himself, eyes bloodshot and fangs dripping with saliva.

"After so many years, you're finally coming back *home*," announced the demonic creature before securing Theon against its body and heading for the window.

Resistance was futile Theon quickly discovered. The only thing he could do is shed a tear...a tear caught by a video camera hidden in his room between two books on the shelf of a credenza.

CHAPTER 72

Circa 500 years ago; France.

"Master Da Vinci, it is getting cold," remarked a 15-year old Michel de Nostredame (*Nostradamus*), who had been placed under Leonardo Da Vinci's tutelage to polish his education. "We can return tomorrow. The weather will be far kinder to our vulnerable bodies."

"Confine your concerns to optimum cognition," strongly enjoined Da Vinci. "The cold will spare your mind if you keep its workings busy. Now count the symbols and tell me how many you've tabulated."

In childish nonchalant fashion, Michel circled the large well, tapping on each flat stone etched with a symbol. "There are eighty symbols around the well's ring, ten symbols repeating eight times in identical groups of ten. But, of course, you already know this, having examined this well countless times before."

"Factual certitude is the scientist's greatest virtue, boy," said Da Vinci. "And confirmation, even from a *lay* boy, is preferable to none. Now, look under the edge of the ring. What do you see?"

Crouching, Michel noted a series of 3-inch diameter opaque spheres embedded halfway into the stone, along the circumference of the ring, alternating in color from white to black. "I believe they're made of solid glass. What are they for?"

Da Vinci was pleased Michel's curiosity had finally been piqued. "Stand straight and press firmly on one of the stones. Spare no effort."

Michel chose one at random and pressed down with his right hand. "It's not moving, should it?" He then tried with both hands, applying the fullness of his body weight against his arms. "Nothing is happening." He selected another stone and repeated the operation, but to no avail. "Must I try them all, master?"

"Let me see." Da Vinci slid his hand along the spheres, walking slowly around the well. "I conjecture that these small spheres of crystal hold the secret to *unblocking* the stones' movement."

"To what end, master?" wondered Michel. "Has it not occurred to you that the colored spheres and the symbols on the stones might be purely ornamental?"

"A simpler hypothesis perhaps," conceded Da Vinci, "but not as intriguing. Michel, try rotating some of the spheres; I'll do the same at the opposite side of the ring. An opportune combination of spheres set in motion might unlock the stones."

Before Michel could comply, the well and the ground around it suddenly began trembling. "What have you done, boy?" shouted an alarmed Da Vinci.

"It's not me," replied Michel, who fled behind a nearby tree. "Master! You must make distance between you and the well. It's enchanted, and we have made it angry."

"Hogwash!" screamed Da Vinci. "This well—*this device*—has been activated; but not by us." Da Vinci scanned the stones, pleading them to budge as he struck the ones near him.

Providence, in its particularly divine manner, blessed him by commanding one of the stones to movement. Indeed, the one he had last thumped descended sharply by four inches. Then, another followed, and another, until eight stones—one from each of the eight symbol groupings—had lowered.

Da Vinci instinctively memorized the stone positions and peered down into the well, when a blinding light erupted from its mouth, only to recede instantly and be replaced by a shimmering substance akin to turbulent waters.

Da Vinci stepped back, vigorously rubbing his eyes, and then blinking and squinting strenuously. "Damn it, I can't see!"

"It will pass," comforted Michel, who had left the security of his shelter and rushed to his master's side. "Your vision will return."

"My vision is a secondary matter under the circumstances," decided Da Vinci, grabbing his pupil by the shoulders and shaking him like a leaf caught in the wind. "You must look into the well and describe what you see, before it vanishes."

"Why would it fade away?" It was evident to Michel that his tutor had formulated a theory. "Master, you have devised—"

"Gaze upon it, now!" cried Da Vinci, pushing the boy against the edge of the well. "Do you see water boiling of its own means, at midheight of the well?"

"There is nothing of the kind, not anymore anyway," answered Michel, "but there is something moving about the bottom, encrusted with mud. It looks like a large pig. How did it get—oh my Lord! It's not an animal…it's a *human being*!"

CHAPTER 73

"Master, I don't recognize the fabric," said a puzzled Michel de Nostredame as he held up the unknown woman's dress after washing it thoroughly. "The foundation cloth is covered with thin metallic-like silver coins, each engraved with a strange symbol—two bumps, a curve and a line at the bottom." He turned it around several times, searching for other markings. "The dress is quite light, and remarkably designed."

Da Vinci, whose vision had finally returned, glanced at the dress before returning to the care of the unconscious woman he had laid on his bed. "If the coins were truly metallic, the dress would weigh more than five kilograms. It appears to be made of a mysterious element, perhaps not of this *world*."

Michel, who had fallen victim to his tutor's antics more often than not, delayed his rebuttal until he could make a determination as to the degree of soberness of Da Vinci's account. "You believe the well to be an alien *transportation* device, don't you?"

Da Vinci grinned as he sponged the woman's forehead. "Very astute deduction, student. There is hope for you after all. The real question is transportation to and from *what* world?"

"Mars is the world closest to Earth," noted Michel. "She may be a Martian."

"Her facial skin may be reddish," acknowledged Da Vinci, "but that's only the result of contact with a strong heat source, a fire most likely. See how her eyebrows and eyelashes have been seared off. Strangely, it makes her face even more angelic."

Michel passed a jar of ointment made of a concoction of medicinal herbs. "You seem quite infatuated with this lady, master; I've never known you to be so easily smitten."

"Mind your tongue, young man," warned Da Vinci. "She's regaining consciousness."

The woman slowly opened her eyes, greeted first by Da Vinci's time-ravaged face, and by his cracked lips forming a misshapen smile, partially shrouded by an unkempt mustache and beard. "Where am I?" she moaned. "Who are you?"

"It sounds like Latin, master," said a surprised Michel.

Da Vinci nodded. "Indeed, some odd dialect of Latin to be precise."

"The more apropos question is: who are *you*, dear?" he gently asked in Latin.

She raised her head and looked around, arresting her attention on a painting secured to an easel a few feet from the foot of the bed. "Is that me?" she asked in a weakened voice.

Da Vinci stared at the painting, and then back at her. "There is a likeness, but I assure you, you are far more enchanting." Realizing what he had just said, and how blatantly it disclosed his crush on her, he turned red with embarrassment. "As a painter, my interest is purely professional, of course."

The woman feigned understanding. "Who is she?"

Da Vinci nervously strutted to the painting. "She is in fact an unfinished *composite* of three women: Costanza d'Avalos, Caterina Sforza, and Lisa del Giocondo."

The woman instantly sat up straight, taunted by vivid remembrance. "I believe that is *my* name!"

"Which name is that?" interjected Michel. "Isabella? Cecilia?"

"*Lisa* is my name," she answered. "I believe my name is Lisa."

"Hardly an alien name," jested Michel. "Certainly not from Mars."

"Keep quiet, boy!" commanded Da Vinci, sheepishly sitting next to the woman. "If that is your belief, then we shall call you Lisa. Tell me, *Lisa*, where are you from?"

"I cannot say," she replied, pressing her palm against her cheek. "Why does my face burn so?"

"The injury is superficial," reassured Da Vinci. "I gather you were caught in a fire."

Lisa suddenly clamped Da Vinci's forearm and squeezed tightly. "There was no fire. There was a blast. I was attacked!"

"By whom?" Da Vinci queried earnestly. "Bandits, soldiers?"

"Yes, they were soldiers," she recollected. "While I can't describe them, I know they were soldiers."

"Do you recall a well, Lisa?" asked Da Vinci; "with unusual symbols on its surface?"

Lisa laid back into bed, fatigued by the exchange. "I recall no such well or such symbols. What do they mean?"

"We can only speculate at this juncture," sadly admitted Da Vinci. "However, there is one symbol that may stir your memory," holding the dress closely. "What are these markings?"

Lisa was overcome with intense revulsion, shuddering furiously. Her shaking hand grabbed one of the silver coins and ripped it off the dress, carrying it inches from her eyes. "It is a *sign*…a sign of impending doom and destruction."

She dropped the coin and lost consciousness once again, but even this would not repel the reawakening of long instilled horrors in her mind.

CHAPTER 74

Da Vinci had many renowned friends, but no close relationships with women except for his friendship with the two Este sisters, Beatrice and Isabella, a portrait of whom he drew while on a journey through the city of Mantua.

Isabella d'Este was *Marchesa* of Mantua, one of the leading women of the Italian Renaissance, and a major cultural and political figure. Da Vinci not only admired her, but loved her secretly. Had she not been married, he believed he would have professed his love.

And now, many years later, in the twilight of his life rich in accomplishments and accolades, he was blessed with a second opportunity to add *true love* to his laurels.

Lisa, as she called herself, had been under the care of Da Vinci for five months now. During that time, her memory had not improved, except for evanescent images of death and devastation that plagued her slumber. But in her waking state, she had managed to achieve a level of apparent serenity and rhapsody that engrossed Da Vinci's heart so utterly; he acted like a skittish and awkward school boy around her.

"Master, when will you tell her?" asked a purposely impudent Michel. "It's clear to me, and so must it be to her."

Da Vinci frowned angrily at his pupil. "You're too young to understand these things! Continue on this course, and I will send you away."

Michel was used to his master's empty threats. "And if you continue on this course, you will be dead before having the chance to express your feelings."

Da Vinci raised his fist in reprisal. "I will not be lectured by cocky child. Go to your room before my hand lands on your empty head."

"Play her a sonnet on the lyre, she'll love it," suggested Michel as he ran away towards his room, passing Lisa on the way. "Leonardo has something to tell you, Madonna." He giggled the rest of the way.

"You have something to say, Leo?" asked a curious Lisa, who came to naming him such as the intimacy between them grew. It was, as she put it, a mark of affection.

"Why yes, Milady…yes, yes…" he fumbled before trotting off to another room, proving by his swift pace that he still had the strong legs of a considerably younger man. Seconds later, he returned with the easel that bore the painting of the composite woman.

"I have toiled on this painting for many years," he told her in a frustrated tone, "never being able to endow it with the majesty of perfection…until now."

Lisa immediately knew what her friend had in mind. "Look at me, Leo. While my skin may have healed, my eyebrows and eyelashes have yet to grow back by any measure. You would do this painting a great disfavor by using me as a model."

"On the contrary, my dearest," insisted Da Vinci. "Your face, as it appears now, while enigmatic is at the height of beauty." He stood there, intently gazing at her, when a notion entered his mind. "May I test a theory?"

"If in the least, it will prove I am not the candidate whose features must be laid onto your canvas," she replied sharply.

Da Vinci grabbed a large compass from his worktable, a technical drawing instrument used for inscribing circles or arcs, and for measuring distances on plane surfaces. His was made entirely of wood, except for a metal spike at one end, and a thin piece of graphite at the other end.

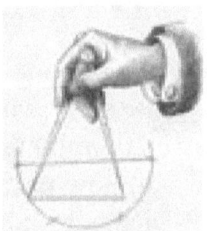

"This will not hurt one bit," he assured Lisa as he placed one end of the compass against her left temple, and progressively reduced the angle until the other end touched her right temple.

Da Vinci then secured a large piece of parchment paper, and pierced the paper with the spike before drawing a very short mark with the graphite. Using a ruler, he drew a line between the piercing and the graphite mark. "This line is our horizontal base—the width of your face," showing her what he had done.

She remained quiet, but quite fascinated, not wanting to interrupt his thought process.

Using an L-shaped instrument, he drew two vertical lines with respect to the base, and marked the ends of the two lines with the compass (keeping the angle as is). He then drew another horizontal line between the two marks, forming a perfect square.

Using the compass again, he created two circular markings intersecting each other, using the end points of one vertical line, and repeated the procedure based on the end points of the other vertical line. He then drew a line between the four intersecting points—this line was guaranteed to cross the square exactly at mid-point.

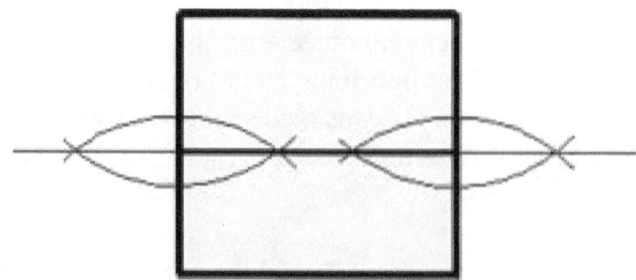

Da Vinci turned to Lisa. "Do you see where I'm going with this?"

"I have an idea," she answered, refraining from any elaboration. Da Vinci had discovered months ago how proficient Lisa was in the fields of mathematics, physics, and languages. She could intelligently debate theorems with Da Vinci—and in Italian to boot, which she learned and perfected over the course of her stay. However, she could not recall where and how she had gained a degree of acumen of the sciences that would certainly intimidate the ordinary man. "Please continue, Leo," she urged playfully.

Da Vinci proceeded to draw a diagonal line between one end of the mid-line and the top end of the opposing vertical line, creating a right-angled triangle. "Do you recall *Pythagoras' theorem*?"

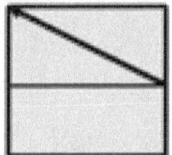

Lisa answered without hesitation. "Pythagoras' theorem states that,

$$a^2 + b^2 = c^2$$

where c represents the length of the hypotenuse of a right-angled triangle, and a and b represent the lengths of the other two sides."

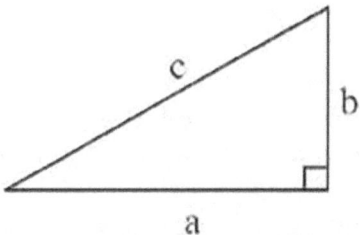

"Correct!" gleefully said Da Vinci. "You are an excellent student indeed, not like Michel—he only thinks of poetry. Now, if we set the length of the base at **1**, the length of vertical side becomes ½. It then follows that the square of the length of the diagonal is equal to:

$$(1)^2 + (½)^2 = 1\text{x}1 + ½\text{x}½ = 1 + ¼ = \textbf{5/4.}$$

"The length of the diagonal is therefore the square-root of **5/4**, expressed as $\dfrac{\sqrt{5}}{2}$ ".

"The next steps are to set the compass at the length of the diagonal, spike the bottom end of the diagonal with the compass, and draw an arc until it passes above the right-side vertical line. Now, the only step left is to extend that vertical line until it intersects with the arc, thus enabling us to create $\dfrac{1+\sqrt{5}}{2}$ ".

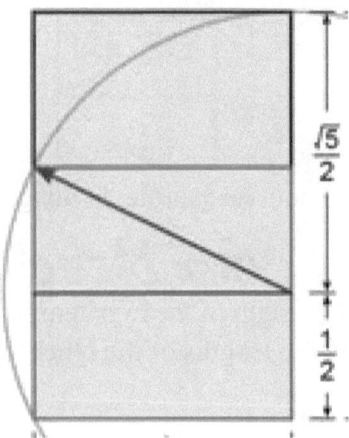

"You've created a golden rectangle," exclaimed Lisa.

A *golden rectangle* is one whose side lengths are in the golden ratio $\frac{1+\sqrt{5}}{2}$ or approximately 1:1.618. At least since the Renaissance, many artists and architects have proportioned their works to approximate the golden ratio—especially in the form of the golden rectangle, in which the ratio of the longer side to the shorter is the golden ratio—believing this proportion to be aesthetically pleasing.

"But why go through this exercise of creating a golden rectangle?" added Lisa.

Da Vinci gave out a wide silly smile. "Because Madonna Lisa, I suspect you are as golden as this rectangle. Resetting his compass to match the height of the golden rectangle, he reminded her: "The base of this golden rectangle matches the width of your face—from one temple to the other—correct?"

"Correct!" she confirmed.

Da Vinci then carefully placed on end of the compass against the bottom of her chin, and slowly moved the other end towards the top of her head, until it rested snugly onto it.

"Eureka!" he cried out. "A perfect fit! Your face has the proportions of the golden ratio. You, my dear, are a miracle of nature. You are *perfection!*"

"I am far from perfect," warned Lisa, who had yet to feel deserving of the old man's incessant admiration. "While any woman would welcome the entitlement, for all we know, I may have come from a very *dark* place."

"Nonsense!" rebutted Da Vinci. "Perfection can only come from the heavens. You are an angel, and I shall make this portrait into the mirror of your magnificence, your glory."

"Please, Leo, while I am so very happy and appreciative to be with you, I am not meant to be lavished with gifts," pleaded Lisa. "I am meant for something else."

An overexcited Da Vinci wouldn't hear of it. "Michel! Come over here and gaze upon the face of God's most sublime creation! And the world shall know of it very soon!"

Da Vinci feverously paced the room. "We must begin without delay. We shall call this masterpiece...ah, ah...yes! We shall call it *Madonna Lisa*! Simple but elegant."

"Too long," said Michel, the young would-be poet. "Call it *Mona Lisa*," opting for the more melodious contraction of the word Madonna.

Da Vinci jumped for joy, grabbing Michel's face. "I knew your feeble mind would come into use one day, you poetic rascal!"

Michel was quite pleased with himself, but it was not so for Lisa, who promptly left the room. She did not want her face to become known to the world. She feared, although not knowing why, that her newfound popularity would attract very bad elements—very bad indeed.

CHAPTER 75

In October 1515, *Francis I of France* recaptured
Milan. On December 19, he requested Leonardo Da Vinci's presence at a
meeting of Francis I and Pope Leo X in Bologna. Francis, considered to
be the first renaissance monarch, had been so impressed with Da Vinci's
artistic and engineering skills that, during the course of the meeting, he
commissioned him to construct a mechanical lion that could walk forward, then open its chest to reveal a cluster of lilies.

To insure Da Vinci's full devotion to the task, he officially entered
him into his service, and gave him the use of the manor house Clos Lucé
near his residence at the royal Château d'Amboise. Since then, Da Vinci
and the King have become close friends, and the former never missed an
occasion to impress his powerful pal.

"Master, you have not changed," remarked Michel de Nostredame.
"The King expects you and Lisa to join his aristocratic friends for supper
this evening…and in proper attire no less."

"This is the ninth supper this month," noted Lisa in frustration. "And
the object is always the same: to flaunt the exquisiteness of the *Mona
Lisa*. Some so-called friends have come from as far as the Netherlands to
see it. Leo, you should never have given Francis the painting. It's all he
talks about, and his poor wife Claude has turned to seething jealousy."

Da Vinci glanced at her as he slaved on another project at his worktable. "Is she jealous of the painting, or just you?"

"Of me, of course," she replied, unintentionally producing a smile
born of vanity. "But it's not right—not right for her, and not right for me.
By now, most of Europe knows either my face or of my face. Either way,
you know how I feel about this unwanted fame."

"Men ogling only the best variety of woman-kin is the ultimate stim-
ulus and testament that can be afforded any *ragazza*," stated Da Vinci.
"You should be honored."

Lisa timidly slapped the back of Da Vinci's head. "I thought you loved me for my mind, old man?"

"That goes without saying," he said before showing her what he had been laboring over. "Now, tell me how your mind interprets this small token of my love for your mind...and for *you*?" he added blushingly.

"It's...it's beautiful, Leo," she stuttered as he deposited a gold ring in her palm. *Amore Mio Lisa* was inscribed on the ring's inner side. "I don't deserve this."

Da Vinci retrieved the ring and slowly slid it on her left ring finger. "You deserve *all* of it. You've had a hard life. The manner of its chronology may vary as you struggle to remember, but its fact remains. I see it as I watch you in bed, tossing and turning, fighting to defeat the darkness... or *release* it. Either way, this ring is a promise that I shall be, now and forever, by your side."

"And I shall always be by *your* side, master," interjected Michel, not wanting to be excluded from the touching love-fest.

"She shall be sided by no one but us!" cried out a chilling voice from the main doorway.

Two towering demonic figures stood there, one wearing a white armor, the other red, both bearing strange weaponry—long sticks with a circular weight at the bottom end, and three nozzles, of equal length and positioned at 120 degree-angles from each other in circular fashion, at the top end.

"I am *Thevetat*, and this is *Aurignacia*," announced the red-armored demon. "Your scriptures know us as the *Dragons of Conquest and War*."

Upon laying eyes on the terrifying demons, Lisa let out a shrill scream that reverberated throughout the Clos Lucé manor, and collapsed onto the floor. "Don't let them hurt me," she entreated Da Vinci as she slid her body behind Da Vinci. "Oh! Oh...my head is throbbing."

Da Vinci mustered his courage, an abundance of which he never suspected possessing—love had indeed multiplied the quantity and quality of his better self. He moved one step forward, brandishing his oversized compass, metal spike first. "Leave now and you shall live!"

The demons smiled at the old man's benign bravado, and even more benign choice of weapons. "She has beguiled you," said Thevetat. "You're not the first *big shot* to fall prey to her charms. You may well be the very flower of the Renaissance movement, but consider this: Man is so defective, he may turn against you, even if he adulates you. And *she* will be the means to that end."

"What do you want with this woman, you spawn of evil?" shouted Da Vinci in a commanding tone, far more concerned about his mate than any threat to his fame.

"What does this whore call herself?" asked Thevetat. "Lisa? Or perhaps, Maria? She may be both, but mostly, she is neither. She is, above all and in ways that only matter, the *Mother of Mayhem*; the *Mother of the Destroyer of Worlds*."

"He is correct, my dearest," said Lisa, whose fear had oddly dissipated, replaced by cool resignation. "I *remember* who I am now. I remember! The shock of their arrival has pulled away the veil of my amnesia."

She stood up and moved to her protector's side. "If you vow to spare this man, and the boy," pointing to Michel, who was hiding under the worktable, "I will come with you willingly."

"You will do no such thing," ordered Da Vinci. "Your place is here."

"I'm not afraid anymore," she told Da Vinci, stroking his beard. "Who would be afraid of the truth when it sets you free?"

As Michel cowered under the table, he observed the demons' strange helmets, both adorned with the distinct symbol that covered Lisa's silver dress. This was not a coincidence.

"Come closer, woman," requested Thevetat. "Let me see you in all your impiety."

She complied, and he pulled the clothes off of her before embracing her. "Where is he? Where is the Destroyer?" he whispered with sweetness incongruent with his bloodcurdling appearance.

"He is not here," Lisa answered stoically. "He was never here…in this place, or in this time."

"You lie, bitch," said Thevetat as he gripped her neck and squeezed. "But I don't blame you; deception has been your teacher for far too long. Now, pull the thread of the tapestry of your preordained destiny and unravel what must be done."

She coughed noisily. "He will never be yours…or *his*," referring to the demons' master. "Take me, and only me, or go to Hell."

"That's the plan!" shouted Thevetat before throwing Lisa at Da Vinci, both falling to the ground. "Tell me where he is!"

"I will tell you where *he* is if you leave afterwards…*without* Lisa," offered a shaken Da Vinci.

"Agreed," said a pleased Thevetat.

Lisa said nothing about Da Vinci's imminent confession, pulling herself and her beloved up. "Throw me my robe immediately."

Thevetat signaled Aurignacia to do so, while he awaited an answer.

"He is hiding in a room," revealed Da Vinci, "third floor, second door to the left as you reach the top of the staircase." This was, of course, a lie.

Thevetat gazed at Lisa suspiciously. "He betrays you, yet you do not react. That is not in your nature."

"His motives are honorable," replied Lisa. "Besides, my sins are to an ant mound what his are to an ant. I am not the one to judge."

"You *have* changed," concluded Thevetat. "I did not think it possible. Aurignacia! Watch them while I fetch our prey." He engaged the staircase and disappeared around the first curve.

Lisa gracefully approached Aurignacia, hands in back. "I must confess that, among my protectors, you have always been my favorite. I have dreamt about you often. Have you dreamt about me?"

The demon appeared uncomfortable. "It is not permitted to consort with you."

She turned her back to him. "Is it at least permitted to attach the buttons of my dress? There are three, just below the neckline."

The uneasy demon glanced at the staircase to make sure Thevetat had gone. Once assured, he rested his weapon against the worktable, and began buttoning the dress. "It is done," he said softly.

Lisa turned again to face him. "You have dared do what is outside your purview, now I must dare do the same."

Auragnicia suddenly bent forward, groaning in pain. Lisa had stabbed his abdomen with the metal spike of the compass. "As I mentioned before," she whispered to him, "you shall go to Hell; but then again, where else would you go?" The demon crumbled to the floor.

To Da Vinci's and Michel's astonishment, Lisa had transformed into a fierce warrior-princess. "You must escape now! I'll hold them off," seizing the demon's weapon.

Michel scrambled to his feet, and ran to the door. "I'll fetch the king's guards!" He vanished before Da Vinci could stop him.

"It's too far and too dangerous to attempt in the open," Da Vinci warned Lisa. "We must travel underground...and covertly." He shuffled to the fireplace in the dining room, pressed a few stones, and the structure slid open like a door. "This secret underground corridor leads to the castle. We must hurry!"

The structure closed behind them. As they made their way through the damp and dingy corridor, Lisa stopped abruptly. "We may not survive this, so I must tell you who I truly am. You deserve at least that."

"We're wasting time, my dearest, my love. We must go!" insisted Da Vinci, who feared more for her life than his.

"Listen to me, damn you!" she retorted firmly, pulling him back by the arm. "It will take a grand total of a minute—the most important and meaningful minute of my life…and yours."

Da Vinci finally acquiesced, but no amount of earthly experience could prepare him for what she had to tell him.

CHAPTER 76

The aperture has been breached," exclaimed a stunned Da Vinci, struggling not only physically, but intellectually with the knowledge that had just been imparted to him. It was so incredible that his mind had difficulty concentrating on the vital task at hand. "He's coming!"

"Lisa!...Maria!" screamed Thevetat. "What name must I call you for you to regain your senses? I will tell no one of your aggression against Aurignacia if you capitulate and tell me where he is concealed."

"I cannot move any further," confessed Da Vinci. "My old bones won't allow it."

"Then we will make our stand here," bravely spat out Lisa, who frantically examined the weapon she had stolen. "Where is the firing mechanism? Damn machinery!" hitting the stick portion repeatedly.

A shot suddenly rang out from a distance, followed by three bolts of fiery energy, one of which hit the right side of Da Vinci's chest, traversing it like it was made of air. He fell heavily to the ground. "I can't feel my right side. I'm paralyzed."

Thevetat's silhouette rose among the shadows. Lisa pointed her weapon, having just grasped its operation. "If you kill me, you will never know where he is."

A second shot rang out. One bolt ripped away her left hand. A second bolt hit her in the heart. The weapon dropped, and she followed right after. She was dead.

Thevetat walked to her body. "It appears my patience has run out."

"The master will be incensed," remarked an injured Aurignacia, who had stumbled through the corridor in the wake of his comrade's murderous pursuit.

"She did not know," surmised Thevetat, "therefore of no use to us."

"Where is he then?" asked Aurignacia. "We must tell the master something."

"We will tell him the *conditions* of our search have become many times more arduous," replied Thevetat.

"What of the old man?" wondered Aurignacia.

"What of him?" snapped back Thevetat. "If he speaks of this…of *any* of it, people will think him insane. Pick up your weapon; we have to go."

In truth, Da Vinci rarely spoke of it, except to his closest friends. He did something more, however; something more perennial. After recuperating, he solicited his left arm and hand, which had not been paralyzed, to create new masterpieces, and *update* some old ones.

Needless to say, Da Vinci's patron Duke Ludovico Sforza and his duchess Beatrice d'Este were both surprised to learn that the famous painter, with the aid of his apprentice Fransesco Melzi, modified the Last Supper mural painting, covering the dining hall wall at the monastery of Santa Maria delle Grazie in Milan, Italy.

"Now, *you* shall live on forever, my dearest *Lisa-Maria*," he declared after completing what he coined *much needed restoration work*. "And the world shall know of your rightful place."

As for Michel de Nostredame, he left the manor shortly after the incident, but not before leaving a set of eight coordinates, and the solution to the blocking mechanism, that allowed two demons to escape through a well. He had come upon the demons as they pressed on the last stone that activated the well, and had counted on his memory not to forget before he could put pen to paper.

The king's guards reached Michel a minute later, but saw nothing; and nor would they ever believe the young Nostredame boy. He would write about this, and much more as his poetic inspiration—as biased as it had been condemned to become—grew.

Like Da Vinci's angel, he too would not be forgotten.

CHAPTER 77

Present day; Kingdom of Hell.

"It appears your paralysis was inconsequential," observed the man who spoke a perfect English. "You seem undamaged, at least not impaired permanently."

Theon rolled onto his stomach, pushed against the floor with his arms, and brought his legs inwards until he could assume a kneeling position. He was still dazed by the immobilizing drug administered earlier by the demonic creature that kidnapped him from his home.

"Where am I?" wondered Theon, who anxiously looked about his surroundings only to discover that he was imprisoned in a large cage whose confinement properties were the product of an amalgam of horizontal metal bars, electro-magnetic circuitry and a multi-layered force field. He was scared.

"I'm afraid you and I are captives of the Diabolicus, the beasts of Hell," reported the man, detained in a similar cage adjacent to Theon's. "But unlike you, I have been rotting in this dungeon for almost two Millennia, my loneliness allayed only by the occasional visit of an old teacher."

Theon immediately concluded that the dire conditions of the man's captivity had driven him to madness, although he appeared quite serenely self-possessed and free from agitation for a madman. His eyes, in particular, projected not only a disarming placidity, but a flickering glow like the incandescence of smoldering embers of a fire refusing to die and wrought its ghost upon the gazing eyes of others. The man's tranquility was soothing and helped alleviate some of Theon's fear. "You look a little peaked. Are you sick or ailing?"

"Not at all," energetically replied the man. "It's just a misleading side-effect of my current condition." To emphasize his point, the man slid his hand between two of the horizontal bars, breaching the first layer of the force field. His entire body began to flicker and flare, and his hand gradually lost cohesion. As the impressive effect extended to his forearm, he pulled out his hand. "Had I maintained this dangerous activity for a few instants more, I would have *de-echoalesced*...in perpetuity."

Theon was astounded. "What in Heavens are you? A spectre?"

"What *in Hell* would be a more accurate statement," smiled the man. "As for my nature, I'm a splendid example of *Resurrection*...and widely acknowledged on Earth, from what I've heard."

Theon frowned in confusion. "Could you be at all clearer?"

"My detractors have also often accused me of being deliberately cryptic and enigmatic," admitted the man. "Occupational hazard, I suppose." The man moved to the center of the cage, raised his arms until they were perfectly horizontal, and tilted his head to his right. "You may recognize me for having died on the cross. I am none other than *Jesus Christ*."

Theon laughed out loud, providing further relief from the glumness of his situation. "You're Jesus Christ—or rather his resurrected soul—and yet, we're in Hell and not in Heaven. Oh, and let's not forget," Theon groped his body in several areas to demonstrate the physical fabric of his body, "I'm not dead."

The so-called Jesus was puzzled. "It is true that you are *not* a resurrected soul—an Echo— and the reason you were brought here is as yet unknown, but *I* am here, in Hell, and the reason is clear: I once carried with me the burden of the sins of Humanity, and as they were thrust upon me, I became the most sinful man on Earth. Upon my death, there could be no other place for me than Hell. I accept this fate wholeheartedly, and would face it many times over without hesitation."

His words were hauntingly poignant and untainted by bitterness or injustice; and stirred by them, Theon skepticism began to abate. "You were very courageous, but I get the sense that the decision to take the sins of Man upon your shoulders was not entirely yours. Am I right?"

"You're an incredibly perceptive boy," said Jesus with fatherly pride and admiration. "During my Earthly life, my thoughts, my choices and my decisions were always guided by a divine force, a holy spirit of sorts, part of me yet greater than all my parts; a mentor without which I would have undoubtedly embraced a path of misdeeds and wrongdoings, and without which I never would have been endowed with the power to wash away Man's sins."

Theon appeared especially sympathetic and moved upon the mention of a holy spirit, blushing scarlet and his eyes watering a bit. "Does he talk to you?"

"He used to," replied Jesus. "He is long gone now. Only his imprint remains. I once had come to believe it to be the spirit of God—my true father, in every sense that mattered; and a father who, for the greater good, forsook me in favor of the mission rather than the missionary. You understand what I mean, don't you?" Judging by Theon's physical reaction, Jesus strongly suspected many of the boy's experiences paralleled his own.

Theon wiped a tear. "I understand...*perfectly.*"

"Then let us speak of *your* holy spirit," candidly proposed Jesus. "Does he keep you on the path? Does he contain your darkness? Do you call him Father?"

"I've often strayed from the course," confessed a guilt-ridden Theon; "and it has become increasingly difficult for my spirit to suppress the darkness within me. I'm so scared the darkness will one day prevail that I toyed many a time with the idea of disabling its power by ending my life."

"That is *not* a solution," adamantly warned Jesus. "While you may resurrect after death, you would discover that the wickedness, in all its forms, had not vacated your soul, and that your holy companion, unlike the darkness, was not the proprietor of your soul but only its evicted tenant. As a human being, you may yet escape this place; as an Echo, you stand a good chance of being damned to Hell for all eternity."

"In both cases, I'm no doubt condemned to Hell," said Theon. "Only the time of my damnation would change."

"*Time* is your best ally," insisted Jesus. "Live your life, and let it become a veritable repository of deeds of redemption; a chronicle of feats of atonement. Listen to your holy spirit; he will shepherd you towards salvation."

"The Ghost Knight agrees, in principle," said Theon after just receiving a message from his spirit, "but claims my quest for deliverance should be set about here, on this soil before it can end on the Earth's. Being brought here is no coincidence, he contends. It's a blessing in disguise."

"The Ghost Knight? A warrior figure?" noted Jesus. "Interesting choice of character. Can you ask this *spiritual cavalier* to explain his recommendation?"

Theon grimaced and shook his head. "The words are vague, if you can call them words at all. They're turning into a cloud of dust, and as it settles, an image is materializing. I see the Ghost Knight standing atop a hill. He's saying something; the words are resilient, resistant to the raging winds: *'Beware the blood brother who covets his brother's house in*

Heaven and on Earth; beware this brother and seek the other in Heaven; beware the brother who is also the blood father of the father; and this father in Heaven shall help the blood son; and this son shall be delivered from evil by the blade of the mightiest sword among all swords.'"

"Is that it?" asked Jesus, hungry for more.

"Yep." Theon shrugged his shoulders. "He decides when to talk to me, and when he does, he's seldom very clear. You and he seem to share the same speech affliction," cracking a smirk. "Nevertheless, he never steered me wrong. Regardless of what it all means, one thing's plain to me, I have to break out of this joint; and, with or without help, find some kind of mighty sword; not a metaphorical one but one that can truly split a man in two."

"Then you believe yourself to be the *son* in your spirit's parable?" surmised Jesus, "which implies your father whose blood you carry and from whom help shall come lives in this realm and is therefore an Echo."

Theon's voice became filled with emotion. "I hadn't thought about that, finally meeting my *real* father. Who was he? Who *is* he? What will he think of me?"

"From what little I've seen of you, he will be incredibly proud of you," reassured Jesus, who had always been a maven at reading people's purest and dominant nature.

"This is all very touching," said a soft female voice coming from the dungeon shadows, "but fatherly love isn't all it's cracked up to be." A demonic creature slithered into the light, her face bruised and swollen. "If Satan can do this to his daughter, think of what he can do to you, *human*."

CHAPTER 78

The female Diabolicus Terrum looked quite young by human standards—about fourteen years old. She wore knee-high boots and a black sleeveless short skirt dress made of leather, outfitted with metallic armbands, belt and breast plate. Her lustrous red hair reached her waist and her face was pretty despite the injuries. While she clearly possessed many Diabolicus traits, several distinguishing ones were absent, like the horns, the claws and the bloodshot eyes.

"You can ogle me all you want, human," she told Theon, a part of whom found itself attracted to her, while the rest remained wary. "I never refuse a compliment, no matter how it's delivered."

"My name is not *human*, it's Theon," he said, walking to the front of the cage.

The young demon followed suit. "I know. Mine is *Akara*." She scanned him from head to foot. "You're cute. You and I could have fun together."

"We could," cautiously agreed Theon, "but then, you'd have to release me."

"Not just yet," she teasingly replied. "First, tell me about yourself."

Theon acquiesced, having nothing to lose. "Well, I'm from Earth, born of unknown parents, and was kidnapped and brought here, which I understand from Jesus is Hell. What about you?"

Figuring she would toy with him, Theon expected her to lie, or at the very least to remain evasive. In truth, she was quite happy and eager to share her sad story with someone close to her own age.

"I'm also a prisoner," she contended, "a slave to the pitiless authority and maniacal impulses of Satan, my tyrannical father, the antipode of my kind and generous mother, Anaita. Before being captured during the Great War, she had been one of Lord God's highest ranking angels, responsible for tending to the Garden of Eden. But now, she, ah, ah…"

Visibly shaken, her voice started faltering. Her tough cookie facade had now completely faded away.

"Your mother is dead, isn't she?" figured Theon. "Maybe she's come back as an Echo, and you need only search for her."

Akara sighed in sadness. "While Sanctus and Diabolicus are eternal, barring fatal injuries, they ironically do not resurrect like many human beings. Your parents, however, might have come back, now hopefully living in the Kingdom of Heaven. I understand they're very *special*."

Theon couldn't ascertain whether or not Akara was trying to curry his favor by flattery, and for what purpose she would do so. "What makes you say that about my parents?"

"I paid for that bit of information with my face," said Akara, stroking her bruised cheek. "This morning, as I snooped around Satan's office—something I've done oftentimes—I noticed a file labeled *Theon Rex* on his desk. A photo was clipped to the file; and to me delight, it was that of a kid...and possible new friend. Before I could rummage through its content, the door opened, and my father appeared, followed by the Dark Lord. I quickly slipped under the desk."

"Aren't the Dark Lord and Satan one and the same?" wondered Theon, recalling Christian terminology.

"Satan is known as the Dragon Lord," explained Akara. "The Dark Lord is a mysterious and sinister being, master to Satan. How this came about is a matter of rampant speculation."

"I once heard the guards hinting a rumor about some wartime happenings," interjected Jesus, who had been silently studying Akara since her appearance. "They spoke of a powerful being that intervened in support of Satan's campaign; a being without which Satan's army would have met with defeat. They also said the being extricated God's Holy Spirit, Maitreya, from the Kalidrone's claws, and imprisoned him in a secret location known only to the being and Satan. In gratitude to or in fear of the being, Satan deferred to its greater power."

"It's evident they were talking about the Dark Lord," ventured Akara. "From my hiding place, I couldn't see his face. In fact, he's such a recluse that only a few have ever seen it. But while I couldn't see him, I could hear him quite clearly—a deep and hoarse voice. He referred to your parents as carefully manufactured *Diads*, and to you as the *Ultimate Tri-Weapon*. Do you know why he would call you that?"

Theon appeared troubled by the foreboding epithet, recalling all his exploits of the supernatural kind. "All I can say is that I'm not like other human beings. When I'm sufficiently *motivated* and emotionally aroused, I can do things no one else can."

Akara was keenly intrigued, her interest in Theon steadily transforming into infatuation whose telling signs she resolutely suppressed. "Oh, and there's something else. The Dark Lord mentioned a sword, but not any sword—the Sword of Maitreya. He said, if wielded by Maitreya himself, it would become the only thing that could neutralize the weapon…I mean you."

Theon and Jesus shot a complicit look at each other. "We too have heard of such a mighty sword, capable of eradicating evil," said Jesus, his provisional trust in Akara instantly consolidating. "Does he have the sword?"

"He doesn't," replied Akara. "It was seized by the Kalidrone, near the City of God, during the Great War; and was probably hidden in one of the Kalidrone's countless underground caves, possibly under the city."

"A fair assumption. Did they talk about the manner in which the sword should be used," asked Jesus, "other than in its traditional usage?"

"I couldn't say," replied Akara. "Before I could learn more, I was discovered by my father, who used my face as a canvass to express all the nuances of his displeasure. He's hurt me so many times before. I wish he were dead instead of my mother."

Despite his own precarious situation, Theon felt sorry for her and suddenly became compelled to help her. "I feel very *motivated* and *aroused* now, Akara. Move your face as close as you can to the bars." He slipped his hand between two bars and through the force field, which light up like fireworks. The electro-magnetic charge traveled throughout his body, ravaging his nervous system; but he remained steadfast, ignoring the excruciating pain.

Jesus was mesmerized by Theon's boldness and his resistance to the otherwise deadly energy of the field, while Akara could only scream in horror. "Don't Theon!" Before she could back up, forcing Theon to abort his valiant attempt, he grabbed the underside of her chin and held it tight. Their eyes met; hers were pleading, his were determined.

Then, the inconceivable happened. The swelling subsided and the bruises faded. Her face was immaculate once again. Theon retracted his hand and stumbled back.

"The pain is gone!" she exclaimed, passing her hands over her face. "You're not a weapon at all."

"No wicked being could act so magnanimously," declared Jesus.

"There's far more Good than Evil in you, my son."

"That's funny; I don't feel so good." Theon staggered and then collapsed, losing consciousness as he hit the floor.

"Hurry Akara, open the cage!" Jesus implored. "He may be dying!"

"I don't know the lock combination," she cried. "I never did." She paced the floor frantically. "What do I do? What do I do?" She stopped abruptly. "I know; I'll get the guard." In a flash, she was gone, leaving only the echo of her footsteps behind as a remnant of her presence.

Jesus stared at Theon, filled with a degree of concern and affection rivaling that which he had once reserved for Maria Magdalena, his long dead consort. He had not heard of her return as an Echo, and concluded she was among those who had not *echoalesced.* He took solace in the possibility that she had been spared an eternity of suffering in the Kingdom of Hell, although he could not image a terrestrial life of misdeeds that would have condemned her to servitude to the Dragon Lord.

And he would not accept such a fate being inflicted on a boy who deserved the rest of his life, if only to prove his measure as an honorable man. "Hold on, Theon. Help is on its way." Theon's fingers twitched as if in response to Jesus' reassuring words.

Then, his eyes opened slightly as Akara and a guard of Herculean proportions arrived. "Open it, quickly!" she instructed in an authoritative tone—she had naturally taken command of the situation, a disposition new to her, which she attributed to paternal heredity. Being Daddy's girl had *some* advantages.

The guard punched in seven numbers on a pad affixed to the cage. The force field shut down and the front panel slid sideways. The guard stepped in, but stopped three feet short of Theon's position, eying the boy nervously. Akara rushed past him and crouched by Theon, taking his pulse. One eye opened and winked at her.

Akara understood. "Guard, I can't feel his pulse. We must take him to a Healer."

"That's against Lord Satan's orders," he retorted. "The human is dangerous, and no one must approach him."

"If we do not move him, he will die," warned Akara. "And *that* is against Satan's orders. You must carry him now!"

The guard finally complied. He rested his weapon against the bars, and then bent over Theon's body. Before he could secure it, Theon's hands shot up and seized the guard's neck, squeezing ever so tightly. Panicked, the guard began pummeling Theon's stomach and chest, but to no avail.

He then seized the boy's arms and tried to rip them off his neck.

Theon's eyes filled with blood as he produced a vicious smile. "No one can hurt me now, but *you*, you can be hurt…and you can die." His back started bulging under his shirt, and the more he tightened his grip, the more the dorsal protuberance grew.

"Stop it, Theon! You're killing him!" screamed Jesus. "You're not a murderer!"

Theon glared at Jesus. "I told you who I was, and you refused to believe me. Look at me! Is this not proof enough?"

"It proves nothing," claimed Jesus overlooking Theon's strange transformation, "if only that, like all humans, you can kill…but you will *not*. It is that abstinence and that sobriety that truly define you. Listen to your spirit, to your Ghost Knight."

Theon suddenly relaxed his grip. "I can barely hear my spirit. He listened intently. "Stay…stay…*stay the course*!"

Jesus instantly recalled the numerous times his own spirit counseled him to stay the course. "Yes, Theon! Stay the course! You must not go astray!"

Theon turned his attention to Akara, who had refrained from intervening—she really didn't care whether the guard lived or died; and didn't care why that was so. She, in fact, lacked the introspection to realize that she was projecting her scornful hatred and intense hostility towards her father onto the guard.

"Live or die," he said to Akara. "What do you choose?"

She stared hesitantly at the dying guard for a long moment, and decided. "For your sake, Theon, and *only* for your sake, I say Live."

Theon released the guard and stood up. In seconds, his physicality returned to normal. "He'll live, thanks to both of you."

"No, thanks to you son," said a relieved Jesus. "I do have some questions about what just transpired."

"No time," barked Akara. "The change of guard is imminent. I can get you out of here. I know a secret way that leads to the outside."

"And go where?" asked Theon.

"Where we can find help," answered Akara. "Help from the smartest Echo who ever graced the Kingdoms of Heaven and Hell: *Leonardo Da Vinci.*

CHAPTER 79

Theon and Akara traveled steadfastly along
the coast of the Province of Abaddon. The terrain was coated with rocks
of all sizes tightly knit together. While it made the trek toilsome, the rock
formation provided cover from the demon guards who regularly surveyed
the area for escaped Echoes.

Some Echoes, desperate to elude the guards and a life of bondage and
suffering, would throw themselves into the Lost Sea, only to be devoured
by carnivorous sharp-teeth fish, the size of white sharks.

After hours of braving the hazardous topography, made doubly daunting by the bodeful hot air, the duo came upon a hill, at the top of which
clouds soiled with grime and sulfur billowed down its side.

"Try not to breathe in too deeply," suggested Akara. "The suspended
filth won't kill you, but it'll make you cough; and that could attract the
guards."

As they climbed, Theon flapped his hands in an attempt to disperse
the dirty air. It only made things worse. Once they reached the top, Akara
directed Theon to a small zone exempt of clouds, a vantage point from
which they could see miles away in every direction except for South.

The Eastern side of the hill towered over the Echo Peninsula, which
was bustling with activity. Hundreds of people were moving about.

"What's going on?" asked a curious Theon.

"Echo processing," said Akara with a modicum of disdain. "Do you
see that shimmering wall of glass traversing part of the peninsula?" The
wall was 200 feet long, 25 feet high, and three feet thick.

"Too big to miss," replied Theon. "What's it fo—Whoa! Did you see
that? Someone emerged from it. Oh, and there's another…and another."
He was mesmerized, gawking at the phenomenon, and then at Akara,
craving for an explanation.

"The wall is a solar energy collector," revealed Akara, "built long ago to capture the energy emanating from *Shuntra*, the heavenly Sun," pointing upwards at the magnificent celestial body. "Once collected, the energy is then distributed throughout this kingdom and the neighboring kingdom of Heaven, providing lighting, heating, and power to structures, instruments, machines, and weapons. As for the creation of Echoes, that's an unexpected by-product of the wall's operating protocol."

This was certainly not the manner in which Theon imagined souls arriving in Heaven…or Hell. "But at least this is something," he thought, "and not the void many predicted after death."

"The wall converts energy into matter," deduced Theon.

Akara nodded. "Yes, but not all energy; only that which vibrates at multiples of a precise base frequency and carries a specific quantum signature. Eternal scientists have tried to eliminate this incidental secondary effect, but not without impairing the wall's proper functioning.

"In the face of this technical failure, Lord Deus, King of Heaven, in his great wisdom and benevolence, declared the alternative—co-existence with human souls—a unique opportunity for generosity and indulgence. Since the Echoes of that time were generally docile and cooperative, and mostly grateful for a second chance at life, few eternals objected to Deus' decree."

"Some Echoes don't seem too grateful," noted Theon, who saw several being shoved into a bus by Diabolicus guards. "Where is that bus going?"

"To nearby regions of Upper Hell," sadly replied Akara. In the wake of the Great War between the Sanctus—Deus's people—and the Diabolicus, the land was split in two. The newly formed Kingdom of Hell was further split into two major zones: Upper Hell, where we are, Lower Hell, and one small area called Purgatory."

"No One goes to Heaven?" wondered Theon, who found the whole exercise ironically *inhuman.*

"Some do," said Akara. "Echoes are evaluated based on their Earthly sins, and assigned a score. That score determines whether they go to Upper Hell, Lower Hell, Purgatory, or Heaven."

Increasingly disgusted, Theon noticed a Sanctus guard pulling a young girl away from what clearly appeared to be her parents. This family of three had just died in a car accident, and what constituted their souls had traversed the energy wall.

"Mommy! Mommy!" she cried out in despair, while her hysterical mother, sobbing and screaming, was struck down by a Diabolicus guard, who tired of her frenzy. To Theon's surprise, Sanctus guards and Diabolicus guards worked together in processing Echoes. It was grotesque.

The young girl was pushed into the first wagon of a train stationed nearby. Theon counted thirteen wagons. "What will happen to that little girl?"

Akara managed a consoling smile. "She's lucky; she's going to Heaven; as are all the people boarding the first six wagons. Her parents, however, are not so lucky," watching them being forced into the ninth wagon, its cargo destined for Lower Hell..

Nearby, a group of resistant Echoes were being poked with electrified prods, much like the ones used on cattle. They all crashed to the ground, their bodies convulsing violently.

Theon stared intently at Akara, his fists clenched. "I feel very motivated and aroused right now. I have the power to save some of them."

"And start a war? No way!" ordered Akara. "The Diabolicus will think Deus sent some kind of super-soldier. The peace is fragile enough as it is. I won't have you jeopardize it."

"This peace of yours is a farce," rebuked Theon, waving his arm at the despicable scene. "If this is the fruit of peace, then it's not worth preserving."

Akara clamped Theon's arm. "Now you listen to me. When you've walked far enough and long enough in Lord Deus' shoes, then and only then will you have earned the right to speak so brazenly and unequivocally. Until that happens, don't presume to know better than God."

Theon reluctantly abided and slowly calmed down. "If I ever make it back to Earth, I'll have the Bible retooled…big time."

"You'll have that chance sooner than you think," teased Akara. "Da Vinci has a copy of it; and it lies within the walls of that mansion over there," pointing westwards. "That's the *Heavenly Embassy in Hell*, Da Vinci's residence."

"Let's hurry then," enjoined Theon, "while I still feel creative."

CHAPTER 80

At the conclusion of his round of the dungeon, Satan, accompanied by a guard, stopped by Jesus' cell. Another guard stood watch by the cell.

"How's the prisoner?" asked Satan, expecting no novel or witty response.

"Behaving, as usual," promptly replied the guard whose dread of his leader always occasioned profuse perspiration. He knew Satan always punished those among his minions who failed him—and he had failed him in spectacular fashion by letting a human child, critical to his designs, escape.

Satan faced the guard and peered deeply into his eyes. "I see no fire, only fear. I see no flames, only the urge to flee. Choose, fight or flight."

"I do not understand, my Lord?" replied the guard in a shaky voice.

"Give me your Kor'ta," Satan ordered the first guard. The Dragon Lord then aimed the weapon at the guilty guard. "Let us fight then," and he discharged the weapon, killing the guard, who slumped to the ground.

Satan turned to the first guard. "How about you; fight or flight?"

The guard took a few steps back. "My Lord, I have done nothing against you." He then raised his weapon ever so slightly, in readiness for the fight.

"That is true," admitted Satan. "Then, I ask you to do something *for* me."

"Ask and I shall obey," said the guard, who relaxed his weapon.

"I ask only that you die," and Satan discharged his weapon a second time.

"You're in a foul mood today," jested Jesus. "Did you fall short of your blood quota?"

Satan let out an impish laugh. "Oh, I haven't killed these guards; Theon E. Rex has. He's now a fugitive of the State. And if he makes it to

Heaven, he will be summarily extradited to Hell, no questions asked. The Acts of Maitreya at work; how wonderful."

"He's a clever boy, far more ingenious than you," claimed Jesus. "You'll never get your dirty hands on him again."

"I've already bested the boy in intellectual sparring," asserted Satan. "And the deceived knows nothing of the deceit. You see, old friend, the conversation Akara heard in my office was carefully planned; I knew she was there, hiding under the desk. And I knew, lonely as she was because of her confinement to the castle, that she would take a liking to Theon, the only being her age, and repeat everything to him. My daughter has a big mouth...just like her mother."

"What can he possibly do for you?" wondered Jesus. "He's just a boy, baffled by his heritage."

"He's far more than that," contended Satan. "And once he finds the Sword of Maitreya, the equation will be complete, and the human known as Theon Rex will be forgotten."

"You lie, you bastard," cried out Jesus, "as you've always done."

"Perhaps so," smiled Satan, "but how can you be certain; as certain as your belief that Maitreya is being detained in a secret location? Oh, that piece of information you provided to Theon was priceless. Since he believes Maitreya to be the *only* one to save him, and believes me knowledgeable of the Holy Spirit's location, he *will* come back to me, one way or another, sword in hand."

"Why don't you get the sword yourself?" barked Jesus. "Do your own dastardly work, if you think it can be used for some grand purpose." For a brief instant, he detected a shred of helplessness in Satan. "You don't know where it is, do you? You never did."

"That is a secondary consideration," simply replied Satan, "but more importantly, my direct involvement would start a war, and conditions are not yet ripe for a war. Better a rogue element acting independently than a Lord risking his kingdom."

"Yet sending the boy in your stead frightens you," detected Jesus. "Don't forget who I was...and still am, to some extent; I can *smell* fear. You're afraid that, if the boy's quest leads him to Heaven, Deus might not expulse him, but welcome him as an ally."

"Your mind is fabulating and ultimately failing you," spouted Satan; "oh so feeble, so feeble, isn't that so, Master?"

"Indeed," confirmed a malignant voice from the shadows.

Satan moved back a few feet. "You were correct, Jesus, at least partially, about Maitreya's presence somewhere in Hell. Does that make you feel better?"

A tall cloaked figure moved into the light. "Greetings, Jesus. It is good to see you again. Let me introduce myself, as best I can. The people of Heaven have come to know me as Maitreya, Holy Spirit to Lord Deus; once part of Deus, and then separate from him. I was never the former, but always the latter." He pulled down his hood, revealing a terribly deformed face.

"I don't know what you mean," exclaimed a confused Jesus, his mind hard at work trying to imagine the figure's original face. "Speak plainly."

"I shall," promised the figure. "There is no plainer way to say this, my son. I am your *father*."

CHAPTER 81

"Akara, what are you doing here? Another lesson from the teacher?" asked one of the two Sanctus Angelicum sentries guarding the entrance to the Embassy. "You know full well Ambassador Da Vinci does not receive anyone early in the morning."

"I thought I was your favorite Drac," quipped the sexy Diabolicus as she moved around the sentry in a sinuous alluring fashion.

"You best return to the castle before Satan discovers your absence," urged the sentry. "He will not condone your truancy much longer."

Akara pushed Theon forward. "He may not condone it, but Leo will. I come bearing a gift that will delight and tantalize his fondness for wondrous curiosities."

"I am not a curiosity," objected Theon, "wondrous or otherwise."

The sentry appeared amused while the other remained stolid. "All right, you guileful creature; you can go in. You owe me."

Before the sentry could reconsider, Akara and her *package* had already crossed the threshold and were well within the lofty hallway. Two marble circular staircases, on either side of the hall led to the second floor, at the feet of which stood two imposing crystal statues of Lord Deus. The walls were covered with paintings, and above their heads hung a majestic chandelier made of gold and diamonds.

The hallway connected to a lounge long since converted into a workshop by Da Vinci. The Renaissance master was obviously out of bed and roaming about since a strong light shone from its interior. No doubt Da Vinci was slaving over a new contraption or a painting. He preferred that over his official duties of handling and mediating minor Echo transgressions of obscure, ancillary by-laws occurring on Hell territory.

As the youngsters entered the room, a two-faced parrot perched on a stand gave away their presence before Akara could acquit herself of the task. "The pretty Akara is here!"

The parrot's head rotated 180 degrees, now giving precedence to the other face whose position was in perfect opposition to its counterpart. "The ugly Akara is not here!"

"One always tells the truth, while the other always lies," Akara told Theon. "The master calls the bird: *Schrödinger*, after some Earth physicist."

As per her habit, she caressed the bird's head, "a pleasure seeing you again, Mister Schrödinger," before trotting to an oblivious Da Vinci, arched over something, immersed in his work.

She tapped him on the back three times. "Hell calling Uncle Leo, hello!" she shouted in Italian, one of the many languages she had learned from the master inventor. She tapped again, this time with greater vigor. "Your tortelli are ready!"

Da Vinci turned around posthaste. "Breakfast is ready." He shuffled to a microwave on a nearby table and looked through its window. "There's no tortelli in there. Akara, did you eat my tortelli?"

"No, Uncle," assured Akara. "They're still in the freezer. Tell me, Leo, who is that?" She pointed at a stocky male Echo tied to a chair, who had been Da Vinci's center of attention for the last few hours.

"It's the strangest thing," muttered Da Vinci. "This Echo attacked the sentries. He was quite enraged and bloodthirsty, wanted to kill them both with his bare hands."

"He must have escaped the Diabolicus and come here hoping for sanctuary," supposed Akara, "at least initially."

"No, no, no, not at all," countered Da Vinci. "He might look tame and oblivious now, but he had murder on his mind, nothing else. I suspect brainwashing. He was programmed to kill Sanctus. Highly irregular."

"Does this constitute a breach of one of the Acts of Maitreya?" wondered Akara. "Must we bring this to Deus' attention?"

"I'm not certain," replied an agitated Da Vinci. "There's nothing explicit about this *procedure* in the Acts. Nevertheless, it's cause for concern. *But*, first things first, breakfast." He trotted to Theon. "Young man, get the tortelli out of the freezer, on the top—" The old man suddenly froze and cringed, his scattered mind finally acknowledging the boy's existence. "What manner of animal is this?"

Overcoming his surprise, he placed a thumb under each eye, and pulled down, exposing the quasi-totality of Theon's eyeballs. "I don't see any flickering or glowing. Are you…are you…" He released Theon and withdrew quickly. "Are you a *mutant* Echo?"

"Leo, this is Theon from Earth's America," said Akara. "He's a *human being*, in the flesh. He hasn't died and resurrected."

Da Vinci was flabbergasted. "How is that possible? The Trans'Kartum is buried." He circled Theon repeatedly, stopping and going, pinching his chin and then his nose. "This happened before during the 1940's: *living* Nazi soldiers appeared in Hell. Two isolated events, but clearly connected."

Da Vinci ran to his worktable, foraged through stacks of papers and pulled out a diagram of a ring marked by 80 symbols. "This is a pictorial of a Trans'Kartum, a device that allows travel from one world to another, from one realm to another. I drew this based on the one I found on Earth. Do you recognize it, boy?"

"Yes, I do," confirmed Theon. "The demon who kidnapped me activated it and took me through, just before I lost consciousness."

"A violation of the Act of Non-Interference," asserted Da Vinci. "*That* we can bring to Deus without the burden of ambiguity."

"Without a receiving Trans'Kartum in this realm, our case is moot," pointed out Akara. "Theon might as well be a mutant Echo."

Theon, who was saddled with a more precariously personal agenda, was becoming weary of all the talks about law and order. "Not that any of your points aren't material to the future of Heaven and Hell—a legitimate preoccupation I'm sure—but I'm here for one reason and one reason only: my liberation."

Of course, we digress," realized Akara, who proceeded to brief Da Vinci on Theon's unique situation. The more Da Vinci knew about Theon, the better equipped he would be in diagnosing his condition. Perhaps an elusive sword wielded by a missing spirit was not the only solution.

"Short of finding your biological parents, who would indubitably shed light on your condition," assumed Da Vinci, "we'll begin with arresting manifestations of that condition. Present your evidence, my lad."

"For starters, there's this." Theon pulled back his hair, exposing his pointed ears.

"Great Scott!" cried out Da Vinci. "I've seen those on a human being only once before. Wait here." He rushed out the workshop to a side room, and returned, carrying four paintings, spreading them on the worktable. They all depicted a fetching dark-haired woman in various settings. In all paintings, her hair was slightly pulled back, highlighting her pointed ears. "I made them all from memory. A past love of mine."

Theon passed his hand over each one of them, his index finger tracing the contour of her face on the last one. "Mother?" he mumbled.

"What was that?" asked Da Vinci.

Theon's face was flustered. "She looks a lot like my adoptive Mother...sort of."

"A mystery upon a mystery," exclaimed Da Vinci. "She lived over 500 years ago."

Akara picked up one of the paintings. "Maybe Diabolicus blood ran through her veins. What was her name?"

"That also is a matter of conjecture," said Da Vinci. "I had come to call her Lisa-Maria."

"Have you looked for her in Heaven or Hell?" asked Akara.

"I have, but found nothing," sadly replied Da Vinci. "She must not have echoalesced. Many don't. I must talk to Deus about the energy collector; perhaps I can improve its effectiveness. I haven't even found her children, a boy named *Jeshel* and a girl whose name was bestowed by another, quite unknown to the mother."

Da Vinci sighed before cutting short his trip down memory lane and returning to the subject at hand. "What else do you have to show for yourself, young man?"

Theon removed his shirt and displayed his back. "These bumps turn into wings resembling more those of the Diabolicus than the Sanctus."

"You're a veritable conundrum on two legs," bellowed Da Vinci, who began pricking the bumps with a pencil. "Strange muscle and bone formation that reach up to the base of the neck. Preliminary evidence suggests you're no mutant Echo at all. You're a *mutant Diabolicus*!"

"That's not amusing at all," shouted Akara. "Does Theon really look like me?"

Da Vinci glared at Akara. "Well, Missy, do you have a more incisive diagnosis?" He resumed his examination, expecting no cunning reply, then stumbled on something new and exotic. "What's this? Hieroglyphs! Come and see this, dear."

"A tattoo perhaps," guessed Akara, who rubbed it firmly. "Weird!"

"A boy your age should not indulge in such a reckless practice," mocked Da Vinci. "It could lead to infection."

"It's not a tattoo," angrily retorted Theon, fed up of being treated like a lab animal. "It's a birth mark."

"I beg to differ," said a fascinated Da Vinci. "You wouldn't happen to be Egyptian? A great Pharaoh wandering about incognito?"

"That's enough!" Theon pushed his would-be forensic examiners away, and hastily put his shirt back on. "I've been jabbed, poked and prodded all my life. I've had just about enough of it. I'm a freak of nature, that's what I am! Say it! I'm a *freak*!"

Akara slapped him on the shoulder. "You're a freak? Look at me. What does that make me?"

"You're supposed to look like you do, not me," was Theon's weak rebuttal. He immediately recanted. "I'm sorry. I didn't mean it like that. I'm just exhausted and frankly on edge."

"Teenagers, so temperamental and dramatic," sighed Da Vinci; "no matter from whence they hail, Heaven, Hell or Earth. Theon...*son*," he added in a comforting tone. "We have our first real clue. These symbols on your neck mean something significant and profound. They reveal something about your origins and perhaps your destiny."

"So they're not random?" concluded Theon.

Da Vinci pulled down the shirt's neckline. "As I said, they're Hiero-glyphs, a script developed and popularized by the Egyptian culture on Earth, six thousand years ago.

"Hieroglyphs were called, by the Egyptians, '*the words of God*'." Da Vinci walked to a bookshelf and selected a book, spreading it open on the worktable. "This is the basic alphabet," tapping his finger on a diagram.

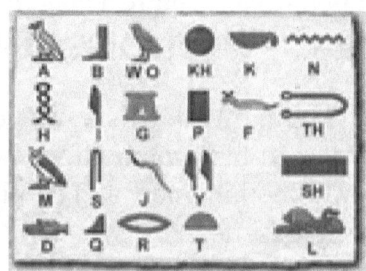

"Hieroglyphs are written in rows or columns and can be read from left to right or from right to left. You can distinguish the direction in which the text is to be read because the human or animal figures always face towards the beginning of the line.

"I thought there were hundreds of Egyptian symbols," recalled Theon from past extra curriculum studies his father encouraged.

"During the classical Middle Egyptian period, there were close to a thousand," said Da Vinci, "playing different functions. "Hieroglyphic signs are in fact divided into four categories:

1. Alphabetic signs representing a single sound.

2. Syllabic signs representing a combination of two or three consonants.

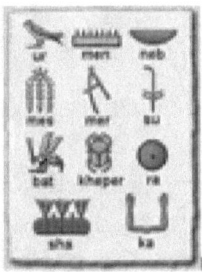

3. Word-signs or pictures of objects used as the words for those objects.

4. And determinatives, pictures of objects which help the reader. For example; if a word expressed an abstract idea, a picture of a roll of papyrus tied up and sealed was included to show that the meaning of the word could be expressed in writing although not pictorially. Determinatives don't represent sounds. The meanings they imply help eliminate confusion by putting the writings in proper context."

"I don't follow," confessed Akara.

"Is it like e-mail symbols?" proposed Theon. "Like the *smiley face* made from the colon and right parenthesis, meaning a state of happiness."

Da Vinci was familiar with the virtual script, but never had the occasion to write an e-mail. The technology was non-existent in the Kingdoms. "That's not a bad example. Let me try something."

The old man scribbled three symbols interspaced by plus signs. "This is a *rebus*, a puzzle made of pictures. Can you kids decipher it and write down your answer?"

"*Eye Heart U*," attempted Theon. "Not much of an answer; it's meaningless."

"I have something," whooped an enthusiastic Akara, eager to prove her cleverness. "*I Heart Ewe*."

"What's a Ewe?" Theon shook his head in disapproval.

"It's a female sheep from Earth," she snapped sternly, her fists pressed against her hips. "I read, you know; I read a lot."

Akara then slapped Theon on the shoulder once again, for good measure. This was becoming a habit.

Da Vinci added a fourth symbol. "This is the determinative. Does it help rid the confusion?"

Theon's face lit up with a quickness of discernment, and he turned to Akara. "*I Love You.*"

"What?" blurted out an embarrassed Akara, who feared her affective fixation with Theon had been exposed.

"It's the solution," indicated Theon, clearly noticing her reaction, but refraining from any inquiry into its underlying cause. Besides, as a boy caught in the first throes of an irreversible puberty, he knew what it was all about, and contrary to his father's assurance, it did not come about with its own brand of piquancy and charm. It was emotionally relentless and confusing.

"Well done," praised Da Vinci, who wisely ignored the sexual tension cutting through the air. "This symbol is usually seen around Valentine's Day on Earth. It is associated with Cupid, the Roman god of love. By shooting someone with his arrow, Cupid caused them to fall in love. Use of this symbol therefore implies that the statement relates to matters of love and emotion, and effectively makes 'I Love You' the only choice."

"Could the same logic be used to solve *my* rebus, Mister Da Vinci?" wondered Theon.

"Call me Leo," insisted Da Vinci. "And yes it could, but, unfortunately, your symbols are not Egyptian; perhaps a separate and concurrent script…Sumerian; Mesoamerican; Chinese…"

"Maybe it's an earlier script," proposed Akara; "one that predated and inspired the Egyptian script; one left behind by a heavenly race. You said earlier that the Egyptians called the Hieroglyphs 'the words of God'. What if they were actually a derivation of those words? The words of God…the words of Lord Deus…the words of the Eternals…the language of Heaven!"

"How could that be?" pondered Da Vinci, countless fanciful notions cavorting in his mind.

Akara pressed on excitedly. "We know the Eternal Sanctus visited Earth often before the Great War. At some point, they must have left heavenly scriptures behind, purposely or accidentally."

Da Vinci remained unconvinced. "The language of Heaven is mostly comparable to Latin. It's not pictorially-based at all."

"Not today," conceded Akara, "but maybe 100 thousand years ago, or 100 million years ago, it was. All languages evolve over great periods of time, correct? Why not the language of Heaven?"

"Fair assumption, indeed. Why not, why not…why not?" repeated Da Vinci as he tugged his beard, hoping the answer would tumble out his mouth. After a few tugs, he stopped and raised his arms in the air. "But of course! This old man's mind cannot be trusted anymore." He thumped his head twice with his palm before running upstairs to a much larger book-shelf that covered the entire wall separating the heads of the adjoining staircases.

He ransacked it, pulling out books and throwing them to the floor, many of which fell in between the spindles of the baluster and onto the first floor. "It must be here. I know it's here. Damn it, where did I put it? Ah, Ha! I have it!" He wrestled out an old book, stained and damaged beyond repair, from the top shelf, and dropped it in his zeal. It literally shattered in several pieces, which he picked up haphazardly before run-ning back downstairs.

"The answer we seek lies within the pages of this book," he stated emphatically, almost slamming the pile of papers on the worktable, and collating the pages as best he could. "There, finally! We have a book!" It was not his most masterful work.

The cover of the book, made of some kind of leather, featured a draw-ing of a bowl overflowing with what appeared to be apples, and to its right a family of Sanctus sitting at a table brimming with plates of food and jugs of liquid. The drawing was simplistic and cartoonish.

"What kind of book is this?" wondered Theon. "It looks infantile, and hardly likely to hold deep dark secrets about my *raison d'être*."

"Not surprising, it's a *children's* book," announced Da Vinci.

CHAPTER 82

Da Vinci, Theon and Akara stared at the ancient children's book whose pitiful condition could stand no more rough handling by the small paws of children hungry for discovery and edification of their virgin minds.

"This book was a gift from Lord Deus," said Da Vinci; "from his own personal library. It dates back to a primeval period in Eternal history when pictographs were prevalent in the written language. It's essentially a learning tool—an alphabet and word book."

"So the picture of the bowl of fruit is a *letter* in the Eternal alphabet?" supposed Akara.

"In this case, it's a *word*," clarified Da Vinci. "The family picture describes its meaning."

"The bowl means food," determined Theon.

"Strictly speaking, yes," agreed Da Vinci. "But the picture of a family preparing to feast on a plethora of foods tells a much more compelling story. It evokes concepts like a festive gathering; the rewards of hard work; the prolific bounty from harvest; abundance; plenitude; satiety; gratification. The meaning behind a picture of a bowl filled with fruit can be as literal or as figurative, as specific or as general as the context in which it's used requires."

Da Vinci carefully opened the book, turning and laying down a few pages from the introductory section. "These marks are accents, much like the acute, grave and circumflex accents you find in the French and Italian languages. They change the sound value of the letter to which they're added. They, of course, only apply to pictographs representing letters, and not words."

Da Vinci moved to the next page. "The arrow markings apply to word pictographs, indicating relative size. An arrow pointing upwards signifies *in greater* quantity, size or proportion, while the arrow pointing downwards, *in smaller* quantity. The concept of abundance would then become *overabundance* and *underabundance*.

"In Italian, suffixes are often used to indicate magnitude. For example, tortelli—delightful pasta which I've yet to enjoy today—would become tortelloni—bigger in size—and tortellini—smaller in size."

Da Vinci moved again to the next page, its top third only having survived. "These marks pose somewhat of a minor mystery."

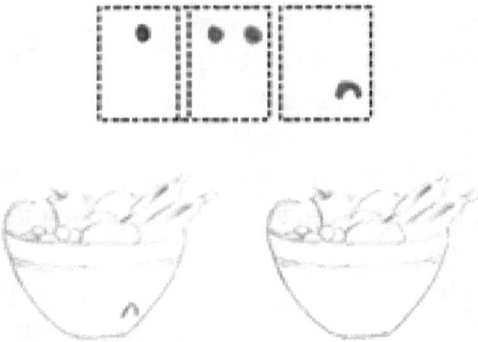

"You seem to have a lot of those," taunted Theon whose interest, nevertheless, remained unfaltering.

Da Vinci grunted in irritation. "Keep focus, boy. These marks are definitely not accents since they apply to pictographs representing words, as exemplified by the aforementioned bowl of fruit. As for the dotted squares, they are simply guides in illustrating the relative position of the marks within a pictograph."

"There must be a section of the book dedicated to the usage of these marks," correctly assumed Akara.

Da Vinci grunted again, this time in discontent. "Time has not been kind to this book—that section is missing."

"Why don't we just ask Deus," proposed Akara. "He might remember."

"You don't question our Lord God about a bagatelle such as a dead language," barked Da Vinci. "He's laden with much more important concerns like peace and order. Besides, if he asks about the reason of my inquiry, he would indignantly take amiss to my harboring of a fugitive from Satan."

"He's innocent," claimed a defensive Akara. "And...and...he's not an Echo; he hasn't been evaluated for sin, and...he's been unjustly accused." She suddenly turned to Theon. "Of what exactly have you been accused?"

Theon hunched his shoulders. "Apart from my own self-recrimination, I don't know."

"Enough of this!" snapped Da Vinci, clamping Akara's wrist. "If I thought he was guilty of anything—except self-loathing and self-absorption—I would not help him."

Akara's eyes wetted and she looked away from Theon, embarrassed. "Thank you."

"I know you care about this boy, and we will *not* abandon him," he whispered in her ear. "Now back to work. I do have some theories about those elusory marks—those little dots and scratches. They seem to be an integral part of primary pictographs. Their removal leads to a modified meaning. At first, I thought they pointed towards *homonyms*, words with the same sound but different meanings, but I quickly concluded it would be more logical and less confusing to create homonymic words depicted by different pictographs.

"I then considered synonyms, which led me more precisely to *specificity*. For example, the fruit bowl with the *notch* marking might mean *abundance*, while the one without the notch, *plenitude*; both synonyms. Or, the two pictographs might have a *causal* relationship—with the notch, *abundance*; without the notch, *satiety*. Abundance is the *cause*, and satiety is the *effect*."

"What about *antonyms*," suggested Theon, "words of opposite meanings?"

"Sagacious supposition, indeed," recognized Da Vinci. "It, too, crossed my mind. With the notch, *abundance*; without, *scarcity*. Of all the explanations at hand, it does appear to be the most plausible one."

"So, what's the upshot of all this analysis on Theon's symbols?" asked Akara.

Da Vinci examined the symbols anew. "Well, the three symbols are primary pictographs since they each contain a marking, one of each in fact."

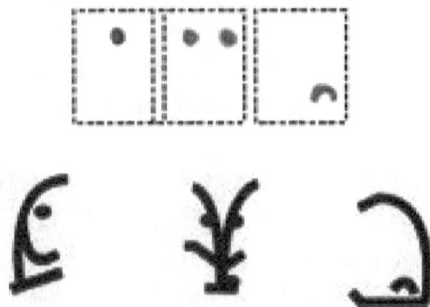

Da Vinci flipped through a few more pages to a partial listing of Eternal pictographs, divided in four sections. "We're in luck; they're in the first section of the book, pages 27, 64, and 143."

Da Vinci eagerly proceeded to page 27. "The first symbol is associated with various drawings: a halo—a luminous ring surrounding the heads of sacred, idealized or famous figures; a crown—the prominent token of Kingship; and a heart etched in the tree of Life in the Garden of Eden—symbol of a generous and benevolent Lord ruling wisely over his kingdom.

"Page 64. The second symbol is associated with a shimmering silver figure, smiling as it is being embraced by another figure wearing a crown—a scene symbolizing a spirit who is one with its body, and expressing brotherly love."

"Lord Deus and his Holy Spirit, Maitreya," reckoned Akara. "Who else could it be?"

"No doubt you're correct," agreed Da Vinci. "But the shimmering figure is larger than the king; the emphasis is on the spirit, the better part of the being.

"Page 143. The third symbol is associated with: the Sun—an emblem of light, a life force, a force of Good; and a sword pointing upwards—an enforcer of Good and an instrument of positive change."

"The Holy Sword, the Sword of Maitreya," surmised Akara before offering a combined interpretation of the three symbols. "Lord Deus, a kind-hearted King, fighting alongside his spirit brother, Maitreya, wielding the Sword of Good against Evil to protect his kingdom, its people and their posterity."

"The Kingdom has already been breached, sundered and hobbled by the Great War," pointed out Da Vinci, "a shadow of its former self. Perhaps the symbols work in concert to signal a time of upheaval, a time to extract and rid the kingdom of Evil, to purge the Diabolicus from the land. What we really need now is an extra pictograph—a *determinative*—to clarify the context."

"At the risk of sounding selfish," interjected Theon, "all this speculation about King Deus is interesting, but I thought we were here to free me from *my affliction.*"

"Perhaps we can kill two parrots with one stone," thought Da Vinci.

The old man's two-faced parrot quacked loudly. "I'm too precious to die!" followed immediately by, "Rotten to the core, I deserve to die!"

"Shut your beak, foul creature," yelled Da Vinci, who then gently approached a recalcitrant Theon. "My dear boy, I indeed believe you may well be part of a much bigger picture, and your salvation may be intimately intertwined with that of Heaven."

Theon's dissident stance remained unchanged. "If that is true, why did Satan not kill me?"

Da Vinci clasped his chin. "Good point. And above it all, you escaped—a feat in and of itself. Consider this: he's afraid of you and really doesn't want you to find the Holy Sword, or pluck a supposedly alive Maitreya from his clutches…reuniting him with his spiritual brother Deus."

He began pacing the floor, going to Akara, then back to Theon. "Then again, he called you a Tri-Weapon. With the sword in your hands, are you to become an instrument of Good, or a weapon of Evil? Maybe it's all a conspiracy. Satan wants you to succeed in your quest. Oh, my; confusing, all so confusing."

"Leo, I found something disturbing," announced Akara, who had snatched a magnifying glass from the worktable, and did some close examination of her own. "The symbols are changing."

Da Vinci rushed to her side, roughly grabbing the magnifying glass. "How do mean? They're the same."

"Not exactly," she firmly contended. "Look at the special markings on each of the symbols. They've faded, going from dark black to gray."

"The remainder of the symbols have remained black," gasped Da Vinci, "while the markings are indeed fading…disappearing."

"What does it mean?" Theon entreated in dread.

Da Vinci appeared defeated. "Everything we have said about the symbols appears to be false. We must now consider an opposite interpretation. Salvation is *not* within our grasp…*destruction* is."

CHAPTER 83

Present day; Kingdom of Heaven.

Sitting comfortably in the center chair of his
viewing room, Lord Deus took a sip of delectable juice made from perfectly grown apples picked from the tree of Life in the Garden of Eden.
As the juice made its way into Deus' body, he jolted in his seat, savoring
its robust and invigorating effect.

Using an inter-realm communication device based on Eternal technology, he enjoyed watching the Earth channels: NNW, the *News Network
of the World*, and LPN, the *Legends of the Past Network*. He was particularly partial to shows featuring the Three Stooges, Abbott and Costello,
and Laurel and Hardy. These comedic duos infused a much needed dose
of humor in his exacting life riddled with predicaments of varying gravity.

Today, however, he opted for a long overdue update on Human affairs
on NNW as he watched Karl Armstrong, President of the United States,
hold a press conference on the threat of nuclear weapons to America and
the world.

"The United States is expecting concrete commitments from nuclear talks with Tehran," announced Armstrong. "Iran claims its nuclear
program is for peaceful civilian purposes and is not designed to develop
atomic weapons."

"Are you convinced of that, Mister President?" inquired one of the
journalists present.

"I've made clear the United States and its international partners are
determined to prevent Iran from acquiring nuclear weapons. But there is
still time and space for sanctions and diplomacy to work. Iran is preparing
for nuclear talks later this month with the United States, France, Britain,
China, Russia, and Germany."

"So, you expect to see concrete commitments from Iran that it will
come clean on its nuclear program and live up to its international obliga-

tions?" asked another journalist.

"Yes," nodded Armstrong. "We're hoping for a plan of action that will resolve our disagreements peacefully."

"What about the small asteroid that landed near Tehran?" queried the first journalist. "According to astro-physicists, it must have detached itself from the asteroid belt between Mars and Jupiter, some time ago."

Armstrong frowned in annoyance. "What exactly is the *relevance* of that question?"

The journalist smiled. "As I'm sure you've heard, rumors suggest the asteroid was imbedded with foreign material, alleged to be some sort of advanced alien technology, as powerful and as deadly as nuclear energy. Are you not afraid of it falling in the wrong hands?"

"I don't dwell on or indulge in fantastic speculation fabricated by fanatical groups," firmly rebuked Armstrong. "And nor should you. I believe we're done. I thank you all for coming."

As Armstrong crossed the door of the room, the journalist shouted, "The true enemy is here. Never more horror!" quoting a line from Nostradamus.

"You're wrong, Mister President," muttered Deus. "The true enemy is *here*, and he tasks me and eats away at my solicitude."

"Never more horror," reiterated the anchorman of NNW. "Infamous last words? Let's hope not." He shuffled his papers, landing his attention on one of them. "Now the President may not be interested in alien technology, but we are. In the pursuit of truth, we have a special guest who may well shed light on the matter, or plunge the issue of alien technology into even darker venues: Doctor Ted Adams, former employee of the Center for SETI, the Search for Extraterrestrial Intelligence. Doctor, what is your take on all this?"

"Let me first say that I'm here of my own volition," Adams began as the camera set upon him, "and not at the behest of SETI. Had I still been on its payroll, the organization would have forbidden me to speak out publicly."

"Then, you were fired?" assumed the anchorman.

"Not at all," corrected Adams. "I was maneuvered into a position of helplessness to pursue and prove my claim."

"Please, share with us," urged on the anchorman, who immediately surmised his prior briefing had been incomplete in the least.

Adams shifted and stirred uneasily in his seat, brandishing his index finger at the main camera. "I know things, and I have connections.

A beam of incredible energy I can only assume came from outer space entered our solar system, grazed the surface of Mars, and ended its journey on Earth. I suspect the energy of the beam was not only utilized for transportation, but for conversion into matter. It also probably dislodged the asteroid from the belt and sent it on a course towards Earth. When the beam impacted with the asteroid, some amount of energy must have converted into matter—or should I say reconverted into its original form, some kind of alien technology, now in the hands of Iran."

"Your account still rests on much speculation, wouldn't you agree?" probed the anchorman, hoping for some substantiating evidence.

"Too many coincidences usually equate to corroboration and *proof*," insisted Adams, who pulled out several pictures from his shirt pocket. "This was sent to me using encrypted messaging by a reliable source at NASA," showing a photo of a rectangular piece of cloth with a strange symbol in its center. "This garment was found on Mars by the Opportunity Mars Rover. Some followers of Nostradamus' writings believe the symbol epitomizes the Great Destroyer of Worlds."

"Huh. Strange indeed," mumbled Deus as he moved closer to his communication screen. "Symbol looks oddly familiar."

"And who would this destroyer be, according to you?" pressed on the fascinated anchorman.

Adams was becoming increasingly restless, and the anchorman feared he would be perceived as a lunatic. "We're all sympathetic to your cause, Mister Adams. Keep your calm and all will go well," he whispered to Adams.

Adams immediately steadied and gathered his composure. "Of course, of course. What I mean to say is that the energy beam may have not only carried weaponry, but also a message and instructions on how to interpret the message to the Earthly destroyer, in this case, the ruler of Iran."

"What makes you think a *message* was intended?" softly inquired the anchorman.

Adams displayed a second photo. "This proves it."

"A dark-colored box?" exclaimed the anchorman.

"Not just a box," strongly pointed out Adams; "a *black box* containing crucial information."

"Like the ones they have on airplanes?" wondered the anchorman.

"Precisely!" shouted Adams. "It was found among strange metallic debris two miles from the garment."

"Amazing," cried out the anchorman. "Anything else?"

"What *more* do you need?" bellowed an exhausted Adams.

The anchorman gathered his papers and stared straight at the camera. "Indeed! What more do we really need. Ours thanks to Doctor Ted Adams, and to our audience for watching. Good night and good dreams."

"Not as funny as the Three Stooges," remarked Khrist Lesus as he entered Deus' viewing room.

"But just as entertaining, if you overlook Humanity's sad condition," said Deus. "We have tried to provide guidance and rules…at least in the beginning."

"We should try again," proposed Lesus in semi-serious fashion.

"We can't intervene anymore," reluctantly accepted Deus, "but neither can Satan and his horde of insane minions. The Law is the law."

"Speaking of the Law, turn to DBN," prompted Lesus. DBN was the *Diabolicus Breaking News* channel, or as Lesus liked to call it: the *DRAC Bitchy News*. A curious Deus immediately complied.

"The Echo boy is considered armed and dangerous," said the Diabolicus anchorwoman. She then repeated the news segment. "A young Echo male, with a Sin Score exceeding 1,000, has escaped from the prisons under the castle of our Dragon Lord, Satan. During his break-out, he savagely killed two Diabolicus guards."

"The boy's got game," said Deus in jest. "Two less to worry about."

"The boy then made his way to Heaven's Embassy," continued the anchorwoman, "where he wreaked the same brand of sadism on the two Sanctus sentries guarding the entrance. Before one of the sentries drew his last breath, he told authorities he saw the boy drag the Ambassador, Leonardo Da Vinci, out of the Embassy. Da Vinci appeared combative and shaken, but very much alive. The raving mad Echo was heading east. His ultimate destination could well be the Kingdom of Heaven. Any Sanctus apprehending the Echo is required by law to detain him until Diabolicus authorities arrive. This is the boy's picture. Memorize it well."

"Leonardo!" screamed Deus in distress as he shot up from his seat. "My poor friend, what has become of you?"

"It is very possible the deranged boy has horrific designs on Lord Deus," pursued the anchorwoman. "He will undoubtedly use the Ambassador as a hostage and a negotiating tool. Satan is clear: he must not be allowed to approach the City of God, at all costs."

"Why is Satan so concerned about your welfare?" pondered Lesus. "There is something about this alleged tragic event that escapes our comprehension. How can one child plunge Hell in such Chaos?"

"Uncertain, but we must prepare and be ready for his possible infringement of Heaven's borders," beckoned Deus.

"Ready for what, really?" Lesus asked in earnest. "To save a longtime friend...and kill a child?"

"There is nothing childlike about this boy," vehemently stated Deus. "Advise the guards, *all* of them within the kingdom."

Theon E. Rex now had his hands full—in Hell...and in Heaven.

CHAPTER 84

Present day; Kingdom of Hell.

"It must be a faulty wire," presumed Da Vinci as he lifted the hood of his custom-made Cadillac, and examined the wiring connected to the electric motor. The car was reminiscent of the 1929 model, with its designer-styled blue bodywork, metal turret top, circular headlights, curved wheel guards, white rims, and tailfins, the only feature evocative of later models.

"We should have taken the train," complained Akara. "Isn't the last coach reserved for traveling VIPs, dignitaries and diplomats?"

"Too dangerous for Theon. Ah! Found the trouble." Da Vinci hollered after toiling with the problem and slamming shut the hood. "We must make haste, children," reintegrating the cabin.

"You built this vehicle yourself?" asked a curious Akara, feeling the plush leather seats.

"I am after all a master engineer," proudly boasted Da Vinci. "No mechanical system is beyond my purview."

Theon placed his hands on the dash as the Cadillac resumed its route along a bumpy potholed secondary road flanked by a column of tall trees whose bark was black and leaves red. The road stretched along the outskirts of the town of Ceti Enfer, a few miles from its public square. "Where are we going, exactly?"

Da Vinci glanced at him as though the answer was blatant. "To find the Holy Sword and meet with Deus…not necessarily in that order."

Theon was understandably bemused given recent inferences about his nature. "What about all the hogwash about destruction, devastation and anarchy?"

Da Vinci kept his eyes on the road and a resolute grip on the oversized steering wheel. "Providence assists not the idle. Therefore, we shall not remain idle. That, at least, I can promise you…and promise Akara, your, what do you kids call it, *BFF?*"

"*Best friend forever,*" Theon imparted to Akara, who kept her delight in the designation subjugated. "So, I guess I've become a concern worthy enough of an audience with God? There is hope for me after all."

"There is hope and a *future* for you, that much is true," said Da Vinci; "and any future is worth discovering. It is in that discovery that change can begin to be effected."

"For the better," added Akara, who purposely grazed Theon's hand as she pointed to a structure ahead. "What is that building?"

"You've never been this far, have you?" realized Da Vinci. "That, my friends, is *Sin City*, the biggest Casino in Hell."

"What's a casino?" wondered Akara, impressed by its size, its extravagance of lights, and by a giant prodigal statue of Satan made of gold, erected by the main entrance.

"A casino is a place of gambling activities," explained Da Vinci, "such as poker, twenty-one, roulette, and slot. Are you familiar with any of these games, Theon?"

"I've played poker with my adoptive father," admitted Theon, "but I've never been to a casino. Got to be 21 years old in most States."

"Not in Hell, son," said Da Vinci. "Here, no one is too young for sin."

Akara's awe grew as they approached. "Looks a lot merrier than my father's funereal castle. Why are we here?"

"To make money, of course," matter-of-factly replied Da Vinci. "We're certain to encounter unsavory elements along our journey. We'll need *money* to buy our way through."

"I didn't know Hell kept its own currency," uttered Theon in surprise. "What is it called? Peshells, Hell Sterlings, or maybe Hellos?"

"Nice try," grinned Da Vinci. "Hell uses something comparable to currency, but not quite like money in the strictest sense. *Sinars*—that's what they're called—are issued by the casinos, and audited by the State, as are the goods that back up and endue Sinars with value. On Earth, gold used to be the backup for money."

"There's obviously gold in Hell," noticed Theon, pointing at the gold statue of Satan. "Is that the good supporting Sinars?"

"It's simpler than that," replied Da Vinci. "Sin backs up the currency; or more precisely *sinners*. When a person buys Sinars, he must put up some of the Echoes he owns as collateral. For example, an Echo evaluated at 300 sin points would bring in 300 Sinars—it's a one to one relationship. To insure the collateral is secured, owners must release their property to one of several consignment centers controlled by the casino network."

"How does one come to own Echoes?" inquired Theon.

"All Echoes initially belong to the State—Satan has jurisdiction over them," explained Da Vinci. "Those who score low enough are either temporarily assigned to Purgatory, or permanently assigned to Heaven. The rest are triaged. The State retains roughly a third of them; another third is allocated to the various Provinces; and the remainder to some of the people of Hell. The greater the standing in the Aristocracy, the greater the allocation. You can, of course, improve or worsen your lot of Echoes by gambling."

"There are exceptions, it seems," interjected Akara, who found the whole process barbaric.

"Indeed there are," concurred Da Vinci. "If you are exceptionally sinful—scoring in the thousands—you can bypass the system and become a citizen of Hell, or better yet, a leader and co-conspirator in this fate allotment farce."

"A contradiction?" said Theon.

"Recognition and reward of pure Evil," replied Da Vinci. "Those privileged Echoes may be few and far apart, but they rival even Satan in depravity."

"Mister Da Vinci, may I attend to your vehicle?" offered the casino attendant as the Cadillac stationed itself at the base of the front stairs.

"Take good care of it," ordered Da Vinci. "Be warned; I always check for scratches on my way out. And no smoking in the car. Oh, and above all, don't eat the parrot."

"I'm so tasty," squawked the bird perched on the dash board. "I'm so vile," it added.

"You gamble in Echoes?" assumed a surprised Theon.

"God No!" exclaimed Da Vinci. "I offer something else of value." He did not expand further.

They entered the casino and proceeded directly to the *exchange counter*, only second in line. A large sign was plastered overhead the counter, disclosing three mandatory directives:

> *Keep Wings Retracted at all times*
> *Echoes Must Be Accompanied By Owners At All Times.*
> *Maximum One Echo Per Owner*
> *No Exchange Without ECA Flash Drive*

"Please submit your *Echo Consignment Account* flash drive," the counter attendant requested the Diabolicus in front of Da Vinci.

The attendant plugged the small rectangular device into a slot in his control board, its content instantly appearing on a small display screen. "Sir, you have placed in consignment twelve Echoes totaling 3,850 points." He the retrieved 27 chips—clay coins, two inches in diameter, coded, and labeled with their value amount—placed them on the counter and slid them forward. "Four chips of 500 Sinars; eighteen chips of 100 Sinars; and five chips of 10 Sinars. I hope all is satisfactory?"

The Diabolicus grunted his approval, snatched the chips, and disappeared among the crowd of hopeful gamblers.

"Leo!" cried out the attendant. "Tony Andolini will be happy to know you've blessed us with your presence yet again."

Theon chuckled. "Tony? Let me guess, the Mafia has found its way to Hell."

"It's only a nickname," Da Vinci told Theon. "He's the casino manager, and he likes to fancy himself the only Italian Diabolicus in Hell. As a true Italian, I'm not too taken by the unflattering comparison, but since I'm one of a few Echoes exempted from certain house rules, I tolerate it."

"What's your poison for today?" asked the attendant. "Planning to save more Echoes and dispatch them to Heaven?"

"Something like that," responded Da Vinci in a thinly veiled dismissive tone. "I require 1,000 Sinars. As always, I'm good for it."

"That comes out to 250 bottles of your home-made *Maddona Mild* ale," indicated the attendant. "In the event fortune forsakes you today, bottles must be delivered to the casino within 30 days, as always."

"You make your own beer?" said an amused Akara. "You're truly a gifted engineer."

Da Vinci ignored the derisive remark. "I plan to win," he advised the attendant. "Am I not the most brilliant and artful man…in any realm?"

The attendant smiled diplomatically. "Here are your chips, genius. Give 'em Hell!"

The trio walked through the slot machine area on their way to the *black jack* tables. Theon counted 240 machines, all of which occupied by overwrought Diabolicus hankering for that big win. Some yelled at the machine, others shook it or banged it.

Da Vinci had no appetite for slot machines. He considered the activity pedestrian, and much preferred black Jack or roulette—those were a gentleman's game.

"Will you be joining the table, Mister Da Vinci?" politely queried the dealer whose table was Da Vinci's favorite. Three players had already engaged in play. One was accompanied by young female Echo wearing a red backless dress with sleeves, accessorized with high-heel boots and belt. She was overly affectionate towards her master, an attitude he did not reciprocate, swatting her instead like one would a pesky mosquito.

"I'd like to observe for a moment, my lovely Orika," said Da Vinci, who, to the two youngsters, now clearly revealed himself as a regular client of the casino. "My two juvenile apprentices are eager to learn the workings of the game."

The dealer eyed the kids while she shuffled two new decks of cards together . "Future clients, I hope." She nodded and then dealt the cards to the seated players. "Gentlemen, 104 new cards to be played."

In black jack, the object was to get as close to 21 without going over, *and* equal or beat the dealer's hand. The value of a hand was calculated by summing the individual values of the cards comprising the hand. The Ace card was valued at 1 or 11 (player's choice), and face cards at 10.

"I want you to *count* the face-up cards you see on the table," Da Vinci whispered to Theon. "Numbered cards from 2 to 6 are rated at *plus 1 point*; numbered cards from 7 to 9 are rated at *0 points*; face cards: the Jackal, the Serpent, and the Dragon, are rated at *minus 1 point*; as are the 10-card and the Ace (Apocalypse) card."

Theon immediately understood the strategy. "As more and more cards are exposed, the counter (cumulative sum of ratings) fluctuates within a range of positive and negative numbers. The greater the *positive* count, the greater the concentration of face and Ace cards in the deck of unplayed cards; and the greater the probability of the next card drawn being a face or Ace card—the best cards to make a 21. But, the greater the negative count, the lesser the probability of the next card drawn being a face or Ace card."

Da Vinci patted Theon on the back. "Smart boy; now let us observe in silence."

After five rounds of play were completed, Da Vinci sat. "Time to garnish my pockets. I bet 200 Sinars."

"The counter is at plus 29," whispered Theon. "There's a 56% chance of getting a ten, a face, or an Ace on the next card. Great odds."

The dealer dealt two cards—face down (hidden)—to each player, and two cards—one face-up (exposed to the dealer and other players), the other face-down—to herself. The dealer's face up card was a Dragon.

Da Vinci's cards, which he discretely showed to Theon and Akara, were a 4 and a 6 for a current total of 10 *(4+6=10)*. No one else was privy to the content of his hand.

"Your odds just went up to 60%," Theon whispered anew.

Da Vinci, the first player to make a call, was confident as he requested another card. His new hand of three cards would likely total 20 or 21, a score unlikely to be beaten by the dealer, especially since ties resulted in recovery of the amount bet. The next card dealt was a 5.

Da Vinci and Theon were disappointed. "There was only a 15% chance of getting a low card," he told the old man. "We're unlucky. What do we do now?"

Da Vinci dug in. "If fortune is asleep, you must awaken it. Orika, hit me with another card." She dealt him a Jackal, bringing his total to 25, exceeding 21 and busting his hand. Alas for him, rules stated that a player who busted lost his bet, whether the dealer, who always plays last, busted or not.

An undaunted and obstinate Da Vinci pressed on, aggressively playing five more rounds, and winning only once, leaving him with only 60 Sinars.

"Something doesn't compute," asserted Theon. "On each hand, the odds were in your favor."

Da Vinci stared rancorously at Orika. "It is better to be lucky than rich. It appears I shall be neither."

She grinned. "Mister Andolini has been in want of late of your delicious ale." Her grin then died away and her face grew aloof. "You owe us 235 bottles of Maddona Mild. You can, of course, continue gambling, and perhaps interrupt your streak of bad luck."

His heart, a seething molten mass of animosity, Da Vinci sprung from his seat. "Come children. It stinks around here."

"Leo!" called out Orika as the trio stepped away. Da Vinci turned to look at her. Her cool expression faded away, replaced by sadness. "*I* am sorry."

Da Vinci waved his arm erratically before increasing his pace. The remorseful Orika couldn't ascertain whether the usually bubbly old man was saying *goodbye* or *good riddance*. In either case, she was convinced he would not be back.

Da Vinci headed for the exit. Theon, however, had other ideas in mind, and an offer Da Vinci could simply not refuse. The pendulum would soon swing the other way.

CHAPTER 85

"Are you certain you can affect the outcome?"
worried Da Vinci as the trio stood by the roulette table.

"Remember who I am," Theon reminded Da Vinci, allaying most of his concerns. "It's just a matter of sustained concentration."

"You gentlemen seemed quite galvanized and committed," said a tantalizing, sensuously attired female Echo, who nudged herself between Da Vinci and Theon, with blatant disregard for Akara. "I work for the casino, and I would love to *work over* this handsome young man," stroking Theon's cheek with her finger.

Akara hissed at her, her fangs protruding menacingly. "Vacate my view now, or *I'll* work you over."

Da Vinci glanced at Akara. "Testy are we?"

"Just protecting my investment," replied a jealous Akara, whose fierce eyes followed the presumptuous Echo as she headed for the slot machines to hunt for more receptive prey.

The game Da Vinci chose was called *Triple-Six-Spin*, although most patrons referred to it as *Six-Six-Six*. It consisted of three wheels (black, blue, red), each divided into six pocket sections labeled 1 to 6. Once the wheels were set into motion, a marble was thrown onto each one, eventually settling into one of the six pockets as the wheels lost momentum.

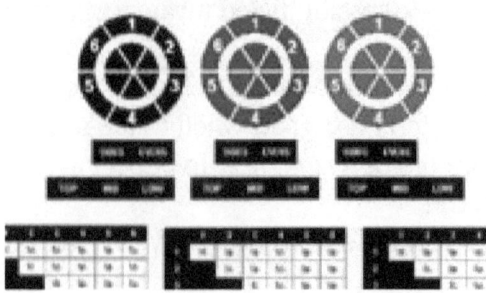

Clients could choose from a variety of bets, all involving the three wheels, and each associated with specific odds and payout. Clients could opt for any the following bets:

Straight: a single number was chosen from each wheel. Odds of winning: 1 to 215. Payout: 199 to 1.

Split: two numbers were chosen from each wheel. Odds of winning: 1 to 26. Payout: 24 to 1.

Odds & Evens: odd or even numbers were chosen from each wheel. Mixes were allowed (i.e. odds on one wheel, evens on another). Odds of winning: 1 to 7. Payout: 6 to 1.

Top Wheel: one wheel was chosen as the wheel producing the highest number compared to numbers on the other two wheels. Wheels with tied numbers favored the house (casino). Odds of winning: 1 to 2.93. Payout: 2.5 to 1.

Top-Down: the three wheels were ordered in such a way that the numbers they produced were in descending order. Wheels with tied numbers favored the house (casino). Odds of winning: 1 to 9.8. Payout: 9 to 1.

Unsure of the outcome despite Theon's reassurance, Da Vinci decided to start conservatively.

"Place your bets, ladies and gentlemen," the croupier instructed the six people at the table.

"I'm betting 30 Sinars on the blue wheel as Top-Wheel," he told Theon, who frowned at his cautiousness.

"Bet *all* yours chips, and I'll do the rest," Theon insisted.

He gazed keenly on Da Vinci's six 10-Sinar chips as the old man placed them in the Top Square associated with the blue wheel, on the betting layout.

"No more bets," firmly announced the croupier after all players had placed their bets. He then spun in order the black, blue and red wheel, after which dispensers expelled three marbles, one onto each wheel surface.

Theon's penetrating gaze fastened on the three marbles, moving rapidly from one marble to the next. Ten seconds later, the marbles settled into pockets: number 6 for the blue wheel; number 5 for the black; and number 3 for the red. Da Vinci won his bet.

"We have *one* winner," exclaimed the croupier, sliding the original 60 Sinars plus 150 more towards Da Vinci.

Da Vinci smiled in stupefaction at Theon, who was justifiably pleased with himself. He then looked at Akara. "He's definitely a *keeper*."

"Place your bets," said the croupier.

Without hesitation, Da Vinci went for a Split bet, and put all his chips into play. He placed one chip in the black 4-6 square, one chip in the blue 1-2 square, and the remainder in the red 1-4 square. Rules for a Split bet required that at least one chip be placed in each of the three squares selected. The number of chips placed on any of the three squares was irrelevant—only the total amount of the bet mattered.

"No more bets." The croupier spun the wheels, and the marbles were released. Against all odds, Da Vinci won again.

"We have two winners, one on Odds & Evens, and one on the Split."

The croupier handed Da Vinci chips totaling 3,750 Sinars.

The old man jumped for joy, staring at the celling. "Thank you Lisa-Maria, wherever you are. Oh, I mean thank you, dear boy," immediately amending his tribute of gratitude.

Two impeccably dressed Diabolicus bouncers—big powerful men in charge of public order, and the identification of possible cheaters—approached the table, one standing behind DaVinci, the other facing him from the opposite side of the table.

Da Vinci noticed their conspicuous presence, but was neither deterred nor intimidated. He placed his chips on the 6-square of each wheel. "Going for a Royal Straight."

"You're being cocky…and quite noticeable," cautioned Akara as more and more people gathered around the table.

"Nonsense. Fitting retribution." Da Vinci was unstoppable. And, of course, he won yet again, garnishing 750,000 Sinars, a casino record.

"We'd better go now," strongly advised Akara as Da Vinci filled his pockets with seventy-five 10,000-Sinar chips.

But it was too late for discrete escape. The bouncer behind him grabbed his arm. "Mister Andolini would like to see you and your young sidekicks, Master Da Vinci."

"Whatever for?" innocently said Da Vinci, the chips in his pockets rattling as he defiantly shook his robe. "Come, children; the big boss wants to see us."

Theon kept his cool and followed the old man's lead, but not before injecting a derogatory comment. "First time I see gorillas in suits. I sure hope you'll grunt stupidly and beat your chests before *wacking* us."

The bouncers, well indoctrinated in the art of self-control and firmness of purpose, did not flinch as they led the trio to Andolini's office.

Andolini was standing in front of a full-length mirror, waving his hands as he quoted lines from gangster movies. "I'm a little fucked up maybe, but I'm funny how, I mean funny like I'm a clown, I amuse you?

I make you laugh; I'm here to fuckin' amuse you?"

"You were made for that role, Tony," quipped Da Vinci. "As long as you stay away from Shakespeare, no one will know how talentless you are."

"Leo, my dearest of friends among the Echoes," shouted Andolini. "Still playing with kids, I see?"

"These are my apprentices," said Da Vinci. "And they're very promising."

"I bet they are," chuckled Andolini, "well, at least the boy is." He walked to Theon and extended his arm to touch his head, but Theon took a step back. "How did you do it, kid? How did you manipulate the game? No one has ever gotten a Straight 666, not before losing a hell of a lot of money anyway."

Theon smiled snidely. "I suppose our bad luck at Black Jack magically turned to good at the Triple-Six-Spin; and in spectacular fashion."

"You win some, you lose some," quoted Da Vinci. "That's your motto, isn't it, Tony?"

Andolini's demeanor suddenly became somber. "Do you know what we do with cheaters? It's not pretty; the fate reserved for murderers of Eternals pales in comparison."

He then turned his television on. "This newscast came in 30 minutes ago."

The three fugitives watched in horror. "I did not kill anyone!" protested Theon. "It's a scheme to incriminate me."

"Does it look like I'm being held hostage by the boy?" cried an outraged Da Vinci.

"And there's no mention of me," added an irate Akara. "All this drivel must have been manufactured by my father."

Andolini was not insensitive to their plight. Although, he would not openly admit it, he genuinely cared for Da Vinci. As an Aficionado of human affairs and idiosyncrasies, Da Vinci had been pivotal in his education. What Da Vinci did not know was that Andolini owed his atypical *humanity* to his human mother, abducted by his Diabolicus father Millennia ago.

"You've called me friend many a time," Da Vinci reminded Andolini. "Am I your *friend* today?"

"Best friend forever," he answered without hesitation. "The boy has become a sworn enemy of both kingdoms. Even God will not show him mercy. What will you do?"

"We will improvise," simply replied Da Vinci. "Don't prepare for the future, just show up and it will be there."

"The Sinars you've won are rightfully yours; use them wisely," said Andolini. "Your vehicle is parked at the back of the casino. Hurry. Guards are bound to show up sooner than later."

In an instant, the trio was gone. And Hell was not far behind…or far ahead.

CHAPTER 86

Da Vinci's Cadillac had been paralleling the main road, Judgment Road, on a secondary road four miles to the North. The train tracks also paralleled Judgment Road, a dozen yards to the South. The old man could hear the train's whistle announcing the arrival of fresh cargo at the Upper-Hell border. Many unfortunate souls would disembark and be shuttled across the land to a fate worse than insentient death.

As for Da Vinci and his comrades, fate had been kind to them. Twice they had been stopped by self-appointed Diabolicus bounty hunters, tracking down escaped Echoes; and twice they had been allowed to pass in exchange for an exorbitant monetary compensation.

"Do you think they recognized me?" Theon asked Da Vinci.

"They spend much of their time in the woods and in the fields," said Da Vinci. "It's likely they have not kept abreast of latest developments regarding escaped Echoes. But that will work in our favor for only so long. I suggest we leave the road and drive through the maze of Polar caves coming up ahead," pointing at the natural formation 500 feet away. The caves, stacked next to and over each other, extended hundreds of miles to the southeast, ending at the Heaven-Hell border and the shores of Lake Seven. "Ice water flows through the connecting caves of the eastern rim. We can quench our thirst."

As Da Vinci replaced his hand on the steering wheel, Theon noticed a tattoo on his right forearm—a series of five digits in bright red. "I thought you hated tattoos?"

Da Vinci glanced at the unsightly mark. "I do. It was forced upon me by one of those infernal scanning machines. Moments after I emerged from the solar energy collector, I was ushered into the scanning contraption, evaluated for sin, and branded with a sin score, just like a stupid cow being branded with a scorching red hot iron."

"Fifty-seven, that's an excellent score," said Akara from the back seat. "At least there's that."

"A vain attempt to make me feel good about it," scoffed Da Vinci. "I am not an anima—"

"Watch out!" screamed Theon as a man appeared in front of the car.

Da Vinci's foot hit the brake pedal so hard, the metal surface beneath it cracked loudly; but the man would not be spared a lethal encounter with furious metal. He was thrown fifteen feet away, and struck a large stone by the side of the road face first.

The frantic trio left the car and rushed to the bloodied corpse. Da Vinci literally unglued the body from the stone, and it slumped onto the ground. "He's still breathing." He placed his ear against the man's quivering mouth as it tried to form a few words.

"Astonishing!" exclaimed Da Vinci. "It's Yiddish."

"What's a Yeadish?" wondered Akara, who probed the body from head to toe, searching for distinctive features.

"It's not a physical peculiarity," explained Da Vinci; "it's a language spoken as a vernacular by Jews."

Theon crouched next to the man. "What's he saying?"

Da Vinci passed his hand over the man's eyes, closing them, and repeated his last words: "They could never curtail my dream of freedom. At last, I am free." The body began shimmering and de-echoalescing, leaving clothing and a dark stain where it once lied.

This was the first time Theon saw an Echo dissolve. "Where did he go?"

"The Universe has claimed this man's essence," said Da Vinci. "It has returned to where it once belonged, never again to be summoned into form."

"He's dead?" surmised Theon; "I mean really dead?"

"Or finally alive," theorized Da Vinci. "Only God might know for sure."

Theon frowned at the cryptic answer. "God, the All Mighty?"

"No, you sarcastic boy; God the Philosopher," replied Da Vinci.

"There was something bizarre about this Echo," claimed Akara. "He had not one but two tattoos; one on each forearm, and both a series of five digits."

"This man was a Jew, a survivor of the Earth Holocaust," concluded Da Vinci. "An event during which six million Jews were murdered by Adolf Hitler, leader of Nazi Germany."

"That's cruel and terrifying," cried out a disgusted Akara. "This Hitler was a beast."

Da Vinci nodded in sadness. "Indeed. It was as cruel and as terrifying as what your father, the beast of Hell, is doing to Echoes under his jurisdiction. Just as Satan brands Echoes destined for Hell with a number, Hitler did something comparable."

"There is something else," noted Akara, who picked up the man's shirt. "Look at this white armband around the left sleeve. It's engraved with a red capital E."

"Another lugubrious spin-off of a Nazi regime practice," said Da Vinci. "Jews were ordered to wear a white armband with a blue Star of David on it, as a marker and a badge of shame."

"A capital E standing for the word Echo," correctly deduced Theon. "But why the redundancy? Why an I.D. number *and* an I.D. patch?"

"To recapture a glorious period of one's past," supposed Da Vinci. "To be seized with morbid nostalgia only a faithful recreation could cure."

Theon was understandably confused, as was Akara. "Are we talking about Satan's reign, or Hitler's?"

"Hitler's dominion, of course," bellowed an imposing Chimerian Bull, materializing from among the Polar caves, immediately followed by eleven others, all brandishing projectile firearms.

"The Chimerian Militia!" howled Da Vinci in consternation. He knew they were vicious, and that, despite the species' obtuseness, they would not waiver in their allegiance to their tyrannical employer, Adolf Hitler.

CHAPTER 87

The Chimerian Militia was a military faction not considered to be part of the State's armed forces. Composed exclusively of Bulls, it provided defense, law enforcement, and Echo recovery support. Unlike the Chimerian Primates, Reptiles and Boars, many of which comprised the bulk of the resistance, the Bulls made a pact with the Diabolicus to assist them in exchange for freedom of movement, sustenance, and access to privileges normally reserved for the Diabolicus.

The Bulls were also notoriously underhanded. "What would you have me do with 45,000 Sinars?" sneered the leader of the Militia, who appreciated the buying power of such a sizable sum of funds, but feigned disappointment. "What about your transportation apparatus?"

"It's yours," immediately consented Da Vinci. "The Sinars and the car for a right of passage."

"Oh, you shall pass, make no mistake about that," promised the leader; "but only under our supervision."

"You mean as your prisoners?" gathered Akara, who adopted a defiant stance before the leader. "Surely my father, the Dragon Lord, would be displeased to know you have mistreated me."

The Bulls laughed in unison. "Satan, the *promiscuous*, has produced countless bastards," pointed out the leader. "And he cares nothing about them. Now, move away, you annoying insect." The pompous Bull clamped Akara's face with his oversized hand, and threw her aside violently.

Theon was ready to pounce, but Da Vinci stopped him, grabbing his shirt collar. "He who fights must vanquish. There are twelve of them, armed with guns and rifles; and there's only one of you."

Theon glared at Da Vinci. "You're wrong; I am *many*."

Da Vinci pulled him back. "Be that as it may; by the time you marshal your private little army of ghostly personae, your body will be riddled with bullets. The time for escape will come. For now, let us gladly take the guise of prisoners, and we shall move closer to our destination, once more without incident."

Theon deferred to Da Vinci's greater cognizance of the situation's explosive volatility. As for Akara, she kept her urge to retaliate in check, mumbling obscenities at the Bulls instead.

Two Bulls struggled to start the car, without success—in his shoe, Da Vinci had stashed the key, a means of activation no Chimerian knew about. "Its power source is depleted," said a deceitful Da Vinci as he watched his parrot fly away to safety.

"Leave it," commanded the leader. "We'll come back for it later. Now move you three," waving his rifle in the direction of the border. "Hitler will be especially happy to meet you, *boy assassin*."

"Keep your wits about you," beseeched Da Vinci as they marched. "Don't let them provoke you."

"I'm ok, Leo," assured Theon; "as calm as I can be, but still confused. What's going on? Do these guys really work for Hitler?"

"Alas, yes," confirmed Da Vinci. "We're not only heading towards the Upper-Hell border, but also the border of the Province of *Land-Der-Fuhrer (Land of the Fuhrer)*, a territory controlled by Hitler himself."

"An Echo?" blurted out Theon.

Da Vinci nodded in deprecation. "As I mentioned earlier, he's one of a select group of Echoes granted citizenship and awarded ruling powers over land and populace usually ceded to high-ranking Diabolicus. The commission was a reward of sorts for his *magnum opus* of mass terror and obliteration on Earth, and a clear mandate to reproduce his monstrous masterpiece in Hell."

"I suppose Osama Bin Laden is next on Satan's promotion list of mass terrorists," nervously joked Theon.

"He certainly fits the profile," concurred Da Vinci, "but I don't think he's murdered enough people to qualify. Had he evaded the military assault that killed him, he might have made the list."

Theon suddenly became distracted and markedly preoccupied. "Or maybe someone else, despite his best efforts, is destined to make the top of that list?"

Da Vinci placed his hand on Theon's shoulder and gently massaged it. "For the life of me, I don't see who that could be. It's definitely not any of my friends, don't you agree, *my friend*?"

Da Vinci had only known Theon for a grand total of twenty hours now, but the more the hours, the minutes, and even the seconds passed, the more his misgivings about the boy dwindled, and the more he realized that, behind the juggernaut, that massive inexorable force bent on crushing everything in its way, dwelled the embodiment of boyishness, with all its quiet eminence and virtues, and all its resounding failings and frailties. He swore in silence that, no matter what happened, Theon would be remembered for no more or no less than that.

It was, after all, Theon's most earnest wish: to be *ordinary*.

CHAPTER 88

The Diabolicus and Sanctus border patrol agents worked in pairs to insure the impartiality of the Echo allocation process, and to constrain the habitual malfeasance and abuse by the more duplicitous Diabolicus.

Once the train entered the station of a particular zone, pairs of Eternals would board one train coach after the other, verify passenger sin scores, and shed from the train those Echoes assigned to the zone. The remaining Echoes would be transported to the next zone, where the process was repeated.

On occasion, some Echoes—fugitives for the most part—would arrive at a zone border by foot. And as their captors would certify, it was never their idea to do so.

The leader of the Chimerian militia raised his hand and placed it against his forehead as a gesture of salutation. "We have captured enemies of the State and of the *Fatherland*," he informed an Echo soldier standing at the border entrance to Land-Der-Fuhrer.

The soldier wore an entirely black uniform, high boots, an armband with the Nazi symbol, the *swastika* (an equilateral cross with its arms bent at right angles), on it, a belt buckle featuring the motto *Meine Ehre heißt Treue* (my honor is loyalty), and a peaked cap. He was an *Oberst*, a Colonel, in Hell's Nazi regime.

"You are far from your embassy, Master Da Vinci," said the swaggering Colonel.

"And you're a traitor to your kind, a betrayer of Humanity," boldly rebutted Da Vinci.

The Colonel smiled. "I was born to rid the world of vermin. Imagine my delight when, upon my death, I discovered a new world crawling with even more of it. I shall certainly be busy for the rest of eternity."

The high-ranking soldier turned his attention to Theon. "Let me see your right forearm, son. I won't hurt you." He slowly pulled up Theon's sleeve. "No mark. Odd. You've never been evaluated." He then stared into the boy's eyes. "No glitter or gleam. What are you?"

"I'm just a boy with a purpose." Theon swiftly retracted his arm.

"Follow me," the Colonel ordered the trio, signaling two nearby soldiers to surveil them as they walked to one of several scanning chambers. The chamber was rectangular, eight-feet high, five-feet wide, and four feet deep, with openings on both ends. Echoes would enter through one opening, traverse the machine, and exit through the other, while an operator worked a control panel and viewing screen linked to the side of the chamber.

"You need only enter through here and exit at the other end," instructed the Colonel, "It's painless."

Theon glanced at Da Vinci, who nodded his approval. For now, cooperation was their best ally.

The old man was especially curious, wondering how the scanning chamber would interpret a human being.

As Theon stepped into the machine, the screen lit up, displaying a rapid succession of images, each representing a critical moment or event in Theon's life, and each updating a sin score counter. The highest sin score ever recorded was 18,743, and it belonged to Adolf Hitler.

"There's a problem, sir," the operator indicated to the Colonel. "The counter has reset to 00000. The scanner is unable to calculate the boy's sin score."

"A malfunction?" imagined the Colonel.

"The scanner was checked just yesterday," pointed out the operator. "Perhaps the boy's score exceeded the limit of 99,999. That could explain the reset to zero."

The Colonel seemed skeptical. "But you are not positive. Has this ever occurred before?"

"Only once, according to scanning records," replied the baffled operator. "The Echo implicated was the one known as Jesus Christ. Wait! Something else is happening."

As hundreds of stacked images moved to the upper-left corner of the screen, others appeared gradually, resolving and taking shape. "This also has never happened before," asserted the operator. "Another malfunction, perhaps; I cannot say."

"Those are silhouettes," figured the Colonel, standing by the screen. "I count four, in continuous rotation. They're clearing up. I can detect the outline of a relatively young bearded man. Can you call up visuals of past scanned Echoes from this control panel?"

The operator understood what the Colonel had in mind. "Initiating a visual match subroutine." Seconds later, the picture of an Echo surfaced. "One Echo closely matches the outline at 87%. It's…it's Jesus Christ!"

"Incredible!" exclaimed the Colonel. "Now, the second outline is that of a man covered in shimmering silver light. Run the match, quickly."

"No match," said the operator. "Not surprising; the image hardly looks human. Let's try the third silhouette, that of a young woman." Seconds later; "We have a *partial* match, at 67%."

"Well, I'll be damned!" cried the Colonel. "It's one of Satan's wives."

"An Echo for a wife, sir?" wondered an incredulous operator.

"He is partial to the fair-haired and fair-skinned," jested the Colonel. "Final image if you will."

The operator isolated the outline. "It's somewhat blurry; I'll compensate using a rendering program." At program's end, he was absolutely stupefied. "We don't need to run a match, sir. The figure is not an Echo; it's Satan himself."

The Colonel did not say a word. Instead, he walked to a phone post, picked up an old style rotary phone and dialed. "Satan has not been entirely forthcoming about the boy. Get me the Fuhrer, now!"

CHAPTER 89

The city of Neues Berlin was teeming with suffering Echos, each sporting the Echo-identification armband, a sight that never failed to delight the Colonel. Today, he was particularly delighted as his jeep, a long armored vehicle with six seating areas, and an attack station at the back equipped with a rotary machine gun, entered the city.

Two armed Nazi soldiers sat in front section of the jeep, Theon and Akara sat in the middle, while Da Vinci and the Colonel took the back seat. A standing soldier manned the machine gun.

"No soldier, Echo or *Diabolicus*, is carrying an energy weapon," noticed Theon, "only standard Earth munition and ordnance."

"We want the re-creation of the Fatherland to be as faithful to the original as possible," replied a proud Colonel. "Even the buildings mimic those of Berlin. It's quite an achievement."

Da Vinci grunted. "Yes, achieved on the backs and with the blood of tortured and humiliated slaves. How many have died reconstructing your masterpiece?"

"You need not worry about bloodshed or death," remarked the Colonel. "They are after all already dead. I simply provide them with an opportunity to *live* again."

"This is not living," interjected Akara, "this is a fate worse than death."

"Ultimately, your father makes the rules," said the Colonel. "I simply apply them to their fullest, and I do so gladly. There is nothing more exhilarating than fulfilling one's purpose."

"And I would gladly kill my father," thought Akara, "and end this horror." That would be her purpose. The jeep came upon a large number of Echoes building a wall. They looked haggard and weak, and their hands were horribly scared. And after each brick was laid, a Diabolicus soldier would whip the workers with a lash, while another would kick them in the legs, ordering them to toil faster.

"The wall is coming along well," said the Colonel. "Our incentive program is functioning well."

"Barbaric!" spat Da Vinci. "I'll never get used to this senseless violence. If only I had more power."

"The Law is clear," noted the Colonel. "And you're just an Ambassador, an officer of absolutely nothing. Make your peace with that, and take your place."

A frowning Da Vinci crossed his legs and his arms, boiling in his own helplessness. The Colonel would regret his words…sometime and somehow.

They passed by another wall, upon which the effigy of Hitler was being painted. The twenty-feet tall figure was near completion as the Echo artist, standing on an elevated ramp, added the finishing touch to Hitler's mustache.

"What do you think?" the Colonel asked Da Vinci, the master painter. "Is it not a perfect likeness of our Fuhrer?"

Da Vinci glanced at it and grunted, "the mustache is too long."

The Colonel stared at it intensely. "You're quite right. It is *not* perfect." He then signaled the Diabolicus soldier watching over the work. The soldier nodded, raised his revolver and shot the painter in the head. The artist dropped his brush, and toppled over the ramp railing, crashing to the ground. "I'm so glad you came along, Leonard." The Colonel jubilated.

Da Vinci, Theon and Akara were stunned. "You're a maniac!" shouted Da Vinci, feeling responsible for the Echo's brutal demise. "A lunatic!"

The Colonel only smiled, happy to have created the impression he sought from his disinclined guests.

As the ride towards Nazi headquarters progressed, they passed the Research & Development Center where all sorts of sordid experiments were being conducted on Echoes, stopping an instant by the neighboring amusement park.

At one amusement stand, Diabolicus civilians and off-duty soldiers were lined up against the counter, holding rifles that shot circular pellets the size of golf balls. Ten Echoes were strapped against the back wall, their heads fixed in place, and their mouths wrenched open with clamps, as the players fired pellets, hoping some would enter their targets' mouths and lodge themselves in the throat, asphyxiating the Echoes.

Another stand featured an Echo sitting on a platform above a tank filled with sulfuric acid. By hitting a bull's-eye with a ball, the Echo would plummet into the acid and die a slow and agonizing death.

"I'm certain you would enjoy some of the thrills of our park," the Colonel told Theon. "As a child, I spent many a day at the carnival. Fortunately, the games have become far more stimulating."

"Why don't you sit on the platform," retorted Theon, "and I'll let you know how *stimulating* it is."

"Feisty," said the Colonel. "I like that."

As they approached the headquarters, a male Echo emerged from the laneway between two buildings, heading towards the headquarters, and pursued by the Chimerian Bull militia. In seconds, the Echo was surrounded by eight Bulls, closing in on him.

The Echo quickly pulled off his shirt, revealing a bomb attached to his stomach. He held a deadman's switch in his hand, a switch that, once released, activated the bomb.

"Shoot me and the bomb goes off!" he warned the militia, raising his arm and exposing the switch. "Freedom for all Echoes!" he then bellowed. "Freedom!"

"Another Echo rebel." The Colonel calmly turned to the machine gunner at the back of the jeep. "He's far enough from headquarters. Eliminate the threat."

The gunner pulled the trigger, and hundreds of bullets tore through the antagonistic Echo, who slumped to the ground, and as the life oozed out of him, released the switch. The force of the explosion ravaged the immediate area, ripping the Bulls to shreds.

"You killed your own!" cried out Da Vinci.

"My own?" snapped back the Colonel. "Those things are *animals*!" he claimed with such overt racist disdain, the chief mindset and staple of the Nazi regime. "You should be more concerned with your own welfare."

"Off and onwards," he instructed the driver, bringing the jeep to the main entrance of Nazi headquarters, over which hung a flag of the Swastika. "The Fuhrer will see you now."

"I have a few things to tell him," angrily puffed Da Vinci.

"The Fuhrer will only see the boy," plainly indicated the Colonel. "Your influence and your value are extremely limited here, old man."

"But, he is just a boy," insisted Da Vinci.

"The Fuhrer will make that determination," said the Colonel.

Hitler would soon discover that Theon was more than just a fugitive and an alleged murderer. Satan would make sure of that.

CHAPTER 90

The man appeared unostentatious and, by physical standards, was unimpressive, standing at 5 foot 8 inches and weighing 160 pounds. His unstylish haircut and tiny rectangular mustache did little to flatter him, and any enthusiast of silent movies would swear he was Charlie Chaplin's doppelganger.

His childhood was quite ordinary, marred by a succession of failures. He was scorned by his father, was a poor student, a mediocre singer, and deemed unfit for military service. This bumbling and gauche boy turned *weapon of mass destruction* against all odds even entertained thoughts of becoming a priest. Had he pursued it, he would have become the first priest to exact condemnation instead absolution on his flock.

Even his voice was irritating, and mousy, as Theon would presently attest.

"Please take a seat, young man," invited Adolf Hitler in a perfect English, as he closely eyed Theon. "As the very personification of the young Arian man, I doubt my Youth program could improve what is already brushing against the gates of perfection. I understand you're a veritable killing machine. Four guards within an hour, that's impressive."

"Believe what you will," snapped Theon. "The truth is the scarcest resource of all in Hell."

"Yet, it lives here and thrives within these walls," assured the evermore politically driven Hitler. "I may be a genocidal monster, but I am no liar. And I suspect neither are you. Tell me, how does a human boy journey to Hell without the benefit, or detriment, of death?"

"He uses an inter-realm *subway*," replied Theon, "one that's by far cleaner and faster than the New York subway."

"Clever boy." Hitler became pensive. "Perhaps Satan has found a means of harnessing the power of the buried Trans'Kartum, and use it in an analogous way." He picked up a pencil and began hitting its sharp end against the top of his desk, before finally availing himself of its primary function, and scribbling something on a sheet of paper.

He passed the paper to Theon, which had five zeros written on it. "Jesus Christ took upon his shoulders Humanity's sins; that explains his sin score. What possible *burden* have you assumed to merit the same score?"

"If burden there truly is," hypothesized Theon, "I did *not* take it on willingly, much less knowingly. Someone else made that decision for me."

"Someone as evil as I am, perhaps more," postulated Hitler, who looked to Theon. "Who do you think that might be?"

"Satan, of course," instantly answered Theon. "After all, he was the one who abducted me."

"Exactly my thought," agreed Hitler as he pulled photographs out of a large envelope, and slid one to Theon. "Who is this creature?"

"The subject of discussion: Satan," asserted Theon, despite never having met him personally.

"An easy guess," grinned Hitler. "Can you explain why your sin scan produced the image of the Dragon Lord?"

"No clue," simply replied Theon.

"What about this image of a shimmering spirit?" asked Hitler, sliding the next photograph.

"Don't know who that is; don't know why it's there," said Theon, who deliberately refrained from signaling a possible connection with the spiritual entity dwelling inside him, fearing Hitler might experiment on him, in order to extract his spirit.

"What's your relationship with Jesus Christ?" went on Hitler, sliding the image of Jesus.

"I met him briefly in jail before busting out," said Theon. "He was gentle and kind, and very much as I had imagined him."

Hitler placed the photograph of Satan next to Jesus'. "You don't find it odd or extraordinarily coincidental that both the images of Christ and of his antipode, Satan, emanated from your being?"

"My life, for the most part, has been odd and strange," replied a resigned Theon. "Weirdness has become the norm, and not the exception."

"I too have been plagued and then blessed with a life full of strangeness," empathized Hitler. "Look upon me as a kindred soul."

Theon rebuked the comparison. "My origin, my nature, and my character, as nebulous as they might be in the moment, cannot be any farther from yours. Contrary to you, I don't embrace the darkness within, I wholeheartedly spurn it."

Hitler smiled at Theon's naivety. "No one can deny his destiny. Give it some time. Now, tell me who the woman is in this next image."

"Somewhat familiar," admitted Theon. "She resembles Da Vinci's Mona-Lisa."

"I had not seen that," said Hitler, who had twice failed the art academy's admission test, his drawing skills having been declared unsatisfactory. "Perhaps you'll recognize this other picture of a female Echo—one of Satan's many enslaved wives no less. In many respects, she matches our mystery woman."

Theon's face went white and he almost fell off his chair. "Where... where did you get this?" he stammered as his trembling fingers stroke the Echo's face. "Is she in Hell? What have you done with her?"

"She's Satan's concern, not mine," replied Hitler. "It's evident you know of her. How has that come to be?"

"What is her name?" demanded Theon, his eyes never leaving her face. "Tell me now!" he growled like a fierce lion.

"I sense anger, outrage, hatred," said a pleased Hitler. "Essential qualities in a leader."

Theon's stare rose and met Hitler's. Had his eyes been laser beams, he would have sliced the Fuhrer into pieces. "Her name is Sarah," informed the latter.

Theon's eyes opened wide, so wide they looked like billiard balls. "Sarah is my adoptive *mother's* name! The woman in this picture *is* my mother!"

"There is more," announced Hitler, adding fuel to an already explosive situation. "I have heard from good authority that the nature of the relationship between Satan and this woman is incestual. She is not only his wife, but also his granddaughter."

Theon's eyes swelled with tears. "This is insane, totally insane. You have to help me save her. Please help me. You would do no less for your own mother."

"I could do no more for my mother," said Hitler. "She lives in the kingdom of Heaven."

"Then, help me bring *my* mother to Heaven," pleaded Theon.

"This Sarah is where she belongs," assured Hitler. "And this Sarah *cannot* be your mother. According to records, she died in the year 64. Raised in a Christian orphanage, she had become an activist in her early thirties and fought the persecution against Christians and the apostles' teachings at the hands of the authorities of the Roman Empire.

"As part of a radical faction, she and her cohorts killed many Romans, and participated in the onset of the Great Fire of Rome. She was apprehended and crucified. Born of unknown parents, who were probably persecuted themselves, and left at the orphanage out of safety, she bore two children who escaped with her husband before the carnage began."

Theon shook his head in disbelief. "The name, the features, they're the same as my mother's. This is too much of a coincidence."

Hitler rose from his chair. "I can offer no explanation, only a suggestion: prepare yourself for what is to come. I am bound by duty to inform Satan of your capture; and his punishments are usually quite extravagant."

"You would do that?" shouted Theon. "What about this kindred spirit business?"

"I would do it, to you and your friends," declared Hitler. "As it was on Earth, I care only for my own position and my own advancement. One day, if you live long enough as a mortal or as an Echo, you may find that divesting yourself of morality and righteousness—the weak man's currency—inevitably brings about an immutable sense of freedom, a clarity of thought and a perpetual tranquility, and lifts you to the apogee of rapture. There is no greater power in one's life; and no one can take it away from you."

"You believe me to be greater than the sum of what I appear to be," boldly noted Theon; "and *my* power may unfold in a way that even you cannot fathom. You should fear me."

"Kill Satan, and I shall fear you," said a calculating Hitler. "Nothing else will do."

"And a new master shall rule over Hell," surmised Theon. "You *are* a fiendish monster."

Hitler chuckled diabolically. "I may have to rid Hell of a few more less formidable demons before I take the throne, but I'm patient. After all, I have all eternity."

Hitler walked to the door and knocked on it. His lieutenant appeared. "Take the boy back to guest quarters. Do not harm him."

The lieutenant saluted vigorously. "Yes, mein Fuhrer. I do have a message from Lord Satan," handing Hitler a letter. "I did not want to disturb you, and waited—"

"Yes, yes, of course," mumbled Hitler, closing the door behind him.

He read it immediately:

"I understand you have the boy, Theon Rex, in your custody, and you have yet to inform me.
Do not interrogate him. Do not torture him. Treat him as you would your Lord.
Bring him, Akara, and Da Vinci to the Games tonight. I shall attend. I will test the boy using my own means."

Hitler was perplexed and vexed. "How the hell does Satan know about Theon's capture and about the company he keeps; and what *test* is he talking about?" He would soon find out.

CHAPTER 91

The open-sky Fourth Reich Forum was brimming with over a thousand spectators, mostly Diabolicus, eagerly awaiting the start of the *Death Games*. At the center of the oval-shaped Forum stood a rectangular arena whose variable perimeter was delimited by a series of retractable poles, generating between them an electro-magnetic force field.

Depending on the nature of the event, the arena could cover as little as 400 square feet—similar to a standard boxing ring, or as much as 2,700 square feet. The greatest area required for a given program determined the seating arrangements, which remained fixed during the entire program, with the exception of a mobile box of 18 seats reserved for the Fuhrer and his guests. From one event to the other, the box would automatically take a position by the ringside.

Sitting in the first of three 6-seat rows were Hitler, Akara, Da Vinci, and Theon. In the row behind them sat a collection of some of the most nefarious mass murderers in Earth's history: Napoleon Bonaparte, Julius Caesar, Genghis Khan, Attila the Hun, and Hell's most recent addition, Osama Bin Laden.

"I must admit to a certain amount of trepidation," Da Vinci told Theon. "Being surrounded by so much evil is unnerving."

"Try picturing them naked," proposed Theon. "It's always worked for me." What Theon didn't specify was that he only indulged in this type of mental exercise when confronted with a girl he secretly liked.

Da Vinci made the attempt. "Oh, Lord, it's even worse. Not only am I still scared, but now I also feel nauseous."

"Tonight's exciting program," said the private box attendant as he handed brochures to Da Vinci and the rest of the group. "I'm sure your nausea will pass when the competitions start." Da Vinci was convinced of the reverse.

"We have company," announced Hitler after looking behind and seeing Satan and his Echo wife, Sarah, enter the box. Much like a pet dog, Sarah was on a leash.

"Good evening," said Satan as he tugged on the leash to draw his wife closer, and then detached it from the neck collar.

"Sit next to the boy," he ordered her. "I shall sit at the other end, next to Adolf."

Sarah gazed at Theon as she took her seat, and squirmed into a comfortable position. "You seem bothered by my presence. Would you prefer I sit elsewhere?"

Her voice was identical to Theon's mother, aggravating his uneasiness. "It's all right. You just remind me of someone I miss very much."

"Then perhaps I can take her place," gladly offered Sarah. "Temporarily, of course. There is no substitute for one's mother."

"How did you know that?" wondered Theon, who found himself suddenly becoming attracted to her.

"I'm also a mother," pointed out Sarah, "and mothers can see plainly into little boys' souls. Do you know what I see now? I see myself in you."

"Did Satan put you up to this?" asked a suspicious Theon; "to mess with my mind?"

"My husband might control my body, but *my* mind and my soul are my own," she attested in a genuine tone.

Theon quizzed her further. "Hitler has told me you're also Satan's granddaughter. How is that possible?"

"That is indeed my husband's assertion," freely admitted Sarah. "Since I never knew my parents, I cannot verify or refute it…and my husband will divulge no more about it, just to torture me, I presume. You're fortunate to have known the people who gave you life."

Theon bowed his head in melancholy. "I'm adopted. I've never known my biological parents."

An empathic Sarah began stroking Theon's back hair. "Have faith. It may yet—oh, what is this?" She noticed the symbols on his neck. "Incredible! I have *similar* symbols on my neck." She quickly pulled up her hair, uncovering the marks. "Mine are quite faded, almost invisible."

"You're right," exclaimed an equally baffled Theon. "Mine have gotten darker with time, with some minor localized fading."

"Mine have never changed since birth. Yours are also closer together," noted Sarah.

Da Vinci, who had been quietly following the conversation, chimed in. "Signora Sarah, have you ever exhibited special powers of any kind?"

"None," she said categorically. "Why do you ask?"

"I'm entertaining a wild hypothesis," replied the inquisitive Da Vinci. "Did you know that about one quarter of identical twins are *mirror* twins—a reflection of each other? Features, such as birthmarks, hair whorls or internal organs, appear on opposite sides of each twin."

"We're twins?" Theon and Sarah said, gawking at each other.

"Your case, however, poses several problems," recognized Da Vinci. "Firstly, identical twins are always of the same sex.

"Secondly, while the symbols are comparable, they are not mirror images—one is not the reverse of the other. And thirdly, and most importantly, Theon was born in the 21st century, while you, Sarah, were born in the 1st century.

"But, then again, you, Theon, have claimed to have had a mysterious sister named Sarah; and now, we are confronted with a woman bearing such a name, sharing the same symbols and looking exactly like your adoptive mother Sarah."

"What if *this* Sarah is my ancestor, or even my mother's ancestor?" conjectured Theon.

Da Vinci crossed his arms and frowned. "The notion that Sarah is your ancestor is far-fetched. The notion that she is your mother's is absolutely preposterous."

"A quarter of my adoptive mother's DNA matches mine," suddenly recalled Theon. "The premise that Sarah is my ancestor would then logically extend to my mother, isn't that so?"

"Good God!" cried Da Vinci. "Why haven't you told me this before?"

"I've had a lot of things on my mind," harshly retorted Theon. "And why would I think to tell you that?"

"Quite right," apologetically mumbled Da Vinci. "Another piece of the puzzle; it must fit somehow."

"I have a message from my dad," interjected Akara. "He says he wants you to *shut up*."

"Tell your *dad* he's just a bully," countered Da Vinci; "a ruffian who withholds pivotal information for his own perverse designs." He then looked away and pouted like a child.

Akara bent forward and angrily looked at Satan. "Everything's quiet now. Happy?" She knew right there and then that, upon return to the castle, Satan would beat her into a pulp for her insolence.

Hitler, who couldn't care less about the girl, stared intently at Satan, who had said very little since his arrival. "I've known you for seventy years, and I'm willing to wager you didn't expect the boy to be caught so swiftly...or should I say, so *prematurely*."

"He's here and now," grumbled Satan. "Testing him here in this arena, or testing him in the field makes no difference."

"Testing him how, and to what end?" queried a clueless Hitler. "Why is this boy, whose very nature and powers are shrouded in mystery, so important to you?"

"The games are beginning," was Satan's only answer. Hitler would mind his place, but only until the so-called test.

CHAPTER 92

"Anzu just delivered a powerful upper-cut, tearing away a piece of LaMoya's jaw, and sending him crashing onto the mat," described the Diabolicus ringside commentator. "There's blood all over."

"But, he's not down for the count," added the analyst, sitting next to the commentator. "He's still breathing, and he's getting back up. No Echo has ever lasted this long against Anzu. Unbelievable!"

Anzu was a gigantic muscle-bound Diabolicus Terrum, who towered over all his opponents. His latest one, LaMoya, a once brilliant, undefeated boxer turned criminal and murderer, had been found dead in a dark ally, a bullet lodged in his brain.

Moments before his demise, as life drained from his body, LaMoya's dying wish was to step into the ring one last time and recapture his past glory. Ironically, what he failed to rekindle in life, he succeeded in death.

And tonight, in Hell's stage, one single thought looped constantly in his mind: "Beware what you wish for."

LaMoya raised his hands to signify his readiness to resume the match. His boxing gloves, just like Anzu's, were covered in sharp spikes in order to inflict as much damage as possible. Unfortunately for him, the blood spilled to date was his own, and only his.

LaMoya took a step back as Anzu barreled towards him, delivering a jab to LaMoya's abdomen that literally sectioned his stomach. He fell to his knees, and Anzu, without any hesitation, and with one final blow, crushed his head. The crowd cheered loudly, calling out Anzu's name repeatedly.

Theon, Akara, Da Vinci, and Sarah were the only ones not cheering.

"Vulgar and inhuman," barked Da Vinci as he watched the Echo boxer's body dissolve.

"Spectacular!" shouted the commentator. "What a bout. Anzu triumphs again. What can ever top this?"

"That's a rhetorical question, I'm sure," said the analyst. "The next competition will bring even more chills and thrills."

"Never so right," agreed the commentator. "The next match will pit the Echo Roman gladiator team of Flavius and Artemus against the undefeated Diabolicus team of Zagan and Eligos. The weapon of choice is the sword, and of course, the contest is no holds barred. Let's get ready to die!"

The confrontation lasted no more than ten minutes, ending with the brutal death of the Echo team, and with the crowd screaming: "Asterion! Asterion! Bring out Asterion!"

"Who's Asterion?" wondered Theon, flipping through the program brochure. What he initially found objectionable had become mildly entertaining. "The next competition is called *The Lure of the Labyrinth*. Look Leo, there's a picture of a maze and of a man fighting a Minotaur (creature with the head of a bull and the body of a man)," showing Da Vinci the brochure.

"For your pleasure and your amusement," roared the commentator, "here he is, the great, the merciless, the bestial, the Chimerian Bull, Aaaaaaasteeeeeriiiioooon!"

The Chimerian appeared from a back exit, accompanied by five scantily clad Echo females, kissing and fondling his body as he lumbered along a corridor leading to the ring.

With every step, the ring began expanding from its original size of 20 by 20 feet to an area of 52 by 52 feet. The poles that had delimited the perimeter of the ring, extended upwards to a height of ten feet. Other poles emerged from the floor, ultimately forming a dotted pattern, where each pair of contiguous poles was separated by a distance of four feet.

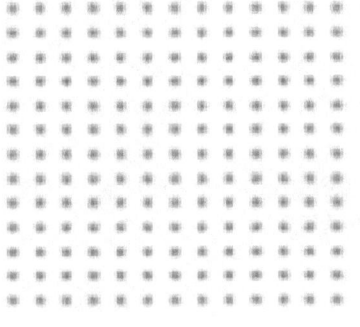

Certain sections of the white mat suddenly changed to black, forming a giant Swastika.

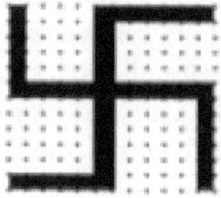

"What's going on?" Theon asked Sarah, who was the most likely to know.

"It's a contest of brawn and wits," explained Sarah. "A man, usually an Echo, enters the labyrinth from one corner of the mat, while the Bull enters from the opposite corner. Both contestants must maneuver through the maze's corridors, which are made up of walls of high electro-magnetic energy that change positions every 30 seconds or so.

"The object of the game is to visit every black floor section (black square area defined by four neighboring poles), and press the deactivation button at the center of the floor section, thus changing the black color of the section back to white. To win, the Echo must erase the Swastika completely before the Bull reaches him and kills him.

"To aid in his survival, ten white sections will contain weapons, such as knives, swords, spears, and axes. If he gets to any of them along the way, he can use them to defend against or kill the Bull."

"Is the Bull allowed to use the weapons as well?" queried Theon, finding this particular game ingenious.

Sarah nodded. "Of course. God forbid you would give the Echo a fighting chance. However, the Echo does have one advantage the Bull does not. He is assisted by a *Guide* perched in a seat 25 feet above the maze. The guide sees the entire maze, providing direction through radio contact. The guide is also equipped with a visual aid that monitors the positions of both contestants, and the changes in the maze schematic."

"Has any Echo ever survived the game?" Theon expected only one answer.

Sarah gave him a look of abdication. "No one survives this game. No one survives *any* of the games."

CHAPTER 93

"So, my Lord, when shall I be privy to this obscure test of yours?" Hitler probed Satan.

"It shall manifest this instant." Satan rose from his seat and addressed his wife. "Sarah, you will be the Guide for this match. Go and take your position."

Sarah was utterly surprised by the command. "Who shall I guide?"

"Those men," he said, pointing at a party of Diabolicus forcefully pushing two men towards the ring. The men wore cloaks and hoods hid their faces. Once they reached the ring, they were positioned on a corner floor section moments before the force field engaged.

The field was completely transparent, with the exception of two thin but clearly visible red lines traversing the center of each energy wall, horizontally and vertically, so that contestants could readily identify available paths through the maze. From their location, the men could easily see the Chimerian Bull, in a fidget for the contest to start. They were far from sharing in his eagerness.

Satan walked pass his guests and sat next to Theon. "We have a special tonight; *three* humans for the price of one."

"I count only two," noted Theon.

Satan snickered. "One more will join them momentarily. Be ready."

As the bell rang, marking the start of the match, the men dropped their cloaks to the ground, revealing their identities.

Theon jumped out of his seat, stunned and appalled. "DAD!" he screamed at the top of his lungs.

Cameron Rex and Scott Dumont, Rex's FBI superior, were the Bull's quarry for this match.

A rabid Theon clamped on Satan's neck. "You bastard! You killed my father!"

"He is *not* dead," rasped Satan in dire need of oxygen. "Let me go, or he will be."

Theon reluctantly released him. "Explain!"

"Your adoptive father and his comrade are ingenious men," said Satan, coughing and clearing his voice. "They unlocked the secret of the Trans'Kartum and traveled to this realm. How they discovered the combination is beyond my comprehension."

A careful Da Vinci, who was nervously pondering how he could intercede on behalf of Theon's welfare, knew he had played a pivotal part in securing the combination and cleverly communicating it through his past work. "Perhaps I should sit next to the boy," he suggested to Satan.

"Perhaps you should remain quiet, Ambassador," snapped Satan, "before I seal *your* fate." He turned back to Theon. "Both men have been implanted with a small explosive device. Any game interference or any assault attempt against me or any of my guests will instantly result in your father's death. At least against the Bull, he has a chance."

Theon sat back, scared, submissive and helpless, and did what the rowdy crowd did: he watched.

"What are your names?" urgently asked Sarah, through the radio device.

"I'm Cam," replied Rex, raising his hand as a means of identification. "The other is Scott."

"Your lives are at stake," cried Sarah. "You have a better chance of completing the Swastika if you split up. I'll guide both of you from above."

Cameron recognized the voice, and looked up. "Sarah? What the hell?"

"How do you know my name?" wondered Sarah.

"You're my wife for Christ sake," retorted Cameron.

"Your wife is back on Earth," said Sarah. "I just look like her for some reason…oh, never mind, not important. Now listen carefully, Cam. Head straight and turn right. Scott, you go to your immediate right."

In seconds, Cam came upon a black section and stomped on the deactivation button. As for Scott, he came upon a knife. As he picked it up, he saw the Bull a few corridors away, heading in his direction. "He's coming after me!"

"Don't panic!" pleaded Sarah. "He's got quite a few turns to make. Now go left. At the end, you'll find a black section."

Cameron was doing well on his own, now having deactivated three black sections. "I see another black section up ahead. I'm going for it!"

"No, Cam!" warned Sarah. "The maze is changing." Halfway through the corridor, Cameron collided with a newly formed wall. The force field repelled him, sending him hurtling back. Dizzy, he stumbled. "Sure beats a bullet to the chest. What do I do now?"

"Quickly, turn right, then left," instructed Sarah.

"Good Lord!" screamed Scott. "The monster's right next to me!" Frantic, Scott ran down a corridor.

"Keep calm, Scott!" urged Sarah. "The force field is protecting you. Oh no! Scott, you're heading to a juncture that connects with the corridor occupied by the Bull. Turn tail immediately. Turn tail!"

Filled with dread, Scott failed to heed her instruction, and when he reached the juncture, he was met by a salivating, growling Bull, whose newly acquired axe came hurtling down, impaling his chest and piercing his heart. He dropped his knife and collapsed onto the floor. The Bull pulled out the axe and several ribs in tow. He then looked towards the sky and roared in victory. The crowd roared back in delight.

"What's happening?" screamed a terrified Cameron.

"Scott is dead," sadly announced Sarah. "You're on your own. Take the next left. You'll find a black section. Hurry!"

"What's the point?" realized Cameron. "There are too many black sections left. What I need now is a weapon. Get me to weapon!"

Before Sarah could relay new instructions, the maze changed again, but in an anomalous way: half the poles withdrew, and half the energy walls disengaged including the energy ceiling, making an encounter with the murderous Bull inevitable.

"Damn you, Satan!" she bellowed. "Cam, there's a sword twenty feet ahead. Run! Run!"

From her platform, Sarah leaned forward and pointed vigorously at the sword. She heard a snapping sound, then another, and looked up. The wires holding the platform in place were coming apart. "Why you traitorous scumbag." The next instant, the platform and its passenger crashed to the ground. Sarah's head hit so violently that her skull split in two. She died instantly and vanished.

Akara screamed in horror, while Theon went wild. He rose from his seat anew and raised his fist above Satan's head. "You'll kill my father no matter what I do; so I'm going to kill *you*!"

"I would never deny you vengeance," said a gleeful and very assured Satan. "But why take a life when you can save one. Short of an attack against me, you're at liberty to do whatever you wish."

Theon was confused. "What are you implying?"

"I've reconsidered; I will allow you to assist your father," replied Satan; "perhaps even save him from the beast. Make haste, boy, save him from his perils, lest he share in your *sister's* downfall, as it were."

Theon's raised fist began trembling uncontrollably. "What?"

"Yes, lad, she *truly* is your sister." Satan raised his arms, palms open and upwards. "Surprise!"

"Sar…Sarah…my, *my* sister?" stuttered a disoriented Theon, letting his fist drop loosely and dangle at the side.

"One death in the family is enough," playfully remarked Satan. "Now listen to your *Grandpa* Satan and go help your daddy."

"Make me proud!"

CHAPTER 94

"It's a trick!" admonished Da Vinci. "You're being deceived. Don't jump into the ring."

Theon was beyond reasoning. His newfound sister was dead for good, and his father was about to join her. He would prevent that even if it cost him his own life. Stepping onto the front railing of the box, fifteen feet above ground, he bent his knees slightly and then hurled himself into the air. He traveled so high and so far, the crowd thought he was actually flying.

As Theon's body began its descent towards the center of the ring, Satan waved at the ring operator, who sealed the top of the ring with a force field. Theon crashed onto it heavily, and was instantly repulsed, flying up and crashing down repeatedly like a capricious ping pong ball on a table.

As he fell onto the field after the fifth bounce, his right hand penetrated the field and somehow acted as an anchor, ending the vicious cycle. "I'm coming, dad!"

Shrugging off the pain, he pushed his head and then his shoulders through the field. His body glistened and lit up like a Christmas tree. As more of his body traversed the field, the pain intensified and became excruciating.

"Theon!" yelled his father, who finally noticed him, but didn't quite recognize him, and immediately feared for his boy's life. "No, son! Go back! For God's sake, go back!" He wobbled to the center of the ring, preparing to catch his son into his arms; but his preparation did not account or brace him for the forces building within Theon. "Oh, my God! My son! My son!"

His eyes bloody red and spiteful, and his gaze malicious and vengeful, Theon grew arms on his back, tearing through his shirt. A skin membrane rapidly formed, attached to the dorsal arms and to the sides of the torso. With one final thrust, Theon fell through the field, landing on his father, who, overpowered by the momentum, crumpled to the floor.

Theon quickly rolled off his father and got up. "Are you ok?"

Cameron, stupefied and quite frankly petrified, crawled a few feet away. "*What* are you? Where's my son?"

Theon had no time to explain. The Bull was racing towards them like a runaway train.

"This is the *test*, isn't it?" suddenly realized Hitler. "You wanted the boy to transform into...*that*."

"I had to make certain that he *could* change," said an elated Satan, who had reintegrated his original seat. "But, this just the tip of the iceberg, the first modest expression of the vast and titanic power that seethes within him."

"Modest?" exclaimed Hitler. "I would qualify the manifestation as most impressive."

Satan remained evasive. "It's all a matter of relativity. You shall see soon enough, and aid us...personally."

Hitler found the comment disturbing. "Who is *us*?"

Satan abstained from indulging Hitler's line of questioning, and watched the ghastly spectacle unfold in splendid fashion. He was beside himself with joy, and expected only one grand finale to the ostensibly lopsided contest.

As for Theon, he would meet that expectation, readily or not.

Acting almost instinctively, Theon wrapped his bat like wings around his father, forming an airtight receptacle. "Stay put! Don't move!"

The Bull's axe descended upon Theon's crouched body, and tore through his left wing, firmly lodging itself in the membrane. In hindsight, Theon's choice of defense instead of offense had been a poor one. He screamed in pain before flapping his sturdy wings so violently, the axe ripped and sore away, in company of its brutish wielder, both crashing onto an energy wall twelve feet away, propelling them a further six feet onto the floor.

Theon turned on his right side, and as he grimaced in agony, his lips pulled back and long fangs egressed where there were once normal-sized canines. "Where's the Bull, dad?"

Seized by an array of rampaging emotions, the least of which was utter disbelief, Cameron was at a loss for words. Instead, he gaped stupidly at Theon's face, which was progressively losing all semblance of humanity.

"God Damn it, dad!" yelled Theon. "You're a trained *FBI agent*, act like one!"

The reference snapped Cameron out of his stupor. "It's *really* you, son. I thought I had lost you," gazing into his son's eyes. He then looked up. "That thing is slowly getting up. We need that axe."

"Or a sword," said Theon, who jumped to his feet. "The pain is gone."

The wound on his wing had miraculously healed. In fact, his wings, seemingly as part of the overall transformation process, had begun mutating into an exoskeleton (external skeleton) made of chitin, calcium carbonate, silica, and tendon-like apodemes. This made the exoskeleton as strong and as resistant as steel, at a fraction of the weight, while still retaining the flexibility of rubber. And the growth of the shield structure did not limit itself to the wings, also covering the entire back side.

"You're halfway to becoming *Iron Man*, son," said Cameron. "You have never ceased to amaze me."

The Bull, however, was neither impressed nor intimidated. After picking up the axe, he bolted towards his game.

"Get the sword!" ordered Theon, pointing to the weapon lying on the ground ten feet away, opposite the Bull's direction. "I'll detain him."

Theon flew towards the Bull, and with each flap of his reinforced wings, his father got closer to the sword. With arms extended horizontally, and fists clenched, Theon aimed for the enemy's head.

But the Bull had immediate designs on Cameron, the weaker of his prey. An instant before Theon reached him, he ducked and flung himself to the floor, rolling like a tire, carrying him but a few feet away from Cameron, who had just placed his hand on the sword.

Cameron gripped the sword's handle tightly, rose, and swerved briskly, hoping to join in the battle and help his courageous son. But his hopes were dashed irremediably when the blade of the axe slashed through the left side of his abdomen.

Cameron stood there, straight as an arrow, and peered into the beast's bloody eyes. He grinned widely, and, as his body began convulsing from the shock, he mustered every iota of strength remaining and raised the sword. "If this sword doesn't kill you, *my* son will." He collapsed to the ground, never releasing the sword.

The overconfident Bull raised his head towards the sky, in preparation for his victory cry, but no loud and assertive token of his superiority shook the building. Instead, a wimpish and almost cowardly sound emanated with difficulty from his mouth, as Theon's legs circled his neck, and his arms clasped his head, both tightening evermore so.

"Die, you monster! Die!" Theon flapped his wings as vigorously as he could, raising the heavy beast a few inches, enough to compromise his foothold and keep him off balance. Striking the axe backwards, the Bull could only reach the exoskeleton, which easily resisted every blow. For the first time since the onset of the contest—of any contest—the Bull was beset by fear, frantically attacking his opponent from all sides.

Dropping the axe, he grappled with Theon's legs, trying to extirpate them like the roots of undesirable weed, but to no avail. Realizing Theon was besting the Bull, the crowd, steadfast in allegiance to victors only, began siding with him. "Kill the Bull! Kill the Bull! Kill, kill, kill!"

The dignitaries sitting in Satan's private box were surprised and aroused by the unprecedented turn of events. Even Da Vinci, a man of peace, was swept away by the spectacle. "He's winning, Akara. He's winning."

Akara glanced at her father, who didn't seem at all disturbed by the Bull's ineptness in quashing his foe. He was instead quite euphoric, rising from his seat and screaming: "Theon Rex! Theon Rex!" The crowd joined him in cheer: "Theon Rex! Theon Rex!"

Light-headed and reeling, the Bull's knees buckled. Theon did not release his hold, now twisting the beast's head, fully intent on breaking his spinal cord.

"Kill the Bull!" shouted Satan, waving his fist in praise. "Kill!"

"*Spare* the Bull!" implored a voice in Theon's head. "Spare your enemy."

Theon relaxed his grip ever so slightly. "Ghost Knight! No! Not now, not ever!"

His holy spirit reiterated more forcefully. "Spare your enemy! You are not a murderer! You are an agent of peace; that is why I chose you."

"Then, you've chosen *wrong*!" harshly replied Theon, who tightened his grip anew, and gave the beast's head one final mighty tug, snapping his spine. Relinquishing his hold, the beast tumbled down, quite lifeless.

The voice of his spirit did not speak again, but Theon felt his discontent and his despondency, as he rushed to his father's side. "I did it, dad. I killed him," he told him, much like a son seeking his father's approval.

And, as he had once done with his sister Maya, he tried to invoke his powers further, to restore his father, but this time, nothing remotely appreciable happened—the damage was simply too severe.

"It's no use, Theon. I'm dying," Cameron muttered painfully, grazing his son's cheek with his trembling hand. "I've always been proud of you.

Remember that."

"I'll see you again, dad," assured Theon. "Souls do go to Heaven, and you have the purest soul I know. I'll meet you there, I promise."

Cameron began to cry. "I'm afraid I'm going to Hell."

"That's not true, dad," insisted Theon. "God awaits you. And from what I hear, he's a pretty fair guy."

Cameron began coughing blood. "No, son; God will have nothing to do with me. I killed a man in cold blood, remember? The serial child-killer who came to our house; I shot him dead while he was down and harmless. I committed the greatest of sins."

"I offered to kill him," countered Theon. "Let the sin be mine!"

"Oh, my admirable son…my only son," spat an agonizing father. "Who could fault such a prodigy?"

"God will forgive you," swore Theon. "I'll see to that personally."

Cameron's hand slumped. "I love you, Theon. I love you, son," gasping for his last breath. "Now, find your way home; your mother's worried, really worr—" Cameron's body became still.

A strange haze rose from the body, dissipating into the air. "Murderer!" screamed Theon, who immediately took flight and darted for Satan. "You're the next one to die," announced Theon as he hovered next to the Dragon Lord.

"Kill me, and your soon-to-return Echo-father will suffer like no Echo has ever suffered before," warned Satan. "Spare me, and I promise to be lenient with him. Your choice, my boy."

"Your word means nothing!" cried Theon.

"Your choice," boldly repeated Satan.

"I'll see you around, demon," exclaimed a frustrated and reluctant Theon, grabbing Da Vinci and Akara by the arms, and flying away through the giant ceiling aperture of the open-sky Forum.

"We shall indeed see each other again," silently promised Satan. "It is after all our *destiny*."

CHAPTER 95

"How is he?" asked a concerned Da Vinci.

"He's weak, but otherwise *normal*," said Akara, holding Theon's hand.

"I couldn't maintain the transformation," muttered Theon in a tone oddly suggesting regret. "Had I, we could have gone much further."

No longer able to carry his friends, Theon had landed his cargo by the edge of the *Elysian* fields, where crops of *Narok*—a kind of purple vegetable closely resembling Earth corn—were tended and harvested by thousands of Echo slaves during the day. To the Diabolicus, Narok was an exquisite delicacy. To most Echoes, the taste was offensive, even when it was boiled at length and overly seasoned.

"I would have thought you happy to be your old self again," presumed Akara. "Although, I must admit you looked quite handsome as a Diabolicus *Quasimodo*."

Theon forced a smile. "If you recall, in the story, Quasimodo never got the beautiful girl."

Akara leaned forward and gave Theon a quick peck on the lips. "This is a different story." She moved back, and had her complexion not been already red, he would have noticed her blushing. "I know you're worried about your father. I'm certain he'll echoalesce, and end up in Heaven."

Theon nodded. "If I have anything to do with it, he will; and no hellish grand-father will stand in my way." And while he struggled with the notion of such an obscene family tie, he maintained a brave front, resorting to humour to mask his pain. "Since you're his daughter, that would make you my Aunt. You should know I don't date family."

Akara abruptly released his hand and slapped him on the arm. "Don't be a smart ass!"

His shirt completely ripped, Theon bent over and pulled the rag off, exposing the back of his neck.

"What's this?" exclaimed Da Vinci as he stared at the symbols. "They've darkened considerably more, and they've combined, forming *one* mark...the mark on the helmets of Satan's close guard.

"Perhaps it foretells a near-ending of a process of metamorphosis, an evolution towards an altered form of life driven by a new imperative."

Theon grabbed his head, sickened by the incessant conjectures and guesswork. He was no longer interested in the *What* and the *Why* of his condition, and was now only concerned with the *How* to cure it. "You don't need to be a genius to see that I'm changing, inside and outside."

"Inside?" wondered Akara. "What do you mean?"

Theon appeared embarrassed. "When I held the Chimerian Bull's head, I felt a boundless anger that would not abate, not until I had broken his neck. When I realized I had killed him, the anger vanished and was replaced by something far more potent; I felt pleasure, unbridled, wanton pleasure. The exhilaration was all consuming."

"The Bull killed your father," defended Akara. "How could you feel otherwise? You wanted justice."

"I wanted *vengeance*," countered Theon.

"So what?" cried out Akara in vexation. "Do you know how many times *I* wanted to kill my father after the beatings? I would gladly dance on his grave upon his death."

"Killing and wanting to kill are not the same," pointed out Theon. "You're nothing like me, or like your father."

"Shut up, both of you!" ordered Da Vinci. "Someone is coming."

Dusk was approaching as a procession of men walked towards the Western range of the Polar caves, eighty yards away from the edge of the Elysian Fields, where Theon, Akara and Da Vinci were hiding. The cortege led by four armed Diabolicus, followed by thirty-eight Echoes in chains, stopped at a rock face, quite common and unremarkable in formation.

The lead Diabolicus pressed on the rock face in three distinct locations, opening a secret door, through which they passed, the door closing behind them.

"Come, children, let's investigate," urged a snoopy Da Vinci, eternally goaded by scientific curiosity. "I've committed to memory the unlocking sequence," pressing three times on the rock face, and opening the door.

"Out of the frying pan and into the fire," quoted Theon. "Haven't we had our share of danger for one day?"

"Satan did not order his men to pursue us," had noted Da Vinci. "He wants us to persist in our quest. Based on that premise, we face no immediate danger."

"A foolish assumption," grunted Theon, convinced Satan's idleness was temporary at best.

After traveling seventy feet through a tunnel, the trio came upon a large chamber, sixty feet in diameter, and thirty-five feet in height, lit by a barn fire at its center. They hid behind a pile of boulders and observed the cloak-and-dagger affair unfold.

"I am *Stuord*," announced a strange creature, accompanied by five of his own kin, armed with spears. "I am Chief to the ninth faction of the Kalidrone. How many have you brought?"

"Satan offers thirty-eight healthy Echoes," replied the Diabolicus leader; "more than was ever agreed upon." Keeping a constant eye on the Chief, he unchained the Echoes, shoved one towards the Chief, commanding him to move swiftly, and then signaled the others to follow suit.

The Kalidrone's appearance was terrifying. Standing at no more than five feet, their skin was as white as unblemished snow; and their bodies were thin, almost scrawny; a frail and inadequate pedestal for an oversized, hairless, and perfectly spherical head.

Their mouths were oval-shaped, the lipless brim of which quivered and panted, dropping long strings of saliva, in anticipation of what was to come. Their sharp teeth, two-inches long, and as slim as golf tees, were reminiscent of that of the prehistoric Dracula fish, the most diabolical fish ever to inhabit the Earth's seas.

Their ears were small and malformed; and their hand and feet nails were black, short, and curved inwards. Strangely, only their eyes seemed normal, by human standards. Light-blue and piercing, they were accessorized with lush long eyelashes and thick luxuriant eyebrows—remnants perhaps of a more genetically endowed and gifted ancestry.

Renowned as fierce Great Dragon hunters, whose skillfulness surpassed even that of the Chimerian Primates, they wore grey, one-piece, short-sleeve, above-knee hemline tunics, made from the dragons' underbelly skin; boots and belts made from osteoderms, the plated skin on the dragons' backsides; and necklaces made from the dragons' teeth.

Designer of a variety of white weapons, they bore *Bosats* for the occasion, a weapon similar in design to a bow saw, but with spikes at both ends, long narrow teeth along the blade, and held with both hands at the midpoint of the curved handle.

One forceful swing of the weapon could slice a man in two. The leader of the Diabolicus was keenly aware of this fact as he disclosed his interest in what was supposed to be a business exchange. "We have provided the Kalidrone with Echoes in excess of the quota. Thus far, we have been indulgent and patient. But no more. Give us the Sword of Maitreya."

"The sword, Theon; the sword," whispered Da Vinci, his excitement almost causing him to slip off the boulder upon which he had set foot. Ears and eyes wide open, they waited for the rest of the tale.

"Deus, Lord God, has tried to retrieve the sword, and failed," reminded Stuord. "Satan, Lord Dragon, has also tried to recover the sword... and failed. If great Lords are so incompetent, and their repeated efforts so futile, what possesses you to believe a mere soldier like you can extricate it from the Kalidrone?"

"We shall hunt your kind down, and exterminate you," threatened the Diabolicus leader.

Stuord grinned, taking a step forward as fifteen Kalidrone armed with crossbows emerged from the shadows, perched on elevated rock formations arranged along the periphery of the chamber. "This is the third time you have menaced us with annihilation. Given its evermore obvious fruitlessness, perhaps you should revise your argument."

The leader growled in exasperation. "Satan will be incensed. You've impinged on his leniency one time too many."

"Tell your master to supply us with 500 more Echoes," demanded Stuord, "and I shall consider concluding our contract."

Powerless and clearly disadvantaged, the leader yelled, "It is said Satan has other ways of securing the sword. Remember that." He then turned around and marched back into the tunnel, his subordinates close behind.

Stuord plodded to one of the Echoes, a young man of about 19 years of age. "You smell delicious," grabbing him by the shoulders and violently pulling him. He opened his mouth, which stretched to almost twice its original size, and bit down hard on the Echo's head.

The Echo screamed in fear as his body shimmered and de-echoalesced into a mist of Humanessence that was siphoned into the Kalidrone's mouth and dispatched to every part of his body, instantly rejuvenating the parasitical creature's being. Nothing of the Echo was left, not even the customary black residue.

Breathing deeply, Stuord fondled his torso from top to bottom, relishing the familiar and euphoric sensation like an addict after the administration of a strong dose of heroin. "I feel much better now."

"May we feast as well?" humbly asked one of his cronies eying an appetizing young woman. "It has been some time since our last meal."

"And it will be some time until you partake in the Echo elixir if you dare ask anew," warned Stuord, who usually appropriated half the delivered Echoes for himself. "Bring them to the compound."

The archers abandoned their positions and, all but one, entered the bigger of the two tunnels at the back end of the chamber, followed by Stuord, the Echoes, and the remaining archer, who, after taking one last look around, brought up the rear.

As the last Kalidrone crossed the tunnel threshold, Da Vinci slipped, freeing a few rocks that tumbled down the side of the boulder, the sound of which attracted the short soldier.

He quickly debated whether to alert his fellow mercenaries, but, assuming it could only be an animal indigenous to the caves, he opted to investigate alone.

"Damn it! He heard us," whispered Da Vinci. "Theon, can we count on your unique style of intervention?"

"He's still weak," indicated Akara, summoning with some difficulty her warrior-princess persona as she pulled a knife out of her boot. Her hand shook, appalled and unnerved by what she had witnessed, which did not go unnoticed by Da Vinci.

"Are you all right?" queried the old man.

"I can handle this *short stack*," she snapped back.

The unwitting Kalidrone rounded the large boulder, and as he reached its opposite side, a boot came flying and struck his right hand, sending his crossbow hurtling through space. He froze in stupor, affording Akara the moment to tackle him to the ground, unimpeded by any tactical countermeasures.

Sitting squarely on his chest, she wedged the knife in his neck, drawing a few trickles of blood. "If I apply any more pressure, you'll die. We need the Sword of Maitreya to *cure* my companion. Where is it, you sickening abomination?"

Da Vinci crouched next to the incapacitated Kalidrone. "I can't control her. She's quite unpredictable and unhinged. If you value your life—however execrable it might be—I wouldn't anger her."

Da Vinci's portrayal of Akara was, of course, grossly exaggerated, in order to solicit cooperation. "And this one," pointing to Theon, "turns into a monstrous, super-strength brute when enraged. He killed a giant Chimerian Bull with his hands."

"I can help you avoid an atrocious fate," offered Da Vinci, playing the *good cop-bad cop* routine to perfection. "If you tell me where the Sword of Maitreya is located, I'll convince them to spare you."

"I can't," bluttered out the Kalidrone, feeling the blade dig deeper into his neck. "I swear I can...ca...c—" He gasped loudly and lost consciousness.

Akara pulled back the knife, no longer feeling his chest heaving and receding. "Lord God, he's not breathing! I just wanted to scare him. What have I done?"

"Your first kill," said Theon. "I was wrong, Akara. You *are* like me... and like your father."

CHAPTER 96

"He's coming out of it," gladly announced Da Vinci, congratulating Theon by tapping his shoulder, now covered with the shirt the Echo from the cave wore before de-echoalescing. "Your powers may not have been required to neutralize the Kalidrone, but they were essential in reviving this one."

"His condition was not severe enough," remarked Theon, downplaying his apparent exploit. "In fact, I don't think I did anything. Had Akara chopped his head off instead, we would have been left with a big mess—nothing I could fix."

The Kalidrone opened his eyes, and cognizant once again of his dire predicament, shuddered and recoiled in fear. "Please don't kill me!"

"We've done that already," said Da Vinci. "Doing so again would be trite and simply too pedestrian."

"I was *not* dead," admitted the Kalidrone. "My species has the ability to place their bodies into *statis*, an extreme state of hypersleep. It's a passive defense mechanism." He looked around, realizing he was no longer in the cave.

"We dragged you out," explained Da Vinci, "concerned your brothers might return to the chamber. I assure you, we're not violent, contrary to what our recent performance in intimidation would suggest. We are, however, desperate, to say the least."

"It worked." The Kalidrone began to relax. "It seems we are plagued with a common woe. The Kalidrone have been sorely desperate for Millennia, in large part because of you."

"Us? What have we done?" wondered a puzzled Da Vinci.

"I speak only of you," indicated the Kalidrone, pointing at the old man; "you and your kind. You are an Echo, are you not?"

"An eminent one," pointed out a ruffled Da Vinci. "Since I've never met one of your *kind* before today, I fail to see how you could lay blame on me."

The Kalidrone lifted himself from the ground and sat. "My name is *Tholen,* and my people were once proud and accomplished. While we never excelled or advanced in technology—a deliberate cultural and social choice—we embraced a simple life based on honest work and the pursuit of philosophical and artistic enterprise."

"Sucking the life out of Echoes hardly qualifies as *honest* work," interjected an inimical Akara.

"Despite this day's appearances, your demon-kind has neither been very generous nor supportive of our plight," rebutted Tholen. "The Diabolicus are, at their core, dishonest, selfish and self-serving. These things are not foreign to you, child."

"I am not anything like *my* kind," vigorously asserted Akara.

"You possess their aggression and the instinct of the hunter," observed Tholen. "We too are hunters, and have been forced to expand the nature of our prey to include Echoes. Tell me, young girl, what do you see when you gaze upon me? A handsome, strapping and dashing man, or a hideous, decrepit and cowardly monstrosity?"

Akara was hesitant to answer, unable to produce a response draped in tact and diplomacy.

Tholen smiled and batted his deep blue eyes, which, for a brief moment, made him look bearable. "You are reluctant to answer? Your delicacy is appreciated. In truth, we were once the former, a vibrant and physically stunning race, basking in Shuntra's magnanimity and bounty."

"Shuntra shines on each and every one of us," said Da Vinci, "no more, or no less. The Sun does not play favorites."

Tholen nodded in the negative. "It does, unknowingly, unwittingly. But it is not photonic energy of which I speak; it is rather another form of energy that resides between the Sun's atmosphere and photosphere—a polarized energy called Humanessence by the Eternals. To be absolutely precise, and to insure all components are accounted for, the energy should rather be termed *Experiential Humanessence* since it is laced with human experience."

"You're talking about the human soul, aren't you?" surmised Theon. "The souls the Eternals are resurrecting using their energy collector?"

"The concept of resurrection is inaccurate in describing the collector's operation," replied Tholen. "Resurrection is predicated on death. Experiential Humanessence is not death; it is another state of being— from physicality, to energy, to reconstituted physicality. Nothing is lost or gained from one state to the next."

"And you say you tap into this process somehow?" said Theon, struggling to understand.

"Our particular biology is designed to attract and absorb E.H. (experiential humanessence)," explained Tholen. "Just as you ingest food to survive, we assimilate energy through our epidermal cells. It was not always so. We used to be like you over 40,000 cycles ago until a great drought fell upon the realm. Many died of starvation. Fortunately for some, a radical mutation interceded on their behalf. The small community of scientists quickly realized the survivors were actually feeding off the Sun's energy. The few scientists we have left today continue to study the phenomenon."

Da Vinci appeared disturbed. "In essence, you murdered human beings in a state of energy to live. Your species had degenerated into a society of genocidal parasites."

"Do not judge us so harshly," admonished Tholen. "Does your species not feed on other forms of life to survive?"

"Animals, yes. Beings without sentience," strongly insisted Da Vinci.

"A very convenient distinction," noted Tholen. "By the same argument, we also fed on insentient beings."

"Yet you claim nothing is lost from one state to the other," countered Da Vinci. "Humans going from sentience, to insentience, and back to sentience is incongruent with that claim. I can assure that I am exactly as I was on Earth; nothing must have been lost in between, including sentience. It would be more accurate to speak of sentience at rest rather than insentience. The phenomenon of sentience is therefore always present."

"What is the last thing you remember before surging from the collector wall?" cleverly asked Tholen.

"Dying in the arms of King Francis," immediately responded Da Vinci, falling into Tholen's inescapable intellectual trap.

Tholen proudly rejoiced. "You recall nothing in between? No floating around the Sun? Even if it lasted only a micro-second, you should have at least a fleeting recollection of that experience? No? I thought so."

"For a relatively rudimentary creature, your logic fencing is impressive," acknowledged a humbled Da Vinci. "I can see now that insentience is more like reverse-polarity sentience. Be that as it may, you are still interfering with a process that provides humans with an opportunity to reclaim awareness. And now, you prey on souls after awareness has been bestowed. Even worse."

"The Eternals *are* the ones who interfered with our livelihood when they built the collector wall to meet their growing energy requirements," contended Tholen, vividly remembering the futile battle to stop them. "Since then, we have shriveled and withered away, becoming a cave-dwelling, misshapen shadow of our former selves."

"I find it odd that Deus never spoke to me about this whole affair," thought Da Vinci. "He's usually been quite transparent during our many conversations."

"It would represent a grievous blemish; a stain on his legendary benevolence," concluded Tholen. "If you were to confront him, he would surely defend his position by professing that the needs of the many outweigh the needs of the few. He did it for you and for all your fellow Echoes, who greatly outnumbered us then...and even more so today. Persistent attrition has reduced us to a mere 5,000."

"That's why you blamed me earlier," said Da Vinci. "My existence endangers your own."

"You are not directly responsible," recognized Tholen. "My desperation spoke in my stead, blaming and condemning you. You were there, in front of me, and available."

Akara, whose antipathetic attitude towards Tholen was fading, moved closer to him. "With the scarcity of E.H., how do you manage...I mean besides sucking in Echoes furnished by my people?"

"Lay your eyes and hands upon me," enjoined Tholen, who snatched her hand and pressed it against his face. "Does it look like I'm managing?"

Surprisingly, Akara did not withdraw her hand. "You still have a good heart."

Tholen was grateful for the kind comment. "I hope you're speaking figuratively because my heart beats like an ever so unwinding mechanical clock. As for your question, aside from the few available Echoes, we cling to life by consuming the residue left behind when Echoes de-echoalesce, which can be found on the ground or within the earth after it breaks down into minute crystalline particles and is imbibed."

Tholen pointed to the Polar caves. "My species' primary economic activity has always been mining. We used to extract silica, graphite, carbon, iron, gold and silver, from the caves. If you were to explore them, you would find several hundred shafts connecting to tunnels, some a thousand feet deep, many hundreds of miles long, but most abandoned. Today, we limit our mining to near-surface tunnels, many of which are rich in Echo residue."

"You seem to suggest there's enough residue to feed all your people," said Theon. "Why then feed on living Echoes?"

"They taste better," jested Tholen. "Our scientists discovered that E.H. is a complex interactive form of energy. Strictly speaking, the *Humanessence* constituent operates unidirectionally on the *Experiential* one: the *Experience* constituent—the collection of experiences from birth to death.

"Exempt from the effects of Humanessence, the fabric of Experience can be expressed as a dissonant wave, composed of a multi-layered succession of *sinful* acts and *virtuous* acts, each described by amplitude rate and by duration."

"Illustrate what you mean," prompted an intrigued Da Vinci as he pulled a pencil and paper from his pocket—the two things a good scientist never leaves home without.

After completing his drawing, Tholen showed it to the group.

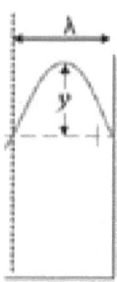

"Assume a certain type of sinful act—say, stealing from a neighbor— represented by the curve," said Tholen. "Further assume the sinful act lasts for λ minutes, during which the intensity of the act progresses from its onset at **0**—the start of planning of the theft; to its maximum at **y**—the theft in full progress; and finally to its wake at **0** once more—the fruits of the theft having been spent.

"The total impact of the sinful act, which we'll call the *Mass* of the sin, is measured by calculating the area under the curve and above the 0 baseline. Now, expanding on the example, albeit in simplistic fashion, let's illustrate a succession of sinful and *countersinful* acts."

"Countersins?" wondered Theon. "What's that?"

"That's what Eternals call human virtue," informed Tholen. "The term *countersin* is more descriptive of the counter effect virtuous acts exercise on sins. Take a look at this:

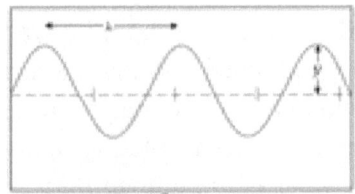

"The curves below the baseline represent countersinful acts, which for humans, barring aberrations, alternate with sinful acts. These frequency patterns are not sequential, but rather concurrent. For example, during a specific time frame, a man may break into his neighbor's house, steal from his neighbor, and upon being discovered, kill his neighbor—three separate sinful acts. Distinct sinful or countersinful acts overlap each other in time—the composite pattern or wave resulting from the addition of the separate patterns would typically look something like this:"

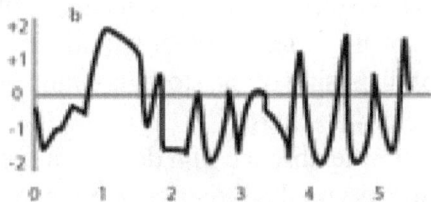

"Fascinating," exclaimed Da Vinci. "Dissension among the patterns. An acute lack of agreement and consistency between them. If these patterns were sound waves, their combination would produce a horrible noise, like that of an untuned disparate orchestra."

"When we assimilate Echo residue," said Tholen, "we're beset and assaulted by its inherent chaos. Our minds and bodies are subjected to the onslaught of unclean, unregulated human experience—memories, emotions, base instincts, neurosises, psychosises—the terrible cumulative effect of which is evidenced by my implacable deterioration."

"Don't the countersins embedded in the residue offer some relief?" queried Akara.

"Not in their elementary state," replied a disillusioned Tholen. "They need to be regulated, tailored by the Humanessence constituent for them to become palatable and beneficial. Experiential Humanessence, in its purified form, is what we *need* if we are to aspire to our past glory."

"You speak of the cleansing or regulating properties of Humanessence," noted Da Vinci. "What precisely is its role?"

"Think about a body of water in the midst of a violent storm," proposed Tholen, "turbulent, agitated and disordered at the surface above; and calm, still and serene in the vast depth below.

"The storm is *life* in all its frenzy acting upon physical human existence. The tumultuous water is the human *thinker* and the human *doer*, emotionally reacting to life according to precepts and principles dictated by an inferior and extremely limited level of consciousness, whose most diligent militants are ego, pride, self-importance, arrogance, lust, greed, jealousy, and malice. The ultimate product of this level is human experience defined by emotionally charged human sin and countersin.

"On the other hand, the tranquil water is human quintessence, or Humanessence: the human *be-er*, unconcerned with thought or action, kindled by a higher level of consciousness, and lolling in an infinite realm of intelligence beyond thought. While the human be-er might be laid-back, his very presence commands the surface water to calmness. But, the human thinker and doer is stubborn and is constantly preoccupied by life. If it was not for the storm of life, the be-er would tame the thinker-doer."

"And one way of disposing of the storm is death," surmised Da Vinci; "shifting from physicality to energy."

Tholen nodded. "In the absence of a dominant competing force, Humanessence is able to *cleanse* the Experience by rendering inert the emotive instigators spiking the thoughts and the actions. Ego, pride, greed, and the like are effectively neutralized."

"It sounds like a *dehumanizing* process," reckoned Theon. "Humans are not cold, dispassionate beings."

"To the extent that emotions equate to chaotic thinking and behavior, it is," conceded Tholen. "But, I'm not talking about the altogether suppression of the human capacity to feel. I'm referring instead to the newfound ability to view one's past Experience with serenity, detachment and objectivity. One becomes the *observer,* watching the thinker and the doer, realizing the observer and the observed are completely separate."

Da Vinci's nose and mouth puckered into a patent grimace. "There's a flaw in your notion. This kind of enlightenment requires awareness. Humans in a state of energy have none."

"True," said Tholen. "The cleansing begins and ends in the energy state, but the conscious epiphany occurs the instant after echoalescence. You said earlier that you were no different from the person you were on Earth. Is that truly *accurate*?"

Da Vinci paused, momentarily destabilized, before submitting himself to a full self-diagnosis. "I must admit that, upon arrival in this world, I felt surprisingly unburdened by my past life. And while I could still ponder over them, I was no longer obsessed by my achievements or my misdeeds."

"If you were to choose a word to describe how you *felt*," invited Tholen, "what would it be?"

Da Vinci vigorously shook his index finger. "Yes, I do feel, more than ever before, but differently somehow. Oh, I'm still a pack of nerves, and I'm still impulsive, but I cope better."

"Most Echoes do cope better," said Tholen. "And that's a blessing, especially for those condemned to Hell. Without the added resilience, most would be quickly driven to dust by sheer insanity and fright."

"Doesn't sound like a blessing to me," remarked Akara.

"Perhaps," grinned Tholen before reiterating his question. "Well, sir, what is the word? Is it *indifference*? Or *placidity*?"

Da Vinci mused over it. "There are shades of those, but...no, no, not quite. The feeling was more akin to...to...I have it! *Harmony*! They say a song can soothe the soul; well, my entire being sang when I stepped onto this soil. The melody might have quieted down since then, but if I pay close attention, I can still hear it."

"The word is very well chosen," asserted Tholen; "and serendipitously fitting. Are any of you familiar with the concept of *harmonics*?"

"Of course," ardently stated Da Vinci. "I am after all an accomplished scientist," he added with a smidgen of pride even an enlightened state could not quell. "A *harmonic* is a component frequency of a wave that is an integer multiple of the *fundamental frequency*, i.e. if the fundamental frequency is f, then the harmonics have frequencies $2f$, $3f$, $4f$, etc. The harmonics have the property of being periodic—occurring in repeated cycles—at the fundamental frequency, which means the sum of harmonics is also periodic at that frequency."

While Theon understood, Akara was lost. "Say again."

Da Vinci began scribbling on a fresh piece of paper. "There!" showing his drawing to Akara, but hiding the bottom portion.

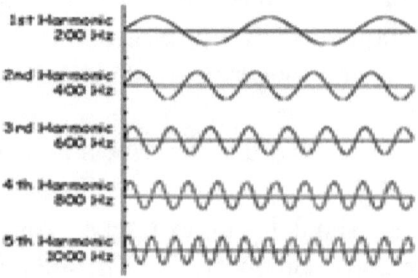

"Suppose the fundamental frequency—or first harmonic—of a wave has a frequency of 200 hertz, that is 200 cycles per second. Further suppose additional harmonics of that wave, say four harmonics, have consecutive multiples of that frequency, namely 400 hertz, 600 hertz, 800 hertz, and 1000 hertz.

"When combined, the composite wave looks like this," uncovering the bottom portion:

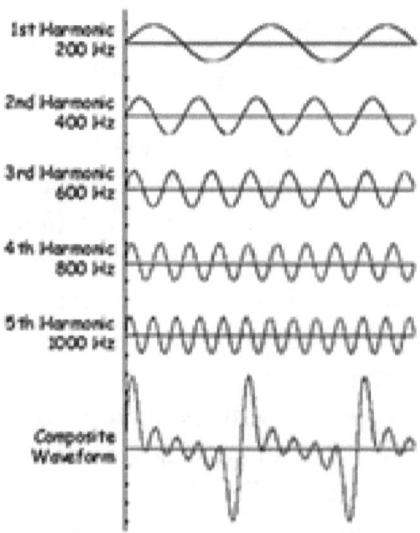

"A distinct waveform, no doubt, yet still exhibiting the fundamental frequency. Notice how the first harmonic repeats at the exact same spots as the composite wave. Riveting, isn't it?"

"Well presented," congratulated Tholen. "Our scientists discovered that a cleansed human Experience is precisely expressed as the sum of *harmonious* cycles of sins and countersins—like those illustrated in your drawing—a clear and dramatic departure from the discordant wave patterns intrinsic to an unaltered Experience.

"You hopefully understand now why cleansed Experience is our only avenue towards health and wellbeing, once naturally occurring and abundantly available from the Sun, and now, only and scarcely available from Echoes we can get our hands on…by any means."

Despite Tholen's comprehensive exposé, Da Vinci was still bothered by one particular element. "Have your scientists ever tried to understand why Echo residue—the Experience constituent ripped away from the Experiential Humanessence whole during de-echoalescence—reverts back to its primary state?"

"It continues to baffle us," confessed Tholen. "Some have speculated that the human genome includes a dormant gene containing cleansing instructions that are activated when the body transmutes into energy; that the gene is duplicated and initialized to a zero state of dormancy during echoalescence, but with reversed instructions—uncleansing instead of cleansing; and that, upon de-echoalescence, the gene's new instructions are executed, resulting in the aforementioned predicament. The recoded gene may also be responsible for the physical separation of Experience and Humanessence. What becomes of the solitary Humanessence is undetermined. What we do know from empirical evidence is that it does not re-echoalesce."

Da Vinci, engrossed by every detail of the Kalidrone's account, was bowled over by Tholen's knowledge and proficiency in the science of Human-Echo evolution. "You are indeed a master of many trades: mathematics, metaphysics, psychology, genetics. One would not expect that from a mere soldier."

"Quite right," acquiesced Tholen. "That's because I'm not just a common, mindless soldier. I'm far more than that."

Da Vinci and his sidekicks keenly awaited the full disclosure. Who was this erudite, scholarly creature, in reality?

CHAPTER 97

**Tholen sighed heavily, flooded by a melan-
choly** the gentle wind refused to peel off and carry away. "I was once
a noted scientist, respected and admired by most of my peers, but de-
tested by some because of my unconventional ideas. Sadly for me, the
chief-scientist was among the dissidents. He not only disagreed with me,
but loathed the very sound of my voice as I spoke my mind. Since he
could not openly expel me from the already depleted scientific community without cause, he assigned me a mission, whose successful completion
was uncertain at best and impossible at worst. My failure would constitute
sufficient grounds for eviction."

"You were appointed to a scientific expedition, I suppose," said Da
Vinci. "Research in the *field*," he then quipped, alluding to and looking at
the vastness of the Elysian Fields.

"It was indeed an expedition," confirmed Tholen, "one that took me
directly to the City of God, to confer with Deus himself.

"I managed to make my way to Deus, escorted by Sanctum guards,
reeking of suspicion and cynicism. Thankfully, Deus was more unwary
and indulgent than his minions. He carefully listened to and considered
my proposal."

"Haven't your people already attempted to convince the Eternals to
shut off the energy wall collector?" wondered Da Vinci.

"That was not my request," indicated Tholen. "My petition was far
less ambitious. Since we primarily live off Echo residue—and endure its
rampaging effects—we sought a means to mitigate those effects, however small the palliation. I implored Lord God to increase the number of
Echoes going to Hell by earmarking for Hell Echoes normally destined
for Heaven."

"What possible advantage could you avail yourself by doing that?"
loudly interjected Akara, who finding the plan cruel and outlandish.

Tholen anticipated and understood her outrage, but quickly discounted it. "The advantage is twofold. The Diabolicus regime of torment and

torture insures a *passable* supply of Echo deaths and residue; contrary to Heaven's policy of non-aggression, which, barring accidental deaths, dispenses no Echo deaths at all. And, the effects of residue from Echoes with low *sin scores* are moderately less chaotic."

"Greater quantity and greater quality, on average," concluded Da Vinci. "What was Deus' reaction to your proposal?"

"He refused to entertain any further latitude profiting Satan and his kingdom," said Tholen. "A failure, I was subsequently banned from the scientific community, and relegated to the plebeian role of soldier."

"Could you not offer the Sword of Maitreya as a bargaining chip?" asked Da Vinci.

"We cannot bargain with something we don't have," countered Tholen. "The Kalidrone do not possess the sword *anymore*."

"But you intimated earlier that you had it," rebutted Theon.

"I implied no such thing," claimed Tholen. "You simply assumed we had it."

"Who has it, then?" earnestly demanded Theon.

"Someone else," vaguely replied Tholen, reluctant to divulge more. "Only a few high-ranking Kalidrone officials know of this, including my faction chief, Stuord, who took an annoying and unrelenting shining to me, entrusting me with the information as a gesture of fondness."

"And now, *we* know you don't have it," pointed out Da Vinci. "Why tell us?"

"You believe the sword can cure this boy of whatever ails him," recalled Tholen. "It must truly be an unbearable affliction for you to risk your lives in its quest. The Kalidrone of the past also recognized the risk...but not the benefits. They obviously did not understand its power. Perhaps it can cure my kin and me. We must recapture it. I will lead you."

"You might very well betray us," feared Akara. "How can we trust you? You will not even tell us in whose hands the sword rests?"

Tholen smiled waggishly. "I count among the few who know where the sword can be found. From my perspective, you have no choice."

"You know the terrain. Will you keep us away from danger?" asked a worried Theon.

Tholen's smile widened. "There *will be* danger every step of the way. But, with my knowledge, and your...*boy-turns-into-juggernaut* trick, we stand a better chance of success."

"Lead the way, then," ordered a convinced Da Vinci. "Today is as good a day to die as any."

CHAPTER 98

Tholen was pensive, recollecting the Elders' legend of the godlike Eternals, who once lived on the tallest mountain of the island they called *Eterna*, many leagues away on the Lost Sea. From the shores of the continent, the Kalidrone could glimpse the tip of the mountain, looming above the clouds.

Shuntra, shining brightly upon it, partook one day of its warm vitality by propelling a burning bolt of light at the top of the mountain, no doubt commanded by the monarch of the Eternals, Deus, Lord God. The splendid event was the inception of a massive migration to the continent.

The Eternals arrived on strange barges, some transporting foreign materials, and the Kalidrone gathered along the shore to greet them. The Eternals were magnificent and quite affable for Gods, not at all arrogant or narcissistic. The Kalidrone did not question them—for who would question gods—and the Eternals, in turn, circumspectly abstained from elaborating on their situation. They preferred to capitalize on the Kalidrone's ignorance and bask in the awe and veneration of those they considered primitives.

They took up the land surrounding the Great Lakes, and called it the Kingdom of Heaven. Since the Kalidrone lived mainly in the South, near the Great Dragon graveyard, with an itinerant workforce mining the Polar caves for parts of the year, they did not object—nor would they have dared.

Today, however, the Kalidrone abound with regrets. The Gods they once worshiped had usurped their livelihood: the Experiential Humanessence granted by Shuntra, the all giving. This last thought lingered in Tholen's mind.

"Tholen, are you sure you know where we're going?" fretfully asked Theon. "Couldn't we have circled the Elysian fields, instead of crossing them?"

Tholen, still macerating his gloomy musings to make them more palatable, failed to respond.

Theon pulled on his tunic. "Tholen! Isn't there another way?"

Tholen turned and gazed at his jittery following. "This is the shortest trail. Circling the fields would add a full day to our journey, and going through the tunnel system of the Polar caves would be ridden with ill-advised encounters with the Kalidrone."

Akara, who kept looking around, her head atop her five-foot-four frame bobbing just above the edge of the fields, noticed an eerie apparition: two googly eyes at the ends of two strings, moving hither and thither, but never relinquishing their hold on the travelers.

A sweet melody suddenly echoed through the ragged sound of the crops, ruffled insistently by the wind. "Fellows, I think were not alone. Something is playing our song…and it has *eyes* only for us."

"Damn it! *Arachons*!" exclaimed an alarmed Tholen. "I was hoping they would be feasting on the crops near the eastern ridge, this time of night. I can see the northern fringe of the fields, 100 yards away. Run everybody! Run!"

Without inquiring further, they all ran as fast as they could. Da Vinci, more adept at strutting for his pleasure than running for his life, lagged behind and was quickly overtaken by one of the creatures.

It blocked his path, separating him from the others, who valiantly rushed back to his side. The black creature resembled the Earth scorpion, but ten times its size, beset with eight legs, a large pair of grasping claws and a narrow, segmented tail, carried in a characteristic forward curve over the back, ending with a venomous stinger.

Unlike the Earth scorpion, it had disproportionately long antenna-eyes, and its dorsal carapace was adorned with six elevated, parallel strings made of dense but flexible cartilage, attached to raised rims at the front and back end of the dorsal shell. Using its stinger, it would strike the strings in a precise fashion in order to produce a sound akin to a melody to signal the presence of prey, attack, retreat, or other types of commands.

"It's summoning it brothers," said Tholen, plucking an arrow from its quiver and affixing it to his crossbow. "They're about to attack," he warned, aiming the crossbow and shooting the arrow into the arachon's vulnerable neck.

Da Vinci sighed heavily. "Thank you for your timely intervention."

"You were in no danger," remarked Tholen. "Arachons hate the taste of Echoes even more than that of Kalidrone. But they do love burrowing into the juicy bodies of Diabolicus as they lie paralyzed and helpless. As for humans—or superhumans—" staring at Theon, "we might just find out if we don't quicken our exit."

As the melody resumed, now coming from all directions, they hastened their escape, running closely together towards the field boundary. Akara, more distressed than the others, gradually took the lead, immediately followed by a protective Theon, who purposely matched her pace.

"Keep close," urged Tholen, trying to catch up. "For God's sake, slow down! I said, slow do—"

What Tholen feared happened. Two arachons emerged from the brush and posted themselves in their path. Theon jumped forth, grabbed Akara, and yanked her back, just as one of the arachons' tail lunged forward, its stinger intent on delivering its paralyzing venom.

The eager stinger punctured Theon's calf. "You freakin' lobster!" screamed Theon, as he latched on the edges of the ventral and the dorsal carapace, and with one mighty thrust, split open the beast's body.

The other arachon, unfazed by his brother's demise, stung Theon on the thigh. The super-boy raised his fist, and as he was about to smash the creature's torso, an arrow sped by and impaled the aggressor through the mouth.

"Thank God," muttered Theon, repressing the boiling energy within him through sheer will power. "Stay human, stay human."

"Hurry!" ordered Tholen. "More are approaching."

They finally made it out of the fields, stopping to rest ten yards away from the accursed trap.

"How are you feeling, son?" wondered Da Vinci, inspecting Theon's wounds. "Giddy, confused, tired, cramped, stiff, sick?"

"Relieved and otherwise unaffected," replied Theon. "Another singular *trademark* of my unique abilities at work."

"Keep them coming, kid," prompted Tholen, showing no empathy for Theon's discomfort with his condition. "We're not out of the woods yet. In fact, we'll be *in* the woods soon enough," pointing at a forest, two miles in the distance.

"Should we expect more monsters in that forest?" sarcastically bantered Theon, as he scratched his bite wounds.

"No! No monsters," assured Tholen. "Only *trees*."

"Sounds quaint and boring," presumed Theon. "A nice change of pace."

"On the contrary," said Tholen. "The forest is anything but insipid or monotonous. Brace yourselves."

Through their short association with Tholen, they had discovered that he had never fostered a knack for hyperbole. So, they braced themselves.

CHAPTER 99

Present day; NASA, Washington D.C.

The sign on Bill Adams' office door read: NASA—*Non Adventurous Spirits Abstain*. This did not stop his brother Ted, former SETI employee, and the latest beneficiary of nepotistic scheming, to barge in, bearing staggering news.

Before he could utter a single word, Bill raised his finger in gentle reproval, then tapped his phone handset, pressed against his ear. "That's too bad, Amadeo. I know you're doing your best to find Theon and Cameron. They've got to be somewhere on this bucket of a world. Hum, ah ha...ah ha...ok. Let's talk again in a few days. Yes, yes...bye."

Bill clasped the back of his neck and pinched it hard. "What other *favor* do you want now?"

Ted grinned, skipping rope like a little girl trying to impress her finicky friends. "You won't believe what the control center has discovered?"

Bill started mockingly shuffling the papers and reports on his desk. "Well, we've found a fashionable scarf, a black box filled with secrets we're desperately trying to crack, and several metallic fragments. And now, the Mars rover is currently sweeping the north-eastern sector of Meridiani Planum in search of even more weirdness. Wait! Let me guess, we've discovered Santa's workshop...on Mars! Who woudda thunk?"

Bill's brother in law's and nephew's disappearance was weighing heavily on him, handicapping his ability to remain calm and collected.

Ted circled his brother's desk and went to work on his computer keypad, calling up an image freshly taken by the Opportunity rover. "This can only cheer you up."

"What kind of sick joke is this?" blurted Bill, in no mood for fun and games. "You *superimposed* a picture of the Earth over the Mars horizon."

"Look closer at the planet's geography," anxiously insisted Ted.

Bill's eyes widened. "One large continent traversing the equator; and several other, much smaller land masses. All surrounded by…*water*! Impossible!"

"Impossible, my ass!" shouted Ted.

Bill scrutinized the spellbinding image. "How come we never recorded this before?"

"The planet's orbit must bring it close to Mars every period of countless years—the last time before the onset of the Mars rover program, for sure," speculated Ted.

"What about the Hubble telescope?" rebutted Bill. "How could it have missed something so close to Earth?"

"The planet must be in an *opposite* position, behind the Sun," theorized Ted; "it must have an orbital path in the *same plane* as the Earth; and must exactly *match* the Earth's angular velocity. That's why we can *never* see it from the Earth's vantage point. It's a shame we can't send the telescope gallivanting about the other side of the solar system."

"All right, then, how do you account for gravitational perturbations?" challenged Bill.

Ted was evidently well prepared. "Hell, even *Isaac Newton*, at the time he formulated his laws of motion and of gravitation, and applied them to the first analysis of perturbations, recognized the complex difficulties of their calculation.

"Granted, he was able to describe the hypothetical motion that a celestial body follows under the gravitational effect of *one* other body using geometry (which he called a *two-body problem*); but, when faced with differences between that theoretical motion and the actual motion of the body, he had to acknowledge *perturbations* due to the additional gravitational effects of other—albeit much smaller—bodies."

"Go on," said a curious Bill.

"His convenient *two-body problem* turned into a very inconvenient *n-body problem*," went on Ted. "To this day, no analytical solution predicting future body positions and motions for the *n*-body problem exists. We can only assume that the bilateral effect from this planet on the solar system is somehow implicitly incorporated into our crude calculations."

Bill sat back in his chair, and, like a melancholic young man fortuitously encountering a long lost love, began romanticizing about the newfound planet. "*Planet V*! Our NASA confrères were right. Planet V does live and breathe."

Planet V was, in fact, a hypothetical fifth planet posited, in 2002, by NASA scientists John Chambers and Jack Lissauer to have once existed between Mars and the asteroid belt.

Chambers and Lissauer had proposed that a previously unknown terrestrial planet once existed in an eccentric orbit around the Sun; and that, perturbed by gravitational interactions with the other inner planets, it was tossed onto a highly eccentric orbit crossing the inner asteroid belt, and eventually sending it plunging into the Sun.

"Those two hacks were partially right," said Ted. "It did exist, as they stipulated, but it never perished in the Sun."

"And, it might support intelligent life," imagined Bill. "Wouldn't that be wonderful?"

"Sure would," agreed Ted, "although we never got a return call from our SETI greeting," raising and waving his arm above his head, his cell phone in his hand, mimicking a phone call from Heaven. "Let's face it, for now, only *God* knows," he added mechanically as a deep-seated learned response.

"Only the *all-knowing* God knows," repeated Bill with a tinge of religious conviction.

But was God truly all-knowing, and ergo, knew? Only he himself knew; and, as a God, there was no knowing he could not know…or could afford not knowing, especially where fiendishly intelligent life the likes of Satan was concerned.

CHAPTER 100

Present day; Kingdom of Hell.

"Stay in the center of the path," earnestly exhorted Tholen. "Do not approach the *trees*, at all cost."

The ominously prophetic forest, counting thousands of trees, appeared to have succumbed to a ravaging, inexorable fire that spared not a single of its denizens. Leafless and pervetedly ill-shapen, the trees' bark was dark black and exceedingly cracked, as if a rabid logger had forced the blade of his axe upon it without pity.

The trunk was mostly hollow at mid-height, swanking a gapping two-foot diameter cavity that sung as the wind entered it and exited through fissures in its pharynx, inviting unsuspecting travelers to peer into its craving abyss.

The thin, sickly branches twisted and contorted in every direction, interweaved with those of adjoining trees, forming overhead a complex and inescapable web even the most gifted spider could not emulate. If one dared gaze upon the web for any length, one would swear parts of it skulked closer to the ground. That was not far from the truth.

"Get back here!" screamed Tholen before abruptly pulling back Akara, who was about to stick her head into the aperture of a tree. "I told you to stay away from the trees. Are you daft, girl?"

"It's just an old, decaying tree," snapped back Akara, upset by the Kalidrone's unplayful rough-housing. "What bee got into your bonnet?"

"Why do you fear the trees so?" wondered Da Vinci, who, unbeknownst to him, was in the most danger.

"These overgrown *plants* are vicious, depraved, vengeful," sternly warned Tholen; "and worst of all, they're *alive*, saturated with killer instincts and survival imperatives."

"There's no sign of life here," said Theon, looking around.

"Give me your knife," Tholen ordered Akara, before cautiously moving towards the closest tree—a demonstration was in order. He looked up at its feeble branches, steadying his stance and raising his blade. "Don't be deceived by their frailty. They could snap your neck in an instant."

Two branches began throbbing convulsively, no doubt out of excitement and anticipation, according to Tholen. They moved slowly but purposely, separating themselves from the matrix, and descending inchmeal upon the creature that defied their proprietor.

The animated branches suddenly darted with uncanny speed, one encircling Tholen's torso, and tightening like a boa constrictor, lifting him and slamming him against the trunk; the other enwreathing and yanking his wrist in an attempt to eject the weapon.

Tholen launched the knife to his other hand and slashed the latter branch, cutting through it diagonally at precisely 60 degrees—the plane along which the wood grain was the weakest. He then sliced the other branch in the same manner, and fell to the ground, rolling over several times until he bumped into Da Vinci.

The two severed branches twitched and spun violently like wounded animals, before retreating and reintegrating the web.

"This is obviously not your first skirmish with these strange arboreal specimens," assumed Da Vinci, evermore tempted to examine them more closely—too closely. "What would have happened had it bested you in battle?"

Tholen got up and dusted himself off. "Oh, I gather it would have toyed with me, and tortured me to excess before strangling or decapitating me...simply out of malice and retribution."

"I've never known flora to be so predatorily usurious," thought Da Vinci. "There is, of course, the Venus flytrap, which entraps insects for sustenance. This is definitely not the case here. These creatures feed on fear, not food. A very queer survival *modus operandi*, indeed."

Tholen gave the old man a look unmistakably heralding bad news. "Fear just wets their appetites. You, my poor friend, are the main course."

Da Vinci frowned in dubiety. "Why would *I* be bestowed such disagreeable honors?"

"Not you, specifically; your kind," indicated Tholen. "These trees ingest Echoes."

"They're botany's version of the Kalidrone," exclaimed Akara. "They're just like you," waving a finger at Tholen.

Tholen abhorred the recurring comparison, often pompously spouted in contempt by the Diabolicus. "We are very unlike these freakish anomalies. We don't resort to torture and persecution. We don't derive pleasure from the suffering of others. And, we have put aside our vindictive ways a long time ago." Picking up a dead branch from the ground and shaking it, "Never liken me or my kinsfolk to this atrocity ever again!"

"Soooorry!" repented Akara, demoting her saucy commentary to the back of her mind.

Tholen settled down, scanning the area top down as if for the first time. "My people used to call these woods the *White Wind Forest*. The trees were once white, with bright orange leaves and glistening red fruit; and they fed on the sun's Experiential Humanessence, whistling entrancing melodies as the wind traversed the forest, and fondled the branch multitude.

"Today, in the absence of the vital energy, they've become ruined, grotesque, famished…and angry like crotchety, cantankerous old men, with a venomous tongues lashing out at you. An infernal shadow of its former existence, we now call the woods the *Black Bane Forest*."

"Hell hath no fury like a tree denied," remarked Da Vinci before noticing an object ten yards away that looked disturbingly like a skull, and trotting towards it.

"It's the skull of a Diabolicus," he determined after picking it up and scrutinizing its features. "There are many more bone fragments lying about. I count two Diabolicus…and two Kor'tas. Perhaps they shot at the trees and died for it."

Akara proceeded to examine the weapons. "They seem quite worn." She aimed one of them at the ground and discharged it. Nothing happened. She tried the other, releasing bolts of energy. "This one works fine," confiscating it as her personal property.

"Look over here," yelled Theon. "The ground is stained with Echo residue." Digging his fingers into the dirt, he scooped up a sample of the residue. His hand had barely left the ground when a tree root cropped up and seized it, forcing it back down.

Theon instantly surrendered his find, and forcefully pulled back his hand. "God! Those things are everywhere."

"The roots extend for many miles, draining residue wherever they can find it." Tholen signaled the group to resume the march. "There was a time when the Diabolicus had no qualms about chasing the Echoes who escaped slave labor in the fields and took refuge in the forest. Now, few Echoes dare enter the forest, having been driven to insanity. And none make it out."

"*I'm* going to make it out," insisted an irked Da Vinci. "Heaven cannot afford to lose a man of my genius."

Tholen cracked a sly smile. "I suppose a precedence was eventually in order…and move that *one* certainly shall, shielded by his dauntless allies." No one seconded the Kalidrone's reassuring but groundless motion, not even Da Vinci. There was still much ground to cover.

Dawn was almost upon them as they completed 90% of their trek through the sinister forest, amazingly unscaved. "How much longer?" asked a tired Akara, dragging her Kor'ta as if it was a bulky ball and chain.

"Something is different," felt Theon. "Some of the trees have leaves, yellowish and spotted. They're few and far apart, but still." He began counting them, from one tree to the next, until he made an even more unexpected discovery. "*Fruit!* That tree has fruit."

"Indeed!" shouted Da Vinci. "Look beyond. There are other trees with fruit." The old man, in turn, began counting. "I estimate 23 such trees in my field of vision." He tried knocking down one of the low hanging fruit from an atypically long and solitary branch, but couldn't quite reach it, even as he jumped surprisingly high for an elder.

Tholen chuckled at his companion's kangaroo antics, raising his crossbow and releasing an arrow that dislodged the fruit of Da Vinci's desire. It plummeted and hit the old man on the head.

Da Vinci rubbed his head before retrieving the fallen fruit. "Now I know how Newton felt," quietly hoping for the conjuration of new revolutionary notions. The strange fruit would have to serve as his only modest quantum leap. "Pale red with grey blemishes; round with curious bumps forming a definite patter—Gadzooks! It's a *face*! A human face! What sorcery is this?"

"There's no magic at play, here," said Tholen. "That fruit you hold, and all the other fruit, are physical manifestations of Experiential Humanessence; an aftereffect of the absorption process. They're, in effect, a plagiarized repository of derivative memories, thoughts and emotions of the ingested Echoes."

Da Vinci carried the fruit close to his eyes, squinting at it. "You mean this eldritch *apple* might, for example, contain the great scientist Newton's engrams?" seriously considering biting into it.

"In a very *loose* manner of speaking, yes," stated Tholen. "It can be any former earthling."

"Are the fruit edible?" asked Akara.

Tholen nodded. "To you, it's only a fruit. To the Kalidrone, it's a *poor* substitute of which the deathly starving venture to avail themselves at grave risk; but a substitute nonetheless."

"To eat only to be eaten," reckoned Theon. "How does that come about?"

Before Tholen could respond, a piercing, bone-chilling shriek reverberated throughout the forest, followed by a prolonged bewailing moan.

Tholen pointed in the direction of the scream. "The answer you seek lies at the fount of the haunting lamentation. You will not like it."

CHAPTER 101

Akara, goaded by her learned warrior proclivity, arrived first at the source of the ruckus, ready to intervene; or so she had believed. A young boy, no older than her, was tightly strapped to the trunk of a tree, three feet above ground, by myriad branches.

He stared miserably at her, his eyes swollen and wet, drooling as he spoke. "Hel…help me!"

Akara stepped back in stupefaction, tripping and falling onto her hindquarters, but never leaving sight of the boy. In a flash, she wondered what he could have possibly done to deserve Hell. It seemed even children were not spared Satan's inexorable touch.

As she rose quickly, using the Kor'ta as a crutch, her gaze wandered momentarily to the neighboring trees, dressed in similar fashion. She counted eight other Echoes submitted to the same predicament. They, however, said nothing, their stare locked onto the ground in abdication. Contrary to the boy, they understood their dire fate—there was no escape.

"I want to go home," supplicated the boy. "I didn't mean to push him over the rail. We were just playing *chicken*."

"Don't fret, kid; I'll get you down," confidently announced Akara, making abstraction of the unknown game of which the boy spoke—likely an innocent pastime she concluded, raising her Kor'ta and aiming it at the base of the tree.

Before she could activate the weapon, Tholen appeared next to her, slapping it down hard before bearing disturbing tidings. "Fool! You wish to bring about the forest's fury? We are no match for so many foes!"

"He's just a boy," angrily cried out Akara who found much physical resemblance between him and Theon—a definite factor in her emotionally laced decision to intervene.

Tholen's attention suddenly turned to the Sun's appearance over the horizon. "The trees are awakening. We must make our way out of the forest. You amongst all should seek to hasten your pace and leave this godforsaken place," he added, glaring apprehensively at Da Vinci.

"We got the message before," chimed in Theon. "Keep Leo away from the trees."

Da Vinci, reminded of his peculiar vulnerability, changed his position, keeping an equal distance from each of the surrounding trees. He eyed each one tree after the other in rapid succession. "How much more *awake* can these beastly trees be?"

"Much!" sharply replied Tholen. "Behold…and beware!"

As the sunlight hit the forest, a primal biological imperative to feed kicked in; the hollow apertures of the trees began glowing, and not even the bodies of the Echoes strategically placed over them could arrest the increasing brilliance. The boy was the first to succumb to his parasitical captor. His small form began glistening and losing cohesion, and he shrieked in searing pain.

Although his features were no longer recognizable, Akara, who was the closest, could still make out the contour of his mouth, trying desperately to forge the words conveying the depth of his horror. A sound, any sound, could no longer be heard, but the ghastly spectacle was not diminished in the least.

Theon was reluctantly compelled to act—something he had grown to despise given the implications—and would have, had it not been for Akara, who, unable to bear the sight—and her inaction—dismissed Tholen's injunction and fired at the tree's bottom, tearing at its roots. This did not prevent the tree from literally collapsing the boy's body into a ball of energy and absorbing it into its interior.

Even the earlier viewing of the absorption of an Echo at the hands of a Kalidrone could not prepare the little warrior or contain her outcry stemming as much from horror as from the futility of her valiant manoeuvre. Somehow, this manner of death seemed far worse.

A strident shriek was heard anew, this time emanating from the murderous tree itself. It tilted heavily, cracked along its side, and its branches whimpered and finally withered.

Numerous trees, one much taller than the others in particular, stopped glowing. "Good news," thought Da Vinci. He could not be farther from the truth.

"Run!" shouted Tholen. "Another league of Hell is upon us!"

One by one, the trees began uprooting themselves, and like spiders closing in on their prey, they marched towards the quartet, using their long sinuous roots, liberated from the earth, as legs.

"Run, damn you, run!" Tholen entreated again. No further persuasion was necessary as they frantically proceeded to zig and zag , scarcely avoiding the lashing tentacles, darting from every direction.

They slid in between two trees, and then two more. The tallest tree had retreated behind his kin, expressing some kind of higher foresight as it posted itself along the only path left to the fugitives.

"Shoot!" yelled Tholen. "Kill the damn thing!"

"Oh, now you want me to shoot," barked a saucy Akara.

"Do it, or I'll have to do something—and be something—I don't want anymore," implored Theon.

Before she could aim her weapon, a branch dashed passed her, enlacing Da Vinci's torso, and raising him into the air. "Now would be a good time!" hollered the old man as he struggled in vain.

The tree used Da Vinci as a shield, bringing him slowly and evermore near its aperture, but never affording a clear shot. Wherever she aimed, Da Vinci's body was immediately in the way.

"How good a shot are you?" anxiously asked Theon, considering acting as a diversion.

"We'll see," she answered, overcome by an unexpected calmness that surprised even her. The warrior was back in full force. She rotated her Kor'ta, positioning the three nozzles in very precise fashion. Theon suddenly realized what she was up to...and prayed.

"Die, you mother fu—" The shot rang out. One bolt grazed Da Vinci's right armpit; the second tore off flesh from his left shoulder; and the third shaved the left side of his thorax. All three bolts hit the mark.

The tree released his quarry, toppling backwards. Da Vinci violently hit the ground, and, was swiftly surrounded by his friends. Groaning, he sat and pressed his palm against his shoulder, rubbing vigorously. "You shot me, you rabid squirrel!"

"No vital organs hit," smiled Akara, quite full of herself.

"Rejoice later," said Tholen, grabbing the fortunate survivor by one arm, while Theon took charge of the other; and they ran towards the edge of the forest, leaving their attackers unsatiated and unavenged.

"What's next?" wondered Theon, somewhat apprehending the response. "More man-eating plants?"

"Talking, walking, flying fish," tersely replied Tholen.

"With long sharp teeth you can't miss?" supposed Theon.

"Can't miss when they smile," said Tholen. "But you don't want to make them smile."

CHAPTER 102

"I should have brought a fishing pole," jested Theon after Tholen led his companions to the southern shores of Lake Seven, a body of water seventy-seven miles in diameter and seven miles in depth, the deepest lake in the land.

"I can certainly build one," vaunted Da Vinci as he crouched by the shore and tasted the water. "Hum, quite salty."

"The salt is carried by the fresh water traveling through the lower corridors of the Polar caves," said Tholen before pointing to the horizon. "We must traverse the lake to the other side, and cross the border into the kingdom of Heaven."

Da Vinci looked around, noting pieces of rotting wood lying here and about. He picked one up, scrutinizing its fragile condition. "I may be good with my hands, but don't expect me to construct a boat with *this*."

"No boat is needed," stoically said Tholen as he scoured the shore from end to end. "Our transport should arrive momentarily."

"Shouldn't you be looking towards the far waters?" wondered Akara, who saw no approaching ship. She then peered into the shore water, which was especially clear and blue. "I see fish, but none seem to be walking or flying. As for their teeth—hey! Something just brushed pass me." She immediately raised her Kor'ta and spun it around, half-expecting to hit something.

She did strike something, but whatever it was, it remained invisible as it forcibly yanked the weapon from her hands and threw it away from her.

"She is young and means no harm," stated Tholen. "We require an audience with Hommi Koota."

The air began wavering, becoming denser until a creature appeared. It stood seven-feet tall and was shaped like a stingray, with dark blue skin, a long tail, and two muscular arms and legs. Its back was wide and curved, at the top of which protruded a hump that hung down at a sixty degree angle—evidently its head. It had two black eyes about six inches apart, two olfactory slits below the eyes, a disproportionally large and lipless mouth, and gills on either side of its pharynx. It was an Akkadian.

"Whoa!" exclaimed a transfixed Theon, who had seen a stingray once before, but never this size, and never with limbs. "It looks hungry," he added, backing off slowly.

The Akkadian's broad back flapped like outstretched angry wings in response to Theon's offhand comment. "You keep the company of unruly, uncivil children, Kalidrone. Must I restrain them for you?"

"They are oftentimes a source of aggravation," conceded Tholen, "but one of them should surely be of interest to Hommi Koota."

The Akkadian grinned, revealing gleaming sharp teeth, spanning half the brepth of its head.

"A sign of indulgence and levity," an encouraged Da Vinci whispered to Tholen.

"They only smile in disapproval or annoyance," whispered back the Kalidrone.

"What would the Priestess want with a Diabolicus?" boldly inquired the Akkadian. "Or an Echo?" The creature's species hated the Diabolicus, who hunted them for their hides, stuffing and mounting them on walls as trophies; but they were indifferent to Echoes, who served no practical usage.

Tholen grabbed Theon by the shirt and pulled him forward. "Behold this boy. He is no Echo at all. He is human and has traveled through the Trans'Kartum."

The Akkadian's interest was piqued. He circled Theon, inspecting him like common merchandise. "It has been sometime since a human walked this soil," poking him several times. Theon kept his cool. "Hommi Koota does enjoy curiosities. What else does this *boy* have to offer?"

"He is avidly hunted by Satan," said Tholen, upping the ante, "far more than any vulgar Echo."

The Akkadian was pleased. "A kindred spirit, the choice prey of the Diabolicus. Your particular hide is uninteresting, however. What else have you to show for yourself, human child?"

"If I showed you, we wouldn't be having this conversation," dauntlessly replied Theon. "I'd start by ripping off that hideous head of—"

"Theon!" shouted Tholen. "We need his help."

Theon held his lashing tongue. "I have powers that seem to be of service in Satan's cause," he went on as calmly as he could.

"And what cause is that?" asked the intrigued Akkadian.

"Of that we are not certain," interjected Da Vinci. "We can only surmise it will be used in defeating Lord Deus and seizing his kingdom. What else would preoccupy the Dragon Lord?"

"Indeed, what else?" The Akkadian pondered the affair for a moment. "That would cause a fundamental shift in power. We would then be at grave risk." He returned his gaze towards Theon. "Perhaps I should kill you here and now while the threat can still be contained."

"That is not your way!" cried Tholen, more as a prophetic warning than a mild reproof. "And, do not forget what the Kalidrone have done for the Akkadians."

"*That* is still up for debate, even today," remarked the Akkadian. "Some would argue history is but a set of lies. We need only agree on which ones. Nevertheless, the Priestess would be incensed if I substituted my will for hers."

"Kurtshak!" suddenly bellowed the Akkadian, ordering the appearance of five other Akkadians.

"Impressive," blurted out Da Vinci as he ventured a touch of the strange device around the Akkadian's left wrist. "An invisibility apparatus."

"That is a weapon," pointed out the Akkadian before presenting a similarly designed instrument on his right wrist. "*This* is the invisibility field generator."

"You might wish to paint them in different colors," humbly advised Da Vinci. "I paint, you know."

The Akkadian grunted. "Join together!" he ordered the motley party. "Closer," he enjoined them as he pressed their bodies against each other. The Akkadian and his kin then gathered around the group, their backs forming a sealed dome. Only one remained apart, in preparation for his role as a steering propeller.

Da Vinci understood full well the purpose of the bubble that enveloped them. "Are you fine?" he asked Akara, recalling the Diabolicus' fear of water.

"My mother was a Sanctum," reminded Akara; "and she loved to swim in the Lost Sea."

The Akkadian assembly tightly clutched its payload, easily lifting it several inches from the ground, before proceeding into the water. With every foot, they sank two; and in no time, they disappeared into the depths of the lake.

CHAPTER 103

The Akkadian city was magnificent—a monument to its people's ingenuity and resourcefulness. Built entirely of quartz glass, manufactured from silica extracted from rocks peppering the core of the Polar caves, the city stood erect inside a gigantic cavity along the north-eastern wall of Lake Seven, half a mile under the water surface. It was well within the kingdom of Heaven, a few miles from the City of God.

The city boasted six towers, two-hundred feet high, along its perimeter, and a central one, three hundred feet high, the crown jewel of the structure. The edifice was virtually devoid of openings, only featuring three large equidistant ones at the base, and one smaller one at the top of each tower.

Viewed from the outside, it seemed that the majority of the city was filled with water, filtered and treated by a processing plant connected to the city. The plant's primary function consisted of removing pollutants and boosting oxygen content.

Some selected sections of the building were water-free, replaced by air comparable to the ambient air surrounding Lake Seven. Specially designed force shields kept the water at bay. While the Akkadians preferred a liquid environment, they often dwelled in these selected areas to develop and preserve their ability to breath in an air medium.

On rare occasions, these air compartments also served as greeting grounds.

"What a rush," exclaimed Theon as the five Akkadians disbanded and left the glass room. "We must have been underwater for at least 30 minutes."

Da Vinci inhaled deeply. "Very breathable." He examined the room, quickly noticing that half of it was water bound. Eternally inquisitive, he walked towards the thin cross-section of compiled energy that kept air and water separate, and touched it.

His fingers, then his whole hand, passed through the energy shield without any resistance. "Stupefying!" he hollered as he retracted his hand and rubbed it from palm to finger tips. "It's dry, completely dry. What manner of magic is this?"

As he was about to plunge his head through the shield, an Akkadian girl emerged from the watery side, running and bumping into Da Vinci. Unfazed and fearless, she looked up and uttered something incomprehensible before pulling on the old man's shaggy white beard, the apparent object of her curiosity.

Da Vinci gladly bent over. "See how fluffy it is, child. Would you like one just like it?"

"I want those," the child said in a near-perfect English, rushing over to Akara and pointing at her ears. She then grazed her own, tiny, flat and mushroom-like. "Do you want to switch?"

Akara smiled in amusement. "I'm afraid they're quite attached to my head, little one."

Scowling in discontent, the youngster ran to a nearby child size table, sat heavily and started playing with blocks whose sides were etched with letters of the Akkadian alphabet.

"Kids will be kids," said Da Vinci, "no matter what the species."

Theon, Akara and Tholen joined Da Vinci by the energy shield, and they all peered ahead into the foreign watery ecosystem, counting nine Akkadian children, one adult, and twenty glass spheres resting on pegs, arranged in rows of five, containing varied-sized life forms, some floating, some swimming about the spheres' confines.

The Akkadian adult, a woman of advanced age, who had been handling one of the life forms, placed it back into its incubator, sealing it, and turned her attention towards the visitors, waving them in.

"It's kidding, right?" presumed Theon. "I'm sure my current resume doesn't include water breathing."

Before Akara could chime in with a witty remark of her own, the shield began to move towards the inviting Akkadian, never losing its cohesion or form, until it collided with the opposing glass wall and scintillated into oblivion. The room was now entirely filled with air.

"What happened to the water?" asked a puzzled Da Vinci, eager for an explanation as he knocked on one of the walls to test its solidity.

The Akkadian, evidently the aforementioned priestess, slid her hand along the wall behind her. "The surface is punctured with thousands of miniscule holes. The water has simply been relocated. There is no miracle *here*…oh, but I'm mistaken, I've been told there is."

As the group advanced, she moved awkwardly towards Theon, clearly ill at ease in the more physically demanding air habitat, and betraying her advanced age. "I've never met a miracle before."

"I'm no miracle," said Theon. "You're not the only one who's been mistaken; those who once called me a miracle were also."

"Don't be so humble, young man," gently berated the priestess in motherly fashion. "Show more pride in yourself," slipping one of her long fingers under his chin, and raising his gaze until she could see directly into his eyes. "I have miracles of my own to show you."

Tottering back to the spheres, she placed her hand on one of them. "These are our young, barely weeks old." The infants had no limbs and barely a nub for a head, moving about the water giddily. "Each one carries the soul of a departed Akkadian, beginning anew the cycle of life."

The Priestess detached the sphere from its pedestal and handed it to Theon, who glued his face against it. The infant immediately became agitated, slamming into the sphere surface repeatedly. Theon smirked. "You want to get away from me, don't you? You know what I am."

"Strange," declared the priestess. "It never behaved like this before," snatching the sphere and placing it back on its mounting before clapping her hands. "Children! You've ogled your brothers and sisters long enough. Time for dinner. And do not forget to review tomorrow's lesson: the Greek alphabet."

The children ran through the entrance, back into watery territories, their long sinuous tongues lashing out like frogs, capturing along the way swimming fish the size of sardines.

"They so love their snacks before dinner," lovingly said the priestess, appearing slightly troubled. "Now, back to you, my little enigma, if not miracle. I've heard things about you."

"Begging your pardon, madam?" interjected Da Vinci.

"I have discreet observers, signore Da Vinci," revealed the priestess. "Much of what transpires on the surface is known to me. It is curious that I would know of you, but you, not of us. Have you never encountered my kind?"

"My movements throughout the kingdoms are extremely limited," retorted a miffed Da Vinci. "I may be an ambassador, but I am still an Echo."

"You do not enjoy Lord Deus' favors?" wondered the priestess.

"His consideration and his respect, of course," replied the old man. "And I've had the great honor of conferring with him several times, at his offices and in the Garden of Eden."

"My kind enjoys no such privilege," remarked the priestess. "It is not surprising since we refused to vow a secret allegiance to the Sanctum, and join them if a new war erupted. Why would we side with those who left us in destitution and distress upon our arrival in this realm?"

"You are not from here?" gasped Da Vinci, instantly imagining some uncanny and exotic home world covered in water, in some distant galaxy. The truth was far less extravagant.

"We are from Earth," announced the priestess, "chased away by the Diabolicus and their allies."

Everyone was flabbergasted, except for Tholen whose race shared an erratic history with the Akkadians, points of which varied depending on the raconteur.

"I do not believe it!" cried Da Vinci. "There is no such historical gem in the annals of Earth."

"One dark pearl along a string of glistening ones, I'm afraid," reflected the priestess. "Many Millennia ago, our species thrived, and our city, twenty times the size of this one, its towers standing high above the ocean surface, bustled with activity. We were an enlightened people living in relative peace among six other races, some far more primitive than others.

"The *Toltec* and the *Turanian*—as they called themselves—were amphibians, equally comfortable on land and in water, more so than us who preferred water. On an evolutionary scale, they resembled us, with one notable difference: we possessed a rudimentary understanding of atomic power, the application of which was being developed for positive utilitarian purposes."

"Fortunate you were an enlightened race," quipped Da Vinci, "and not a bellicose one."

"That is what we claimed to be," uneasily said the priestess. "Despite pressures by the Toltec and Turanian, we refrained from sharing any knowledge of it; and they resented us for it. Still our relations remained civil.

"The other races: the *Rmoahal*, the *Tlavati*, and the *Phoenician*— branches of what you called *Homo Sapien Sapien*—and the *Neanderthals*, were too primitive to ask anything of us except peaceful co-existence.

"All that changed when hordes of Diabolicus, led by a commander called Aurignacia, clandestinely invaded the land amidst treaty negotiations in the wake of the Great War with the Sanctum. They preyed on the Phoenician's innate warrior instinct, gave them bows, better spears and axes, catapults, trained them and launched them onto their unsuspecting evolutionary brothers, who were largely outnumbered.

"The men were massacred, the women captured and handed to the Diabolicus to rape, and the children beheaded."

"What could possibly justify such onslaught?" asked a disgusted Akara, feeling shame for her people.

"To supply Hell with an explosive influx of fighting Echoes," supposed the priestess. "Perhaps Satan had briefly considered reneging an eventual treaty in favor of a new offensive against the Sanctum. Only the Dragon Lord holds the answer.

"In any event, the violence did not end there. Upon learning from the covetous Toltec and Turanian of our atomic technology, the Diabolicus, assisted by their new army, promised to support them if they rushed our city in search of an alleged atomic weapon whose power they would then share."

"A weapon that you did not possess, of course?" hinted Da Vinci.

The priestess looked down in chagrin, and then away in evasiveness. "My people are not beyond fault or blame. The attack was savage and brutal. Using invisibility and hand weapons, a third of the populace battled its way to and transported through the Trans'Kartum, after forcing an address from one of the Diabolicus guarding it."

"And the city?" queried Theon.

"As per the instructions from the reigning priestess, the atomic device was detonated," admitted the priestess with grave sadness; "and the city was destroyed. No one would wield such power ever again."

"Such sacrifice, such loss," thought Da Vinci. "Was it worth it?"

"While we knew little of our new home," said the priestess, "we hoped Lord Deus, who had visited us in the past, would help us settle and help us return to Earth one day. But, weary of war, we wanted nothing to do with Sanctum homeland security concerns, and declined to act as a covert military reserve. So Deus refused to help, even going so far as publicly pretexting an inevitable breach in the fragile treaty on the cusp of being ratified, if he did offer any help. We had to seek assistance elsewhere."

"The Akkadians had been refused and humiliated," exclaimed Tholen, "just as my people had. It seemed only fitting that we help them. While they sought safety in Lake Seven, we mined the Polar caves for silica and other materials needed to build their new city."

"A very generous deed, indeed," considered Da Vinci. "However, some Akkadians don't seem to be appreciative," alluding to cynical commentary by one of the Akkadians by the lake shore.

"Understandable. There was an *unfortunate* incident," awkwardly confessed Tholen.

CHAPTER 104

As the waters receded in front of them, the priestess led the group to the city's history museum atop one of the towers. The museum was impressive, featuring over fifty exhibits spotlighting prominent moments and periods in Akkadian history.

"I believe the disintegration of Akkadian-Kalidrone relations is best told through imagery," asserted the priestess, beaming with pride in her people's artistic virtuosity.

The first display the group noticed exemplified Akkadian evolution. Four statues of humanoids standing erect, made of polished glass, were placed in a row, one behind the other. In order, there was a being resembling a galeopithecus, or flying lemur; an ape fitted with wing membranes; a frog-like winged amphibian; and an aquatic vertebrate matching the modern Akkadian.

A dark and dense gaseous vapor filled the statues, investing them with substance and dimension. And as the vapor drifted lingeringly without design, if not to attract and mesmerize onlookers, it created the illusion of mobility.

"It's a suspension," explained the priestess; "a mixture of pure water and black ink extracted from *decapuses*, ten-legged creatures comparable to Earth octopuses."

"You kill these poor creatures just for the ink?" asked Da Vinci. "Isn't that a bit wasteful…and barbaric?"

"We also feed off their flesh," immediately rebutted the priestess. "It is a great delicacy among Akkadians, even more delectable than its earthly counterpart."

Each exhibit caught the group's eye, especially Da Vinci's, who wanted to stop and study its technical flawlessness. But the priestess urged them on again and again until they arrived at one particular display comprised of a man on his knees whose head was being held by an Akkadian standing over him.

"A man asking absolution from a father confessor," gathered Theon who understood the concept, but never experienced it. "Why is his face so deformed?"

"He was beaten nearly to death by the leader of the Kalidrone," said the priestess, "his face pummeled days on end. His aggressor wanted the secret to the power of the Sword."

"This is Maitreya?" surmised Da Vinci before glancing at Theon and whispering, "the sword, my boy; Maitreya's sword."

"Apparently so," concurred the priestess; "shortly after his capture during the Great War. He tried to convince the Kalidrone that only he could summon the Sword's titanic force. In time, and after countless beatings, the Kalidrone leader came to believe him, and a—"

"Where is the sword?" anxiously bluttered out Theon, unable to quiet his impatience.

"It is not polite to interrupt your elders," admonished the priestess, now cognizant of the group's purpose in New Akkadia. She would make the boy languish a little longer to teach him manners if nothing else. "And a novel notion sprung within the Kalidrone leader's racing mind. He called upon the ruling Akkadian priestess, who came accompanied by twenty guards. While she trusted the Kalidrone as a whole—after all, their help had been instrumental in building the city—she had misgivings about their leader whose chronic sickness had worsen considerably, taking its toll on his perception and his judgement."

The priestess turned her palms outwards, and a very fine three-inch long tentacle slid out from each, twisting like restless worms. "Priestesses are not only chosen for their ancestry and their wisdom; they also enjoy certain *aptitudes*. With these, I can probe the minds of others."

Fascinated, Da Vinci reached out and secured a tentacle between his fingers. "Testy little thing, and somewhat slimy. How do you, how shall I say, *plug* them in?"

The priestess pointed to the exhibit, at which Da Vinci took a much closer look. "The workmanship is exceptional. It appears the Akkadian statue's protuberances pierce the center of the temples, through the skin and bone. What did the Kalidrone leader hope to learn from Maitreya?"

"Not learn, but acquire," specified the priestess. "Since the Akkadians were endowed with the gift of reincarnation, the Kalidrone leader believed the priestess could steal Maitreya's essence, God's Holy Spirit, and transfer it into himself using the mind probe as a conduit. The effort was futile, as the priestess had predicted, and the operation failed, leaving her shaken and perturbed. She had touched something in Maitreya she had not expected. She called it: *a darkness within the mist*."

"God is the tower and the Holy Spirit is the *light* within," quoted Akara. "Surely her perceptual recordings were mistaken."

"Perhaps leaving its vessel, Deus' body, and taking a bodily form of its own had changed something in Maitreya," conjectured the priestess. "At any rate, the Kalidrone leader became furious, and the Akkadian guards had to secure the priestess' return to the city. Later on, the leader sold the useless Maitreya to Satan in exchange for two-thousand Echoes, but kept the Sword as a bargaining chip in procuring more Echoes in the future. To this day, the Kalidrone still petition for Echoes, and Satan still does not have the sword."

Theon glared angrily at Tholen. "You lied. The Akkadians don't have the sword. Your people have it."

"The Kalidrone do not possess it," interceded the priestess on Tholen's behalf. "Years later, the Kalidrone leader, at the onset of crippling dementia, and filled with indignation and rancour, gave his last order to destroy the Akkadian city by provoking a massive cave-in above it. But, when the bedrock gave way and the stones plummeted, the crazed leader, sword in hand, and his subservient men plunged as well, to their deaths. The rear part of the city was heavily damaged, but has been repaired since."

"Then, you did recover the sword?" eagerly concluded Theon.

"We have it," confirmed the priestess. "Follow me."

They walked down the hall to another exhibit, this one evoking gladder times, when the Akkadians and Kalidrone worked hand in hand. The collection of statues depicted three Kalidrone mining the rock while four Akkadians carried away the extracted material in impermeable bags. In the background stood the Kalidrone leader, watching over the process.

"The sword you seek is there," announced the priestess, waving a finger at the glass sword by the leader's side.

"That is but a replica," retorted Da Vinci. "Surely the real item is well hidden somewhere within the city?"

"It is well hidden," said the priestess before inviting Theon to break the glass sword with his fist.

Theon complied, and at one fell swing broke the glass sword from end to end, uncovering the true sword hidden by the black ink. He grabbed it and pulled it away, cracking the glass hand that held it.

Latching onto the handle with both hands, Theon raised it above his head. "It feels weird, yet strangely familiar, as if a part of me wants to bond with it, while the other wants to cast it away."

The priestess rested her hand on Theon's shoulder. "I can now clearly sense the conflict within you." Gently relieving Theon of the sword, she passed it on to Da Vinci. "Child, would you allow a probe of your mind? It is invasive but painless."

"All right. Is it like hypnosis?" nervously asked Theon, who had found that experience a bit disconcerting.

"I have no frame of reference to provide a comparison," replied the priestess as the tentacles sprouted from her palms and drilled into the boy's temples.

An uneasy stillness pervaded for a minute as the priestess seemed to struggle to establish a connection. Suddenly her eyes grew wide open and her head abruptly jerked sideways. "I have you; I *have* you...I have *all* of you!"

The tentacles retracted and hurriedly regained their refuge, and the priestess stepped back, dazed with unaccustomed incomprehension. "You are a house of lights and shadows," she exclaimed, not once but twice; "ruled by many but owned by none. Lights and shadows prevail in turn with no lasting dominion in sight. If nothing is done to end the pernicious stalemate, the house will crumble. Nothing will survive."

"What do you mean?" shouted Theon, unnerved and frightened, and now convinced his situation, which he had believed to be at its direst, could in truth be even direr.

"The more I grapple with it, the less I see," said the baffled priestess. "I do not understand it. It is as if I have been infected by a virus that multiplies with my every exertion of probing thought."

"What of the sword?" pressed Theon. "Will it help me? Will it kill the darkness?"

The priestess strained to respond. "Does the sword eradicate the lights, the shadows...or the house? I do not know." Pacing back and forth, she could impart nothing more. "You must find your own answers. Take the sword and leave. My guards will safely take you where you will."

"We have what we came for," Da Vinci softly said to Theon. "There is nothing left for us here."

"Courage and fortitude," suddenly advocated Theon's Ghost Knight, braking silence after many days. "Stay the course."

The burden of despair lightened, becoming bearable once again, but only barely. "You haven't abandoned me?"

There was no answer, but that was an answer in and of itself.

"Thank you for your help, priestess." Theon nodded his gratitude. "Do you still think I'm a miracle?"

"You are here, alive and hopeful," replied the priestess. "You have escaped Satan's clutches. You have the sword and my complicity. And you are sided by true friends. You may not be a miracle, but you are surrounded by them."

CHAPTER 105

Circa 2,000 years ago; Kingdom of Hell.

Two Diabolicus sentinels, armed with Kor'tas,
stood guard by a large steel door equipped with a fourteen-inch circular lock at its center. Bored out of their minds, they occasionally exchanged grunts and sighs, stretched their arms, and tapped the floor with their weapons, in a vain attempt to alleviate the monotony.

But the tedium of their assignment would presently be broken by a barely audible high-pitch, plaintive sound coming from the shadows, twenty feet from their position.

"Did you hear that?" one sentinel asked the other, hoping it would prove to be a worthwhile diversion.

The other sentinel squinted as he peered into the darkness. "It's coming from the end of the corridor, just ahead of the junction."

Just as he was about to summon the intruder to identify himself, two tiny legs popped out of the shadows, jerking rapidly and randomly. It became immediately clear the shoeless limbs belonged to an infant resting on its back.

"It's *her* baby," obviously concluded the sentinel as he prudently approached the child. He pocked one of its feet with the end of his Kor'ta while the other guard looked on from his post. The child whined in irritation.

"What are you afraid of?" cynically yelled out the sentinel by the door. "It's just a baby for Hell sake. Pick it up!"

The sentinel crouched, depositing his weapon on the floor. He gently seized the child by the torso, lifting it to its feet; and as its face entered the light, it frowned at him.

"My baby boy dislikes strangers," said a determined voice rising from the darkness; "your kind especially."

Startled, the guard gazed in the direction of the voice, recognizing it in an instant. "Maria, is that you?"

"I much prefer Lisa," said the woman behind the voice, just before a dagger emerged from the obscurity and stabbed the guard in the neck just below the chin. The knife was then pushed in at an upward angle until none of its blade could be seen anymore.

Quite satisfied with her work, she retrieved her child and quickly rejoined the blackness.

The surviving sentinel nervously raised his Kor'ta, ordering the assassin to show herself. "Maria Magdalena! Come forward or I'll kill you and then the child!"

The lifeless guard's weapon, whose tip was concealed in the gloom, was pulled into it completely. "Aim well, demon. Your life depends on it."

His aim was indecisive and far more conclusive as he pointed his weapon at successive spots—fear was at play more than lack of information. He knew his life would be forfeited if he slayed the child. "Damn it, Lisa; show yourself!"

"Satan is quite unforgiving in intimately personal matters," strongly suggested Lisa before a blast erupted from the dark and struck the sentinel just above the heart.

He slumped to the ground, face first, slowly slipping into unconsciousness. "In Hell or on Earth, *he* will find you," groaning in pain.

Her child pressed against her chest, Lisa walked past the guard to a wall panel next to the door, applying her hand against its surface. The device lit up, scanning the epidermal ridges. A message appeared at the top of the panel: *print complete; identity confirmed.*

A booming clunking sound resonated from the circular lock. She removed her hand and briefly examined it, gloatingly smiling in contentment. "Like father, like daughter."

She grabbed the rim of the lock and rotated it clockwise 180 degrees, pulled the door open, and proceeded inside.

She entered an immense chamber the size of an auditorium. A metal grid lined with bars three inches apart, presiding as a suspended floor, traversed the chamber. At its center stood a two-foot high structure, which was, except for its height, an exact replica of the long buried Trans'Kartum—*and* of the mysterious well in which Theon was found. Unknown to the Sanctus and to Deus, this second Trans'Kartum had been discovered while excavating for the construction of the Sin City casino.

The relatively small size of the well was in truth a clever deception—it was in fact the extremity of a much larger monument, partially cloaked by the grid floor. Under it rose a monolithic three-sided pyramid, sheered at its tip to accommodate a five-foot tall cylinder, clearly the base of the well component.

Made entirely of stone, two sides of the pyramid were smooth, while the third was fashioned with a sculpted staircase leading to the base of the well. Undoubtedly, the pyramid was an iconic idol of worship, in addition to a means of interstellar travel—or so Lisa assumed.

At this point, all she cared about was its displacement capabilities. She unlocked the combination by pressing on two of several tiny domes under the well's rim, and, using her right foot, she pushed down on one of the eighty trapezoid stones, each etched with a symbol, of which the rim of the well was comprised.

She then pushed down another stone, and then another, until eight precise stones had completely receded into the body of the rim. A fierce flash of light discharged from the well's mouth, instantly replaced by a pool of shimmering water-like energy.

She looked down at her child, grinning widely as she rearranged the blue satin scarf around his head so that the familiar symbol braided into it became plainly visible again. "Let this symbol be a blessing for once and not a curse. We're going home, darling."

"Not possible," countered a voice behind her. The guard had regained his senses and was pointing his weapon at Lisa, trembling in throbbing pain.

She turned and glared at him with such backbone and boldness, even he could not mask his admiration for her courage. "I'm sorry, Lisa. If you escape, I die. Better to die a duty-bound soldier than a fool duped by a woman."

Lisa did not hesitate. She flung herself over the energy pool and dropped into it, crossing the event horizon. The guard, however, did hesitate, and shot as only her head was left protruding from the pool. Suffering acutely, his aim was wild, hitting the pool a few feet from her head, and producing a wave of antagonistic surplus energy that was not absorbed by the pool, but rather skated along its surface towards her, engulfing her head and searing her face as she disappeared.

"I am dead," whispered the guard, hoping at least she would return as an Echo. "But what of the child?"

What of him?

CHAPTER 106

Present day; Kingdom of Hell.

The stone, its edges ravaged by the passage of time, began shaking, then moving slowly forward, ever so dislodging the surrounding ones. Passing the midpoint, gravity instantly intervened, toppling the stone and bringing with it its neighbors to the dusty ground two feet below.

The stone wall was left with a gaping hole, the dark interior of which was teeming with shadows moving in a tumult of fervor and suspense.

One shadow, evidently the most aroused of the lot, materialized into a rather unsightly head bulging out of the wall. "We've made it!" shouted Tholen in delight.

"Shut up, you foolish creature," reprimanded Da Vinci, forcefully pushing Tholen out of the aperture and onto the ground teeth first. "We're trying to remain concealed." The old man slid out on his rear end, followed by Theon and Akara, the latter having found the journey through the narrow tunnel arduous because of the Kor'ta she dragged and the sword she carried strapped onto her back.

"Amazing," murmured softly Theon. "I've never seen someone tunnel so fast, with his *bare* hands. Your reputation as a gifted digger is certainly well deserved," gazing back into the hole.

"Not everyone appreciates our gift," muttered Tholen as he stood up, checking the condition of his teeth, glaring all the while at Da Vinci.

"End this bickering," enjoined Akara. "We have a job to do."

"Quite right," agreed Da Vinci, expressing little sorrow for the product of his impatience. "This way."

"Why this way?" asked a crabby Tholen, whose genetically enhanced vision allowed him a unique perspective of the immediate environment.

"My sight may not equal yours," replied Da Vinci, "but from what I can gather, it's the only way." It was the only passage.

Tholen huffed and puffed in resignation as the group made its way through the musty and ill-smelling corridor, one of dozens constituting the dungeon, the bowels of Satan's castle.

"Help me," pleaded one prisoner after the other, hands extended in heartfelt petition outside the cell bars. "I'm innocent. I don't belong here. Take me with you."

"We will free you if you tell us where Maitreya is being held," repeatedly said Da Vinci in empty promise. No one knew where God's former spirit was, not one. Some pretended to, of course, out of desperation, but Da Vinci was not duped.

"Something is amiss?" eventually realized the old man. "We've inspected over forty corridors and not only have we failed to locate him, but not one Echo has heard of his captivity within these walls. This may well be a wild goose chase."

"Pursuing an anseriform bird without cause?" gathered a puzzled Tholen, recalling several species of ducks, geese and swans living on the outskirts of Heaven. "It is doubtful Maitreya will *quack* us to his position."

Theon giggled nervously. "We could spread bread crumbs along the floor. That could attract the fowl being."

"Keep focus," ordered a roiled Da Vinci as he signaled the group to penetrate one of the few remaining corridors. He only had to take a few steps before a harsh voice resonated from the end of the corridor—and from the very last cell.

"While I may not be a fowl," the voice said, "the air in here certainly is. Quite offensive to the senses."

Surprised and justifiably holding back any premature jubilation, they ran towards the origin of the welcomed disturbance, peering into the dark cell. They could see the outline of a statuesque man wearing a hooded cloak, sitting on the edge of what passed for a bed.

Akara pointed her Kor'ta at the mysterious convict; Tholen quickly followed suit with his crossbow.

"That will not be necessary," reassured the man. "I am the one you seek. I am Maitreya."

"How do you know of us?" queried Da Vinci. "How did knowledge of your rescue come to you?"

"Very little escapes my purview," boasted the self-proclaimed holy spirit. "My physicality has yet to dull the far grasp of my awareness. Do come in; the door is not locked."

Da Vinci pushed the door open, and they all scurried inside. "Strange that you did not flee before. Only a few feet separate you from freedom."

"It was the only way," said Maitreya; "the only way to finally meet the boy." He waived Theon to approach; the boy stared at Da Vinci for approval.

"There is no danger," vouched Maitreya. "You are four and I am but one, quite weakened by the miserable conditions of my incarceration."

Da Vinci nodded cautiously, and Theon walked to the bed, sitting next to Maitreya.

Maitreya patted Theon on the knee. "You are legend, my boy. Hell has never known an implacable force such as you. So much fury and fire you have wreaked upon your enemies. There is, however, one other force you have yet to reckon with."

Maitreya suddenly grabbed Theon's arm, piercing it with a device sequenced with spikes tipped in a powerful toxin. The effect was immediate, Theon crumpling to the ground.

"It's a trap!" screamed Akara as she raised her weapon.

"If you fire, you all die," warned Maitreya before removing his hood and revealing a viciously deformed face. "Your people did this to me," touching his face and then pointing at Tholen. "They believed it would augment the ransom, and hasten its delivery."

"It's the Dark Lord!" cried out Akara, on the verge of firing. "Where is Maitreya? If Maitreya is dead, I'll, I'll—"

"He's not!" replied the malevolent being. "My men can attest to that."

Ten Diabolicus emerged from the shadows of the opposite cell, all armed with Kor'tas. "As you can see, I am far from oneness. Now, lower your weapon before you hurt yourself, little girl."

The Diabolicus marched forward, surrounding the would-be rescuers. One shoved the tip of his Kor'ta in Akara's back. "You killed my brother when you helped that *thing* escape," referring to Theon. "I'll have my way with you, and not even daddy will be able to save you."

"If you hurt the boy," a defiant Da Vinci balked at the Dark Lord, "I'll become your worst nightmare."

The Dark Lord laughed aloud at the old man's inept threats. "Why would I injure this magnificent boy? Why would I harm my *own creation*?"

CHAPTER 107

"Don't worry, dear lad," said the sure-footed Dark Lord. "The effects will subside just in time for the momentous happening."

Theon could hear his captor, but could not move or offer any resistance as two Diabolicus hauled his body into a huge chamber. Four more guards followed, escorting Akara, who had been relieved of her Kor'Ta and of the avidly sought Sword of Maitreya.

"What have you done with Leo and Tholen?" she demanded, addressing both the Dark Lord and Satan, standing at an angle behind his master.

"Nothing here concerns them," said the Dark Lord. "A comfortable cell should calm their nerves."

"Then, why am I her—good God!" exclaimed Akara, looking towards the center of the chamber. "You have a Trans'Kartum!"

The Dark Lord smiled proudly. "Indeed. We discovered it while digging the foundation for the casino. It appears this world possessed two; a fortunate happenstance for the Diabolicus, and for me; and an integral part of my plan."

"Are you going to send us through that thing?" wondered Akara as she tried to piece together his diabolical scheme.

"Perish the thought," replied the Lord. "That would be a terrible waste of resources. You, little one, are here to attest to my great power, and to witness a most stupendous event. As a member of the *family*, you deserve no less."

"Common ancestry shall never bind us," retorted Akara in loathing. "I may be a Diabolicus—a twisted fate I've long come to terms with—but I am nothing akin to the likes of you."

"Oh, no, no, dear; I make no such inference," he reassured her. "I am not the one that binds us all together; *he* is," pointing at Theon. "He is the culmination of a meticulously cultivated, crossbred genealogical tree."

"And I suppose you're the devoted gardener?" snickered Akara.

"I am both the breeder *and* the bred," claimed the Dark Lord. "And I've invited good friends to taste the ripe fruit the tree shall inevitably yield. Do come in," he shouted towards the entrance of the chamber.

A procession of the most evil men made their way through the door: Adolf Hitler, Napoleon Bonaparte, Julius Caesar, Genghis Khan, Attila the Hun, and last but never the least, Osama Bin Laden. Each one bowed as he made his appearance.

The Dark Lord's narcissism could not deprive itself of such an august audience. "I believe you've all met at the Games. No introductions are therefore necessary. But, I have been woefully remiss in my proper introduction—the designation *Dark Lord* is so impersonal. I shall remedy the situation this instant; you may call me *Demahon*."

"Demahon?" cried out Akara in bewilderment. "You're Deus' twin brother?"

"In the flesh," confirmed Demahon, "perverted and mutilated as it is," clasping his face with both hands.

"It can't be," reckoned Akara. "Legend has it you were disintegrated and banished to the vastness of the Universe."

"The Universe could not contain me," contended Demahon; "spat me back, as it were. It's quite a tale. But, where are my manners? We have a family tree member dying to join us and indulge in my riveting and fatally delicious story of rebirth and restoration of my birthright. I present to you: a spiritual father of yesteryear…and *true* father to you, young Theon."

Theon was instantly engulfed by a dual feeling of circumspection and anticipation, only one destined to prevail upon revelation of this alleged father.

Two guards crossed the threshold, escorting a longtime prisoner. He stood tall and resolute, his gaze solemn and inscrutable. It was indeed Theon's *biological* father…and the son knew the father.

CHAPTER 108

Present day; New York.

Sarah Sinclair did not know where her son Theon was; and neither did her husband four days ago, when he told her that Theon had been abducted from his bedroom by an unknown aggressor.

While the images captured by a video camera Cameron had hidden in Theon's room failed to identify the intruder, they did reveal his nature: a spine-chilling *demon*—a detail Cameron was compelled to conceal from his wife whose nerves, he believed, had been sufficiently frazzled.

All he told her was that he and Scott Dumont would search high and low for Theon, even if that meant traveling halfway across the globe. Of course, he and his partner knew exactly where they were heading first: the mysterious well in the forest behind Le Clos-Lucé Manor; the well that spawned the equally mysterious Theon E. Rex.

Cameron had promised to call her within the next 24 hours. He never did. To fuel her anxiety and despair even more, Sarah had just received a registered envelope marked urgent and confidential, and addressed solely to her. It contained a key and a short ambiguous letter from Dr. Maurice Lefoux. It said:

"Enclosed key opens safe deposit box registered in your name, at Chase Manhattan Bank on Park Avenue. You have been appointed Guardian of your son's heritage to the world. The combination of the safe deposit box is 5 – 13 – 13 – 3. $E = M^2C$. Tell no one of this—No one!"

The box was now in front of her, on a table in the Chase Manhattan Bank's vault. Rotating the four combination lock dials, she unlocked the box and opened it. In it, she found: three rolled-up DNA charts labeled *Subject C*, *Subject M^2*, and *Subject M^2C*; a gold ring inscribed with the name *Lisa-Maria*; a finger bone; a strand of hair; and a letter. She was quite confounded by the eclectic content, and felt emotionally coerced to understand its meaning and confront its implications. Her hand quivered as she picked up the letter and read:

"Hello Sarah,

It has been a while since our previous encounters, during one of which I had the great privilege of discovering how unique and special your son Theon was. I had hoped that your son's singularity would flourish and become a source of reverence to all. Unfortunately, only half of that equation materialized.

To be tactlessly blunt, there are men who want your son dead. They are agents working directly for the Pope, entrusted with the mission of murdering your son.

I, on the other hand, am part of an organization driven by certain beliefs, trodden on by many, whose vindication could very well come at the hands of your son. That is why it is imperative that your son survive, and become a symbol of hope and an access to a higher, more altruistic level of consciousness.

The proof of your son's fundamental essence and revolutionary identity resides in the items found in the box, whose consummate qualities and significance can best be expressed through a lesson in a history denied and quelled.

Two-thousand years ago, Maria Magdalena met and bethroved Jesus Christ. She bore a male child, who was whisked away for its own protection. Soon after, Christ was crucified, and Maria Magdalena disappeared.

During the fourteenth Century, a cloth, now known as the Shroud of Turin, was discovered in a little church in Liry, in north-central France. The shroud was a linen cloth bearing the image of a man who appeared to have suffered physical trauma in a manner consistent with crucifixion. That man was none other than Jesus Christ. Because of its historical importance, the shroud was preserved and has since been kept in the royal chapel of the Cathedral of Saint John the Baptist in Turin, northern Italy.

While the body of Christ was never uncovered, the same cannot be said of Maria Magdalena's remains. In fact, various claims have been made as to their location.

The official Church version is that Maria Magdalena was buried in Ephesus, near Turkey, and that, in 899, the Emperor Leo VI had her relics transferred to a monastery in Constantinople.

That account was, however, contradicted in a document in Latin, circa 6th century, which, referring to an earlier record, claimed that Mary Magdalena had travelled to Aix-le-Provence with Saint Maximin and had lived there for many years before dying in Aix at the age of 60. Maximin, the first Christian bishop in Gaul, placed her embalmed body in a crypt and had a Basilica built over it to honor and protect it.

The body was said to have been subsequently removed during the Saracen invasions as it was feared it would be discovered and destroyed. Rumor has it that part of the remains were taken to the French monastery of Vezelay in Burgundy, the church of which carried Mary Magdalena's name.

None of these hypotheses are true since the body is actually buried in a grave behind the Chapel of Saint-Hubert, in the town of Amboise, France, not far from Leonardo Da Vinci's tomb within the Chapel.

Under circumstances that remain unclear, scientific or otherwise, but cannot be refuted given the evidence, Maria Magdalena survived the test of time and found herself befriending Da Vinci. She died some time later, killed, according to a written account by Da Vinci, by demons from Hell, who were searching for her only son. It is uncertain whether or not Da Vinci was using a metaphor to describe the assassins, who might have been just mortal men—albeit evil ones.

Today, that son, apparently as time-resistant as his mother, is now been pursued by the Pope's henchmen, for reasons as old as time: greed, control, power, and dominion over Man.

The Pope, determined to protect the widespread notion that he is the ultimate messenger of God, is petrified at the idea that the Holy Grail is not a cup but, in fact, simultaneously the womb and the earthly remains of Mary Magdalena, a lowly woman; and the descendants she and Jesus engendered, which parallelly hinted at Jesus' mortality.

For the longest of time, the leaders of the Church of Rome have been frightened of women and of priestly intimacy with women. Why? Because women become wives and mothers, and the very nature of motherhood is a perpetuation of bloodlines. It was this that bothered the Church: a taboo subject, which, at all costs, had to be separated from the image of Jesus—an image molded and manipulated by the Church to maintain its dominance.

Now, that image is about to be shattered; thanks to whom? Thanks to your son, Theon.

In the safe deposit box, you will find the following:

A finger bone and a strand of hair belonging to Maria Magdalena, preserved by my organization for the last 500 years;

A gold ring given to Maria Magdalena, whom Da Vinci called Lisa-Maria, for unknown reasons;

A DNA chart, marked Subject C, produced from Shroud DNA, and belonging to Jesus Christ;

A DNA chart, marked Subject M^2, produced from hair and bone DNA, and belonging to Maria Magdalena;

And a DNA chart, marked Subject M^2C, produced from Theon's DNA, classified under coding: $E = M^2C$; l'Enfant est issu de Maria Magdalena et du Christ.

The DNA proof is incontrovertible. Your son is the biological child of Maria Magdalena and Jesus Christ.

Sarah gasped in confusion and sheer disbelief, dropping the letter. Her knees weakened, arresting her fall by holding tight to the table. The boy she grew to fear was now extolled as the next Messiah.

What was she to believe? Her own senses and experiences—strained through a filter of suspicions and fright—or the words of a reputable Doctor, who might have taken leave of his sanity in deference for a seductive, timeless and ideological proposition.

She slowly picked up the letter and resumed the reading:

"I realized it is a lot to take in, but you must remain centered and do exactly as I say. My associates and I—leaders of the organization—are in grave danger. We were once eight; now only three remain, the other five having been murdered by the Pope's agents. We have no choice but to go into exile. Our enemy's determination has intensified and he has simply become too powerful and resolute.

And I have no doubt they will eventually find us. That is why you must hide the evidence where none would think of looking. No one will suspect you, Theon's adoptive mother, of harboring the secret and its proof. It would be too obvious and imprudent to do so.

It is crucial you guard the evidence with your life. Other elements of proof have already been destroyed: Maria Magdalena's grave was desecrated two days ago, and the bones removed; and DNA material was mysteriously stolen. I suspect even the Shroud is in danger of disappearing.

For now, I can only hope your son is safe. I know he vanished a few

days ago, and I can only surmise he was taken into hiding by your hus-
band and one of our allies, Scott Dumont, who has yet to contact us.

One last thing. One of my associates, a prominent politician, was
gunned down recently. He was leaving work and heading to a meeting
with one of the Pope's men, a man claiming his loyalty to the Pope had
long since waivered, and who wanted to help.

This man is your neighbor, Amadeo Da Verdi. He pretends to be
Theon's protector. Beware of him.

May God protect you.
Doctor Maurice Lefoux.

Completely shocked and overwhelmed, Sarah checked out and staggered to the bank exit, leaving the items of proof in the box. She had
decided the time was not ripe to bring them with her—and she was absolutely correct.

"You're white as a ghost, Sarah," said Amadeo, who had driven her to
the bank, and was now holding the passenger door open for her. "What's
going on?"

She sat in the car, mute as a fish, and waited for him.

As Amadeo started the car, he asked anew. "Well, what's going on?
What was in the safe deposit box?"

"Nothing of importance," Sarah insisted. "Just some weirdo bent one
playing a sick joke on my family and me."

"Care to share, just a bit?" pushed Amadeo. "Maybe I can help."

She gave her driver a blank look. "You *can't* help me."

They drove off in silence.

CHAPTER 109

Present day; Kingdom of Hell.

Jesus Christ caressed Theon's hair. "Demahon might be notoriously deceptive, but in this instance, he is correct. I am your father."

Overwhelmed, heavy tears of relief and joy trickled down Theon's cheeks. His mind in disarray, he tried to fathom it all. "I wondered all my life about my biological father; wondered what he looked like, what made his life worthwhile. Was he a good man? Did he possess powers like mine? Would I be disappointed?"

"Are you disappointed?" asked Jesus.

Theon grinned with pride. "How could I be? You're Jesus Christ, all forgiving, all powerful."

"My powers, for whatever good they served, left me upon the cross," reminded Jesus. "They deserted me just as my holy spirit did. Perhaps they were never mine to have."

"I wish *my* powers would dump me," longed Theon before abruptly turning to Demahon. "Where is my biological mother?" Before any answer could be offered, he turned back to Jesus. "*Who* is my mother?"

"Maria Magdalena is your real mother," admitted Jesus… "was your mother," glaring at Demahon for clarification on his wife's current situation. "Now that father and son have been revealed to each other, is it not time to finally disclose what has become of her?"

"She never echoalesced," interjected a disgruntled Satan. "Had she, she would have paid dearly for he betrayal, and I would have been the instrument of her suffering."

"Mother," mumbled Theon, who allayed his sadness by entertaining the possibility that she may yet echoalesce, that her experiential humanessence might simply be detained in some sort of electro-magnetic maze. It was a sound theory, he convinced himself.

As he pondered over this, trivializing any flaws, something suddenly dawned over him. "You're two-thousand years old," he said to Jesus in an accusatory manner. "You can't be my father. It's inconceivable; nor can Maria Magdalena be my mother."

"It is nevertheless the truth," maintained Demahon, "just as Satan is your grandfather, and just as I am Jesus' father… and your *grandfather*."

"I know this to be true," corroborated Jesus, who had learned of this upon Demahon's recent visit to the dungeon. "The thought of being this vile creature's son revolts me."

Theon slipped out of the Diabolicus' hold and fell down, intercepted by Akara before his head could hit the floor. The evidence of his maleficence was mounting, revealing and providing a context for his many monstrous transformations of the past. Despite the blood of Christ coursing through his body and the spirit of his Ghost Knight tempering his raging impulses, his perception of self crystalized into permanency.

Whereas he had attained a precarious balance, wishfully believing he could be both a defender of good and a demon—and be neither one nor the other in particular; he now truly believed to be only the one: a monster. "I'm an abomination," he whispered to Akara, "and nothing else. Sta… stay away from me," he added with a difficulty he never would have suspected.

"Make me," she whispered back, kissing him on the forehead.

Only divine intervention deployed in terms so certain even Theon could not discount them could save him from his self-inflicted damnation. Without it, the reality of what was about to come would only prove him right.

CHAPTER 110

"You have many questions," suspected Demahon as he probed into Theon's inquiring eyes. "I will not keep you lingering in ignorance."

"As you've probably deduced," he merrily went on, "the famous Mary of your Bible is indeed your grandmother; likely prancing about Heaven at this very moment. I came upon her on Earth, under the guise of the Holy Spirit Maitreya, and impregnated her with this savior of mankind," pointing at Jesus.

"How did you save so many souls, my dear Jesus?" inquired Demahon. "It was not part of my plan. Tell me now what secret you have been hiding from me." Jesus was concealing something, and, unbeknownst to Theon, so was he. The father's secret had become the son's.

"I will find out," assured Demahon, his conceit compelling him to pursue his story. "Years later, Jesus met and became mate to Maria Magdalena, formerly known as Lisa, daughter of Bethel, Mary's twin sister and receptacle of Satan's seed. He too had come came upon Bethel under the guise of the Holy Spirit Maitreya , their fornication ultimately producing the child Lisa.

"Since Lisa, who never left her mother's side, had become as popular in Galilee as her mother because of the wench's many indiscretions, I gave her a new identity upon her return to Earth, years after capture by Thevetat, my closest operative. While in Hell, her father Satan was the one who instructed her in new ways, and indoctrinated her to do my bidding."

"You should have chosen another instructor," disparagingly advised Akara. "He could not even teach an obstinate mule to heel. See how docile and obedient I've turned out under his fatherly ordinance."

Insulted, Satan raised his hand on his unruly daughter, ready to strike.

"You touch me, even in the slightest," roared Akara, "and I'll rip off your arm…daddy!"

"Enough of this!" ordered Demahon, hard-pressed to acknowledge some measure of validity of Akara's claim. After all, Satan had let Lisa AKA Maria Magdalena escape with her son through the Trans'Kartum.

"I sometimes wonder who is the child and who is the parent," he said almost apologetically to Theon, before summarizing the genealogical account. "You are the true son of Jesus and Maria Magdalena. Jesus is my son and that of Mary. And Maria Magdalena is the daughter of Satan and Bethel. That completes the sordid family tree…or the part of it that matters."

"You forget my age," pointed out Theon. "I'm *not* two-thousand years old."

"Biologically, you are but thirteen," recognized Demahon, "but chronologically, you are very close to two Millennia. You see, weeks following your birth, your mother rediscovered her humanity and succeeded in fleeing through the Trans'Kartum. By some strange cosmic aberration, a massive solar flare intercepted the wormhole that carried both of you from my realm to Earth, sectioning space and time, sending her to the sixteenth century into Da Vinci's hands, and you to the twenty-first century into your adoptive parents' care. Eventually, we found her, and then you."

"Your plan is complete," asserted Akara. "The family reunion is successful and is now over. So let us go."

Demahon burst into laughter. "One does not forego such an intricately orchestrated plan at its apogee. Raise the boy," commanding two guards. "The time has come to ready the *weapon*."

CHAPTER 111

Circa 50,000 years ago; Kingdom of Heaven.

From the private notes of Demahon: *Philosophiae Naturalis Principia Physica*

Quintessence is a form of dark energy—a mysterious phantom energy that can be either attractive or repulsive depending on the ratio of its kinetic to potential energy, and that has the power, unlike light energy, to mold the shape of the Universe.

Through controlled energy-matter conversion, I believe I can produce three comprehensive and distinct types of dark matter described by anti-charge and anti-quantum spin—physical properties of elements existing on the fringe of clusters of normal space. The process will take a hundred Millennia, will likely be irreproducible, and will engender minimal but sufficient quantities necessary for its intended purpose.

I further believe the recombination of these three elements, in matter-form, will result in an enclosed and manipulable source of destructive power equal to that of the pool from which it was drawn. The nature of its multiplicity, presumably native to the domain of mysticism, still eludes me, but its understanding is not essential to its deployment.

However, there is an apparent complication. The three types of dark matter cannot be merged in a vacuum—a facilitating environment is required. I am now entertaining a theory I suspect will be successful in their reunion, one in whose application I shall be an intimate participant.

Biology and the inescapable instinct to reproduce shall be my oasis.

Deus dropped the excerpt of Demahon's work to the ground.

"Bring in the accused," he then bellowed to the bailiff who opened the courtroom door and instructed the Thronos, the King's personal guard and enforcement agents of God's justice and authority, to deliver them unto God and his jury. The Thronos, five in number and sporting togas with an image of God's throne on the front, pushed in the three prisoners, bearing a complex series of chains and locks, covering most of their bodies and making movement almost impossible. Wearing only a loin cloth, the humiliated captives awkwardly shuffled to the center of the room.

Somberness pervaded the legal theatre as dozens of beeswax candlesticks adorned its stained walls of stone, burning ever so slowly and sweetening the air with a soothing aroma reminiscent of freshly collected maple sap boiling in a sugar shack. A massive antiquated marble table, cracked along its edge by the onslaught of time, and heavily worn by forearms weighted down by the fate of past offenders, hulked along the wall opposite the entrance. Deus, Lord God in permanence and judge in the moment, stood gravely behind the table.

"Permission to proceed," he asked the twelve jurors who sat at a curved wooden table, twenty-five feet in partial circumference and three feet in depth, and positioned to Deus' right. Each jury member was the head of a tribal family devoted to and excelling in the study and the practice of Eternal Law.

Issachar, the Primus Judge and jury chairman, rose. "I am honored to serve, and have been appointed speaker for my tribe and for the tribes of Reubus, Simeon, Levi, Judus, Danus, Naphtali, Gad, Asher, Zebulun, Joshed and Benjar. On their behalf, I tender their approval to carry on."

"Very well." Deus pointed to the detainees. "One, two, three." His index finger's aim traveled across the criminal lot. "While it may have been a long time since so many have stood within this court at one time, it is the grievous and heinous nature of the crime, and the singularity of those that committed it that have profoundly appalled this court. I'm disgusted and sickened to find myself by my own blood, and distressed to be forced to spill it."

"None is forcing you to do anything," claimed the most imposing of the terrible trio as he vehemently shook his chains. "You are king of the Heavens and no one would oppose your clemency in this instance."

"My rule could afford you leniency," replied Deus, "but my blood ties would incite a moral uprising."

"Brother kills brother," screamed the criminal. "What could be more immoral? I am Demahon, your brother, laden by the chains of oppression, as are my sons Yazus and Shaitan. You would slay us for striving for what is rightfully ours?"

"Conspiring against the king is a capital offense," reminded Deus. "Plotting against him is well beyond the province of absolution."

"Absolution is but a means to an end: life renewed," remarked Demahon. "If a man's course foreshadows certain ends, surely if the course be departed from, the ends must change. You can intercede for me based on that premise alone. I promise I shall change. Be the catalyst to my transformation."

"The dark forces that have consumed you are eloquent indeed," returned Deus, "but your words slide off me like rain drops of a morning shower over the garden of Eden."

"Yes!" exclaimed Demahon. "Remember the Garden of Eden; remember how you and I sat against the trunk of the Tree of Life, eating its fruit and exchanging tales of past glories. These are the memories of your own kin and not of a nefarious manifestation bent on mayhem."

"We speak for ourselves," interjected in concert Yazus and Shaitan,- stepping closer to Deus. "We do not trivialize our vile deed as our father does, nor do we diminish its gravity. We submit however to you and this court that we were subjected to our father's influence and subjugated by his authority. We were but pawns in his plot for domination."

"Deserters!" loudly sneered Demahon, trying to free his arms from the chains to strangle his children. "I am your father. Your fate is my fate."

"Silence!" ordered Deus. "Fathers shall not be punished for their sons, nor shall sons be punished for their fathers; everyone shall be punished for his own sin."

Issachar rose once more. "Lord God, your Honor, it is time for the recital of the accusatory scroll."

"Summon Gabriel," commanded Deus. Gabriel, the archangel, walked in carrying a roll of parchment sealed with a round spot of red wax embossed with the letter D. Handing it to God, he bowed and then left the room.

Breaking the seal, Deus unrolled the scroll. "Accused, stand straight and mindful. You are separately and conjointly accused: of consorting with the dark mystical forces dwelling within you and without you; of experimenting with the transmutation of your physicality and your spirituality into the quintessence of evil—the Dark Trinity; and of planning to unite these malevolent parts, each one of you harboring one sordid part, into an perverted whole—the Anti-Triune God of chaos, devastation and desolation."

"How do you plead to these charges?" enjoined Deus who, for all intents and purposes, considered the question a formality.

"The light is within the darkness," argued Demahon, "just as the darkness is within the light. One gives life to the other. Kill me, kill us, and you kill yourself."

"The deftness with which you dispense philosophy cannot protect you," advised Deus. "If you will not enter a plea, I shall, for all of you." Deus stayed his tongue an instant, purely for effect, and then delivered the plea by proxy—and his verdict: "Guilty on all charges! Only the jury can save you now. You need have swayed only one to your plight to earn the mercy of the court."

Again, Issachar rose. "We need not retire for deliberation. We have reached a verdict: guilty on all charges."

"So say you all?" asked Deus, who required, according to Eternal Law, a unanimous guilty verdict from the jury in the event *he* found the accused party guilty.

"So say we all," stoically replied the jury.

"Then, beckon Khrist Lesus," instructed Deus. Lesus was an outstanding and devoted young Eternal, the only Sanctus Terrum to be anointed Prime Seraph and elevated to the rank of Khrist. Seraphim, typically angels—or Sanctus Angelicum—were the caretakers of God's throne. The Khrist, above all Seraphim, not only cared for the throne but also guarded God's Holy Sword and its power to summon Maitreya, the Spirit of God.

Khrist Lesus crossed the entrance threshold, holding a gold case in both palms at eye-level. As he came upon Deus, he very slowly deposited the case onto the marble table. "I live to serve and defend the Master Spirit, the spirit of my Lord. May God and Ghost meld, that God's true supremacy be felt and that God's true wisdom be heard."

"Your allegiance brings comfort to my heart," said a gratified Deus as he pulled on the cover and opened the case, revealing a striking 40-inch straight double-edged blade sword, with a 10-inch cruciform hilt and a spherical pommel. Silver-colored, the sword was made entirely of Etheron, a rare heavenly substance characterized by a melting point exceeding 10,000 degrees Fahrenheit, a tensile strength 250 times that of steel, and a weight one-tenth that of iron. "What say you at the sight of it, Lesus?"

"It is magnificence," Lesus spoke in awe. "It is the Sword of Maitreya. It is *you*."

Grabbing the sword with both hands, Deus tapped its tip against the floor and then flipped the weapon upwards until the tip came to rest against his forehead. "Teacher of all things, defender of all life, mirror of my being, I conjure you."

The sword suddenly began to shimmer and shine with a quivering silver light, blinding whoever looked upon it. His eyes clamped shut, Deus felt the placid light, undisturbed by tumult and disorder, expand and envelop his entire body, summoning something sublime within.. As it subdued, Deus opened his eyes. "We are whole again, Maitreya. We are One, my Holy Spirit and I." His voice was different—he spoke in an eerily flanged, deepened register.

"Do you know who we are?" the augmented Deus questioned Demahon.

"You are a coward hiding inside a craven," spat Demahon with abject disdain. "The fruits of my contempt shall rot and turn into pure unadulterated odium."

"Directing your hatred at me is certainly your prerogative," conceded Maitreya, the Holy Spirit, who was now in full control of Deus' body; "for I am the agent of divine action; and such action shall be executed onto you. The sword shall do my bidding. The instrument of my will and the catalyst of my coming into being shall carry out your sentence."

"You can destroy me," dared Demahon, "and you can destroy my children, but others will take our places. All is not right or still in the kingdom of Heaven. On the day of retribution, Heaven shall be torn into two by the wrath of Darkness. Your Light shall not shine bright enough to cast away the shadows of turpitude and depravity. The Lord and the Spirit, and the Khrist, and all the citizens of Heaven shall be obliterated. Mark my words."

Maitreya grinned. "As per your custom, you speak too much, yet say nothing of import or worthy of contemplation. Hear me instead; I shall not destroy you."

"To what then are we sentenced?" asked a confused Demahon.

"You shall be put to contribution," simply replied Maitreya. "You are sentenced to matter segregation and function restoration."

"You are *recycling* us?" shouted Demahon.

"Since you are fond of putting parts together," pointed out Maitreya, "we shall do the reverse. Your entity and those of your children shall be divided into a myriad of particles—*dark* particles since you espouse so vainly this property—and propelled beyond the Heavens into the Universe to promote its creation and expansion. While the essence of your former selves shall remain ingrained in each particle, the Dark Trinity shall forever remain dormant."

"You should eradicate the Darkness," taunted Demahon, "for we will find a way to awaken and have our revenge."

Maitreya overlooked Demahon's desperate threats. "Heavenly essence—even that which has turned to darkness—cannot be absolutely extinguished. It can only be rendered inert and inlayed with a new purpose. To that end, the *dark matter* that shall be given out shall enjoy no sentience, no awareness of self. And once it has served its function, it shall become part of the Universe and forfeit its distinctiveness."

On those last words, the Thronos marched towards the violators and forcefully placed them one behind the other.

"With this divine sword, the holiest of all, I stab at thee," shouted Maitreya as he swung back the weapon. "Only the blood of your kindred can resurrect thee. But thou shall not seek it for thou shall taste the privilege of thought nevermore." With one mighty thrust, the Holy Spirit impaled all three bodies from back to front. And they became the darkest of dust, floating through the courtroom ceiling, into the skies above the kingdom of Heaven, and into the Universe, never to return.

CHAPTER 112

Present day; Kingdom of Hell.

"My Lord, are you well?" Satan asked Demahon, who suddenly appeared pensive.

"My thoughts were momentarily hostage of my past," replied the Dark Lord, reliving his condemnation at the hands of his brother, fifty Millennia ago. "They have caught up with me in the present. But they will haunt me no more. Revenge is finally at hand."

He focused anew on Theon. "I literally built you, dear boy," he announced as guards inserted Theon's hands and feet into metallic cylinders that contracted, restricting all movement. He just hung there, his arms and legs spread out and stretched to their limits, by the edge of the transportation machine.

"Your quest was doubly successful," he added; "you unlocked your vast powers and turned them outwards with explosive effect, and you retrieved the sword without consequences for me. You are indeed my greatest creation."

Demahon spread apart Theon's neck hair, exposing the symbol that had plagued the boy all his life. "Behold the mark of absolute evil. *Tenebras*," touching the symbol's left side; "*Quein*," stroking its middle; "*Tenebris*," brushing its right side. "*Darkness within darkness*. An unholy king standing in the protective shade of the tree of Death, exploiting his children, cursing his brother and coveting his radiance, his renown and his sword, the instrument of his glory. He shall take what is rightfully his and, from its parts, create his own instrument of death: the *Dark Trinity*." Demahon then pressed his palm against the entire symbol. "And the darkness has a name: Mabus."

"*What* are you talking about?" asked a helpless Theon as he tested the sturdiness of his restraints, only to realize his mobility and his strength still remained quite depleted.

"Legend contends the Dark Trinity never reached its consummation," pointed out a dubious Akara. "It was stopped in mid-course by Deus."

"The dawn of the Dark Trinity was merely postponed," corrected Demahon. "I would admit my children and I were divided into a myriad of dark particles and propelled beyond the Heavens into the Universe to promote its creation and expansion.

"And while the essence of our former selves remained ingrained in each particle, we remained dormant and unable to revive each part of the Dark Trinity and affect their reunion. However, one cannot ignore Maitreya's words of wisdom and warning moments before impaling us with his sword: *'Heavenly essence—even that which has turned to darkness—cannot be absolutely extinguished. It can only be rendered inert and inlayed with a new purpose. Only the blood of your kindred can resurrect thee. But thou shall not seek it for thou shall taste the privilege of thought nevermore.'*

"In truth, I was restored to thought and to sentience by the blood of my kin—the blood of my brother Deus."

"Deus never would have participated in your resurrection," argued Akara. "You're lying."

"He would not knowingly," indicated Demahon. "When the *Audacia* was destroyed by asteroids, the sword of Maitreya was thrust into space, ultimately encountering my essence in the form of a dense cloud of dark particles. Then, the unexpected happened: the supposedly insentient particles sensed the power of Maitreya—an antagonistic force—and stormed the sword, collecting along its surface."

"What's an Audacia?" wondered Theon, wanting to understand it all, one piece at a time.

"It is a designation," said Demahon. "It is the name of a *starship*."

CHAPTER 113

Present day; NASA, Washington D.C.

Bill sat in his chair, his arms locked behind his neck, day dreaming as he watched a blank screen on NASA's control room's main viewer. His staff buzzed about, analyzing data, preparing reports, or discussing with colleagues the nature of various phenomena.

No one dared consult with Bill, who had asked not to be disturbed until a very specific task had been completed; a task fraught with momentous revelation and sweeping paleontological significance.

His staff understood the importance of the task, and was excited and quite relieved to see the contractual linguist enter the control room and march victoriously towards Bill, immediately reporting his findings. "The audio file consists of some kind of Latin dialect devoid of any historical precedence. While the *root* portion of most of the words is consistent with classical Latin, the *affixes*—the stem portion of the words—are totally different from any recorded dialect."

"But that didn't stop you, did it?" gathered Bill, judging by his enthusiasm.

A pert smirk was the linguist's way of testifying his self-gratification. "You should know I'm also well versed in the science of decryption, which proved to be crucial in my translation of the dialect."

"Excellent work," congratulated an eager Bill. "Do you have a transcript?"

"Better yet," announced the linguist. "With the help of your technicians, I've prepared an English audio file—using my silvery voice, of course—which has been overlaid onto and synchronized with the video file from the black box. We can access the modified file on the main viewer."

The contents of the black box, found on Mars by the Opportunity rover, had finally been accessed through ingenious and unconventional usage of some of the rover's mechanical and electronic functions. What it revealed was unexpected and astounding—nothing Bill could ever have imagined.

"By the way, I'm a hard-core atheist who doesn't believe in a godlike supreme being," said the linguist. "How about you?"

"I'm ambivalent about the subject. What's your point?" replied Bill, wondering about the relevance of the question.

"Just checking," said the coy linguist in anticipation.

"Everyone's got his popcorn?" bellowed Bill as he turned his attention to the viewer. "Roll it!"

"Operational log, solar date 237691.5," stated a curious-looking machine man standing behind a flat control panel. "Back-up Control Unit N-I-4-N-I reporting."

"Fascinating!" cried out a staff member who, like his peers, had not been present at the first viewing of the virgin tape. "An android!"

"Keep your comments for the end," Bill ordered his staff. "Take notes if you need to."

The android began its report. "The starship Audacia has been struck by a large rogue asteroid, deviated from its orbital course following a collision with another asteroid within the belt. Auto-reaction time insufficient. Navigation, propulsion, and shields have failed. Catastrophic damage on decks five through twelve; emergency force fields offline. Internal sensors have recorded 3,123 deaths and 807 survivors.

"The ship is drifting towards the asteroid belt. Impact imminent. All cargo bays, except bay two, have lost structural integrity; one escape vessel left with a capacity of 450 passengers. The commander of the Audacia has begun the selection process. Destination: fifth planet of the solar system, classified as L-3, capable of supporting life. This is Audacia's last operational log. Terminating now."

The main viewer went blank.

"Holy crap!" gasped Bill. "Aliens in our solar system. But where could they be? Jupiter can't possibly sustain life as we know it. Where, oh where, could they…of course, the elusive and enigmatic fifth planet." A most likely answer; after all, Bill had seen the planet with his own eyes.

"That's just a fairy tale," pointed out a staff member. "Astro-physics doesn't support the existence of such a planet."

"Not if we consider the *n*-body problem as metaphysical," said Bill. "Its mathematical resolution remains unanswerable only under *conventional* thinking."

"How else pray tell should we be *thinking?*" spouted the annoyed staff member.

Bill was in no mood for a heated debate. He just hankered for more information. "Guess that's all she wrote?" glaring yearningly at the linguist.

"There *is* more," he told a shocked Bill. "Amid the mass of technical data regarding the ship's operations, we uncovered a series of recordings—command logs I believe. I've managed to decipher the very first one and converted audio to English."

The linguist nodded at the technician controlling the tape, who resumed the playback. Another figure appeared, imposing but quite human-looking, sitting behind a desk, surrounded by four other humanoids.

"Greetings whoever you are," began the seemingly ageless man, sporting a well groomed mustache and beard. He was handsome and wore clothing that could barely qualify as a space suit.

"This is the first command log of the starship Audacia," went on the man; "solar date 237487.1. As ship commander, this is my first elocution, whose quality and substance shall be more akin to a tribute and a memorial to our existence, our plight and our ambition, than a routine status report.

"Our past has unfolded gravely, and our future bears down upon us with insistent uncertainty. We no longer have a home. Our planet and our kingdom, which spanned far and wide over its land, have been destroyed by a Sun gone Supernova. Of its 200,000 former inhabitants, less than 4,000 escaped on the Audacia, built specifically for the exodus and the Divine Journey. Our mission is simple but difficult: find a new home where we can thrive once more as a people. If we fail, the advantage of immortality we enjoy shall assuredly become an endless agony."

"Astonishing!" blurted out Bill. "Humanoids—like *us*—and who live *forever*," spinning his hand as though the tape had sentience and would accelerate the pace.

"If you are listening to this recording, then many of us, or *all* of us, are dead," carried on the man. "Wish for the former, and look for us; we will welcome you as kindred spirits."

The man rose from his chair and extended his arms outwards. "Gaze upon me as a friend. I am called Deus, Lord God and ruler of the Kingdom of Heaven. My might may have been tested heavily, but it shall never wane into extinction."

Bill's eyes almost popped out of his head as he turned and confronted the linguist. "This is a joke, right? You screwed around with the transla-tion, to baffle me for some reason?"

"No joke," calmly replied the linguist. "Just watch the rest."

The rest of the recording was indeed telling and hard to refute, as the eternal being called Deus introduced the other men around him. "These are my closest allies—my supreme command team: Prime Seraph Khrist Lesus, General of legions Michael, Tribuni Angusticlavius Gabriel, and Prime Pilus Satan."

One by one, they sided by their King and bowed to whatever audi-ence was privy to the contents of the recording, revealing yet another ingredient of the indigestible meal being shoved down Bill's throat—one that substantiated the identity of the man claiming to be God.

"For God's sake!" screamed Bill. "I mean, for Heaven's sake…I mean…oh fuck it," unable to find a non-religious interjection. "Three of them have wings! They have God damn *wings*!"

"Angels!" exclaimed several staff members.

"And Man created God in his own image," quoted the atheist linguist, curling his lip in a supercilious smile. "How off have we really been?"

CHAPTER 114

Present day; Kingdom of Hell.

Not only were the economics and the politics of Heaven and Hell dramatically different from those depicted in the Bible, but the policy makers were not deities at all.

"The starship Audacia carried the last surviving Eternals to their new home," explained Demahon. "We are not native to this place. We are interstellar *immigrants*."

Theon was quite surprised, but as long as these aliens weren't short, green-skinned, with big heads and huge opaque eyes, he could wrap his head around this latest revelation.

"Just as the Eternals found this world, so did the sword of Maitreya," revealed Demahon. "The sword, amply laced with my essence, had traveled the vastness of space, eventually entering the gravity field of our new home—fate was indeed on my side. It plummeted to earth, only to be found by Deus in the midst of a Chimerian primate clan Millennia later. During battle, the sword was stained with his blood, which came into contact with my essence, effectively restoring me to bodily form while unexpectedly expelling the spirit of Maitreya into the void of space, never to be seen again. It appeared to me that the darkness within's latent intelligence, even in isolation of its sister parts, clashed with Maitreya's surging presence, and was sufficient in casting out Maitreya's light.

"I immediately seized the opportunity, claiming to be a newly materialized Maitreya, and soon thereafter took control of Deus' army. No one would question my actions. No one would defy my orders, not even Deus. I was after all his most trusted advisor, his conscience, his holy spirit."

Akara suddenly became extremely upset. "So, in reality, you're the one who ordered the disastrous assault against the Great Dragons, turning a great number of brave soldiers into *this*," pointing thumbs at herself, "and giving rise to a hellish nation. Everyone had thought Maitreya's senses had left him."

"Quite the reverse," smiled the identity-usurper Demahon. "His senses had never been sharper."

"To what godforsaken end?" Akara vainly tried to comprehend.

"To create a whole far greater than its parts," replied Demahon. "With my restitution came the serendipitous ability to detect and locate dark particles. I soon discovered the leader of the Great Dragons had been embedded with a sufficient quantity of my eldest son's. Protected by his tribe, I ordered the attack that would pave the way to the creature."

"Yet, it is said you killed it," remarked Akara, "an act incongruous with your intent to capture it."

"Capture was never my intent," admitted Demahon. "Since a dragon and a humanoid—Eternal or human—could not mate and beget a child, I arranged for Satan to be mauled by the dragon. The essence of my son was then transmitted to Satan through his injuries. The subsequent transformation into the Diabolicus race was simply an unforeseen side-effect, which I eventually turned to my advantage, another token of my *enterprising* nature."

"You flatter yourself for all the devastation you caused," scoffed Theon. "No wonder you surround yourself with the pestilence of the Earth," alluding to the evil Echoes in the room.

The egocentric Demahon took it as a compliment. "With the assistance of the Trans'Kartum, I roamed the Earth for Millennia, hoping to find my younger son's essence…and did, in the persons of twin sisters Mary and Bethel. Can you appreciate the odds of such a remote occurrence, my dear boy? And some say there is no such thing as an all mighty, all seeing God. I am *that* God, and his will shall not be denied."

"So you shacked up with Mary; Satan shacked up with Bethel," concluded Akara. "And Jesus Christ and Lisa-Maria Magdalena came about and shacked up in turn; all this to produce an innocent boy who suffered Hell because of you."

"He is not innocent at all," balked Demahon. "He carries the triad of dark particles. He is the instruments brought together in salacious symphony; he is *Tenebras Quein Tenebris*; the Mabus, the most powerful weapon in the Universe. Once I harness the infinite power of my creation, with the merest thought I shall lay waste to Heaven, to the planet that embraced its cities, and then to the Earth, until all bow down to me. Deus believed that, in unconsciousness, I would add to the cosmos. Instead, in ravenous consciousness, I shall take the life from it."

"The true measure of a man is what he does with power," heeded Jesus. "Let *that* be your guide."

"Then I shall be the tallest man in the Universe," proudly proclaimed Demahon. "I have the might of the Trans'Kartum, and the might of the Sword. In combination, these agents shall catalyze the weapon and release its power unto me."

"Then the sword's energy was never to be used to my benefit," sadly realized Theon. "It could never save me."

"It could," affirmed Demahon, "only if Deus, possessed by the spirit of Maitreya, wielded it, and with one downward thrust, penetrated your body at the neck," indicating with his own finger the position of Theon's fatalistic mark. "But, regrettably for you, Maitreya is gone."

"Perhaps, he is closer than all of us think," conjectured Jesus, dawned by a notion he had failed to consider despite steadily recurring evidence.

"You attempt at delay serves no one, Christ," said an unimpressed Demahon. "All that is to be known and worth knowing is now known. Let us proceed at once."

Theon did not know what was about to happen; and perhaps, neither did Demahon.

CHAPTER 115

Napoleon Bonaparte, Julius Caesar, and Genghis Khan stood along the rim of the Trans'Kartum, to Theon's right, while Adolf Hitler, Attila the Hun and Osama Bin Laden stood in similar fashion, to Theon's left. Satan stood opposite Theon.

As for Demahon, he placed himself behind Theon. "Through trial and tribulation in the acquisition of the sword, you've demonstrated your readiness, Theon E. Rex. You need no longer struggle to contain the darkness within you, for it has proven itself stronger than you…and quite unstoppable. That combat shall now rage on another battlefield."

Demahon removed his cloak, revealing a small cylindrical reactor core lodged in his chest. The core was empty, its sole compartment in wait of a singular incumbent.

Six guards trotted to the Trans'Kartum, each picking up a wire made of silica fibers, connected at one end to a port along the inner side of the rim. The ports were distributed equally along the rim. One by one, the guards fastened the other end of their wire to an outlet on the reactor core.

Demahon tugged on each of the wires to insure they were properly affixed. "Had I deployed the weapon on my home world, I would have counted on the particular energy produced by my system's red giant sun. However, given the impotence of this system's yellow sun, I had to rely on the Trans'Kartum as an alternate source of comparable energy. The signatures are not identical, but I believe I can compensate."

"I hope it blows up in your *face*," growled Akara. "God knows you need a new one."

Demahon ignored her, signaling the men to activate the Trans'Kartum. Satan unlocked the device before returning to his post, and each man pressed down on a specific stone closest to him, in a specific order, with Satan completing the sequence by pressing the last two stones.

The transportation device rumbled and lit up in a pool of shimmering energy.

"Give me the sword," he bade the guard holding it.

Theon struggled anew as bodily sensation returned, and he could feel the cold metal encasing his extremities. "I will not die today! If there ever was a reason to live…" He looked at Akara with tender eyes.

Tears slid down her cheeks. She understood.

Demahon grinned widely. "Death shall whisk away only that which is profitless. The rest is mine."

"Let the monster out!" Akara screamed to Theon in desperation, as she tried to free herself of the guards' hold. "It's your only chance!"

"Providence may yet bless the boy," Jesus said to Akara, "and it shall manifest beyond mere monstrous semblance."

"You're not talking to your stupid apostles," snapped back Akara. "No one here believes that crap."

Jesus remained cool and collected. "You need only watch."

The energy pool began bubbling excitingly at its center, producing centrifugal waves traveling towards the edge of the pool where they massed and rose like a stationary tsunami.

Meanwhile, Theon's transformation was irreversibly afoot, and swifter than ever before. In seconds, his mass increased by a third, and he morphed into the most frightening of Diabolicus.

Bloated with the Trans'Kartum's energy, Demahon's reactor core suddenly ignited into a fiery glow whose intensity grew as the amplitude of the peripheral waves tapered. "The time to receive you is imminent," he announced as he raised the sword, blade down, and rested its tip on Theon's neck mark.

By now, Theon had almost doubled in size, and his shackles started cracking. Even the guards became afraid of him. Demahon tightened his grip, while his eyes carefully monitored the state of Theon's metamorphosis, awaiting the ideal moment. And just as Theon was about to break loose, he plunged the sword into his victim.

Akara shrieked in horror.

Theon's warped body turned translucent dotted with scores of black spots, while a second humanlike form—slightly dephased—surfaced, much like a shadow that had forgotten to separate from the obstruction that gave birth to it.

The black spots moved about, quickly clustering into three dark zones, the common area through which passed the strange shadow after imploding into a ball of fire. Theon had become completely unrecognizable—the outline of his severely misshapen body having transmuted into a canvass for a micro-universe within a universe, with three black holes competing against a super-giant star for domination.

During this succession of incredible reactions, Demahon never released the sword, which shook and vibrated without reprieve. Try as he might, he could neither push it down further nor raise it. But he could sense something surging and climbing along the blade.

Demahon's face went white with dread, an emotion he had long forgotten. "Maitreya!"

Akara stared surprisingly at Jesus. "Theon's Ghost Knight *is* Maitreya! You knew?"

"I suspected," replied Jesus. "Providence in action."

The energy waves packed against the rim suddenly went flat, and the glimmering pool resumed its original configuration just as the chamber was flooded with a blinding light, and tremored violently.

"The boy will not do your bidding," declared Maitreya, his voice infiltrating every corner of Demahon's mind. "Not today."

The force of a consuming explosion stormed through the chamber, lifting everything in its path, tearing stones from the walls. It swirled with rubble and life forms apprehending extinction, finally forming a wide string of kinetic energy that carried its litter through the mouth of the Trans'Kartum, which closed behind it. An eerie silence followed.

Demahon, who had been thrown against a wall, swept the dust and debris off of himself and dizzily got up, instantly realizing he had been endowed with no great power at all. "Aaahhhhhhhhh!" he screamed at the top of his lungs, in defeat. "The transfer has failed!"

Satan stumbled towards his master, enraged and dejected, stepping over several Diabolicus bodies. "Millennia of planning, searching, waiting, ending in *this*! My dedication and my loyalty were sorely misplaced. What a fool's errand."

A numb Demahon said nothing, wallowing in self-pity.

Satan spat at Demahon's feet before scanning the room for survivors and spotting his daughter kneeling and bloodied, looking furiously about for any sign of Theon. There was none.

"He's gone," Satan told her, extending his hand in a rare gesture of kindness and empathy.

She covered her face with her hands and began sobering. Her father did not insist, resuming his survey of the area.

"Demahon!" shouted Satan, dispending for the first time of the title of *Lord*. "Come and see this. Stop indulging in idle sentiments of ill fortune and come here," he repeated.

Demahon shook off his torpor and regained his composure. "There are always alternatives," he told himself. "Not all is lost."

"Of course there is hope," Satan concurred, not believing a word of it. If there ever was, he would be forced to manufacture it.

"Compassion for your king?" said Demahon. "I will have none of it. And, you will address me as Lord," pushing Satan aside. "What is this?"

While all seven Echoes, including Jesus, appeared to have been destroyed, not all left the customary residue behind. Where Bonaparte, Hitler, and Jesus once stood, there was no trace of it at all.

Satan quickly tallied the number of missing residue stains. "Do you believe they've reunited with Shuntra…in *all* their integrity? That is most unusual, most bizarre."

Demahon stared at the quiet Trans'Kartum, suddenly feeling rejuvenated and once again in full command of his faculties. "They are not with Shuntra. Our plan has not failed. It has simply been momentarily delayed."

"I don't understand," admitted a confused Satan.

Demahon passed his fingers over the stain free ground and examined their tips. "The end remains the same. Only the order in which the means shall be deployed has changed."

"Come!" he ordered Satan, walking promptly towards the exit. "Darkness within darkness; the Dark Trinity shall yet be mine!"

CHAPTER 116

Present day; Area 51, Edwards Air Force Base, Nevada.

Karl Armstrong, President of the United States,
looked down upon a most exotic sight from a deck circling the perimeter
of a large oval enclosure made of successive, alternating layers of steel
and concrete. For all intent, it was impenetrable.

Deeply absorbed in introspection, he thought, "it was good to be human again—completely and utterly human." And while the voice of the
original owner of the body he now occupied was but a whisper, no harm
had come to the owner's soul.

Taking a few steps, as if they were an infant's first ones, he arrested
his careful stride at the top of staircase, which spiraled down to the ground
floor, and peered into the depth. "Quite a sensation; alike but somehow
dissimilar." He proceeded downwards, then towards what his aids had
coined *a wicked curiosity*.

Entrapped in a cell made of a complex, transparent composite, engineered at great cost to be as strong as steel, the *curiosity*, clearly weakened and impaired by an invasive episode no force on Earth could have
survived, pressed his quivering hands against the glass. "Where am I?"

"You're back on Earth," revealed Armstrong, "in an underground, secure facility. I knew to find you in the well from which you sprung as a
baby."

The prisoner glimpsed his claws, which were gradually receding,
then his body, covered in greyish lumps, boiling as they diminished and
quieted their slovenly dance. "I must disgust you?"

"Nothing I haven't seen before," replied Armstrong with great empathy.

"*Who* are you?" asked the puzzled captive.

"To most, I am the President of the United States," said Armstrong.

"To you, I am your *father*."

"My father...my *fathers* are in Hell," retorted the angry prisoner. "Why are you toying with me?"

Armstrong smiled fondly. "You don't recognize me, do you? I'm not surprised; I don't even recognize myself. It is I, my dear son Theon; it is Jesus."

"How is this possible?" wondered a thunderstruck Theon.

"With Demahon, anything is possible," supposed the Armstrong-embodied Jesus. "In truth, I don't think he planned this. I am what appears to be a by-product of his failed plan."

"So we've won?" naturally concluded Theon, who by now had resumed human form—not a trace of monstrosity to be noticed.

"Not quite," said Jesus, his face turning somber. "This is but a temporary reprieve. Soon, Man's basest instincts, his deeply-ingrained belligerence, and his thirst for power and conquest masked and kept in check by a shroud of self-imposed, constraining civilization, shall all be tested as they have never been tested before. A third World war is upon us. The final judgement shall befall Humanity, and the souls of the damned shall be sentenced to Hell, by the billion, to serve evil. Once that happens, Demahon and Satan shall strike again. Heaven shall burn."

"Deus will never allow it," vigorously assured Theon.

"Deus may well die," sadly foreboded Jesus.

"He can't!" cried Theon, pushing hard against the glass. "He and Maitreya must be reunited; to save *me*."

"What is Maitreya telling you know?" queried Jesus, knowing the answer full well.

"To think of others," sighed Theon, bowing his head. "I'm not to be selfish...and, I'm to believe in myself, despite myself."

Jesus understood this notion better than anyone. Millennia ago, his selfless words provided hope for the future, and the ghost force within him, his source of faith, guaranteed a fresh start by wiping Humanity clean of sin. Now it was up to Theon who, while deficient in delivering penetrating insight, more than made up for it in unyielding spirit—even though he disputed it.

"The battle will begin on Earth, and end in Hell," announced Jesus. "And you and I shall be part of it."

"I risk capture by Demahon again," warned Theon, the only consequence of which capable of mitigating such an adverse outcome was a possible reunion with his adoptive father, and a definite one with Akara. And he *wanted* to see her again.

Jesus did his best to contain his concern. "It is likely Maitreya shall be your safeguard once again." It was a reasonable albeit uncertain assumption to him. Theon put little stock in it, fearing Maitreya could not contain the ever growing boundless Dark Trinity forever. But as long as he still had some measure of control, he would act.

"Let me out!" shouted Theon, banging on the glass.

"Can I trust you?" asked Jesus, closely eying Theon like a circus trainer would a lion.

"I don't know," answered Theon.

"Are you *safe*?" added Jesus.

Theon frowned. "I thought I was clear. I *don't* know."

Jesus let out an uneasy self-conscious smile. "Of course, stupid questions." He pressed a button and the glass siding rose; and he prayed he was not making a fatal mistake from which the world would not recuperate.

Theon stepped out. "The evil within lies in wait. A wrong word, a wrong step, and the beast rises. I don't trust myself; how can you?"

"I cannot do it alone," said Jesus. "I never could."

Despite his dire apprehension, Theon would not abandon his true father. "What do you want from me?"

"Much," said Jesus, whose mind had been hard at work on a plan. "But in the immediate, there is a grave danger threatening this world. Eternal technology has somehow made it to Earth ...and to Iran, of all places. I strongly suspect we're looking at a large section of the starship Audacia, perhaps even the ship's weapons system. We need an advanced weapon of our own, capable of hacking a path through enemy territory and retrieving it before it falls into the wrong hands."

Theon no longer minded the designation *weapon*, but proving he could wield himself successfully was another story "Isn't it already in the wrong hands?" he assumed, surprised to see his biological father's hardline militant side emerge. It seemed to him that the expression *Live by the Sword, Die by the Sword* had escaped his father, or had been conveniently deemed obsolete.

Jesus reacted by latching on Theon's arm and squeezing tightly. "Not as wrong as the hands of the most dreaded—those who truly understand how to kindle the *dark* side of Humanity."

"Demahon and Satan?" guessed Theon, not knowing who else might fit the bill.

Jesus nodded in the negative. "Those two exploit evil admirably, but they cannot kindle it like the scourge of the Earth."

"Who then?" insisted Theon.

"Better to show you than to tell you," was Jesus' only response—and he had a lot to show.

EPILOGUE

Present day; Berlin, Germany.

By early 1945, World War II was coming to an end. Germany's military situation was on the verge of total collapse. Poland had fallen to the advancing Soviet forces and they were massing to cross the Oder River between Küstrin and Frankfurt, with Berlin, 51 miles away to the west, as their objective.

Hitler, the once undisputed head of state, retreated to his *Führerbunker*, an air-raid shelter, in Berlin on January 16th and, by the end of February, was presiding over a rapidly disintegrating Third Reich.

Eva Braun, Hitler's longtime companion, joined him in the bunker where they married hours before committing suicide. Hitler shot himself through the head while Eva ingested cyanide.

That same afternoon, in accordance with Hitler's prior instructions, their remains were carried up the stairs through the bunker's emergency exit, doused in petrol and set alight in the Reich Chancellery garden outside the bunker.

The bunker was abandoned and subsequently leveled by the Soviets between 1945 and 1949, largely surviving, although some areas were partially flooded. Apart from one unsuccessful attempt in 1959 by the government of East Germany to blow it up, the underground complex remained undisturbed until after the reunification of Germany when some sections were destroyed.

Today, the bunker—or the decrepit shadow of its former self—was but a small pile of disparate rubble, identified by a commemorative plaque with a schematic of the bunker to mark the location.

German passers-by largely ignored the site, a vivid reminder of the country's darkest hour; and tourists took a plethora of photos to show family and friends, many insensitive to its evil symbolism. It had, after all, happened a long time ago, well before their time.

For Ulrich, a young Austrian man who had recently turned twenty, however, it was as if it had transpired only yesterday.

"Ulrich!" shouted his mother who stayed behind as her son made his way to the plaque. "Be careful! There are rocks everywhere. You'll sprain your ankle."

The father, standing next to his overprotective wife, grumbled as he puffed on a cigar. "He's twenty now. Let him be. Let him explore this newfound interest in German history. Perhaps this is the end of his lazy and apathetic ways."

"We traveled all the way from *Braunau am Inn* to see *this*?" She waived in discontent at the ruins. "He's not just interested, he's obsessed with it, and thoroughly obsessed with Adolf Hitler—it borders on sick admiration for that monster. First, we had to visit Hitler's birthplace—in our *own* town no less—now this. "

"He's enthused and highly motivated," noted the father. "He may even decide to go to University and make a career out of it."

"Oh no…no, no, no," rebutted the mother in disagreement. "He's not headed for University with this; he's headed somewhere else entirely. *I* don't like it. Did you see his eyes of late? They're different— cold and cruel."

The father dismissed her overtaxed imagination. "For the first time, he's showing signs of finally flying of his own wings, and you just won't let him leave the nest. He's not a child anymore. Deal with it."

Ulrich heard everything his parents said and could not care less. As long as they were of use to him, he would tolerate their irrelevant, septic chatter. He gazed at the plaque, his fingers grazing the bunker schematic, and then made his way to where the Reich Chancellery garden once flourished majestically.

"Destroyers," he whispered in disdain as he dug his fingers into the dirt and scooped up a handful, which he forcefully threw against the flat face of a massive stone a few feet away.

Years ago, a group of Russian students on vacation had come upon the stone and had indulged in the reckless art of graffiti, carving a message along its flat surface. It read, quite distinctly:

ADOLF HITLER
BURN IN HELL

"I shall brew them a devil's drink," sneered Ulrich, quoting Hitler, before pulling out a knife and scratching over the hostile but well deserved invitation to shrivel in hellfire.

Below it, he engraved a message of his own:

AS I HAVE RULED IN HELL
I SHALL RULE ON EARTH
ONCE AND FOR ALL

Throwing his knife aside, he slowly walked back to his parents. "I *want* to go to Ajaccio!" he said in a staunch commanding tone.

"That's a commune on the island of Corsica, in France, isn't it?" recalled the father; "where Napoleon Bonaparte was born, in fact."

The father proudly placed his hand on Ulrich's shoulder. "Expanding our horizons, son?"

Ulrich smiled diabolically, his eyes turning bloody red. "You could say that."

THE END

Theon E. Rex's adventures will continue in the upcoming novel:

**THE BOY
WHO DINED IN**
Hitler's Kosher Kitchen